"Kaye's luscious d   s are
a great touch as s   ys of
Red Hook series.   view)

Back to You

"Passionate and poignant . . . an emotionally gratifying
contemporary romance."   —*Kirkus Reviews*

"Heartwarming, sexy, and definitely enthralling. . . . Ms.
Kaye delivered it with style, complete with humor and a
swoon-worthy hero."   —Under the Covers

"If you like contemporary romance with a nice sizzle . . .
I definitely recommend *Back to You*."

—The Romance Dish

FURTHER PRAISE FOR
ROBIN KAYE AND HER NOVELS

"Robin Kaye creates characters that reach in and grab
your heart."   —LuAnn McLane

"Charming readers with her wit and style, Kaye creates
an extremely sensual romance."   —*Booklist*

"You'll be in romance heaven."

—Night Owl Reviews (top pick)

continued . . .

Also by Robin Kaye

Hometown Girl
(A Penguin Special Novella)
You're the One
Back to You

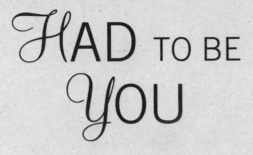

HAD TO BE YOU

BAD BOYS OF RED HOOK

ROBIN KAYE

A SIGNET ECLIPSE BOOK

SIGNET ECLIPSE
Published by the Penguin Group
Penguin Group (USA) LLC, 375 Hudson Street,
New York, New York 10014

USA | Canada | UK | Ireland | Australia | New Zealand | India | South Africa | China
penguin.com
A Penguin Random House Company

First published by Signet Eclipse, an imprint of New American Library,
a division of Penguin Group (USA) LLC

First Printing, February 2014

ISBN 978-0-451-41357-4

Printed in the United States of America
10 9 8 7 6 5 4 3 2 1

To Margie Lawson and Michael Hauge—two of the most inspiring, knowledgeable, and gifted writing instructors I've had the good fortune to know. They teach me something new every time I see them, hear them, or take an online course with them. I'm blessed to count them among my dearest friends as well as instructors. If not for their classes, I would never have been published and stayed published.

ACKNOWLEDGMENTS

I'd love to tell you I wrote this book all on my own. After all, part of the writer's mystique is the solitary life we live. For me at least, the solitary part is a load of bunk; I believe it takes a village to make a book. Here are some of the people who have helped me:

I'd like to thank Barbara Perry, LCSW-C. Barbara is a therapist who specializes in childhood and adult trauma. If not for Barbara, this book would never have been written. She spent countless hours with me, answering questions and talking about Slater's childhood and how one in his position would live through his trauma and become a successful, loving man in spite of it. If there are mistakes, they are all on me; if I did a good job with it, Barbara deserves all the credit.

I'm lucky to have the love and support of my incredible family. My husband, Stephen, who after twenty-three years of marriage is still the man of my dreams and best friend. My children, Tony, Anna, and Isabelle, who despite being teenagers are my favorite people to hang out with. Alex Henderson and Jessye and Dylan Green, whom I love like my own kids. All of them make me laugh, amaze me with their intelligence and generosity, and make me proud every day. My parents, Richard Williams and Ann Feiler, and my stepfather, George Feiler, who always encouraged me and continue to do so.

My wonderful critique partners, Laura Becraft and Deborah Villegas. They shortened my sentences, corrected my grammar, and put commas where they needed to be. They listened to me whine when my muse took a vacation, gave me great ideas when I was stuck, and answered that all-important question: Does this suck? They helped me plot, loved my characters almost as much as I did, and challenged me to be a better writer. They are my friends, my confidantes, and my bullshit meters.

I owe a debt of gratitude to their families, who so graciously let me borrow them during my deadline crunch. So, to Robert, Joe, Elisabeth, and Ben Becraft, and Ruben, Alexander, Donovan, and Cristian Villegas, you have my thanks and eternal gratitude.

I'd also like to thank my writing friends, who are always there when I need a fresh eye or a sounding board—Grace Burrowes, Hope Ramsay, Susan Donovan, Mary Freeman, R. R. Smythe, Margie Lawson, Michael Hauge, and Christie Craig, all the Killer Fiction authors and my RWA chapters, WRW-DC, Valley Forge Romance Writers, Maryland Romance Writers, the Golden Network, and PASIC.

I wrote most of this book at the Starbucks in Mt. Airy, Maryland, and I have to thank all my baristas for keeping me in laughter and coffee while I camped out in their store. Josh, Garrison, Lamar, Ginny, Amy, Edward, Sue, Eric, Ann, Ashley, Maggie, Jena, Blair, Julie, Nick, Molly, Nate, Holly, Sam, Lauren, and Tara. I also need to thank my fellow customers who have become wonderful friends: Anne, Mike, Doug, Jerry, and Ann.

As always, I want to thank my incredible agent, Kevan Lyon, for all she does, and my team at New American Library—the cover artists for the beautiful job they did and my editors, Kerry Donovan and Jesse Feldman, for all their insight, direction, and enthusiasm. Working with you has been a real pleasure.

CHAPTER 1

The last time Slater Shaw had climbed up a fire escape outside his foster father's Brooklyn bar, he'd been helping his brother out of a jam when they were kids. Showers of iron flakes fell with each step he took. The fire escape had been rickety back then. Ten more years in Red Hook's sea air hadn't helped.

Slater cursed under his breath as the telltale scent of cigar smoke permeated the alley where he'd been unloading a crate. He'd noticed his foster father, Pete Calahan—the curmudgeonly ex-cop turned heart patient, who went against doctor's orders as often as possible—on the roof, puffing away like a teenager smoking in the boys' room.

Slater wasn't ready for the role reversal, but the consequences from Pop deep-sixing his doctor's orders were worse than Slater's fear of confronting the old fart.

He'd thought about going into the apartment and taking the stairs to the roof, but then he'd have to explain Pop's bad behavior to ten-year-old Nicki—his dad's newest stray. When Slater reached the top, he threw his leg over the low wall and tugged himself onto the roof.

Pop watched, shaking his head, not even bothering to hide the smoking evidence. "Do you have a death wish, boy?"

Slater wiped his hands on his pants. "No, but it seems you do. Shit, Pop. Put that damn thing out and go inside."

"One cigar isn't going to kill me." He took a couple puffs and then examined the growing ash. "I don't know what all the stink is about—it's not like I inhale."

"I don't care. I've come here to help and you've turned me into a glorified babysitter for you, Nicki, and her big-ass mutt. What the hell were you thinking taking on a little girl to raise at your age?" Nicki was a cute enough kid, but every time he looked at her, he got an eerie *step-on-your-grave* type feeling.

"I was thinking Nicki reminded me a lot of you boys—that's what. She needed a home, and I gave her one."

"You can't handle her on your own." Slater didn't know the first thing about little girls and wasn't really interested in finding out.

"I don't have to. I have you boys to help out. I'll be back to normal soon."

"Not if you don't follow the doctor's instructions. You've only been out of the hospital two months and you're exhausted after working a few hours. You don't know how long it's going to take for you to recover fully." Slater looked out over the bay, and the Statue of Liberty stared back at him. How ironic that the symbol of freedom stood before him, when all he felt was a sense of losing his own. Knowing that the doctors swore Pop was out of danger didn't make Slater sleep any better. He was a grown man, but he couldn't understand why losing his dad scared him to his marrow. His fear wasn't rational, so he did what he always did—he compartmentalized.

Pop sat on an Adirondack chair and looked at him. "Last I heard, you weren't due home for a few more weeks. Then I walk in yesterday and there you are with a chip on your shoulder the size of the Flatiron Building. I'm glad you're here, but what the hell happened to have you running home early? What put you in such a shit mood?

"What makes you think something happened?" Slater put his boot on the edge of the other chair. They both needed a fresh coat of paint. He'd never cop to being played and dumped, especially not with Pop. How could he have missed that Dominique was engaged? She'd used him like a disposable plate to be thrown away after dessert. He was Chinet and no matter what he did, he'd never be Wedgwood. Fuck.

"I know you, son. Did you finally get your heart broken?"

Slater tried to freeze his features, keep them locked in place, but he knew he failed.

Pop had that *gotcha* look in his eyes. There was a reason he'd been a great cop before retiring to run the Crow's Nest.

"No. I'm not heartbroken. I'm pissed. Dominique measured me on her high-society ruler and I came up short in every way." Every way but the length of his dick and his skill in the sack.

Pop raised his glass of scotch. "Yup"—Pop took another drag off his stogie—"you got your heart broken."

"Close, but no cigar." Slater reached over and plucked the stogie out of Pop's hand and ground it out on the tarred roof.

"Shit, why'd you have to do that?"

"Because I won't let you kill yourself."

His dad studied him like a jeweler studying a diamond, searching for just the right place to make the next cut. "There's more to this than you're telling me. I know it and you know it. Whatever it is, it's embarrassing—I can tell by the color of your face. So you got taken in by a woman. Congratulations—every man does at least once." Pop stood. "If you want to talk about it, I'm here."

"Thanks, but there's nothing to talk about." He'd take this one to the grave.

"Yeah, that's what I thought. Now come down through the apartment the right way, the last thing I need is Nicki watching you play Spider-Man—she already has an unhealthy fascination with Wonder Woman."

Pop turned and took the stairs down to the apartment and Slater reluctantly followed.

He slipped out into the alley undetected, used the crowbar, and ripped into the crate entombing the one thing he did love. He hammered the crowbar under the wood, urgency pumping his blood in time to the throbbing of his temples.

He had to get to her.

He wanted her.

He wanted her with the same burning desire a pubescent boy wanted a centerfold.

Another board fell to the ground and a flash of chrome shone through the darkness. Baseball-sized knots in his upper back and shoulders loosened enough to give his neck free range of motion. He'd been home for less than twenty-four hours and he already needed to escape. Escape from the apartment, escape from his past, escape from Red Hook.

He ripped another board off the crate and threw it

against the brick building with more force than necessary. He'd lived in Seattle for two years, and when he'd left, it had surprised him that there was no one he cared to say good-bye to. And for the first time in his life, that bothered him.

Slater tried to erase Dominique from his mind but it wasn't working. No matter what he did, no matter how far he'd come, the only chance he had to clean off the stink of poverty was to sign that contract with OPEC. The money they were offering more than made up for his crack-shack beginnings.

"Whatcha doing?"

Slater jumped. Shit. He couldn't believe Nicki had snuck up on him. He looked over his shoulder; her long curly brown hair whipped in the icy late-fall wind. The girl was all legs and feet, too skinny for her height, and her jacket swamped her slight frame. Clothes that were three sizes too wide and three inches too short hid her bone-thin arms and legs.

"Just unloading my bike."

Nicki hesitated before moving closer. He saw himself in the haunted, wary look in her eyes, like she'd seen someone use a crowbar as a weapon instead of as a tool. He didn't know what was worse, how much she reminded him of himself at that age, or that she'd probably seen that kind of violence. Both made the unsettled feelings he had about Nicki even worse.

"Pop said he'd buy me a bike this spring. Maybe you or Logan or Storm can teach me to ride it in the park. Bree won't let me ride on the street—she's weird about stuff like that."

His brother Storm and sister-in-law Bree were on their honeymoon. They'd grown up together and from what Slater remembered of Bree's overprotective mother, the fact that Bree wouldn't let Nicki ride her bike in the street wasn't all that surprising.

"It's not a bicycle, Nicki. It's a motorcycle."

"Oh." She turned a little red and kicked a piece of broken pavement into a pothole. "So, can you take me for a ride sometime?"

"I guess that's up to Pop." He gazed at the second floor of the building and wondered if the old man had sent her down to keep him company. "If Pop says it's okay, I'll take you for a ride. It's pretty cold this time of year." Way too cold for a kid with no natural insulation.

Nicki's hair flew across her face and she pulled the jacket tighter. "I'm going in to ask Pop right now, okay?"

"Sure, but it's getting late." He needed to take a long, cold ride. Not the kind of ride he'd take with a slip of a girl on the back of his bike. No, he needed to let out the throttle and go balls to the wall. He needed to rid himself of the antsy feeling he'd fought all day with nothing to do but roam the apartment. "Even if it's okay with Pop, I'm not taking you out tonight. We'll have to do it when it's still light."

Nicki's shoulders slumped, making her look like a longer-haired version of a Dora the Explorer Macy's Thanksgiving Day Parade balloon with a bad leak. "You promise?"

He looked at her, got that déjà vu feeling again, and fought off a shiver that had nothing to do with the dropping temperature. "If it's okay with Pop, then I promise I'll take you for a ride. But if Pop says no, it's no."

Nicki's eyes rolled around like a Magic 8-Ball landing on *Don't count on it* and she dug her sneaker into the pavement. "Pop and Bree don't have to know everything. I'm not a baby, you know. I'm almost eleven."

"That old, huh?" The girl was actually trying to work him. "Good try, Nicki, but I'm not gonna shake Bree's cage. I'll be here awhile, and believe me, when Bree gets back from her honeymoon, I plan to stay on her good side. I heard she took a cast iron skillet to Storm's hard head—"

"You should have seen Bree hit him with the frying pan of truth. It was epic."

"Not so epic for Storm, but it couldn't have been that bad—he married her. I have no problem learning from my brother's mistake. I'm not gonna mess with Bree— even for a kid as cute as you."

Nicki studied her shoes. "You're not gonna snitch on me, are you?"

"No, but I'm not falling for your charm either. I'm immune." Something else he got out of his relationship with Dominique—he figured it was like an inoculation. He might have been sick as a grass-eating dog when he'd gotten it, but he wouldn't fall prey to that emasculating disease again.

"You think I got charm?"

He let out a laugh. "Charm—kid, you've got so much charm, you have everyone in the family wrapped and you know it."

She stuffed her hands in her pockets and shrugged. "Not everyone. I'm gonna go do my chores before I ask Pop if I can go for a ride on your bike. Maybe then he'll say yes."

"Good luck, Nicki." Slater watched her sneak back into the restaurant's kitchen. And she was sneaking. She'd even stuck her head through to make sure the coast was clear. He'd heard Skye tell Nicki that she wasn't allowed in the alley alone. Nicki hadn't been alone, but it damn sure didn't look as if she'd asked permission to join him.

Slater rolled his bike out of the crate and cleaned up the rest of the wood. He straddled his bike, the only woman who just wanted him to ride her fast and hard and never asked for anything else. His blood pressure dropped a good twenty points when he put on his helmet. As always, she started on the first try, he gave her some gas, let out her throttle, and took off.

A part of him was trying to outrun his demons. Here in Red Hook, they were not only too close, but there were too many to count. Maybe he just needed to make peace with being made a fool of, make peace with his father's health crisis, and make peace with spending the next five years living and working between the Middle East and Vienna. He sped down the straightaways at breakneck speeds, took the turns too fast, and flew through the icy wind coming off the bay until he lost feeling in most of his appendages.

He drove fast, skirting the edge of control through neighborhoods he remembered from his youth. Ones he'd never planned to revisit and had successfully avoided for years. Yet here he was in Red Hook. He'd serve his one-month sentence helping Pop with the bar and Nicki, and then he was off to Bahrain.

Slater returned to the Crow's Nest and parked his bike out front—in a spot so perfect, Dominique would have called it princess parking.

Too bad it wouldn't be any easier to run from his demons there than it was in Red Hook. He'd traveled the world and no matter where he went, his demons were always licking at his heels, singeing his consciousness, waiting to possess him.

Slater squared his shoulders, took a deep breath, and tried to prepare himself to step into his not so rosy past.

He pulled the heavy door open and walked into the Crow's Nest.

He'd hoped the ride would clear his head. It hadn't worked—his mind tumbled like dice on a craps table—Dominique, his dad, Nicki, Red Hook. The result: emotional bankruptcy.

He pushed his way through the crowd—and it was a helluva crowd, which, when it came to the Crow's Nest, was a new one on him. If he hadn't seen the sign outside, he would have never known it was his father's place.

The only thing he recognized was the huge carved antique mahogany bar. The rough longshoreman crowd—gone. The stained drop ceiling—gone. The cheesy prints and cheap barstools—gone. They were replaced by an upscale clientele, high-back stools, and a tin ceiling with crown molding that matched the bar. The chipped plaster walls had been ripped down to exposed brick with the patina of age. Damn, the place was nice. High-back booths lined the wall opposite the bar, round tables filled the center, and Tiffany-style lighting set the mood. But the lighting and decorations were nothing compared to the sultry, sexy voice of the woman singing an Adele song on the stage. He couldn't see her—the stage was just out of his line of sight.

With the number of people packed into the place, he'd expected the normal raucous *shout-if-you-want-to-be-heard* noise level, but all he heard was her. She had the crowd enthralled: the men mesmerized, the women envious.

A big guy behind the bar nodded to him and finished pouring a drink. He slid the glass in front of a customer, grabbed her cash, and rang it up. Strange silver eyes met Slater's head-on. "What can I get you?" the bartender asked, and tossed a napkin on the spotless bar in front of him. The singer announced that she and the band, Nite Watch, were taking a break.

Slater waited for her to stop speaking before he answered. "A Sixpoint Bengali Tiger IPA and a shot of Jack."

The bartender gave him an assessing look and Slater assessed him right back. Slater's too long hair and badass leathers made people wonder if they should have the cops on speed-dial. He supposed he should be glad the bartender kept an eye out for trouble, but lately he'd had a hard time working up much in the way of appreciation.

A minute later his drinks were delivered. Slater pushed his hair out of his eyes, tossed a twenty on the bar, and watched a cool platinum blonde with her back to him fill a glass with water. She had short choppy hair, a long neck made for a man to nibble, and an upper back and shoulders that told him she'd been a pretty serious dancer in the not too distant past.

He didn't know what she was doing behind the bar in a long dress. She turned and he realized it was only long in the back, the front was so short, the dress was just a tongue-lashing away from indecent.

He didn't mind that it looked more like a bathing suit cover-up than a dress. The wild tropical print on the layered, floaty material didn't cling to her, but ensured that every curve demanded attention. She belonged barefoot on South Beach in Miami, not in a corner bar in Red Hook in December. He had the urge to offer her his jacket just to cover her. Shit.

Slater had ordered the shot to warm up, but one look at the blonde and he didn't need it.

The slash of fluorescent blue that sliced through her side-swept bangs covered one eye, and pointed to a wild streak. He couldn't see her eye color, but he'd bet his

Harley they were blue. He'd always had a thing for blondes with blue eyes, and wondered how she felt about bikes.

She said something to the bartender and then walked the length of the bar in heels so high and pointed, they were an engineering marvel—not to mention what they did to her legs.

He downed the shot. She had one hell of a walk. It highlighted every muscle in her legs, every curve of her ass, and made her breasts even more drool-worthy.

Unfortunately, he should do anything but follow. No, he was the last person who should be looking at a woman. Any woman. He'd learned from experience it was much safer to clear his head by flying down the streets of Red Hook on a motorcycle on a cold night. He might have frozen his balls off—but that was what he'd needed. He just wished it had worked.

Slater took a pull off his beer and still felt antsy. Maybe it was being back home. In his mind Red Hook was like the Munsters' house in that old TV show—gloomy and gray, with a big cloud hanging directly over it. That was why, when he'd been old enough to enlist—he did.

The navy had been the only way Slater knew to get the hell out of Red Hook and make something of his life. He and his brothers had each made his escape and left Pop here to fend for himself. Now it was his turn to come back and take care of Pop, the Crow's Nest, and Nicki. But unlike his brothers, he wasn't getting sucked back in. He was giving it a month. One month—then he was out of here.

He roamed the bar and was amazed at the amount of food still being served this late. The kitchen was doing decent business—something that hadn't happened when he'd been a kid. The stage lights came on and he checked his watch—almost ten, time for the band to start. He wasn't sure why they'd been playing earlier, but he'd figure it all out in time. Running the place would be his job starting tomorrow. Today, he wanted to see how things worked before anyone found out who the hell he was.

CHAPTER 2

Rocki O'Sullivan stood center of the stage, belting out one of her favorite Kirsty MacColl songs—a little bit Latin, a little bit sexy, and a whole lot funny. She'd chosen her dress carefully, with this song in mind. Short, sassy, and comfortable—the perfect combination for making a man wonder how long it would take to get her out of it. It worked perfectly paired with her favorite pumps, mirror platforms that picked up the cobalt blue of the shoe and added a good five inches to her already long legs. The kind of shoes that made a man think twice about taking them off before carrying a woman to bed.

And putting thoughts in men's heads was one of the reasons Rocki chose most of her shoes—that and she was a total shoe whore.

The electric buzz of eyes on her was normally something she relished. But tonight something, someone, had set off her heat sensor. Rocki scanned the crowd and her gaze landed on a man who threw her so far off her game, she missed the chorus. She never forgot the words. Thank God Tessa, Mark, and Kirby were singing backup and covering her ass.

Whoever he was, he seemed to have an invisible barrier around him. No one stepped into his space. He stood still, a bottle of beer in one hand, the other hooked into a belt loop.

He wore a kick-ass black leather biker jacket, scuffed black boots that'd been driven hard miles, and his long legs were tucked into tight black jeans that seemed as if they'd been tailor made to cup all his intriguing parts.

An image of him straddling a hot bike flashed through her mind. He was tall—really tall with curly chestnut brown hair that looked as if it was absentmindedly tucked behind his ears. It was too long to be respectable—but then respectability was way overrated. On any other man the curls, which were big enough to slide three fingers through and probably hung like ringlets when wet, would look feminine, but on this guy there was no hint of softness.

He filled out his Under Armour turtleneck like a superhero might—pecs and abs clearly defined against the hot lights that hit him, his muscles delineating the shadows and highlighting a bulge that made her mouth water.

Rocki had always liked men and was well aware that they liked her right back, but she'd never had one look at her quite the way he did. His eyes flared with so much heat that she wouldn't need a tanning booth if she were naked.

Mark nudged her, bringing her mind back to the song.

She sang to the bad boy as if he were the only man in the room.

He didn't move to the music. He didn't move a muscle. The only thing that moved were his eyes. His gaze scanned her body, trailing heat from the tips of her toes to her tits.

It was a little disconcerting. She was used to guys checking her out, but no one had ever looked at her with such intensity that it was all she could do to get through the song without forgetting the words.

She checked the playlist taped to the floor. The song she'd just finished was about being propositioned by several different men, and the next was no better. When she sang about watching a man shower, it was him she envisioned. When she sang about picturing her telephone number, his brow rose in question. Oh my god. This guy was good and so hot that even though she never dated, she'd date him in a Brooklyn minute.

She was relieved to get back behind her trusty piano for the next song—of course it was about telling a man that if he wanted her, where exactly he could find her. She never realized before that the entire playlist was a come-on of ginormous proportions.

She looked up from the piano and saw that he'd moved right into her line of vision. She sang about wondering about him—all kinds of questions ran through her head about the man who could carry on a conversation with a quirk of his lips, the rise of a brow, and the way his Adam's apple bobbed when he swallowed.

Wendy, a cocktail server, stopped to ask for his order, and it didn't look as if he'd even heard her. He never took his eyes off Rocki and she wasn't able to look away except to check the playlist.

After remembering the next song, she wondered if it had been too long since she'd dated. She flirted a lot, but she made it a point to always go home alone. Still, when looking at the playlist with a critical eye, she had to admit it looked as if it were written by a horny woman. It was too late to do anything to change it. Mark was already tuning his guitar to go into the next song. The lyrics of which practically begged a man to take care of her in all ways possible.

Rocki's face heated as she sang about being full of desire—which she was, but damn, she certainly didn't want to give Mr. Rough-and-Ready the wrong impression. She needed to get off the stage and find out who this guy was.

She signaled the band to play one more song before they took a break. Mark drew a question mark with his guitar head and she answered it with a shrug. Just great. The next song was Carly Simon's "Nobody Does It Better." She threw herself into the intro and closed her eyes, blocking him out while she sang, only to imagine him lying naked and tangled in the sheets.

Rocki finished the song and didn't take her fingers off the piano keys until quiet filled the bar. "I'm Rocki O'Sullivan and we're Nite Watch. We'll be back." She was just glad Pete wasn't sitting at the bar keeping track of her breaks.

The rest of the band lit off the stage and one of the bartenders switched on the music.

Rocki took a fortifying breath—she couldn't sit there hiding behind her piano forever. When she got the courage to look, the guy had disappeared. It was probably for the best. She rose, grabbed her water for a refill, and went down the steps—there was no jumping off the stage in her heels. When she hit the floor, an arm reached out from the hallway to the left and gently pulled her in. She should have felt threatened, but she didn't.

"Looking for someone?" His deep voice was as soft and smooth as top-shelf whiskey.

Her eyes rose and met his. Damn, he was a big one. In her heels she was pushing six feet two and he had at least a couple of inches on her. He looked as broad as he was tall. Solid. Hard. Dangerous—with a twist of naughty. The naughty part came on loud and strong in the quirk of his full lips. Lips a girl could sigh over and wish she had a matching pair. On anyone else they'd look girly—but on him, like a beautiful red apple, they just made her want to take a bite.

"I wasn't looking for anyone. But it looks as if you are." He stood so close she caught a whiff of the sea on him mixed with leather and yummy man. He didn't wear aftershave but that only made her want to stand closer and drink in his scent.

He leaned against the wall and looked her up and down, just like he had while she was onstage. His gaze lit her up like a sparkler on the top of a cake and she was dessert. No one had ever done that to her and she wasn't sure she liked it.

"I wasn't looking for anyone either—then I saw you."

The *you* came out on a purr and she felt the rumble in her chest. "Is that a good thing?"

"You tell me."

Rocki wasn't the nervous type, but this man looked at her in a way that set her hormones jumping, her heart pounding, and made her wonder if he had X-ray vision. She thanked the gods she wasn't wearing granny panties. His intense scrutiny had her trying to cover herself even though she was fully clothed. "I think it's too early to tell but it has definite possibilities."

"I'm more interested in probabilities. What's the probability of you letting me buy you a drink?"

Rocki looked at her watch. "Pretty good, but I have to be back on stage in about fifteen minutes."

He nodded to an empty booth. "No problem." He

placed his hand on her lower back, heat searing through the thin gauze of her dress, and steered her across the room. He leaned in close. "What do you want?"

She swallowed back a few racy retorts. She didn't know anything about this guy. "I'd love an Orange Crush."

"Done." He flagged down Wendy, the server he'd ignored earlier, and ordered her drink and another beer for himself. He settled into the booth across from her and seemed to take up the entire side. If she were sitting beside him, she'd have been pasted to him whether she wanted to be or not. She didn't think she'd complain.

"You have an amazing voice."

"Thanks. I'm glad you think so."

He took a sip of his beer. "Where else do you play?"

"Nowhere. We're the house band. We're here Tuesday through Saturday nights."

"Seriously? Why?"

He didn't look as if he meant to be offensive, so she chose not to take it that way. "Why not?"

He leaned back and shrugged, and if she wasn't mistaken, he looked disappointed. "You could be playing all over the city. Why would you choose to play in Red Hook?"

She took a sip of water and shrugged. "It's a steady gig, the band is happy to have to work only five nights a week. Most of us have day jobs, and no one is interested in pounding the pavement looking for gigs. Besides, Pete Calahan, the owner, is a great guy to work for. It's steady, and since I have simple tastes, the money is enough."

"Do you have a day job?"

"I work when I want. What about you?"

He leaned back and stretched out. "I'm kind of in between jobs. My next contract doesn't start until after the first of the year."

"What do you do?"

"IT security."

Wow, that didn't compute—the man was seriously built, he looked as if he was an athlete turned model—she so couldn't see him sitting behind a computer. "You're a techno weenie? Where's your pocket protector?"

One side of his lip quirked up in a sexy half smile as if a full one would take too much effort or would be too overwhelming for mere mortals. "I left it with the rest of my uniform—you know, plastic black-framed glasses taped together, white button-down shirt, high-waisted chinos that are a few inches too short, white socks, black shoes."

She tried to picture it and failed. No matter what this guy wore he'd look hot. He was a hot nerd.

"So, you said you worked when you wanted to." He leaned in close. "What do you do and does it require a uniform?" His deep voice dipped another half an octave and made her feel as if he were picturing her in a French maid costume.

She took a drink of her tepid water to wet her parched throat. The man had a way of driving her mind right into the nearest gutter. "Me?" God, did she just squeak? "I do voice-overs, sing backup and some voice acting—no uniform required, except this," she motioned to her dress.

His mouth quirked into a full smile. "That definitely beats chino waders."

Wendy brought over her Orange Crush and Rocki thanked her before taking a healthy swig. "I like to play dress-up when I'm onstage and whenever the mood strikes. For everything else I can get away with yoga pants and a T-shirt if I feel like it, but I prefer dress-up."

"You certainly excel at it." He cleared his throat and shifted in his seat.

He was definitely picturing her in a French maid costume. She almost told him she had one, complete with feather duster and fishnet stockings but stopped herself just in time.

"What is voice acting?"

"I record audiobooks—different voices for different characters, that kind of thing. It's fun and it keeps me in shoe money. What can I say? Shoes are my only vice."

One of his eyebrows rose and he shot her a sexy smirk. "You're sure about that?"

She had a feeling that if she spent more time with him, before she knew it, she'd have a long list of vices. The man was potent, and the way his eyes raked over her sent goose bumps skittering across her chest and shoulders. She was afraid it wasn't the only physical response he could see.

"Your occupation and only vices are certainly more interesting than mine—IT security can be pretty boring."

"You don't look as if you lead a boring life—just the opposite. I'm seeing a hard-nosed cyber warrior. But then I've always had a vivid imagination. So, what are your vices?"

"Fast bikes, faster computers, and beautiful women with sultry voices and strange shoe fetishes—not necessarily in that order."

"My shoe fetish is not strange." He didn't look as if he believed her, or maybe he would just prefer it to be strange and sexual—not that she'd know what shoes had to do with sex except maybe having sex with shoes on. . . .

"You don't have a New York accent—"

She laughed, almost glad for the change of subject. "No, but you do."

"So where are you from?"

"The Midwest and New England. You?"

"I'm from here, but I've traveled all over."

"Wanderlust?"

"No, navy."

"Join the navy, see the world?"

"That's what they say." He peeled the label off his bottle of beer. "Some parts are better than others. Still, it got me out of Red Hook."

"And yet here you are."

His eyes met hers and seemed to transmit a warning. "Temporarily."

Okay, so he was going off on another adventure. "Where are you off to next?"

"Bahrain most likely."

"The Middle East? Well, that's certainly not a place a man with very many vices would be comfortable living."

"Tell me about it."

"Don't they frown on the whole wine, women, and song thing out there? Isn't it an Islamic country?"

"Yes, it is. Bahrain is Middle East lite. It's a definite rub, but the job is challenging, the money is amazing, and there's nothing keeping me in the States."

"No wife or family?"

"If I had a wife, I wouldn't be buying you a drink. No wife, no girlfriend, and as for my family—they're used to me being away. Between school and the navy, I've been gone ten years. At least with this job I'll be able to visit a few times a year. I'll probably see them more than when I was in the navy."

She checked her watch and realized her time was up. The rest of the band had taken the stage and the music had been switched off, and all that could be heard was the low murmur of conversation. "Well, that's my cue. Thanks for the drink." She took a long swallow and set down the empty glass.

"You're welcome. Thanks for the company." He stood and offered her a hand. Damn, he even had manners. He helped her out of the booth and she almost got lost in his dreamy hazel eyes. "I hope we can do it again."

Rocki blew out a breath and decided there were a hell of a lot of things she'd like to do with him, the least of which was having a drink between sets. "Maybe. You know where I work . . . some of the time at least."

Slater watched Rocki O'Sullivan saunter back to the bar with a host of hungry eyes following her. The woman collected attention like a magnet collects shards of metal. He knew all about the laws of attraction, but had never experienced attraction this strong.

Damn, he wished Rocki wasn't his father's employee. Sleeping with the help was bad business.

Rocki hadn't blinked when he'd told her he was here only temporarily. She hadn't gone running off because he wasn't going to be here long enough to get attached, and after Dominique, the last thing he was looking for was attachment.

Attraction was one thing; attachment was another. All he wanted was a way to let off some steam, someone to have fun with, and if he was lucky enough to see Rocki wearing nothing but those funky shoes of hers, all the better.

She rounded the bar and shot him a teasing smile before slipping under the pass-through. After refilling her water, she moseyed toward the stage, stopping to say hello to a few people who looked like regulars and to hug a big guy Slater recognized immediately. The tendons in his neck and shoulders tightened as if someone had taken a ratchet to them. "Shit. Frankie DeBruscio."

Frankie had spent his entire high school career beating the crap out of Slater and his brothers.

Slater had always heard that when someone returned to their childhood home, everything looked smaller than they remembered. Unfortunately this wasn't true of bad-ass bullies like Frankie.

Their eyes locked and a smile cut Frankie's face in half—either he was happy to see Slater back in the 'hood, or he was looking forward to another fight.

Slater grabbed the back of his neck and tried to loosen his spasming muscles. It was way too late to pretend he hadn't recognized Frankie. All Slater could do was thank God he was a lot bigger now than he'd been at eighteen—the last time he'd tangled with Frankie. Luckily, he'd hit a few growth spurts. He'd grown four or five inches and packed on seventy-five pounds of muscle. He was no longer the scrawny kid Frankie used as a punching bag.

He cursed under his breath. The last thing he'd expected on his first full day home was to see Frankie. Slater figured Frankie would be in prison by now. But then a few people probably thought the same of Slater.

Frankie grabbed the hand of the woman beside him and made a beeline for Slater. Shit. He recognized the woman too—Patrice Taylor. She was just as beautiful as he'd remembered. Her mocha-colored skin shimmered and her long dyed blond hair fell in perfect order around her shoulders, as if she were starring in a shampoo commercial. When she spotted Slater, her smile widened, and her bright eyes locked on him. He groaned, praying it wouldn't be a painful reunion—he was not in the mood for a barroom brawl.

"Slater Shaw! Well aren't you a sight?" Patrice threw

her arms around him, going in for a hug, and a kiss on the cheek. "My, my, look at you. I always thought you'd fill out. I just had no idea how well."

He cringed, waiting for Frankie to pound him into dust—or at least try.

"When did you get back home, and how long are you staying?"

"I flew in yesterday. As for how long I'm staying? Maybe until the first of the year. How are you, Patrice? You're as beautiful as ever." He spoke to her but watched Frankie over her shoulder.

"You remember my husband, Francis, right?"

Husband? The school bully married the prom queen? "Francis?" Frankie had always beaten the crap out of anyone who dared to call him Francis—even the teachers. "Married. Wow. Congratulations."

Frankie slid beside his wife and took Slater's hand in a crushing grip, pulled him into a guy-hug, and pounded his back, almost knocking the wind out of him. "Good to see you back here, man."

"Really?"

"Pete must be thrilled to have you home."

Slater wasn't sure if Pop was thrilled, but whatever—he didn't even want to contemplate the reason for the less than thrilled reaction he'd received from the old man.

Patrice waved to Rocki, who had just started singing.

Slater couldn't help but notice that Rocki's eyes almost bugged out when she saw the three of them together. He wasn't sure why, but Patrice grabbed his hand and dragged him toward the booth he'd just vacated. "Now sit down and tell us all about what you've been up to. Pete said you left the navy and went to grad school in Seattle. And you worked for Microsoft?"

Frankie pulled Patrice into the booth beside him. She

snuggled up and rested against his big broad chest. "Give the man a minute, woman, and for God's sake, take a breath."

"I am breathing, you big galoot." Patrice elbowed Frankie—make that Francis. "I'm excited that Pete's last little rooster has returned to the nest."

Slater had never been referred to as a rooster, a cock maybe, a rooster no. He looked from Patrice to Frankie—it was just too surreal. "I didn't know you and Pop were close."

Francis shrugged. "I've been working for Pete since shortly before Logan left. I caused Logan to need a few stitches, and Pete told me I could work for him to pay off the hospital bill or he'd call the cops. Your old man helped me, believed in me. I became a paramedic and I still help out here on my off time."

Leave it to Pop to take on another troubled teen. And Frankie had been as troubled as they came. "You've worked for Pop for the last ten years?"

"On and off . . . whenever he needed a hand. We're close to Bree too. When Pete had his heart attack, we did all we could to help her out. The woman had her hands full with Nicki and the bar, and Pete in the hospital."

Patrice waved a hand in front of her husband. "Francis, enough about us. I want to find out about Slater. So?"

"So what?"

"Tell us everything. And don't you dare leave anything out. We haven't seen you in forever. Of course, Pete's mentioned what you've been up to, but it's always better to get the story right from the horse's mouth."

Slater didn't even know where to start or why they were so interested. "I'd much rather hear about you two. How long have you been married?"

Patrice spun her wedding ring around her long finger.

"Almost seven years. We got married right after I graduated nursing school. We had our daughter Cassidy a year and a half later—she's five and a half—and our second, Callie, is three. I work three days a week at Methodist and run roughshod over the family the rest of the time. Now, what about you?"

"What about me?"

Patrice gave him a *don't-even-try-to-mess-with-me* look. "What have you been up to?"

"I was in the navy for eight years. When I got out, I went to Digipen Institute of Technology and got my master's in computer security."

"You work at Microsoft?"

"I had a paid internship; now I'm waiting on a contract with OPEC. They want to buy a program I developed and hire me to implement it."

"OPEC? As in oil?" Frankie asked.

"Yep, that would be them."

Patrice leaned forward. "Where will you work?"

"Bahrain to begin with—if all goes well." If not, he'd be looking for a job but couldn't imagine going back to Seattle. No. He'd find a job someplace else. Someplace that was Dominique-free.

Drinks were delivered and both Frankie—make that Francis, damn that was going to take some getting used to—and Patrice thanked the server by name.

Patrice took a sip of her margarita and licked the salt off her top lip. "Bahrain." She looked as if she were searching her internal database. He saw the spark the moment she retrieved the data. "Isn't that an island in the Middle East?"

Slater took a drink and peeled the edge of the label off the cold bottle, not meeting Patrice's penetrating golden brown eyes. "That's correct."

"What's a guy like you going to do in an Islamic country?"

"A guy like me? What the hell is that supposed to mean?"

"Dude, Patrice meant a single guy like you." Frankie took a swig of his beer.

Patrice interrupted. "No, I meant the girl-in-every-port kind of guy. I've heard all the stories."

"You have? From who?"

"Storm and Logan."

Francis looked a little sheepish. "Patti has a way of dragging information out of anyone with a pulse. Still, isn't it gonna be a bitch trying to get a date there?"

"I don't know. I really hadn't thought about it." All he thought about was getting away from Dominique, Seattle, and Red Hook. Oh, and making a shit-ton of money. So much money that after five years, he would make Dominique and her new fiancé look like paupers. "It doesn't matter. The last thing I need is a woman to complicate my life."

Patrice pushed her long hair behind her shoulders and nailed him with her golden brown stare. "Complicate your life? Sounds to me as if you don't have much of a life to complicate. You've been gone almost ten years, and all you've talked about is your job. Granted, it sounds as if you've been plenty busy and very successful, but do you have a life? A life outside work? It doesn't sound as if you've taken much time to smell the roses."

"Patrice, there aren't many roses in the middle of the Arabian Sea, and since I left the navy, I've been working my ass off to get through school. I've been busy. Smelling the roses hasn't been an option."

A smile spread across Patrice's pretty face, the kind of smile that made him wonder if she knew something he didn't, and made the hair on his arms prepare to evacuate his skin. "Well, you have a month or so to just sit back and smell all the roses you want. And don't think I didn't notice how you watched my girl Rocki walk away. She was sitting here with you for her entire break, wasn't she?"

Shit. "Rocki seems very nice."

"Of course she's nice. She's one of my best friends and she's single."

Yes, they'd established that. "She's also Pop's employee, and since I'll be helping out here at the Crow's Nest and plan to be out of here come the first of the year, it's probably best not to complicate matters."

"Oh that's right. You don't need a woman to complicate your so-called life."

"Right." Not unless Rocki was into some very uncomplicated, hot, explosive, mind-numbing sex and could keep it on the down-low. Still, the gleam in Patrice's eye told him she already saw too much.

"Hey, you're both adults, and as far as I know, Rocki doesn't like complications either. She dates, but she's never had a long-term relationship in the three years that I've known her."

Francis wrapped his arm around his wife. "Now, Patrice, keep your nose out of his business."

Patrice waved away her husband's warning. "What? So I want my friends to enjoy themselves. They're both single adults and they're both not looking for"—she held her fingers up to make air quotes—"complications. I think they'd be perfect for each other. Temporarily, that is, and from the sparks shooting between them while they were tucked into this booth earlier, they're not going to be able to stay out of each other's pants for long anyway."

Patrice slid out of the booth pulling Frankie along with her. "You know what I always say, if you can't beat them, you might as well just cheer them on. It's like rooting for the Cubs—you know it's not going to end well, but it's always fun to watch."

CHAPTER 3

Rocki loved her friend Patrice like a sister. She'd never had one, but she knew from having a brother that sometimes you could love your sibling and want to throttle him or her at the same time. On her way to the stage, she'd given Francis and Patrice a hug, refilled her water, and then started her next forty-minute set. She sang, played the piano, and watched Patrice make a beeline for the hot biker dude whose table Rocki had just left.

To her amazement, Patrice proceeded to hug and kiss him like they were lifelong friends. Shit. To say that Patrice was known for sticking her nose in everyone's business was like saying that Congressman Weiner was known for sexting—it was the God's honest truth. Patrice would know the poor man's life story before she let him leave the booth.

Thinking back, Rocki realized she hadn't even gotten the guy's name. She'd been too busy mentally divesting him of all clothing to ask pertinent questions. Sometimes she wondered about herself. Was she so sex starved she'd jump the first man who floated her boat? Unfortunately the boat was a naval vessel. Great. She had no problem imagining him in dress whites or out of them apparently. Of course, when it came to men, her one weakness was a man in uniform and if they were sailors, all the better. That was why she always made it a point, during Fleet Week, to stroll through South Street Seaport daily and check out the scenery.

The trio retired to the same booth she and hot biker guy had shared. The poor man looked as if Patrice had just read him his Miranda rights. What the hell was she up to? And how did she and Francis know him? Sure, the guy said he was from Red Hook, but he'd also said he'd been away for ten years.

Rocki made it through her set without messing up the words, which was a true miracle, because the entire time, she found her gaze landing on the booth and the man.

Francis's discomfort came out strong and clear in the chagrined expression covering his face more often than not. When she caught the flash of Patrice's satisfied, *I've-done-my-duty* smirk, Rocki knew she was in trouble.

Having Patrice as an ally was always a good thing since the woman's machinations were ingenious, but Rocki didn't like being the object of Patrice's latest intrigue. She needed to put a stop to it and the only way to do that was to avoid the three objects of her interest at all costs.

Rocki finished her set, gave her taking-a-break spiel, grabbed her water, and hightailed it to the bar without even looking in the direction of Patrice's latest inquisition.

"Hey, Simon, do you have time to pour me a drink, or should I come back there and take care of it myself?"

It was always so much fun to see any of the Crow's Nest bartenders' reactions to her offer of help. Simon didn't disappoint—the man looked like an albino who'd just seen a ghost.

Rocki knew where her talents lay, and behind the bar was not one of those places. She hated covering for the bartenders, so, in order to avoid that, she might have played up her ineptitude just a bit. It worked—maybe too well. For God's sake, she didn't want to give the poor man a stroke.

"Another Orange Crush, Rocki? Or is there something else you want?"

She wanted to find out what Patrice was up to, but she refused to ask. She knew Patrice was waiting for her to do just that. "Orange Crush is fine, Simon, and would you refill my water, please?"

The look of relief was almost laughable. She took a seat at the end of the bar next to Simon's girlfriend, Elyse. "So, what do you know?"

Elyse grinned so broadly, you'd think she was starring in a toothpaste commercial. Rocki wished she wore shades. "I know you're off your game tonight. I don't think I've ever heard you forget the words before."

"You forgot the words?" Pete's deep voice boomed from behind her. "Are you feeling okay?"

"I'm fine." Rocki ruffled her hair until it matched her mood. "So, I've been a bit distracted—sue me."

Elyse looked over her shoulder to stare at the hot guy.

Pete's hold on Rocki tightened and followed Elyse's gaze. "The guy in the leather jacket is your distraction?"

Elyse nodded. "But what a distraction. Rocki sure knows how to pick 'em." She made a slurping sound.

"For God's sake, Elyse, wipe your face." Rocki wished Simon would hurry up with her drink. She checked her watch. Shit, she still had fifteen minutes left on their break. She looked from hot biker dude to Pete.

His eyes held a brightness she hadn't seen in way too long with a twist of something she didn't understand and wasn't sure she even wanted to—undisguised humor. It looked like he fought off a chuckle.

"I'm sorry about the brain fart. It won't happen again."

"No need to apologize, it's nice to see someone has the power to ruffle those pretty feathers of yours. I don't believe it's ever happened before. Your armor might be made of fabric, but until now, I've wondered if it was impenetrable."

"Pete—there will be no penetration with hot biker dude. You know me. Flirtation is one thing—the man is definitely a temptation—but that's as far as it goes."

He looked over at hot biker dude and those bright eyes flashed again. "I guess we'll see. He doesn't look the type to give up easily."

Simon delivered Rocki's drinks.

Pete grabbed a handful of pretzels. "Simon, give me a scotch."

"I'm sorry, Pete. I can't do that. How about a soda water with lime?"

"Boy, if I wanted a soda water with lime, I'd have asked for it."

"You know I'd be the first one to pour for you, but damn, between Rocki, Skye, and Patrice, the women will have my head, and Elyse over there will chop off a few other important parts. Sorry. Fire me if you must, but I'm more afraid of them than I am of you."

Simon took off for the other side of the bar and left Pete giving her his *I'm-disappointed-in-you* look.

"I can't believe I can't get a drink in my own bar. I thought you were on my side."

Rocki put her hand on his and gave it a squeeze. "I am on your side, and I want to make sure you're here for a long time, so do us all a favor, listen to your doctors. I don't want to lose you too." Rocki's eyes filled and, to her embarrassment, the water level increased with every blink. First she forgot the words to a song she knew as well as her own name—her real name—and now she was about to cry. "I don't think I could take it, Pete."

"Sheesh, leave it to you to pull out the heavy artillery." Pete kissed her cheek, and shook his head.

Elyse signaled Simon and he grabbed another beer for her and a soda water for Pete. Simon delivered them both and leaned over the bar and kissed Elyse. "Did you tell her yet?"

"Tell me what?" Rocki wondered if someone spiked the tap water with Love Potion Number Nine. First Simon fell hard for Elyse, and then Storm and Bree got back together and ended up married, and up until today, it looked as if Logan and Skye were on the fast track to the altar. Evidently they seemed to have hit an oil slick— not that anyone would give her a clue as to what the hell happened. It was all she could do to go into the kitchen to deliver Logan's message to Skye without coming out sporting a meat cleaver. It was bad. Where they'd end up was anyone's guess.

Elyse shot Simon an annoyed glare with a twist of a *just-wait-till-I-get-my-hands-on-you-later, sexy* promise. "What is it with men feeling the need to rush everything?"

Pete just stood there wearing his knowing grin and trying to look like he enjoyed drinking soda.

Rocki's gaze shot from Pete to Elyse. Then she tried to sneak a peek at the third finger of Elyse's left hand but couldn't—she was sitting on her hand. "Let me see it."

"See what?" Elyse was one of those sweet girls who blushed all the time. She was about Rocki's age, maybe even older, but compared to Elyse emotionally, Rocki felt ancient.

"The rock Simon gave you. You know, the engagement ring?"

Elyse shook her head, but the bright red blush covering her face told the story better than any words could. "Come on, let me see. I promise I won't say anything."

Elyse pulled the hand from beneath her leg and ran it nervously through her thick dark hair and then held it out for Rocki's inspection. "Nice." She'd seen some beautiful, expensive rings in her day, but this was over-the-top gorgeous in a totally artsy, Simon way. "This is Simon's work no doubt."

"He said he sketched it out and asked the jeweler to make it."

"It's so beautiful, he should consider designing jewelry full-time. It's gorgeous, girlfriend. Congratulations. I'm thrilled for you." And she was. She was just wondering what her life would be like once everyone else got hitched. Patrice was married and couldn't get away often because of the kids and Francis, but it had never bothered her because she always had Bree. Now Bree and Storm were off on their honeymoon and it was anyone's guess how much girl time they'd have now that Bree had taken the plunge. Elyse had joined them for their girls-night-out dates since she and Simon became an item, so now Rocki and Skye were the only single girls left.

"You don't look thrilled." Disappointment draped Elyse's face.

"I am happy for you. Really. It's just I'm the last one in the group who's single. Well, depending on what happens between Skye and Logan anyway."

Pete grumbled something about Logan getting his head out of his ass.

Elyse's eyes widened. "So it's Logan's fault? I heard Skye took off all upset. It sounds pretty serious." Her *I've-got-my-happily-ever-after* gaze landed on Rocki and she patted her hand. "Don't worry. You'll find someone."

Rocki wanted to run. Oh God, not again—why did couples feel the need to set up everyone who was happily single? She needed to stop this nonsense right now. "Oh no. I'm not looking to settle down. I feel as if I just got my independence—"

"You were in a relationship?"

Pete's bushy eyebrows rose.

Shit, shit, shit. Rocki took a deep breath. "No, not exactly. But there was always someone else controlling me—telling me how to live my life, where to go to school, what to study—"

"Parents can be such a drag. I know."

Rocki wished she had her parents to blame, but then her parents would never have imposed their will on her or sent her away so she wouldn't be a bother. Her uncles were nothing like her parents. She'd often wished she could do a DNA test to prove her theory that her father had been adopted. "I like my life now and I'm in no rush to change it. The last thing I want to do is give another man control over me."

"Hey." Elyse sat up straighter. "I might be getting married but that doesn't mean Simon controls me. I'm my own person; I just choose to share my life with Simon."

"Of course, and that's great. It's just not for me." Rocki searched for a way to escape this conversation and she still had another ten minutes before her next set started. She looked around, trying to find someone else she had to talk to. Unfortunately, when she did, she spotted Patrice heading her way. Damn. "If you want to keep your news a secret you'd better sit on your hand. Patrice is on her way over. Pete, not a word, you hear?"

He let out a laugh. "Yeah, good luck with that. I'm getting out of Patrice's way. Be good, ladies."

Rocki gave Pete a kiss on the cheek before turning back to Elyse. "Just be cool and don't look Patrice in the eye."

"Like you're not going to tell her."

"Hey, you have no idea how good I am at keeping secrets." Hell, she could hardly believe how good she was. She spent more time with Patrice than anyone else besides Bree, and the woman didn't have a clue. Maybe the secret to keeping secrets was never to let anyone know you have one.

"Rocki?" Patrice took the seat beside her. "Are you avoiding me?"

Rocki couldn't help but laugh. "Avoid you? As if it would ever work. What would be the point in trying?"

"Girlfriend, if I didn't know you adore me, I'd wonder."

Rocki let her smile unfurl like a flag in a soft wind and did her best not to wince when Elyse kicked her ankle. Damn, that was going to leave a bruise. She kept her eyes on Patrice. "So? Go ahead. Bring it on. I know you want to."

Patrice looked around her to Elyse. "Do you have any idea what she's talking about?"

No one could pull off the innocent look as well as Elyse, probably because it wasn't much of a stretch. She was the most innocent person Rocki had ever known— at least until she'd hooked up with Simon.

"Maybe she's referring to the man you and Francis were just questioning. The one who distracted Rocki so much she actually forgot the words to a song I've heard her sing at least a hundred times."

Patrice's brows rose to the height of the Empire State Building. Simon's little innocent Elyse was turning into a first-class traitor. If she hadn't been snitching on her, Rocki would be almost proud. Oh yeah, Elyse was getting more than just her groove on lately.

Patrice did her seventies Cher hair flip; the woman had the move down. "So, I saw you and Slater cozyin' up in the booth."

"His name is Slater?" Oh God. "Slater, as in Pete's son Slater?" Shit, the first guy she'd been interested in longer than she could remember and he was off-limits. "He's practically family. Not family, exactly—it's not as if we'd have two-headed children or anything—but there is no way in hell I'd ever get involved with one of Pete Calahan's kids."

Patrice's face lit up like a Times Square billboard. "So you already thought about taking him to bed? My, my, my, you do move fast. I'm impressed, girlfriend. If I wasn't happily married, I'd take him for a spin too."

"But he's Pete's son." Rocki groaned and thought about ordering a shot. Pete knew. God, no wonder he was so damn happy.

"Is that a problem?" Patrice looked dangerous and way too proud of herself.

"Hell, yeah, it's a problem. Pete's worse than a Jewish grandmother having a coffee klatch with the village yenta . . . or you. Pete already knows everybody's business before they do. I've managed to stay out of his peripheral vision for three years and I'm not about to have him homing in on me like a vulture circling fresh roadkill." Shit, shit, shit, he was probably already working on his flight pattern.

Patrice and Elyse stared at her with their mouths hanging open in silent shock.

"Look, I know Pete's heart attack scared him, and that ever since he's come home from the hospital, he's been doing his damnedest to see all his boys settled. Which is understandable as long as one isn't settled on me. I'm not daughter-in-law material."

Shit, bugger, bugger, shit! Why hadn't she connected the blasted dots? A sailor, a computer geek—she'd heard all about him. She'd been so damn enamored with his body she'd obviously gone brain dead.

Patrice didn't have to feign shock—she was really and truly stunned. "You didn't know?"

"No! If I had, I never would have—" What? Come on to him? No, she would have run in the opposite direction.

Patrice put on her evil queen face—she was obviously unaware of her tell, but Rocki had been a willing participant of her high jinks long enough to recognize it. "I think Slater looks like a perfect temporary distraction for you. He's out of here come the first of the year. And you have to admit that it's been forever since you've dated anyone. And like you, he's not looking for Mrs. Right—just a Ms. Right Now, and that's your M.O." She shrugged. "For you it's always been Mr. Right Now, or at least it has been since I've known you." Patrice hit her with her *tell-me-all* stare that for some strange reason always worked.

Rocki looked away to make sure her penetrating gaze wasn't some kind of voodoo truth serum.

"Have you ever had a real long-term relationship?"

"No, and I'm not looking for one." She still refused to look at Patrice. She didn't want to take any chances.

"Good. Then a little fun, frolicking, and mattress tag

with Slater would be great for both of you. Sounds like a temporary match made to get your mind and body back in the game. A woman shouldn't go that long without an orgasm that's not self-induced."

She caught Patrice's gaze in the mirror behind the bar, hoping Patrice's mojo couldn't work due to the reflection. Still, she felt the pull. She rubbed her bare arms, trying to chase away the goose bumps. "Don't knock BOB. All he needs to get me going is three C batteries and he's even good in the tub or shower. Besides, Patrice, you know how Pete is. He's—"

"A grown man who knows his sons aren't virgins. Heck, I'd be willing to bet that he even knows you're not a virgin."

Rocki held her head in her hands and then ran her fingers through her hair, which was already standing straight up. "Forget about it, Patrice. The last thing I want to do is disappoint Pete or have him think less of me. No, the only thing I'm going to do with Slater is practice avoidance." She chugged the rest of her drink, grabbed her water, and signaled Simon to switch off the canned music. It was time to start avoiding the most fascinating man Rocki had met in eons. "I gotta get back to work. Night, ladies." With any luck, they'd both be gone before she finished up at two. Too bad it was a Friday night— they could be here until close, and knowing her two friends, that was exactly what they had planned.

Slater spent the rest of the night watching Rocki perform. He couldn't believe she played here at his dad's bar instead of going somewhere she and her band would be discovered. It would be one thing if they'd lived in the middle of nowhere. But the woman worked in a town loaded with people who would be more than happy to make her a star. Rocki had it all—the looks, the person-ality, the talent . . .

He pulled out his phone and googled Nite Watch, and from what he could find, the band didn't even have a Web site. What the hell?

He googled the Crow's Nest's Web site and cringed. It was a one-page disgrace with a picture of Pop and the gang, and a description of the food and music, the ad-dress, and the hours. It didn't even have an app that would offer directions. It was worthless.

Patrice slid into the booth next to him and took his phone, looked at what he was doing, and then handed it back to him but not before she hit the kill button. "I don't know about your chances with Rocki. She didn't know she was flirting with one of Pete's kids."

"I'm hardly a kid, Patrice."

"Doesn't seem to matter. She's under the impression that since his health scare, Pete's trying to get you boys married off."

"Is he?"

Patrice shrugged. "I don't know. It could be that you're all of a certain age—the age people tire of living alone and start looking for their other half. I guess before you do that, you have to know yourself pretty well, and as far as I can tell, Rocki's still trying to figure herself out."

One look at Rocki told him the woman knew damn well who she was and what she wanted. That was one thing that attracted him to her in the first place.

"Why do you say that?"

"I don't know. Rocki's different from anyone I've ever known. It's as if every day is her birthday—she cele-brates her life, she doesn't simply live it. I love that about her. I don't think I've ever heard her wish for anything she doesn't have. Well, except maybe for a man with a body like Storm's, but I think she only did that to give Bree a hard time."

"Is she running from a broken heart?"

"Rocki? No. Rocki loves me and Bree, and the people who work here, but like I said, she hasn't had a relationship since I've known her."

"What about before you met her?"

"I don't know. I guess it's possible, but she's never really been one to talk about her past."

"And that worked with you? Hell, you just finished giving me the third degree. You know more about me than my own father does. How does she get away with it?"

Patrice shot him an incredulous look. "You know, I never really thought about it. She tells me everything—"

"Obviously not, since you don't seem to know much about her before she started working here."

"I know she had just graduated from college in Canada somewhere."

"Wow, that's specific."

"She has a degree in music."

"What about her family?"

Patrice's brow pinched. "I don't know." She looked over at the server walking toward them. "Wendy? Do you remember Rocki ever saying anything about her family?"

"She has a family?"

Patrice cocked her head and gave Wendy the *don't-you-know-anything* head shake. "She wasn't hatched from an egg, girl."

Wendy set her tray on their table and stretched her back. "She's always just talked about all of us like we were her family—Pete, Bree, you and Francis, and the staff. I think she even celebrates most holidays with Pete and the gang. You know how we always end up back here after everyone does their family thing. She takes a couple of vacations a year, but all I've been able to get out of her was that she had a relaxing time. I don't even know where she went. She came back with a great tan and joked about it being an all-over tan. I figured she went to one of those nudist colonies in Florida or something."

"Girl, are we talking about the same Rocki O'Sullivan? A nudist colony? I sincerely doubt that. You just have a dirty mind."

Wendy laughed. "Maybe, but do you know where she went?"

Patrice's brow furred. "Bree and Pete must know."

Wendy shook her head. "Not Bree—the two of us spent the entire two weeks guessing. We tried to get it out of her when she came home. She was all mum. We even accused her of being in the CIA."

Slater ordered them another round and Wendy headed to the bar. "So how can you, the neighborhood busy-body—"

"Hey, I resemble that remark."

"Yeah, I gathered that. So how is it you know so little about someone you obviously think of as a best friend?"

Patrice was stunned speechless.

"Kind of makes you wonder, huh?"

"Maybe she's just a private person."

"Like me?"

"Fine." Patrice raised her hands and held them out as if she were holding her own cartoon bubble. "I can't explain it."

"Yet you know everything about her since she moved here. I asked her where she was from and she said the Midwest and New England—no specifics. She's good at dodging questions." Which did nothing but make him more curious. "The band doesn't even have a Web site."

"Not everyone has a degree in computer security, Slater."

"Yes, but you can pay someone to build a Web site. If she's looking to make something of her band and her talent, she needs a Web site and a Web presence. It's as if she's trying *not* to be discovered, as if she's hiding in plain sight."

"Hiding?"

"Well, Red Hook is hardly the hotbed of the music world. That's L.A. and Manhattan—just across the bay. Name one band that came out of this hole?"

"Red Hook isn't a hole. And don't you be letting Bree hear you talk like that. She's spent the last five years working with the Red Hook Revitalization Committee. They brought in IKEA and the Fairway Market—the place is really changing for the better."

"Fine, but you have to admit it's not Manhattan. If you want to be discovered you play the hot clubs in the city, not a neighborhood bar in Red Hook."

Patrice shrugged. "Rocki is happy with her life. She likes doing what she's doing. In her mind, she's successful. She has a full life, great friends—"

"Great friends who don't even know where she came from." He watched Rocki playing her heart out, singing about loneliness and hurt. She was a damn good actress, or she could relate to the familiar lyrics. She looked so . . . broken . . . that he fought the urge to jump up onstage just to hold her—if there was one person who looked as if she needed a hug, it was Rocki. She finished the song and stared at the piano keys, letting the sound die a natural death. Then he watched her shut that part of herself off. The pain he'd seen came out in her music, and when she looked up and saw him staring, her face flamed. Yeah, she was busted and she knew it. He'd seen that part of herself she thought she hid from the world, and she was not happy that he was the one who discovered the crack in her soul.

Patrice waved a hand in front of his face. "Earth to Slater? What the hell are you saying?"

"I'm just saying that the woman is intriguing."

CHAPTER 4

Rocki had never tried to sneak out of the Crow's Nest before; tonight she tried to be invisible. A little hard to do, considering her outfit and the fact that Slater seemed to stare holes through her. Why couldn't she be one of those New York women who always dressed as if they were going to a funeral? Still, it was too late to change now, so she hunched down and followed Mark out.

"Where are you headed?"

Shit. Slater had snuck up on her. She spun around to look at him and almost ran into his broad chest. If not for some fancy footwork on her part, she'd be plastered to him. "Mark usually gives me a ride to the F-train."

"I'll drive you home."

"No, thanks."

"Rocki, it's two in the morning. I don't want you running around the city alone this time of night."

She shoved her hand in her pocket, grabbed her tiny bottle of pepper spray, and aimed it at him. She didn't release the safety, but it took everything in her not to do exactly that just to scare him. "I'm armed and dangerous and I've been making the trip alone for three years. I've never had a problem." At least not one she'd mention to anyone here. "Besides, I'm hardly dressed for a ride on your bike. If you haven't noticed, it's cold outside—"

"And raining. I have Pop's keys. His car is parked right out front."

"Look, Slater, I appreciate the offer, but I don't need an escort."

"What kind of car does Mark drive?"

"A white panel truck. Why?"

"Because it looks as if you've missed your ride."

"What? Mark would never leave without me."

Slater's innocent grin reconfigured into a naughtier than naughty smile—one that had her sucking in a deep breath to make up for a sudden lack of oxygen.

"He would if I told him I'd be taking you home. It didn't hurt that Patrice and Francis vouched for me. Mark's very protective of you."

"It must be comforting to know you have company on my shit list. I just added Mark's name right below yours on my mental dry-erase board in bright red lipstick." She pulled out her wallet, scrounged around for her debit card, and then dug for her cell. "I'll just call a cab."

"Come on," he said, stilling her hand, "save your money and let me give you a ride. What are you afraid of?"

Other than losing her panties and her mind, she wasn't sure, but she wasn't about to cop to that. "Slater, if I can handle the New York subway system, I can handle anything and anyone. You certainly don't scare me."

"That's good, because instilling fear is not what I'm going for."

Her plan to avoid the man was failing miserably, but she didn't know how to get out of the pickle jar she suddenly found herself trapped in. "What exactly are you going for?"

A slow sexy smile said all she'd feared. He was going for her and she didn't want to be gotten.

"Just to get to know you better. We spent fifteen minutes talking and I learned one very important thing."

"What's that? What I like to drink?"

"Orange Crushes, but that's not important. I learned that you're a master of deflection when it comes to anything personal. All I know about you is that you're from New England and the Midwest—no specifics. You left me with more questions than I had when we sat down together, and believe me, only a few of those were sexual."

It wasn't the words that shocked her, it was the way he said them. The man made her want to grab her panties and hold on tight—he didn't look like the kind of man who needed to add to his collection. He was a good two steps away but she felt as if he were in her personal space—not just her personal space but her private, private, private space, and she wasn't sure she didn't like it. If he moved any closer, not only would she be unable to breathe, but she'd also lose what was left of her wits, and that would be bad. Very bad. "I'm not playing hard-to-get if that's what you're wondering. You're a nice guy, but I'm just not interested in dating one of Pete's sons. I don't mix business with pleasure, and as soon as I found out who you were, I firmly placed you in the nothing-but-business category."

Slater tossed a set of keys in the air and caught them. "Okay, you can have it any way you want it, Rocki." It was just so wrong that every word out of his mouth made her think of sex. The worst part was he knew exactly what he was doing. "What can I say? You have me intrigued on multiple levels. I find it fascinating that you're skillful enough to dodge your best friend Patrice's questions. She's a tougher interrogator than Pop—and that's saying something. It's amazing that you were able to pull it off without Patrice ever realizing it. Well, not until I pointed it out to her."

"You didn't!" God she wanted to wipe that sexy smirk right off his face with her pair of killer combat boots— too bad she wasn't wearing them. "I can't believe you would sic Patrice on me."

"Why not? From what I saw this evening, Patrice is willing to share her extensive knowledge about everyone with just about anyone. How else did you expect me to get to know you? It's a hell of a lot safer to get the info out of Patrice than to pick the lock on Pop's filing cabinet and read your dossier. Oh, and don't think for a minute he doesn't have one on you." Slater took a step closer. "I might just have to resort to that since it's obvious I'm not going to find a damn thing about you on the 'Net. Your band doesn't even have a Web presence. So come on, put me out of my misery and let me take you home. You can tell me all the interesting things Pop wouldn't know—the info on what kind of undies you're wearing, if any, is optional."

Rocki pushed away from the wall and stomped out the door, drawing the collar of her coat close to keep the rain from streaming down her neck. By the time she slid into Pete's car, her equilibrium returned.

Slater held the door for her while she pulled her dress down over her legs and checked to make sure she wasn't flashing him. When she caught his eye, she almost groaned. The man wore that self-satisfied grin she was beginning to recognize.

Most men who stood in the pouring rain looked like wet dogs, but, unfortunately, Slater just looked like a man who had been sprayed down for a modeling shoot. His eyelashes were so thick, raindrops clung to them and sparkled in the light of the streetlamp. His hair curled in corkscrews just like she'd imagined it would. He was a walking, talking wet dream. She should be cold, but instead was just the opposite—she was tempted to turn on the air-conditioning.

After she was settled, Slater closed her door and ran around to the driver's side—even the way he moved was predatory and graceful like some kind of jungle cat. He slid in beside her, taking up all the available space and oxygen, started the car, and turned on the heat and the defroster—yeah, she'd already fogged up the windows with just the heat of her thoughts.

"So, where do you live?"

"Chinatown."

Slater wiped the rain off his face and pulled into traffic, heading toward the Manhattan Bridge.

Rocki expected a barrage of questions—questions she didn't want to answer. She'd happily lived in her perfect little world for three years and, now, one day in Slater Shaw's presence had blown it all to hell. They drove in silence so thick, it made it difficult to breathe. By the time he'd turned onto the Brooklyn-Queens Expressway she was at her wits' end.

She turned in her seat to face him, which didn't help. Still, she refused to utter a word but couldn't stop the growl from escaping. Lord, he was driving her crazy.

He glanced her way. "Are you too hot?"

"No, I'm not hot at all." A voice in her head screamed *liar, liar, panties on fire* and that little voice sounded suspiciously like Patrice's.

"Want me to turn up the heat?"

"Isn't that the reason for this little trip?"

"No." He didn't even bother to pretend the double entendre wasn't intentional. "But I wouldn't complain if it did. I don't know what's going through your mind, Rocki O'Sullivan, but I'd love to. So, since something is obviously bothering you, why don't you just come out with it?" His gaze raked her from head to knee and sent a shiver through her. "But then maybe not. If I learned everything about you, you'd lose that whole woman of mystery thing you've got going."

"There's no mystery. I just don't feel the need for everyone at the Crow's Nest to know my life story."

"I'm not everyone. And believe me, I know how to keep a secret."

"That's nice." She patted his shoulder. "Still, for some reason, I don't have the urge to share. You should understand that." She licked her bottom lip and then scraped her teeth across it. "Think classified information."

"Don't worry." He leaned closer. "I have Top Secret. Sensitive. Compartmentalized. Information. Clearance."

All she could do was stare at his lips. "I'll just bet you do."

"So?" He leaned closer still, his breath brushed her ear. "Are you going to tell me?"

So much for her equilibrium. She needed to stay far, far away from Slater Shaw. "That's need-to-know information. I'll leave you to work it out."

"Oh, a challenge. I love challenges almost as much as I love puzzles and you're both." He shot her an *I've-got-this-covered* grin and let out a laugh. "I guess it's a good thing I have a diverse skill set."

"Great." She'd succeeded in doing the one thing she didn't want to do—she'd practically dared him to dig into her background. But without her real name, he wouldn't get far. Would he? She'd been using her stage name ever since she hit New York, and she used it for everything. She just wished she knew it would work.

Slater's hacking skills were part of the Crow's Nest's lore. Rumor had it he'd been caught hacking into his school's computer when he was just a child. He'd probably improved since then. She'd heard tales of him hacking into the NYPD database and deleting his and his brother's juvenile criminal records. She wasn't sure it was true, but looking at him now, she wouldn't put it past him.

She caught him staring at her and hoped he had good peripheral vision. "What?"

"I didn't mean to freak you out, Rocki. Are you in some kind of trouble? Is that why you're keeping such a low profile?"

"No. You've been watching too much TV. I'm not in witness protection or anything. Is it against the law to be afraid of someone digging into your past? I share what I want to share, and the rest of my life is just that—mine. It's not any of Patrice's or your business, so just leave it alone."

"Okay, but that's sad."

"Sad? Sad that you don't have permission to snoop about me?"

"No, what's sad is that you don't trust anyone enough to open up. Not even your best friend. What's got you so scared?"

"Nothing."

Slater shook his head and his usual easy grin turned suspiciously empathetic. "You know sometimes we build things up in our minds until they seem so much bigger and more important than they actually are."

"Are you speaking from personal experience?"

"I don't know. I haven't figured it out yet, but I'm letting it marinate. Maybe you should do the same."

Rocki had never been so happy to see Canal Street in all her life. "Make a left on Canal and I live just on Mott."

Slater took the turn and drove—not bothering to fill the silence, which was just fine with her. "Mott's the next cross street. Make a left and stop in front of the restaurant."

"Which one?"

"Here on the right."

She expected him to just stop and drop her off but no, he was out of the car and had her door open before she could pull her collar up. He offered her his hand and she almost groaned. There was no way to avoid it. She placed her hand in his and before she could pull away he'd linked his fingers through hers. She'd never been big on hand-holding because it always felt awkward, but for some ungodly reason, this time it felt right—like his hand, arm length, and proximity was just perfect for holding hers. She couldn't wait to get out of it. "Thanks for the ride."

"I'll walk you up."

She pulled away and tried to quell the feeling of loss when she did. She dug through her bag for her keys. "Thanks, but there's no need."

"Humor me." He held out his palm, obviously waiting for her to hand him her key.

She rolled her eyes and held the key to the outer door out to him. "I've been humoring you all night, but that's going to stop at the door to my apartment. Don't expect to be invited in."

He opened the door and held it. "What floor are you on?"

"Just one up. I can take it from here."

"I'll see you to the door."

"Fine." She pushed her wet bangs out of her eyes and trudged up the steps, cursing under her breath. It was dangerous having Slater so close. She stood in front of her door, facing him, and then she remembered he still had her keys.

The smile on his face said he knew she was back in the pickle jar. He looked through the keys and found one with a bright red rubber piece surrounding the head. "Is it this one?"

"Yes."

He leaned in, rested his left hand on the doorjamb, blocking her in, and fit the key into the lock.

She pushed back against the wood, the slats digging into her back. He was so close she smelled the rain on him. He was so close she felt his breath brushing her cheek. He was so close she felt his heat, but he didn't touch her. Not that she wanted him to—much.

"When you go in, make sure you lock up."

All she could do was nod.

"Sweet dreams, Rocki."

Right. With the way her day was going, those dreams would not only be sweet, they'd be wet.

After a night of too little sleep due to way too many thoughts of one particularly hot blonde who had the ability to steal the spotlight while fading into the woodwork and some serious trust issues, something had woken Slater and, unfortunately, it hadn't been Rocki.

He'd finally been out for the count and now he was wide awake. Shit. One glance at his watch and he let out a groan. It was too early to be awake. He rubbed his eyes and felt the foot of the bed dip. What the hell? There was a kid in his room. And a dog. "Nicki, what are you doing in here?" Hadn't she ever heard of knocking? He pulled the sheet up and thanked God he wasn't flashing her. Still, he was uncomfortable. He'd never before been naked under nothing but a sheet in the presence of a ten-year-old girl and her dog.

"D.O.G. needs to go out."

"So, take him out."

Her hair looked like a rat's nest—curls stuck straight out from what looked like matted knots.

"I'm not allowed to take D.O.G. out by myself and Pop's still not up for it. D.O.G. pulls too hard and it hurts Pop's chest, and sometimes D.O.G. pulls me right over. I scraped my knee. Wanna see?"

"No." He was afraid if he'd said yes, the kid would take her pants off or something and the last thing he wanted was for them both to be without pants.

"It's right under the hole in my jeans here." The kid lifted her knee to show off her ripped jeans. "Skye put some stuff on it that made the stinging stop. She's nice."

"Yeah, okay."

"Mr. Francis came up before he and Ms. Patrice left last night and took D.O.G. for a walk since you weren't around, but that was hours and hours ago and D.O.G. has to pee."

Shit, he'd forgotten all about the mutt last night. He'd never had a dog. He knew no more about what to do with a dog than he knew about what to do with a little girl. He did have a very strong suspicion he would no longer be sleeping in the raw.

"I'd have brung you coffee—"

"Brought."

"Whatever." Nicki pushed her hair out of her eyes and he looked away. How a ten-year-old, fifty-pound girl could give him the willies he'd never know.

"I would have brought you coffee but I don't know how you take it." She shrugged and she and the dog leaned against the bed watching him. "Storm and Logan were always nicer when I waked them up with coffee but Skye's nice all the time. I guess it depends on the grown-up, huh?" She tilted her head to the left and crossed her bony arms over her chest. "Or is it only boys who are always cranky in the morning?"

"I'm not cranky. Why don't you and your buddy there get ready to go and let me get dressed."

"You want me to pour your coffee?"

"Sure. I take it black."

"Sugar?"

"No, I'm sweet enough as it is."

The kid actually cracked a smile and let out a little giggle. "Hurry up and get dressed. Maybe we'll run into Skye and Pepperoni. Then we can take both dogs to the dog park and let them play and you can buy us bagels. Logan always buys us bagels before school. He promised he'd come home, you know."

"He did?" Slater hoped the kid wouldn't be disappointed if Logan had a sudden change of plans. After all, it sounded as if he and Skye had some kind of blowup.

"Sure. He loves Skye and Skye loves him so of course he's coming home. People don't leave people they love."

From what Slater had seen, love was temporary at best. Nicki obviously had read one too many fairy tales. What was it with little girls—hell, big girls too—and love? Until last night, he didn't think he'd ever seen a couple who were really in love.

Nicki worried her lip between her teeth and backed out of his room. D.O.G. eyed him warily and followed her out.

"Nicki, close the door."

When the door snicked shut, he picked up his jeans off the floor and tugged them on.

If Francis and Patrice weren't in love, then they had been doing a hell of a job of faking it last night. He'd watched them dance and almost felt like a voyeur. The way they danced and looked at each other made him uncomfortable enough to look away. It was so intimate, so personal, that even though they weren't doing anything at all sexual, the two of them should have gotten a room. He'd never seen anything like it.

Slater headed to the bathroom with Nicki's words repeating in his head. *People don't leave people they love.* He loved his father and his brothers, but he had no problem leaving them. He guessed it would be different if he loved a woman, but since that had never happened, he had to be immune.

He ran his head under the faucet—the only way to deal with his bed head—brushed his teeth, and dragged on a Henley before grabbing his jacket.

Nicki stood by the door holding D.O.G.'s leash in one hand and a travel mug of coffee in the other. "Thanks for taking us out."

"No problem." He took a swig of coffee, tapped his back pocket to make sure his wallet was still there, and grabbed the keys. "Let's go."

Nicki handed him the leash. "You first, but be careful, he gots to go bad, so he'll pull you down the steps."

"Thanks for the warning." And it was a good thing she'd told him because if she hadn't, he was sure he'd be on his ass. He hightailed it outside and waited for Nicki while D.O.G. took a leak on the nearest tree.

She shook her head. "Told you he had to pee bad."

"You sure did." The rain had stopped and the skies had cleared and it was unseasonably warm. He took off his jacket and asked Nicki, "Why don't you show me this dog park and the bagel shop? We can let your boy here play and bring back breakfast."

"Okay." Nicki grabbed his hand.

He'd never held a little girl's hand before and he wasn't sure why he was now, but he didn't think it would be cool to ask. He didn't want Nicki to think he didn't like her.

"I'm not allowed to cross the street without holding a grown-up's hand."

Great, he'd better start doing a better job of hiding his discomfort around the kid.

"The park is this way." Nicki skipped across the street and let him go as soon as she hit the sidewalk. "Bree's pretty weird about things like crossing the street and she has spies everywhere. It's just not worth taking a chance on getting caught."

He figured she was more than old enough to cross the street alone, but then what did he know? All he wanted to do was get the dog walked, buy breakfast, and get home.

Slater watched Nicki and D.O.G. play and wondered if he'd blinked and missed winter. It felt like spring. Nicki had dropped her coat on a bench so Slater picked it up and watched her and D.O.G. race around the park.

He took a deep breath—fresh air filled his lungs, and heightened the sense of expectation. His blood buzzed through his body. It was a perfect day. If the weather report was accurate, the mercury would hit seventy and he wasn't going to miss his last chance for a comfortable ride.

"Come on, Nicki. Time to go. Patrice is going to pick you up to go to see the Intrepid Sea, Air and Space Museum today."

Nicki ran all out toward him. He held out a hand and caught her.

"It's a museum." She strung the word out like a piece of taffy until it broke. "Do I have to go?"

"The Intrepid is awesome—it's an Essex class aircraft carrier. You'll get to check out the whole ship. Plus there's the space shuttle, and they even have a Russian space capsule. It's a really cool museum."

"If you think it's so great, how come you're not going?"

Smart-ass kid. "I wasn't invited."

Nicki took his hand. "That's okay. You don't need an invitation. You can come with us."

She tugged him toward the gate and he wondered how the hell he'd get out of it. Then he realized he didn't want to—it would be fun to check out the *Intrepid*, to be on board a ship again, even if it was only a museum. It wasn't as if he couldn't go with them and then take off early if he was bored. And Patrice might be happy to have a little help. He didn't think he could handle watching a three- and five-year-old, but he'd been helping out with Nicki this morning and he hadn't lost her yet. "How about I take you to Patrice's house? We can take my bike if it's okay with Pop, and then we can ask Patrice if she wouldn't mind me going along."

Nicki shot him a look that told him she was way too proud of herself. She thought she'd played him like Parcheesi and what the hell, he'd let her bask in the illusion.

Nicki had one hand on D.O.G.'s head while she skipped all the way to the apartment. For once she looked like every other normal kid. The kind of kid with a real family, the kind of kid who never went hungry or wondered when she'd eat again. The kind of kid who knew the meaning of love and trust and security. For just a few minutes, they both could bask in that illusion.

CHAPTER 5

Rocki took the last slug of coffee, stepped up to Patrice and Francis's house, and let herself in. "Patrice, it's me."

Patrice bopped out of the kitchen, and it was a bop, followed by a shimmy, and sometimes a sway—the woman looked like she moved to a Motown beat that played on a continuous loop in her head. She didn't walk, she didn't saunter, she did a modified conga.

Patrice wiped her hands on a towel. "I'm just putting together a few snacks for the trip." She stopped talking, walked up to Rocki, and eyed her new boots. "Uh-huh." She placed her hands on her hips and struck an irritated pose. "So, girlfriend, what's the problem?"

Rocki did her best to look bored. "No problem. I just saw these in a window and had to have them."

"Right. So nothing had you running out for emergency retail therapy? You said you were going to work this morning; that's why we're going at noon. You didn't have time to shop, remember?"

"I didn't shop."

"Yeah, so tell me what's in the bag?"

Shit. Rocki was tempted to hide the bag behind her

back but it was already too late. "Just a few ribbons I thought the girls would like for their hair."

"Hm-hmm, yeah, that's not shoppin' all right."

Rocki let out a breath and prayed for strength. "So, I'm blocked—nothing I wrote worked. I was just making a hash out of the whole piece. I had to get out. Shopping is not a crime. I paid for everything—I even paid way too much for these boots, but you have to admit they're gorgeous."

Patrice cocked her hip and looked down her nose. "Girlfriend, you best be careful because you're in for a shock."

"I already know what the boots cost me. It's no longer a shock."

"That man affects you like the moon affects the tide, and you don't even know each other—yet. But you will. I have a feeling you definitely will."

"I will not." Her retail therapy had served its purpose. She'd hardly thought about Slater since she started. Okay, maybe that wasn't entirely true. She'd thought about him, but she hadn't pictured him naked—not in the last hour.

"Ha, you didn't even have to ask what man. You and I both knew who we were talking about. Just sayin'." Patrice gathered the kids and helped them with their backpacks. She opened the door, ushered them out, and stepped onto the front stoop before looking over her shoulder. "Rocki, are you coming?"

No, but damn, she wanted to. She practiced her deep breathing. Maybe she needed more oxygen to the brain. "I'll be out in a minute."

The door closed—yeah, she needed a minute. A minute to finish putting herself together. The kids squealed in the front yard and she knew Nicki must have arrived.

The pumpkin orange boots were drool-worthy but were slouching so she tugged them over the knees of her black skinny jeans. She'd brought her black leather jacket to wear over her long-sleeved T-shirt even though she didn't need it. It rounded out the outfit, and who knew how long the freakishly warm weather would stick around. She checked her lipstick in the mirror by the door, ran a hand through her hair, making the top stand up, and hoped there'd be a few sailors on board the USS *Intrepid*. Maybe a man in uniform would replace the vision of the one she'd been picturing with and without clothes.

Rocki opened the door, looked out, shook her head, and blinked, hoping the vision in front of her was just the result of her extremely overactive imagination. But this one was different—in this one, Slater was dressed. She rubbed her eyes only to open them and see the very man she'd been trying to erase from her mind since last night. "What are you doing here?"

Nicki bounced beside him. "Slater's coming with us, but he's going to have to ride his motorcycle since there's not enough room in the car. I want to ride with him, but he said no."

Slater's eyes traveled the length of Rocki's body and he took his time, hitting all the highlights, and sending a trail of warmth all the way from her head to her toes. "Nice boots."

"Thanks." She hadn't realized she'd stopped midway down the stoop, so she started walking again. "I didn't know you were invited."

"It was a last-minute thing." His eyes homed in on hers and the quirk of his lips told her he'd planned this. "Nicki wanted me to come, and Patrice was nice enough to include me."

Patrice stood beside him wearing her *this-is-going-to-be-so-entertaining* grin. "I've always found it helpful not to let the kids outnumber the adults. Now we're even. Since Francis was supposed to go with us before he got called into work, we even have an extra ticket."

Rocki pasted what she hoped would pass for a smile on her face and did her best to inject cheer into her voice—she never had a problem when she was voice acting, but looking at Slater made her feel anything but cheerful. "Lucky us." She averted her eyes and walked right past him toward the car.

Rocki held the door open for the girls and couldn't believe Pete let Nicki ride with him. If Bree found out, there'd be more than one skillet flying.

Patrice buckled Callie in and then looked over the top of the car at Rocki. "He sure looks good straddling that bike."

"I hadn't noticed." Rocki got into the car and ignored both Slater's and Patrice's annoying laughter. She wanted to strangle Patrice, but she couldn't do it in front of the kids and Patrice knew it. She'd just avoid him the rest of the day.

Slater started his bike and the purr of the engine slid over her—it wasn't one of those obnoxiously loud Harleys; it was a either a classic or was made to look like one. It was hard to tell since the bike was in pristine condition. It had beautiful lines and as much charisma as its owner. A powerful machine made for a powerful man. A dangerous combination.

He waved and took off ahead of them. Maybe they'd get there and lose him. Maybe she could just take one of the girls and either take off ahead or lag far behind—anything to avoid spending the day with Slater.

*   *   *

An eternity later, Rocki climbed down the gangplank and held on to Cassie's hand.

Cassie looked up at Rocki and gave her a smile that matched her momma's—a little bit sweet, a little bit evil, but Cassie's evil tendencies weren't as well developed or effective. Still, at five, the kid was fishing for tasty information. "So what did you learn, Rocki?"

She'd learned that there wasn't a ship large enough for both her and Slater. But she couldn't say that. "I learned the *Intrepid* is an aircraft carrier and it's really long."

"Mine's longer. I was on the USS *Ronald Reagan*." Slater's breath brushed Rocki's ear and his deep voice sent her pulse skittering. "I hear size matters."

They'd been on the ship for a couple hours and every time Rocki turned around, Slater was there. Every passage they went through, Slater helped her over. Every retired sailor they'd met, Slater had made an impression. The whole ex-navy thing must have been tattooed on his forehead in invisible ink seen only by fellow sailors. Maybe it was the ease with which he moved around the ship, or the way he held himself. Whatever it was had all her girly parts standing at attention, and a few even gave him a salute. That was so not good.

Nicki skipped past Rocki on her way to the car, Patrice and Callie followed, and Slater brought up the rear.

Rocki turned to face him and walked backward toward the car. "I guess I'll see you around."

A slow half smile came to his lips—as if a full smile would have been just too much trouble. "I was wondering if you were free. I thought we could grab a bite, maybe go for a ride through the park. It's probably the last nice day we'll have until spring, and I don't know about you, but I'd like to enjoy it. What do you say?"

She looked around, not sure how to get out of it, not

sure she even wanted to. Okay, she didn't want to get out of it, but she knew she shouldn't go. "I don't have a helmet."

He pulled one out of the saddlebag and handed it to her. "I have an extra."

She stared at the helmet, wishing she had the self-control to hand it back to him and get in Patrice's car.

"I bought it today so Nicki could ride with me." Slater raised a shoulder and Rocki saw a shadow of the tall, lanky geek Patrice had told her about.

Rocki's concentration was shattered when Patrice slammed the car door, looked over the roof at her, and waved. "I'll call you later, Rocki. You two have fun."

"Wait!" By the time she yelled, Patrice was already driving away. "It looks like I don't have much of a choice."

"You could always take the subway home, but it's a hike to the Port Authority, and my bike is more fun. There's nothing like the feeling of seventy-five horsepower between your legs."

She wanted to smack herself—he'd played her like Pavlov played the dogs when he rang the bell. Her conditioned response had her mind going from slightly pissed to over-the-top horny in a nanosecond. The last person she wanted to be horny with was Slater. She stuffed the helmet under her arm, put a hand on her hip, and a *don't-give-me-shit* cock to her head. "Did you and Patrice have this planned?"

"No."

She stared into his eyes and knew he wasn't lying. "Just so you know, this isn't a date."

He took the helmet from her and tossed it from one hand to the other like a basketball. "Okay, if it's not a date, what is it?"

"It's nothing."

He stepped toward her, placed the helmet with a full face mask on her head, and tightened the chin strap. "That's good because I've been looking forward to doing nothing with you since the first time I saw you." He flipped the visor down, effectively cutting her off from saying any more. It was a good thing the helmet covered her mouth; she'd hate for him to see her drool.

Slater straddled the bike and held his hand out to help Rocki.

She ignored it, grabbed his shoulder, and threw her leg over.

"Wrap your arms around my waist and hold on."

"No, thanks. I'll just hang on to the bars back here."

"Suit yourself." He took off, knowing her back would hit the backrest, and her arms flew around his waist before he was out of the parking lot.

"You did that on purpose."

Damn straight he did. But then there was no reason to tell her she was right. She knew it. "Are you hungry? We could have a picnic in the park." He took the turn onto Twelfth Avenue a little tight and her arms squeezed his waist, her thighs squeezed his hips, and her breasts flattened against his back.

She didn't answer but then he didn't really expect her to. The bike and the beautiful day were working their magic. It's hard to say no to a longer ride on a perfect day, and with Rocki holding on to him, he was having a hard time seeing anything that wasn't perfect—well, except for the fact that Rocki really didn't want to be with him. She wanted on the bike—sure. She wanted to take a ride—hell, yeah. But with him—not so much.

He headed uptown, turned onto Fifty-Eighth Street to Columbus Circle and Central Park West, and wondered how to handle Rocki. And by God, he did want to handle her. He parked the bike, removed his helmet, and offered Rocki a hand.

This time she took it.

He helped Rocki off. "I'm not going to take it personally."

Rocki tugged at her chin strap. Confusion furred her brow. "Take what personally?" She pulled the helmet off and then raked her hand through her hair until it stood up again.

He looked deep into those eyes he couldn't get out of his head. "I'm not a threat, Rocki. I don't want to take over your life. I just wanted to be friends."

"Friends? That's why I'm getting the full-court press?"

Leave it to Rocki to put it all out on the line. He thought he was direct. He shrugged. "I want to get to know you." Oh yeah, and that was the truth; he wanted to know everything about her. What she hid from the world, what she felt like in his arms, the sounds she made when she was excited, and he wanted to see the look on her face when she came. Slater blew out a breath and prayed the tightness in his jeans wasn't too noticeable. "Unfortunately you won't give me a break just because I'm Pop's son."

He sat on the bike and looked up at her. Damn, even with helmet hair she was gorgeous. Taking a deep breath, Slater swung his leg over and got off the bike, standing so close to her, he saw the flecks of silver in her irises that made her eyes go all soft and gray. He set his helmet on the seat. "If I were anyone else, I have a feeling we'd get along just fine, better than fine."

"We get along." Rocki stuffed her hands in the pockets of her jeans as if she didn't trust herself not to touch him. He should know since he was doing the same thing.

"Right. But I'm Pop's son, so that puts me on your do-not-tangle-with list. Even though everything I see tells me you'd like nothing better than to get all tangled up with me." Her eyes dilated and her breath came out in soft puffs. He stepped closer. "A tangle of tongues, a tangle of arms, a tangle of legs. Yeah, and I want to get all tangled up with you too—temporarily."

Rocki's breath shot out of her as if she'd just taken a blow to the diaphragm. Not a good sign.

He took her hand and pointed to a gourmet deli he'd found when he was roaming the city before he'd gotten the guts to go home. "Come on. Let's get some food, and you can decide what you want. Once you do, I promise I won't argue."

She knew what she wanted and Slater knew it was him. She wanted him every bit as much as he wanted her. It showed in the way she breathed a little too heavily, the way her eyes sparkled a little too brightly, the way her face flushed hot. He just hoped she didn't let her fear get in the way.

CHAPTER 6

Slater had been in Red Hook for more than a week but it felt like a year. Being back home was as bad if not worse than he'd expected. In the last week he'd seen Skye quit, met her four brothers, and was forced to watch Rocki flirt with every last one of them. He wasn't sure why, but he didn't like it. Not one bit. If he'd been another man he'd swear he felt jealous. But Slater didn't do jealous—not even with any of the girls he'd dated and slept with, and technically, he hadn't done either with Rocki. Not for lack of trying on his part.

He tentatively touched his jaw, worked it from side to side, and winced. It hadn't helped that he'd allowed his brother Logan to beat the crap out of him. Sure, he had it coming after accusing Skye, Logan's girlfriend and chef extraordinaire, of doing the same thing Dominique had done to him—dumping him after finding out he was a stray mutt with no parents, no prospects, and no pedigree.

Deserving a beating was one thing, but Slater just wished Logan hadn't gone for the face. Slater could have taken him without even working up a good sweat, and

Lord knew Logan wasn't much of a fighter—thank God—but he had a hell of a right cross. Slater's left eye was still swollen, his jaw still ached, and his face was more colorful than a gay pride parade.

His face would heal—eventually, but he wasn't sure about his ego. It had taken a hit after he'd said good-bye to Rocki after their nondate. She'd told him she wasn't interested in being more than coworkers. He saw the lie in her eyes but had said he wouldn't push, so he didn't. He just wished he knew what she was hiding, and he couldn't help but feel that her secrets were the reason she wouldn't see him.

He ran his hands over his face. He couldn't seem to concentrate on anything but the maddening woman who either ignored him or treated him like a pesky kid brother. Rocki stirred him up more than anyone he'd ever met. She made him crazy, curious, and hard—not necessarily in that order. When it came to Rocki, he had a whole catalogue of feelings for and about her—the least of which was brotherly. No, lust was at the top of the list, followed closely by admiration and intense interest, but he could guaran-ass-tee he'd never look at her like a sibling.

No matter where he went, it seemed as if he couldn't get away from her—not that he really wanted to. Rocki was in the bar playing something classical and he knew for a fact that she played it by heart. He'd checked her sheet music—it was nonexistent.

He sat behind his computer at his dad's desk and eyed the drawer where Pop stashed his personal files, fingering a paperclip and wondering how hard it would be to pick the lock.

He hadn't been able to find out a thing about Rocki. He thought about hacking into the DMV but decided against it. After all, he'd told her he wouldn't and he never went back on his word. But he hadn't told her he wouldn't see what Pop had in his files.

Slater had googled, Facebooked, checked Twitter, and every other social networking site known to man. It brought him zilch. It was as if Rocki O'Sullivan didn't exist. She was a ghost, an enigma, a puzzle.

When he couldn't get anything off the Internet—and he specialized in Internet searches—he'd decided to do some more old-fashioned investigating. He'd talked to everyone he could about Rocki, hoping someone would know more about her than Patrice. With all the people he'd spoken to, he hadn't found one person who hadn't loved her. Hell, most of the employees at the bar considered her their best friend, but when it came right down to it, no one knew anything concrete. It was as if Rocki appeared three years ago and took over the joint.

The only person who would know would be Pop. Pop, the ex-cop that he was, made it his business to know everything about everyone who worked for him. He wouldn't have taken Rocki under his wing, let her help take care of Nicki, and become part of the family, if he didn't know all. Still, the fact that Pop knew didn't mean he'd be willing to share the information. He'd probably hold back just for shits—after all, the old man hadn't had a lot to laugh about recently, and since Slater had come home, he seemed to be Pop's court jester of choice.

He opened Pop's top desk drawer and found cigars. Now that Bree and Storm were home from their honeymoon, Pop had better hope Bree didn't find his stash or she'd box his ears.

Slater didn't know what Bree had done to make Pop fear her, but he'd heard that she'd taken a cast-iron frying pan to his brother Storm's thick head before he'd fallen in line and in love.

The office door opened and—think of the devil—Pop walked in and gave him a once-over. "Damn, son, you're looking rough. How's the face feel?"

"Never better." Right. He cleared the screen on his laptop—the last thing he needed was for Pop to catch him trying to get information on Rocki.

Pop sat in the chair opposite the desk. "What are you working on?"

Slater realized he still toyed with the paperclip he'd considered using to pick the lock and dropped it, hoping it would go unnoticed. "Just programming stuff. Nothing important."

Rocki started to play another one of her classical pieces.

"Pop, what the hell is Rocki doing here?"

"Sounds to me like she's playing Tchaikovsky. Why do you ask?" Pop tried to rock back in the chair and it didn't work. He looked like a parent sitting in a kindergarten-sized seat during a parent-teacher conference. Slater didn't imagine Pop had ever been in that position, since he and his brothers were almost teenagers by the time Pop took them in. If he'd done the whole parent-teacher thing for preschoolers, Slater figured that's how Pop would have looked.

Slater tried to hide the smile that he knew would do nothing but cause him pain, not to mention get him a smack on the back of the head. Shit, he couldn't win for trying. The man was an ex-cop and a master interrogator. It didn't take a genius, which Slater was, to figure out that his father was as good at deflecting interrogation tactics as he was at getting information. He might as well give it up. "Just curious."

Pop raised an eyebrow.

"Fine. Rocki doesn't belong here. What's a woman who

knows classical music like she does doing working at the Crow's Nest? She should be performing at Carnegie Hall for fuck's sake not playing at a bar in Red Hook. She's got a shit-load of talent. and she's wasting it here with that band of hers."

Pop held out his hand.

Slater eyed the open palm, wondering when it would turn and smack him upside the head. "What?"

"Pay up. Bree charges everyone five bucks for cursing. That's another ten spot for Nicki's college fund."

"Bill me. Besides, Nicki's not even here. I should be able to curse as much as I want."

"Don't matter." Pop shook his head and Slater almost groaned when he saw the *you're-gonna-get-a-lecture* look crossing his father's face. Slater might be pushing thirty, but he knew he'd never get too old to receive a talking-to from Pop. He just wanted to know what the hell he did to deserve it this time. He'd been home a week and he felt like he was back in high school.

"You gotta clean up your language if you're going to be spending time with Nicki."

Slater had been walking Nicki to school and home every day, taking her damn dog out, and even helping her with her homework. In other words, he'd been dealing with everything he hadn't wanted to deal with. "Nothing against Nicki—she's a great kid—but the last thing I want to do is spend more time with her."

"What the hell is that supposed to mean?" Pop sat forward in his chair, and if the damn thing wasn't too small, Slater was sure Pop would be flying over the desk. The man still had one hell of a temper when he thought someone was dissing one of his kids.

Slater held up his hands to calm his old man, but still stood his ground. "I meant what I said." He ran his hands through his unruly hair. "It's nothing personal— Nicki's a great kid but that doesn't change the fact that I'm taking off in a month. Nicki doesn't need to get attached to me when we know I'm only here temporarily. Hasn't the kid had enough loss in her life without me adding to it?"

"Nicki has seen more than her fair share of loss, but you're her family. Just because you're going to the Middle East doesn't mean she shouldn't get to know you. It's not as if either of you are going to leave the fold—not for long at least, and Nicki needs to feel as if she's part of us. All of us."

Pop looked around and pushed himself out of the too-small chair. He might have lost a ton of weight since his heart attack, but he was still a big man. "Get out of my chair, son. I can't think on this side of the desk."

Slater waited half a second before standing. He didn't want to be on the other side either. That was the lecture side and he'd spent more than enough time there as a teen to ever be comfortable.

Pop took his seat behind the desk and Slater leaned against the wall, stalling. He shoved his hands in his pockets and forced himself not to slouch.

"Sit down, son. I don't have the patience to crane my neck up at you."

Pop had that determined frown that meant business— serious business. Like the time he'd found out Slater had hacked into the NYPD database and deleted his and his brother's arrest records. Pop had been mad as hell. He hadn't turned him in but made sure that he'd never do it again. That was the one and only time Slater had wondered if three hots and a cot wasn't such a bad idea.

Slater felt a lump settle in his gut that had nothing to do with lunch and everything to do with impending doom. He wasn't superstitious or anything, but Pop's whole demeanor was off. It was as if whatever he was about to say was not something Slater wanted to hear. Was his dad's health worse than he'd been told?

Slater fell into the chair, crossed his arms, and waited for the inevitable mind-fuck. The lump in Slater's stomach expanded exponentially.

Pete opened his drawer, fingered a cigar, and checked the clock, wondering if he could put this conversation on hold and suck on a stogie before he blew Slater's world apart. He mentally adjusted his balls, leaned forward, and looked Slater right in the eye. "I don't know how to tell you this, son, so I'm just gonna say it—"

Strains of Tchaikovsky splunked into a teeth-jarring mess.

The scrape of the piano bench.

The *clickity click* of Rocki's heels racing across the wood floor.

The muscles in Pete's neck seized like the first time he broke in his barrel as a rookie cop—all twitchy fingers and adrenaline overload.

The door crashed open, missing Slater by half an inch and Rocki stumbled in. One look at the pasty complexion of a person who had just received the worst news imaginable had Pete up and around the desk, pulling Rocki into his arms. Whatever was wrong was bad. Really bad.

Rocki clung to him. Her unintelligible mumbling between gasps, heaves, and sobs made him wish for an interpreter. He caught about every fourth word. Brother. Accident. Coma. New Hampshire.

"Slater, get the Macallan and three glasses." This was going to be a high-dollar session. Not the time for Jack, Jim, Ron, or Jose. He thought about calling for backup, but the only other set of good-looking legs with a decent head on her shoulders would dump his scotch.

Slater was out the door like he was chasing a highball.

Pete sat Rocki down and handed her a box of tissues. He'd never needed Kleenex with the boys—even when they'd had colds. They had plenty of sleeves and there was something to be said for toilet paper. But ever since Bree moved into his office, Pete had to embrace his sensitivity. That meant investing in Kimberly-Clark paper products. He was turning into a regular Oprah.

Slater skidded in and set the glasses on the desk. He filled two, and downed a shot before handing Rocki hers.

"You could have poured me one, son."

Slater shook his head. "Oh no. I'm not dumb enough to contribute to your delinquency. Pour at your own risk and don't even think about lighting up."

Rocki downed her shot and held the glass for a refill. For a girl who rarely drank anything without an umbrella, this didn't bode well.

Pete poured his own and sipped it. Someone had to appreciate a fine scotch. "Take a deep breath, and tell me what you need."

"I just did." Her eyes filled all over again, her face was pale and blotchy, and she was shaking.

"Once more, without the sound effects."

By the time she garbled her way through the story, Pete knew three things. One: Her brother had been hurt in a skiing accident. Two: He would never, ever give Rocki two shots of Macallan. Three: She needed a designated driver—destination, somewhere in New Hampshire. And he knew just who to send. "Slater, you up for a road trip?"

"Me?"

"Storm and Bree can cover the bar. Take Rocki where

she needs to go and take care of her while she's there."
Pete put his hand on Rocki's shoulder. "This girl's family
and she needs us. Go pack your bags."

"I never unpacked. I'll be back in thirty seconds."

"Good. Grab the extra box of tissues in the linen
closet. I have a feeling you're gonna need it."

Pete pulled his keys out of his pocket and tossed them
to Slater. "Take my car. I'll pay the speeding tickets."

Slater had almost made his escape by the time he heard
Nicki's feet stomping up the steps, announcing she'd
come home from school.

He'd checked his watch. He'd completely forgotten
that someone had to pick her up. Logan must have and,
knowing Logan, he'd probably sent Nicki to the kitchen
for a snack and promptly returned to pouting in his personal booth in the bar.

Slater didn't understand Logan's behavior. Logan had
never been one to pout like a girl. Hell, the man could
never stand still long enough to get attached to much of
anything—not even women. They were similar in that
respect. Slater didn't expect it to take more than a few
days for Logan to shake off the ego bruise Skye had laid
on him when she dumped his ass. Slater had been sure
that by now, Logan would have taken one of the women
who'd been trolling by his table up on the offer of a good
time. Okay, it sucked being dumped—Slater should
know—but shit, it had been almost a week and Logan
was still walking around like a zombie.

Nicki flew through the door to the apartment, skidded
to a stop, and caught Slater with his duffel over his shoulder. "You're leaving?" She tossed the backpack that was
almost as big as she was onto the breakfast bar and drew
her hands to her hips. "You just got here."

He looked at her, trying to figure out why he felt so off around her.

Nicki dug her sneaker into the carpet. "Slater?" She'd caught him staring. Her eyes bore into his with a combination of fear, hurt, and frustration. Damn, she was already getting attached.

"Rocki's brother was in an accident in New Hampshire and we have to check on him but I'll be coming back before I have to leave again."

Nicki's eyes practically tripled in size. "Rocki has a brother too?"

"Apparently. You didn't know?"

"No, she never talks about her family. I just figured we were it. Around here, family is what you make it. You know what I mean?"

"Yeah, Nicki. I know." He knew all about being a part of a family with no blood relation. He couldn't even remember his own parents.

"Is he hurt bad?"

"Who?"

"Rocki's brother. Duh."

Right. Rocki's brother. Slater scrubbed his hand over his face not knowing what to say and settled on a shrug. Head injuries were iffy at best. The guy could die or he could come out of the coma and be just fine. Slater didn't want to lie and tell her everything was going to be all right when he didn't have a clue. It didn't stop him from having the urge to say whatever it took to wipe that worried and scared expression off Nicki's face. "It's too soon to tell. They should know more in the next day or two. I'm sure we'll be checking in with Pop."

She didn't look any less worried. God, he really sucked at dealing with kids.

"Look, Nicki, I have to go because it's a long drive and Rocki needs to be there for her brother."

"Okay, but wait a minute. I have something to give her."

He must not have stifled the impatient grunt as well as he meant to because Nicki stopped and shot him an annoyed glare before running to her room. A second later she returned holding something behind her back. She looked up at him and smiled before she held out a rock the size of a softball. She shrugged her little shoulders and dug her foot into the carpet again. "It's my lucky rock. Nothin' bad happens when I have it, so it might be lucky for Rocki too. Will you give it to her to borrow? Maybe it'll make her feel better."

He dropped the box of tissues and his duffel, knelt down, and looked into eyes so familiar he knew he'd seen them before. "Sure, Nicki. I'll tell Rocki you're lending it to her. It's really nice of you. I'm sure it will help."

She handed him the rock and then moved in close. She smelled like Johnson's Baby Shampoo and little girl and peanut butter.

"Did you get Rex to make you another peanut butter and bacon sandwich?"

She bit her lip and shrugged.

"You'd better brush your teeth before Bree sniffs you out."

"Okay." She threw skinny arms around his neck and hugged him.

Slater had no choice but to hug her back. It wasn't as if he didn't want to, but the feel of her—so small, so freakin' fragile kind of weirded him out. She felt like a delicate little bird—he was afraid to squeeze because she might break. He was ready to take off but couldn't because she was still wrapped around him like a monkey. He gently lifted her and set her away. "You be good for Pop, Storm, and Bree while I'm gone. I'll be back as soon as I can."

He picked up his stuff and hurried out the door. The last thing he wanted to do was get caught up in Nicki's all too familiar gaze again. He shook off the chill making its way down his spine. He'd never thought of himself as a coward, and for the first time in his life, he'd begun to wonder if he'd suddenly turned into one. Nicki was an amazing kid. She deserved better, and running away like a coward was not his best. He forced himself to turn and face her.

Nicki stared back with eyes that held hurt and worry. She reminded him of the way he'd felt as a kid every time he had known his time was running out at one of his foster homes. Nicki was scared. "Hey, Nicki. Come here." He crouched down so they were eye to eye.

Nicki bit her lip and walked the few steps toward him.

He took her little chin in his hand and tipped it so she met his eyes. "Look, kiddo, nothing's happening except that I have to take Rocki to see her brother. Nothing else is going on, so there's no reason for you to worry."

"You promise? First Skye left, and then Logan came back but he's sad all the time, and now you and Rocki are leaving too. . . ." A tear dripped down her cheek and he brushed it away with his thumb.

"Logan and Skye have grown-up things to work out, but that has nothing to do with you. As for me, all I can promise is that I'll come back and stay for a while at least. We'll figure everything else out then. I promise I won't leave you high and dry, Nicki. Okay?"

She didn't say anything; she just nodded her head and looked as if she was doing her damnedest to staunch the flow of tears. The next thing he knew she had her arms wrapped around his neck and her wet face burrowing into him. "Shh, it's okay, Nicki."

"No, it's not. Nothing is okay." She let out a gulping hiccup.

Someone cleared his throat behind him.

Nicki looked up, pushed out of his arms, and ran to Pop.

Slater rose, knowing he'd been right. He sucked at dealing with kids.

Pop caught Nicki and shot him an apologetic look before turning his attention to the little girl in his arms. "What's going on, Nicki? What's with the tears?" Pop pulled Nicki over to his favorite chair and she climbed on his lap. "Slater, you go ahead down and I'll be there in a minute."

Slater should have felt relieved to hand the crying ten-year-old off to his father, but what he felt was anything but. He didn't know what it was, and with Rocki downstairs waiting for him, he didn't have time to identify it.

Nothing made sense. He was so confused—not something he'd ever experienced before. He couldn't wait to get away from Nicki, but then felt as if he shouldn't leave her.

He'd wanted to get to know Rocki and didn't like the way she'd avoided him all week. He especially didn't like the way she flirted with every man between the age of two and eighty-two. He'd wanted to spend one-on-one time with her, but being trapped in a car for six hours while she was upset and sniffling was not exactly how he'd envisioned it.

He didn't know if he suffered from a Sir Galahad complex or what, but he wasn't able to let a damsel in distress fend for herself. Even if Pop hadn't suggested he escort Rocki to New Hampshire, he would have volunteered. Whatever the complex, he had no option but to take Rocki to her brother and stay until he knew she'd be all right.

When Slater returned to the office, Rocki was right where he'd left her, looking like her world had imploded. Lost, alone, and shaking. The only difference was that she wore her coat and hugged her purse to her chest. Her red-rimmed eyes were circled with what was left of her mascara—the black rings looked like shiners and accentuated her unhealthy pallor.

"Are you doing okay?"

It seemed to take a minute for her to register he was even there.

Rocki rose from her chair like an arthritic geriatric and looked right through him before turning and walking out.

"Pop, Rocki and I are leaving."

Pop met them in front of the door and grabbed his arm.

"Is Nicki going to be all right?"

Pop gave him a look Slater couldn't decipher—surprise mixed with something else. "She'll be fine. Change of any kind makes her nervous—it was the same with you boys. I guess I should have expected it but it's been a lot of years since any of you were in that position." He stepped closer. "Here, you're not going to have time to stop for cash, so take this." He held out a wad of money.

Slater didn't want anyone to think that he expected to be paid to help Rocki out or, God forbid, he needed the cash. He didn't. "No, I'm good, but thanks."

Pop dragged Rocki into a hug and whispered something in her ear—something that brought a wobbly smile to her lips.

Rocki kissed his cheek and refused his cash too.

He ran his hands down her arms and slipped the wad of bills into her coat pocket before stepping away. "Call me when you get there. We'll be here praying for him, sweetheart." He dragged Slater into a hug, and then gave him a slap on the back. "You take care of my girl, son. Drive safe."

"Will do. Come on, Rocki. Let's go." Shit, the way Pop talked made it clear that he thought of Rocki as a daughter. Slater was beginning to appreciate the hell Storm must have gone through growing up and wanting to date Bree—the daughter Pop had never had. He couldn't imagine that Storm had an easier time of it as an adult. Maybe the fact that Pop always seemed to take in strays wasn't such a good thing. It certainly cut down on his sons' dating prospects.

CHAPTER 7

Pete slipped into his office, pocketed a stogie, and wondered, not for the first time, what the hell his kids were going to do when he bellied up to the big bar in the sky. When that happened, he wanted to be able to kick back and shoot the shit with St. Peter, and not worry about his kids.

He knew if he weren't steering them in the right direction, the lot of them would be chasing their own tails. As entertaining as it was to watch them do just that, it got old fast. Since his heart attack, he worried he wouldn't be around to make sure his kids were finished with the tail-chasing part of their lives—both their own and the tails of the opposite sex.

He was sure Storm and Bree were going to be okay, thanks to him—though Storm would die before he'd ever admit it. He'd even thought he'd had Logan and Skye on the right path until Logan went and screwed it all up. Screwing up was one thing—after all, what the hell did Logan know about being in a loving relationship? For Logan, learning relationship rules was akin to a blind man feeling his way around a crowded room without a guide dog or a cane. Pete shook his head. It was a painful process. He was going to have to step in soon because Logan's inaction was just making matters worse.

"That better not be a stogie I see in your pocket, Pete."

Bree. Damn the woman. She had amazingly bad timing. Where was she when he'd needed her? "Oh come on. Who died and left you my keeper? I've been doing the job long before you were born, young lady."

Marriage obviously agreed with Bree—she and Storm had spent the last month in New Zealand and Australia—much of that time on a boat or beach from the look of her tan, and he'd never seen either of them so happy. Bree was a redhead and it surprised the hell out of him to see her normally pale skin bronze. He couldn't remember the girl ever having a tan before. "I'm glad you're home, even if you are a royal pain in the ass."

Bree crossed her arms and tapped her toe. "I'm only a pain in your ass when I catch you. I swear, I'm going to every smoke shop in Brooklyn and will threaten the life of every store owner. If I can't stop you from buying those foul things, I can do my best to keep the owners from selling them to you."

"You can try." Pete couldn't keep the smile off his face. He was glad that Bree and Storm were back home and happy. Things were just the way they should be. He only wished he could say the same for his other two sons.

"Where's Nicki? Rex said she seemed a little off after school. Is something really wrong or was Nicki just tugging on his heartstrings so she could wrangle a PB&B sandwich out of him?"

"Both. Rocki had to take off for New Hampshire—her brother's been in an accident—".

"Whoa—Rocki has a brother? Since when?"

Pete sat and rocked back on his chair. "Her whole life, since he's three years older than she is."

"How could I not know this?" Bree sat down opposite him and shook her head, looking both hurt and bewildered. "Rocki's my best friend."

"Bree, there are reasons people keep things to themselves. I'm sure Rocki has a good one."

"Is he . . . God, I don't even know his name. . . ."

"Jackson."

"Is Jackson going to be okay?"

"We don't know. He's in a coma. From what I gather, he was in a skiing accident. Rocki was so upset, I could hardly understand her. I didn't want her driving. Besides, I'm not even sure the girl has a license, so I gave Slater my car and told him to take care of her."

"Slater? What the hell were you thinking?"

Pete smiled and stuck out his hand.

Bree's eyes rolled like a slot machine, and he just hit the jackpot. She stuffed her hand in her pocket, fished for a Lincoln, and slapped it onto his palm.

He added it to the ten he'd taken from Slater earlier, making sure he didn't expose his cigar. "Slater's hardly hidden the fact that he's interested in Rocki, and since he could use some breathing space, he might just find it and all the answers to his questions about Rocki in New Hampshire." Pete leaned forward and put his elbows on the desk while surreptitiously closing the drawer, hopefully hiding the contraband. "It was like killing three birds with one stone. It was ingenious if I do say so myself."

"No wonder Nicki's upset. Slater just got here, and now he left right after Skye took off. The poor kid doesn't know who is coming and going. Her life's been like a revolving door lately."

"I know, Bree, but both Logan and Slater were in such prickly moods, if the two of them stuck around, one of them would end up taking another swing at the other and I'd be forced to get the bat out again. How could I explain that to Nicki? I think 'boys will be boys' only works once. It's definitely better this way." Pete wished he could light up and follow it with a glass of scotch. "I think it will be good for Slater and Rocki to help each other deal with the changes they're facing in their lives. And since you just returned, it's not a good time for you to leave. Nicki's been waiting for a month for you to come home. Leave Rocki to Slater for the time being. We'll know soon enough if I'm right—and I haven't been wrong yet."

· Bree shook her head. "You'd better be careful, Pete. People don't like feeling like pawns on a chessboard of your own making. No matter how right you are." She leaned over the desk, gave him a kiss on the cheek, and swiped the cigar right out of his pocket before turning on her heel and slipping out of the office.

It was a damn good thing he had more where that came from. He just prayed that Bree didn't make good on her threat to talk to his suppliers.

Slater drove to Rocki's place and searched for a parking space as soon as he turned onto Mott Street.

"You can park here."

"In the loading zone?"

"It's fine. I know the owners—they'll say I'm waiting for a delivery." She got out of the car, went to the restaurant, stuck her head in, and spoke to one of the women by the counter.

Slater waited on the sidewalk and then followed her up to her apartment.

Rocki opened the door, and when he stepped in be-hind her, he was greeted by a wall of shoes—the entry-way had nothing but shelving from floor to ceiling. The floor space in front looked like a Payless after a blowout sale. Shoes were scattered hither and yon. There were so many bright colors it made his head hurt.

He couldn't imagine what one person did with that many shoes. He had his running shoes, his biker boots, and a pair of hiking boots. That was all he needed.

Rocki pointed to the door at the end of the hall. "Bathroom's through there if you need it."

The hallway opened into a large room containing a baby grand piano, a twin-sized daybed with rumpled sheets, a dresser, and a small bistro table and two chairs. Clothes littered just about everything. There were two laundry baskets beside the bed, one full of clothes in a heap, and the other containing neatly folded clothes.

"Do you want a water?" She pointed to a kitchenette so small it looked as if there was just enough room be-tween the oven and the refrigerator to open the oven door—maybe. "I don't have much else. There might be a yogurt or something in the fridge, but do yourself a fa-vor, check the expiration date before you dig in. The last thing I need is a chauffeur with food poisoning."

So he was a chauffeur, huh? He gave her a look that said *no-fuckin'-way*, but didn't voice his opinion. He didn't need to.

Her return volley was an expression that told him in no uncertain terms, he could think anything he wanted. In her mind, he was nothing more than a glorified cabbie. Great. "No, thanks. I'm good." And he was, when it came to just about everything, including sex—he was good for way more than a ride.

She cleared the clothes off one of the bistro chairs

and tossed them on the bed. "I'm just going to pack a few things."

He slid his laptop out of the messenger bag he was never without and sat down at the bistro table. "Do you have Wi-Fi?"

"No. I use the restaurant's. The password is *chopsticks*."

"Original."

She shrugged and raided her dresser, pulling out all the small silky things he'd spent the last week imagining. She had all the colors of the rainbow in her lingerie drawer. She definitely wasn't the white-cotton-panty type—not that there wasn't something to be said for little white cotton panties. Or none at all. He shifted in his seat; the last thing she needed was a freakin' chauffeur with a raging hard-on. Not now at least.

Rocki got on her hands and knees to search beneath her bed, her black leggings hugging and accentuating her long legs and heart-shaped ass. The oversized T-shirt or dress she wore—he wasn't sure which—slipped over her hips and showed off the dimples on her lower back and enough pale, smooth skin to make his mouth water and his jeans tight. Shit.

She rose, pulled a bag out from under her bed, and dusted it off. The woman would never be confused with Martha Stewart. Rocki tossed the selection of undergarments into her weekender along with a few pairs of jeans—something he'd never seen her wear—sweaters, and, to his surprise, a white cotton granny nightgown.

She didn't strike him as the kind of girl who wore granny nightgowns to bed. No, he'd pegged her for something sheer and silky, or nothing at all. He wasn't sure which he preferred, but damn, anything was better than the Grandma Moses thing she held.

Slater kept his eyes trained on his screen and thanked God his peripheral vision was exceptional. She moved around the place with a nervous energy that made him wonder if it was more the rule than the exception. "What's the number for the restaurant downstairs? I'll call in an order—it should be ready by the time you're done packing."

"I'm not hungry."

"You need to eat anyway."

"Fine." Rocki grabbed her phone. "I have it on speed dial—I'll order. What would you like?"

"Just order me whatever you're having, I'm not picky— just make sure they give me a fork. I can't drive and eat with chopsticks."

"I hope you don't mind it spicy."

Spicy worked for him. "I can take anything you can dish up."

"I guess we'll see." She dialed the phone, shoved clothes under her arm, and headed to the bathroom speaking Chinese.

Well, shit. This woman was just full of surprises.

"It'll be ready in five minutes."

He heard the bathroom door close and stopped pretending to be riveted to his computer and stood. He had five minutes, so he took the time to study the studio apartment, looking for anything that would tell him who Rocki O'Sullivan was—other than a bit of a slob.

Sheet music littered the piano. He paged through it and realized it was all original work. Serious work. Amazing. The woman not only played classical music, but she also wrote it.

One piece rested on the music rack and looked as if it was a work in progress. She'd titled it "Him." Him who? The paper had been erased more times than a grade school chalkboard and showed some serious wear. Entire bars had been scratched out and rewritten. Notations in the margins pointed out which parts needed more work. He scanned the room looking for any evidence of a man in her life—after all, she'd written the piece for someone.

Slater sat at the piano more confused than ever, took a deep breath, and let his eyes wander. Rocki must have spent a lot of her time sitting right here, considering the amount of music she'd written. His eyes landed on a photograph—the only one in the apartment.

He slid off the bench, skirted the piano, and picked up the four-by-six shot of Rocki on top of a ski slope with a blond-haired man. They had their arms around each other, as if they'd stopped midrun for a kiss and a cuddle.

Rocki looked happy—too damn happy in Slater's opinion. Shit. He put the picture back where he'd found it. The sight of Rocki touching another man—any man that wasn't him—did funny things to his insides. Things he wasn't used to feeling. Feelings so foreign to him, he wasn't sure he even recognized them. All he knew was that he didn't like whatever the hell it was. If Slater had been standing next to them, he'd have put his fist through the guy's face and ripped Rocki right out of his arms. That knowledge alone was enough to make Slater want to get as far away from Rocki as humanly possible. Unfortunately, he couldn't leave. He would be stuck like Velcro to the woman for the next day or two at the very least. "Fuck."

"Problem?"

Slater turned so fast he almost tripped over his size-thirteen feet. "No." Other than he'd just freaked himself out. "I didn't hear you." When he got his balance—both physical and, he hoped, mental, he wondered how much of his klutziness she'd seen. He pulled himself together, took a good look at her, and almost fell over again. She must have washed her face because she wore no makeup. Not even a hint, much less the outlandish, yet weirdly attractive color choices he'd seen her sporting over the last week.

Rocki had changed into jeans. Another first and they weren't even skinny jeans. They were a little baggy and looked as if they were a good size too large for her. She'd paired them with a big, shapeless sweater, and stood before him looking like a teenager.

"How old are you?"

"Almost twenty-five. Why?"

"You look like you should be singing in a high school chorus not a bar."

Rocki tugged on a pair of rag-wool socks and reached to the top of her shoe wall to pull a pair of flat boots down. She blew the dust off them and sneezed.

"God bless you."

"Thanks." She stuffed her feet into the boots, tossed a ditty bag into the suitcase, and zipped it up. "I'm ready when you are."

He blinked and did his best to hide his shock while he tried to make some sense of this new side of Rocki O'Sullivan. She didn't bother to mention her sudden style change. In his limited experience there was never a good time to ask a woman about her fashion choices — especially during times of stress like this, so Slater did what every smart man would in this situation — he kept his mouth shut. Still, his silence did nothing to keep him from wondering if the woman would ever stop surprising him. He packed up his computer, tossed the strap of his messenger bag over his shoulder, and gave her a nod. "I'm ready, Rocki. Let's go."

*   *   *

Rocki slid into the passenger seat of Pete's car, threw her coat over the back, and prayed she didn't ralph. She'd been in such a state; she hadn't even noticed her stomach rebelling. Maybe doing shots of scotch hadn't been the best idea.

Slater had insisted on paying for their meals. Of course, he charmed Anita and Rosemary Chin, the beautiful and single daughters of Mary and Charlie—the owners.

The man was annoyingly attractive—which is what she'd told her friends in broken Cantonese.

By the way the two of them batted their eyelashes, they didn't find Slater nearly as irritating as she did.

He closed her door and went around to the driver's side.

She waited for him to buckle his seat belt. "Just what do you think you were doing in there?"

He started the car and checked traffic. "Paying for our food. I should ask you the same thing. You were the one speaking Chinese, not me, and you seemed to have an awful lot to say."

"I just told them I was going to New Hampshire. That's all."

"Did you tell them about the accident?"

"No."

"Why not? I thought they were your friends."

"They are. Just because they're my friends, doesn't mean I'm going to weep all over them."

"Telling them your brother's been in an accident isn't weeping."

It would have been if she'd so much as mentioned it.

"And there's nothing wrong with tears. Hell, you can cry as much as you want. At least if you're crying, you're not hiding your feelings."

"I don't hide my feelings. I tell it like it is. Just ask anyone."

"Your opinion is one thing, your feelings are altogether a different story. I know you have no problem expounding upon your views."

"Are you saying I have trouble expressing my feelings?"

"I don't know. Do you?"

If she expressed her feelings, she'd explode. Right now, it was all she could do not to fall apart. Jackson was in a coma. If she expressed her feelings, she would be hysterical and Rocki didn't do hysterical. Okay, maybe for a few minutes there at the Crow's Nest she'd rubbed up against the fence separating her from full-on hysteria hard enough to leave some skin on the barbs, hard enough to leave her bleeding, hard enough to taste the metal, but she never stepped through or over, and she'd never even thought about ducking under. No. Rocki knew the danger of going there and she'd never travel that terrifying path again.

If she expressed her feelings she'd have to face the fact that without Jackson, she'd be alone. She didn't know if she'd survive losing Jackson and she didn't want to find out. She knew all too well what it felt like to lose the people you loved most in the world. She'd relived losing her parents more than once. She'd had nightmares of the car accident for years afterward.

Rocki blinked away the image of her mother staring at her through lifeless eyes, the metallic scent of blood, and the shrill of her own scream when she realized her parents were dead and she was alone. Their bodies might have taken up space in what was left of the front seat, but Rocki had been alone, cold, scared, and trapped.

She wasn't sure how long it had taken for someone to

rescue her. Hours? Days? She'd been in and out of consciousness and the blackouts reset her mental clock.

She awoke in the hospital with Grace holding her hand and Teddy beside her, praying. They were probably doing the same thing now with Jackson. They'd always been more than just the caretakers of the lake house. Grace and Teddy were the closest thing to parents that she and Jackson had. They were the reason the lake house was still where she considered herself at home.

Jackson hadn't been in the car accident all those years ago. Jackson had never lived the nightmare that made her scream from the pit of her being, cutting like glass all the way up, and echoing in her mind—clouding the edges of her vision.

Jackson had been spared that horror.

The only reason she'd survived was because she had no choice.

The only reason she'd survived was because she had more to think about than herself.

The only reason she'd survived was because when their parents died, Jackson had become her lifeline. Without Jackson, she would be alone in the world. All alone, just like she'd been in that car.

Slater took his eyes off the road and zeroed in on Rocki. One minute they were talking about expressing feelings, and the next she stared through him as if she were in a trance. She might be sitting beside him, but she was light-years away. Rocki had looked pale before but now she looked ghostly. "Rocki?"

She didn't move. She didn't blink. She didn't breathe.

"Rocki?" He hadn't even hit the West Side Highway and already he was in trouble. He didn't know what the hell to do. He took her cold hand in his and thought about dropping it to bump up the heat but he didn't want to let go of her. He gave her hand a squeeze, then brought it to his lap, sandwiching it between his hand and his thigh, trying to rub some warmth into it. Shit.

He dropped her hand, flipped the heat up to roast before reaching for her and cursing the console between them. There was something to be said for bench seats. He did his best to tuck Rocki under his arm, and kissed her chilled forehead. "Come on, sweetheart. Say something. I'm good with silence, but at least answer me so I know you're okay."

Rocki didn't say anything; she just burrowed into his side, her face tucked against his neck, her soft-as-silk hair brushing his chin.

Slater didn't know what to do to make Rocki feel better. He couldn't tell her that everything would be all right. No, in situations like these, platitudes were insulting. The only thing he could do for her was keep her fed, hold her hand, and listen if she felt like talking. He was almost glad she wasn't the talkative type since talking was definitely not his forte. It wasn't as if he was insensitive—at least he didn't think he was—but until they got up there and saw firsthand what the situation was, there wasn't much to say. He'd done everything he could do. He'd bought food so she could eat. He hoped she'd relax enough to sleep. He'd be there for her if she needed him. Other than that, he was completely out of his depth. Just like he'd been with Nicki.

Shit. He felt like slamming his head against the steering wheel. He'd forgotten all about Nicki's rock. "Rocki, reach into my bag. There's a rock in there—take it out." He thought she'd ask what the hell he was doing carrying around a rock, but she didn't.

Rocki didn't so much as blink, but did as he asked.

"Nicki wanted to lend you her special rock. She said it's her lucky charm and swears nothing bad happens when she carries it. Nicki thought it would do the same for you."

Rocki curled up against the console with Nicki's rock in one hand, and her other holding his in a surprisingly strong grip. Good thing he could steer with his knees. He didn't want to drop her hand to turn on his blinkers to merge onto the Cross Bronx Expressway. "Why don't you close your eyes and try to get some rest?"

She didn't answer him but after a half hour, he felt her grip on him loosen, her breathing evened out, and her head lolled against his shoulder. He wasn't sure if he was relieved or not. At least when she was awake, he could focus on Rocki and her problems. Now that she was asleep, all he had to think about were his.

CHAPTER 8

Rocki's neck hurt. She tried to find a more comfortable position, but the pillow felt ... hard? Boney? It was as if she slept on someone's shoulder. She didn't sleep with people. Ever. She opened her eyes and realized where she was—in Pete's car. And who she was sleeping on—Slater. She hoped she hadn't drooled or anything. Then she remembered why she was in Pete's car with Slater—Jackson.

"We're almost there. How are you doing?" His deep voice was like a soft blanket, warm and comfortable, tempting her to wrap herself in it ... in him.

How was she doing? She was doing as well as could be expected, considering she was living a nightmare. She kept telling herself that Jackson wouldn't dare leave her. He was young and strong and too damn stubborn to die. But her parents hadn't been, and she knew they'd done everything they could to live. The fear she'd seen in their eyes had been for her, not for themselves. Until their last breaths, they'd tried to live for her. She remembered the anguish in their eyes when they realized they were losing the battle.

And then it hit her, the fear she had was for Jackson, of course, but it was also mixed with a huge helping of another kind of fear. Jackson was her rock, the one person she knew she could always count on to care about her. The only person who really knew her—all of her. The good, the bad, the snarky, the emotional wreck, and the scared little girl who used to wake screaming on a nightly basis. Her nightmares had been so bad, she'd never been able to have roommates at school, which did nothing but further isolate her.

When she moved to New York after college and met Pete and the gang, Rocki made the first friends she'd had in years. She'd hid her background and the parts of herself that had isolated her since her parents' deaths.

She looked at Slater and cringed. She'd been so upset, she hadn't thought of the consequences of falling apart in front of Pete and Slater. She'd been so upset, she hadn't realized what that one mistake would cost her. But looking at Slater now, she wasn't sure she even regretted it. Not yet anyway. As much as she didn't want him to be here, the fact that he was gave her more comfort than she could have ever imagined. "Thanks for this."

"This?"

She realized he was still holding her hand. His hand was big, warm, solid, and seemed to ground her. She felt protected, which was something she hadn't felt for so long. "Driving me to the middle of nowhere, letting me sleep on you, taking care of me. I know you're just doing it for Pete, but I appreciate it. Since I don't know if I'm going to be in any shape to thank you later, I thought I'd better cover all my bases and do it now."

Slater squeezed her hand and blew out a breath. "Rocki, I have a lot of reasons for making the trip with you, the least of which is an order from Pop. I'd have insisted I take you to see your brother either way. That's just the way I roll."

She didn't believe that for a minute. "You pick up virtual strangers and drive six hours to take them to see an injured relative?"

"We're not strangers."

"We met a week ago."

"Whether we explore it or not, we have a connection that makes us more than acquaintances."

"A connection?"

"Damn straight. Don't pretend it doesn't exist. We don't have to act on it. And hell, it might be better for both of us if we don't, but something is there, and that something is the reason I'm here. Simple as that."

Slater was way too smart for her to hide anything for long. As soon as he learned who she was, any connection he thought they shared would change. It always did. It would also change every relationship she had in the life that she'd worked so hard to build in New York.

Maybe she could ask him to leave as soon as she got to the hospital. He didn't have to know. Maybe she could salvage this disaster after all.

Rocki caught Slater staring. Time to ease into it. They'd be at the hospital in about ten minutes. It was either now or never.

"You can just drop me off at the hospital and then go back to Red Hook. There's no need for you to come in." She didn't look at him but she could feel his stare.

"I'm not leaving you alone."

"I'm not going to be alone. Grace and Teddy are there."

"You call your parents by their first names?"

Her parents? "No. Grace and Teddy are ... family friends." Not exactly the truth, but not a lie either.

"Are your parents on their way?"

Shit. "No."

"Why not?"

Her face heated and she looked down at the rock in her hand. "Because they're dead."

"I'm sorry. I didn't know."

She couldn't look at him. She hated seeing the pity in people's eyes. No one knew—well, no one in Red Hook. Keeping parts of herself to herself had been a way of life for so long, even if she wished she could change it, it was too late. Her friends wouldn't understand her reasons, and no matter what they said, if they knew the truth, everything would change. She wouldn't be one of them anymore. Now she could lose Jackson and everything else in the world she loved.

"When did they die?"

"A long time ago." Eleven years this month.

"What happened?"

"A car accident when I was thirteen. It's just me and Jackson now." To her embarrassment, the last word ended in what sounded like a sob but she refused to cry.

"What did you do?"

"What do you mean?"

"If it was just you and Jackson, and you were only thirteen, who did you live with?"

"No one. Our uncles sent us to boarding schools."

"That's rough, but it beats the hell out of foster homes."

"Not yours."

"Yeah, well, you didn't see all the others. Compared to most of the homes I was placed in, a boarding school would have seemed like heaven." It looked like a bank of storm clouds shadowed his face, turning it to a sharp-edged granite slab. It was as if each muscle in his body tensed.

His knuckles whitened on the steering wheel.

Rocki didn't know anything about Slater's life before Pete had taken him in. Patrice must not know either since she never mentioned it. Maybe she and Slater had more in common than she'd thought.

"Pop was definitely an unusual foster father and I mean that in a good way." His voice sounded mechanical, emotionless, removed. "Still, Red Hook wasn't what it is now. If things were still the same, you wouldn't be working there—that's for sure. I'd bet your boarding school was a damn sight safer."

"Maybe." But then he didn't know what it was like. It may have been one of the ritziest boarding schools in Europe but it felt like a jail. She'd been ripped away from everything she loved and stashed with a throng of overindulged debutantes who hated her from day one. She'd never fit in.

"It wasn't as if you were alone. You had your brother, didn't you?"

"No. We were sent to different schools." When Jackson turned eighteen, he'd tried to get custody of her, but their uncles fought him. No judge in America would give the care of a fifteen-year-old girl to her eighteen-year-old brother who wanted nothing more than to remove her from her world-class boarding school.

Jackson—living away from him then had been hell. She wasn't even allowed to visit for Christmas. She'd spent her Christmases alone in her room. Sometimes Rocki would get a pity invitation to a teacher's home to celebrate the holiday with their family. After trying it once, Rocki realized she'd rather spend holidays alone than to be reminded of everything she'd lost.

"Rocki? Are you with me?"

"Yeah. I'm fine."

"Worrying isn't helping your brother, you know."

She'd prayed, but then she'd prayed the entire time her parents had been dying—it hadn't helped.

"Are you two close?"

"Very." Even though they weren't geographically close, she couldn't imagine going more than a few days without hearing his voice. She couldn't imagine living without Jackson. He was the one person in the world who knew everything about her—even the woman she showed to no one else—and he loved her despite it. They'd promised each other that they'd always be close. They'd promised to take care of each other—no matter what. They'd promised each other they'd always be together.

Slater watched Rocki become more and more nervous. It was strange that no one at the Crow's Nest had known Rocki's brother even existed before today except maybe Pop. Pop didn't seem shocked she had a brother—he just seemed shocked to see Rocki fall apart.

"We'll be there soon." He pulled her closer and kissed her temple.

"I know you want to help, Slater, and I really appreciate it, but I'll be fine. Why don't you just drop me off at the hospital? There's a hotel a few miles down the road. You can go there and get some rest before you head back tomorrow. I'll call you just as soon as I know anything."

She was trying to get rid of him. He didn't know why; all he knew was that she needed him and didn't want to. That's the way he'd prefer it himself. This was an extraordinary circumstance—Rocki wasn't a needy person, he knew that right off. She needed someone and it scared her. His only question was why? Was it the fact that she wasn't completely independent? Was it something to do with all the other questions rolling through his mind? Was she afraid he'd get his answers? "Thanks for the easy out, but I'm here because I want to be and we'll see this through together."

She looked like she was going to say something else, so he saved her the time and trouble. "Rocki, Pop is waiting for me to give him an update. I can hardly do that without knowing what we're facing, and if I want to live, I'm not going back to Red Hook without knowing you and your brother are going to be just fine."

He thought knowing people cared would make her feel better; instead it just seemed to agitate her more. She was tense to the point of shaking, and the hand he still held lost whatever warmth he was able to pump into her. "What's the problem with me staying?"

There was a wealth of information scrolling over her face at lightning speed. If it were code, he'd be able to read it without a problem. But Rocki was a woman, and women used a mystery code he'd as yet been unable to crack, though, truth be told, he'd never really tried that hard. He'd never wanted to before. Now, for some strange reason, he did. He just wished she spoke C++, Java, PHP, or any other computer language. Instead she looked confused, scared, hurt, and completely conflicted.

She opened her mouth and closed it, as if she was unable or unwilling to tell him.

He wanted to kiss the worried look off her face. He wanted to hold her until her shaking stopped. He didn't think either would help. "I'm staying until I see that you're okay and your brother is too. Then if you want me to leave, I will. That's the best I can do."

He pulled into a parking space and she was out of the car before he turned off the engine. He grabbed their coats and hauled ass inside.

Rocki was already pressing the elevator button like a woman driven to vengeance would push a button to shock a cheating ex.

When the doors finally opened, he barely got his butt inside before she gave the button to the ICU floor the same treatment. *Driven* wasn't quite the right word he'd use to describe her, but then he didn't know what was.

When the doors opened, Rocki flew through, her long legs eating up the distance to the nurses' station. "Jackson Sullivan. Where is he?"

Sullivan? Slater thought her last name was O'Sullivan.

The nurse lifted her gaze to Rocki. "And you are?"

"Racquel Sullivan. Jackson's sister." She looked from Slater to the nurse and back again. All the color in her face disappeared like the picture on an Etch A Sketch after a good shake.

Her name was Racquel? He guessed Rocki was a nickname. So okay, that made sense, but Sullivan didn't.

"Racquel?" An older woman—a woman who looked as if she could pose for a picture in a dictionary under the word *grandmother*—rushed past him and grabbed Rocki in a crushing hug. A big man stopped beside the women and looked Slater up and down.

"How is he, Grace?" Rocki asked.

"There's no change. They put a tube into his skull to release the pressure on the brain from swelling and put him in a drug-induced coma. We should know more tomorrow." Grace looked from Rocki to him.

"Grace, Teddy," Rocki said, hugging the old man and kissing his bristled cheek, "this is my friend Slater Shaw. Slater, this is Grace and Teddy Watkins."

Slater shook hands with Teddy and felt very much like a boy meeting his girlfriend's father for the first time on the way to the prom. "It's nice to meet you both."

The nurse cleared her throat. "You can go in two at a time, but you can only stay for five minutes."

Grace patted Rocki's shoulder. "You two go ahead. We've been in and out of Jackson's room all day. It will do him good to hear your voice, Racquel. I believe coma patients can hear so be sure to talk to him."

Rocki grabbed Slater's hand and held on so tight; she was practically cutting off the circulation. They trailed the nurse to a glassed-in room and she held the door open for them.

Slater followed Rocki in, looked over her shoulder, and broke into a cold sweat. He swallowed back bile, his salivary glands went into overdrive, and he prayed he wouldn't be sick. It was as if he was reliving a nightmare. Tubes and wires, machines, the beeping of a monitor, the swoosh of a respirator, the IV hanging beside the body of a man he'd never seen before. He shouldn't feel as if he was going to lose it. He forced himself to take a deep breath through his mouth. He didn't want to smell the scent of antiseptic. He didn't want to hear the squeak of rubber shoes against the linoleum. All he wanted to do was escape.

He had the urge to drag his hand from Rocki's and run as fast and far as his feet would take him. The glass wall seemed to cage him in. His heart pounded a dirge beneath his breastbone and he rubbed his chest—pain, or the memory of it, speared his consciousness. He grabbed the cold metal bedrail beside Rocki to anchor himself in the present. He had to be there for Rocki.

She paled even more. The constant pressure of her hand on his increased, and her lip quivered. "Jackson, I'm here." Her words were a whisper. Tears slid down her cheeks.

Slater wrapped his arm around her, drawing her to his

side, praying he didn't pass out himself. It was all too familiar—the smell, the sounds, the machines. It was as if he'd been there before. He was certain of it, but he didn't know when or why. Nothing made sense except the feel of Rocki's shaking body holding on to him. Rocki needed him. He stuffed the half memories into his external hard drive and concentrated on her. "You need to speak louder."

Jackson's head was wrapped in gauze with a tube coming right out of it draining something. He was as white as Rocki looked, as white as Slater felt, but since there were no mirrors, he couldn't tell for sure. The bruise blooming on Jackson's swollen face was the only color Slater could see. If not for the respirator filling Jackson's chest with air, moving it up and down, he'd swear the man was dead. He'd never seen anyone so still, so motionless, so lifeless.

Rocki let out a sob and turned her face into Slater's chest.

Comfort. He could do that for her. He turned his back on her brother, on all the machines, and concentrated on Rocki. It was easier to do that than wonder what the hell was going on with him. He kissed the top of her head and slid his arms around her. "It's going to be okay." He didn't know how he knew it, but he did. He just hoped to hell he wasn't wrong. "Come on, sweetheart. Just talk to him. It'll get easier. I promise."

She looked up at him with those wide, blue eyes—the kind of eyes a man could get lost in.

"You can do this. Just take a deep breath and try again. I'm right here for you. We'll all get through this together."

She pulled her hands from his, scrubbed them over her face, took a deep breath, and then gave him a nod.

"Jackson, it's Rocki. I'm here. You need to wake up. God, please wake up." She reached over and took his lifeless hand in hers. She was still shaking, but she was doing what she needed to do. Just like he was—trying to hold it together. He just didn't know why he was falling apart.

Rocki was so screwed. She wasn't sure how it happened, but then she'd pretty much been in a state of shock since she'd set eyes on Jax. By the time she and Slater had stepped out of Jax's ICU room, visiting hours were over, and Grace had ordered them to follow her and Teddy back to the lake house using what Grace always used— logic. There was no reason for them to stay, they wouldn't know anything until the morning, and besides, they were all upset and tired.

Grace forced Rocki's hand by issuing an order wrapped with a pretty bow to look like an invitation for Slater to stay at the lake house. Rocki's family home—the only part of her parents' estate that she and Jax hadn't liquidated.

It wasn't as if they needed to liquidate any of it. They could have kept the whole package since money had never been an issue—only the root cause of many of the problems, for Rocki at least.

They'd kept the lake house because it was where her family had spent all their summers and most of their winter vacations. It was where most of her happy family memories took place. Nothing bad ever happened at the lake house. Unfortunately, by bringing Slater there, chances were pretty darn good that the track record would end.

The lake house was the last place she wanted to bring Slater, Mr. Perceptive, Mr. Curiosity, and her personal, though obviously tortured, hero, all rolled into a six-foot-three Michelangelo body with a da Vinci intellect. But then after she'd seen the way Slater had looked when he stepped into Jax's room—like Superman wearing a Kryptonite cape—she could hardly send him off to a cold hotel by himself.

She'd never seen a man so close to falling to his knees and expiring. Never seen a big—and lord he was big—strong, larger-than-life, vibrant man-in-charge go from superhero to vulnerable and back in less than a minute. If she hadn't seen it with her own eyes, she'd swear it wasn't possible.

One minute he was holding her up, playing the hero—something she had a feeling he did more often than not—and the next, he nearly shattered, turning green and looking as if he were going to pass out, hyperventilate, and be sick all at the same time.

When she'd looked into his frantic, confused, and fear-glazed eyes, it became apparent—if only to her, one who'd been there, done that, and dealt with the flashbacks—that he was reliving a battle he'd already fought and probably lost.

She was living proof that a person could lose the battle and still survive. She didn't know what he'd endured, but she knew with certainty that Slater was nothing if not a survivor.

Pain had radiated through him—a pain so monumental she'd felt it. She'd seen the way he rubbed his chest, the same way Pete rubbed his scar tissue, and wondered if it was a war injury, but then with his background as a foster kid—he might have just survived his family.

Slater had been amazing—he hadn't succumbed. He turned around, slammed whatever personal hell he'd experienced away with the ferocity and determination of the warrior she would always see him as, and pulled back on his superhero suit. He held on to her, calmed her, and talked her through one of the most horrifying experiences of her life.

As they followed Grace and Teddy back to the house, her mind raced faster than the cars blowing past them on the rural highway. All she could hope was that since Slater obviously had his own secrets, maybe he wouldn't out hers.

Slater drove with one eye on Rocki—or should he say Racquel?—and one eye on Grace and Teddy's car. It was late—too late and he was done.

Whatever happened at the hospital had drained him like a hose drained the gas tank when he and his brothers used to siphon instead of buy the stuff. Tired wasn't a fit description of how he felt. He wasn't sure if there was one. It was as if someone had taken his body and soul and wrung it out and then beat it against the sidewalk a few times just for good measure—not that there were sidewalks around here.

He stared at the scenery as far as the headlights reached on the dark mountain road. There was nothing but trees—and not the pines he was used to in the Pacific Northwest—these were deciduous trees. With the light of the moon behind them, they glowed like eerie skeletons. Breaks in the trees showed a lake—a big one they'd been driving around for miles. "Where are they taking us?"

"To the lake house. We're almost there."

She didn't sound happy about it. First she'd been trying to get rid of him; then in the hospital she'd held on to him as if she was afraid he'd disappear. He wasn't sure if it was for his benefit or hers. He just hoped she didn't ask for an explanation for his behavior because he didn't have one to give her. He didn't even have one to give himself.

The Watkins signaled a right-hand turn onto what was obviously private property if the stone fence and lion statues on either side of the well-tended entrance were anything to go by. The grounds screamed money—a lot of it. They continued on the private drive, climbing in elevation through a vast amount of property and past five or six huge houses before stopping at what could only be called a mansion.

Teddy and Grace parked their SUV in front of a six-car garage beside the main house.

Whoever these folks were, they were rich—rich on the level of Dominique's family. Rich as in way out of his and Rocki's league. Rich as in he and Rocki didn't belong and wouldn't—probably ever. No matter how much money Slater made, he could never run in their circles. There were some things to which a lowborn dude like him just couldn't aspire. He might not know much, but if there was one thing he'd learned from Dominique, it was that there were some things money couldn't buy, and class was one of them. "Rocki, the only people welcome in a place like this have old money and the kind of class that's inbred—not purchased. I don't have it—I never will. I can't stay here."

"Sure you can. Believe me, Slater, the people who own the place couldn't care less about how much money you or anyone else makes. And as for class—you have more class in the tip of your little finger than most people have in their whole body. Not all rich people are snobs."

"All the ones I've met are. Let's just go to that hotel you told me about."

She shook her head. "We'll hurt Grace and Teddy's feelings if we leave now. Come on, it'll be fine."

Rocki said the words but didn't look as if she believed

them. Still, she got out of the car—a car that was at least ten years old. "Do you want me to park someplace else?"

"Why?"

The Watkins drove a Range Rover, and the other car in the drive was an Aston Martin DB9. He didn't have to be a *Sesame Street* aficionado to know the song "One Of These Things (Is Not Like the Others)." "Because Pop's car looks like a piece of shit—that's why. Just parking this old Jeep here is going to lower their property value."

She leaned into the car and rolled her eyes. "Slater, I had no idea you were such a snob."

"Me? I'm not a snob."

Rocki grabbed her purse and the rock Nicki loaned her. "It sure sounds to me as if you are. You're judging Grace and Teddy by the price of the car they drive. How is that not snobby?" She didn't wait for a response before going around to the back and opening the tailgate of the jeep.

Slater turned the car off so the fumes didn't suffocate them—the beast was burning oil—and he listened to its death rattle while he watched Grace and Teddy go up to the side entrance of the mansion and walk right in without unlocking the door. He couldn't believe people around here didn't lock their doors. What were they? Nuts?

He got out and stomped over to Rocki, grabbing the bag right out of her hand. He might not look like one, and sometimes he didn't act like one, but it wasn't as if he didn't at least try to be a gentleman. "I'm not judging anyone. I'm just trying not to piss anyone off."

"You're not doing a very good job of it. You're pissing me off royally."

If he weren't so damn done, he'd appreciate the way Rocki's eyes blazed and the color that lit her face. The part of him that wasn't still in shock from his earlier hospital escapade did, but the part that would have done something about it was temporarily out of order—at least he hoped it was temporary.

Slater barely had the energy to follow Rocki up the steps and into what they probably called the mudroom. The mudroom was the size of Pop's living room. Ten-foot-long pristine white benches sat beneath hooks for coats, scarves, and hats. Beside the benches, ski and sports equipment racks were filled with first-class gear, skis, boards, snowshoes, and the like. There wasn't a speck of mud to be had. He was afraid to put down his battered duffel.

Rocki dumped her purse and her coat on one of the benches like she owned the place, so Slater set the bags on the floor beside her stuff, afraid to scuff the furniture.

He looked down at his own clothes and realized he was incredibly underdressed and wished he'd bothered to change before they headed out of Brooklyn. If he'd known where they were going, he would have done better than to wear his old threadbare jeans and beat-up boots. He didn't have much in the way of dress clothes, but he could have worn a newer pair of jeans, and maybe a shirt that wasn't faded. The thermal Henley he wore used to be red, but now was muted due to years of washing. He pushed up the frayed cuffs, hoping to make them less noticeable. If anyone walked in, they'd surely think he was the help.

"Addie left a pot of soup cooling on the stove," Grace called out to them. "I'll have it heated in a flash."

Rocki gave him a *you-better-eat-it-and-like-it* look before slogging up the steps to the kitchen.

The kitchen had two commercial stoves, miles of granite counters, and more cabinets than he could imagine filling. It was twice the size of the restaurant's kitchen. A farm table that had to seat ten sat in front of a fireplace on a braided rug beside floor-to-ceiling windows overlooking what he assumed was the lake. The place looked like something out of *Lifestyles of the Rich and Famous*.

Slater blew out a breath and asked for directions to the restroom to wash up.

Rocki waved a hand. "Just go through the butler's pantry and it's there on the right."

Slater didn't know what the hell a butler's pantry was, but he figured it out pretty quickly. He walked down a long hallway with glass-fronted upper cabinets and full lowers with more counter space on both sides. The cabinets were filled to overflowing with more china and gleaming silver than they stocked at Pottery Barn. Shit. It all looked old and expensive. There must have been enough dishes to serve more than a hundred. He had no idea what people who lived in a house—even one as big as this—would need with all that stuff.

He slipped into the bathroom and washed the sweat off his still bruised face, thankful Grace and Teddy hadn't mentioned it. He wished he could jump into a shower, wished he could get the hell out of there without losing his dignity, wished he could just erase the roller-coaster ride of a day from his memory bank.

CHAPTER 9

Rocki took a sip of the hot tea Grace set in front of her. The warmth of the fire chased the chill out of her bones, and she groaned in appreciation. The tea was heavenly, heavy on the honey with a splash of lemon — just the way she liked it, just the way Grace had fixed it for her all her life.

Grace's hand slid across Rocki's shoulders as she passed by. Grace touched everyone. Always comforting, always there, always steady. Grace and Teddy had been the only constants in her and Jackson's lives since their parents died, when it seemed that the rest of their world was falling apart.

Rocki turned to her and wrapped her arms around Grace's waist, resting her head on the woman's not so flat stomach, and closed her eyes, holding back tears.

"Jackson's strong and he has a reason to live. Don't give up on him, Racquel. He won't give up on you. You have to know that." Grace's hand stroked Rocki's hair like she had since Rocki was a baby.

"But Mom and Dad—"

"Didn't have the medical attention Jackson's receiving. Honey, don't do this. History will not repeat itself. Jackson won't let it, especially now that he knows you're here."

"Thanks to Slater. I don't think I could have gotten here without him." Rocki didn't need to look up to see the expression on Grace's face. Just to stop the questions, she cleared her throat. "He's been a really good friend."

When Grace didn't answer, Rocki knew she was in for it—maybe not tonight but sometime soon. Grace was like an elephant; she was good at holding on to things. She'd drag it out as soon as she was sure Rocki least expected it.

Someone cleared his throat. Slater.

Grace patted Rocki's shoulder and leaned over to kiss her brow. "It's good to have you back. I'm just sorry this is what it took for you to come home. You've been gone too long."

Only six months, but Rocki didn't say that. Instead she snuck a peek at a very uncomfortable-looking Slater while Teddy brought over bowls of thick, creamy chowder.

Teddy set Rocki's before her and squeezed her shoulder. "Addie just came back from Kennebunkport and brought over a bushel of clams and a half dozen lobster. The lobster will keep until supper tomorrow."

She did her best to smile but it felt as if her face was frozen. The smile must have been brittle at best from the sad look Teddy gave her. God, she was a mess. "That's a treat for us. You're okay with shellfish, aren't you, Slater?" She looked at the chowder that, any other time, she'd be salivating over. "You're not allergic or anything, are you?"

"No, I love seafood." He waited to start eating. When Grace came back to the table with the bread and salad, Slater stood and held her chair.

Grace beamed at him. "Thank you, dear."

Great. As if Rocki wasn't in enough trouble with Grace, Slater had to play the consummate gentleman.

Grace didn't give Rocki a choice; she filled her salad plate and pulled off a hunk of crusty bread and set it in front of her. When Rocki didn't dig in automatically, Grace leaned over. "You need to eat. You'll not be losing any more weight on my watch, young lady."

"Yes, ma'am." Rocki ate. She was sure the chowder was wonderful—no one made chowder as well as Addie—but Rocki didn't taste it. She stared into the bowl and only saw Jackson with his head all wrapped up, his eyes closed, machines breathing for him. It was all she could do to choke down half the bowl and a few bites of salad.

Slater seemed to have no problem eating, but then he probably hadn't eaten since breakfast and, she reminded herself, it wasn't his brother lying in the hospital bed. The Chinese food still sat in the car—neither of them had touched it.

When Grace finished, she pushed her bowl away and collected the dishes around the table. "Racquel, I made up the blue room for Slater. Teddy has already taken your bags up. Why don't you show Slater to his room and get some sleep? I set fresh towels out for you. You two look like you're about to pass out in your bowls." She shot Slater a look. "I have a picture of Racquel sound asleep in a bowl of spaghetti when she was just a little tyke." She smiled at the memory and put her hand out to illustrate how short Rocki had been at the time. "Bald as a cue ball she was. I think she was two before her hair came in, just as blonde as corn silk. Her mother and I used to tape bows to her head so people would know she was a girl."

Slater shot Grace the first real smile Rocki had seen on his face today.

"Don't encourage her, Slater. If Grace gets out the photo albums I swear I won't come to your rescue."

"That doesn't sound like much of a threat. Just think of all the ammunition I'd have."

The thought was scary, or would have been had she been able to feel anything. She seemed to have gone numb. "Yeah, well, whatever." She waved her hand and grabbed a few glasses to carry to the sink.

Grace took them from her. "Teddy and I have this. You go on up to bed. You know where we are if you need us. The hospital will call if there's a change. I gave them both our numbers." She placed the glasses on the counter and gave Rocki a hug, kissing both cheeks. "Just say a prayer, dear. There's not much else we can do."

Tears threatened again so Rocki just nodded, giving Teddy a wave.

He winked and in his face she saw love and understanding—he'd seen her like this before. He knew she couldn't talk right now.

She left the kitchen, heading to the main staircase through the dining room like she'd done a million times before. The house looked the same—dark hardwood floors were buffed to a shine, and it smelled the same, like lemon furniture polish and the flowers Grace always arranged, but it felt empty. She felt empty—as if someone had hollowed her out like an avocado, leaving only the skin. Even though Slater padded behind her and Grace and Teddy chatted in the kitchen, she felt more alone than she had since her parents died.

She dragged herself up the steps, concentrating on the comfortably worn oriental runner held in place with brass rods that shone in the light of the milk-glass overhead pendants. She made the turn and counted the last four steps. The wide hall greeted them, the runner softening the sounds of their footfalls.

The door to Jackson's room stood open, a pair of tennis shoes looked as if they'd been kicked off next to the pair of jeans lying on the floor beside them. She stopped herself from going in and picking up after him. She stopped herself from dragging in the air that still carried the scent of his aftershave. She stopped herself from curling into a ball and crying. She held on to the wall, staring through the door wondering if Jax would ever return.

Slater's strong arm came around her and pulled her to his chest. "He'll be back. I know he will. He'll be okay."

She wished she could believe him.

Slater ran his hand through her hair, massaging her neck muscles, and holding her close. "Which room is yours?"

"I'm just across the hall. Yours is right next to mine."

He turned, opened the door, and led her through.

"What are you doing?"

"Getting comfortable." He toed off his boots. "Go get changed."

"What?"

He pulled down the duvet. "I'll just stay until you fall asleep. You don't look like you should be alone." He wiped the tears off her face and kissed her forehead. "Go ahead."

She rummaged through her bag and grabbed her cotton nightgown. "You don't have to do this. I'm a big girl." She was more than capable of crying herself to sleep—she'd had a whole lot of practice.

"Yes, I do. If I want to get any sleep tonight, I need to know you'll be okay." He pulled his Henley over his head; his T-shirt rode up, showing off washboard abs and a thin trail of dark hair disappearing into his threadbare Levi's. He tugged the hem of his T-shirt back into place, tossed his shirt on his boots, pushed the pillows against the headboard, and settled in. "I'm not going to leave you alone until I know you're sleeping soundly. You need the rest."

"So do you."

"Rocki, don't argue with me. There's not much I can do to help. This is something I can do."

He looked so sincere, as if the fact there was nothing he could do to fix things, to fix her, made him feel impotent or worse, useless. Slater didn't strike her as a person who suffered either well.

She didn't know what to say; her thanks sat like a stone lodged in her throat. She'd never be able to thank him for all he'd done for her. She just wished she had something to sleep in other than the ugly cotton nightgown Grace had given her last Christmas. She'd never worn it—why would she? She didn't wear PJ's at her apartment. It was so hot, she had no choice but to strip down to nothing. Even with that, she kept a window open all winter. But here at home, Grace never thought twice about walking into her room to wake her. Besides, it was cold here—much colder than in the city or maybe it just felt that way.

Whoever said granny gowns weren't sexy had never seen Rocki O'Sullivan—or Racquel Sullivan—wearing one.

Rocki stepped out of the attached bathroom and the light behind her outlined her body, leaving nothing to Slater's imagination. He'd spent the last week imagining Rocki naked. He thought he'd exaggerated her qualities, but he hadn't. If anything, he hadn't done her justice.

Rocki was covered from chin to toes but with the light behind her, it didn't matter. She might as well have been naked.

When she stepped back into the room, the light no longer illuminating her body, she still hadn't lost any of her appeal. Even her walk was sexy and the part of him he thought had been temporarily out of order roared to life as if someone had just yanked on his starter and opened the throttle. Shit. It had been a long time since seeing the silhouette of a naked woman could get him half hard. Hell, even seeing a naked woman wouldn't cut it. Rocki seemed to defy the laws of attraction.

Skirting the bed, she slid between the sheets on the far side, and shivered.

"Rocki, if I wanted to be this far away from you, I'd have gone to my own room." He wrapped his arm around her waist and yanked her across the bed and into his chest. The damn nightgown didn't slide like the silky kind did; it just pulled tight against her body, which didn't help his ever-growing problem. There wasn't much he could do about it so he chose not to let it bother him any more than the physical discomfort already did. They were both adults, and hell, in his book, his being turned on without even a kiss or a grope was a true compliment.

Rocki's cold feet hit his shins and he sucked in a Rocki-scented breath. Her nose slid over his neck, sending chills through him.

"You're an iceberg."

"And you're a heater. How can you be so warm?"

With her lying against him, he was more than warm—he was downright hot, but he couldn't tell her that. "I'm a guy. Guys are always hot."

Rocki's hand slid over his chest and he caught it in his and held on. He hoped it would look as if he was trying to warm her when in all actuality he was just trying to contain her movement. The last thing he needed was for Rocki to realize his predicament.

Cupping the back of her neck, he set her head to rest on his shoulder and slid his hand down her back so she straightened her body and leaned against his side, which was safe. All he wanted to do was warm her while he did his best to concentrate on everything but the press of her body or the way her breasts pillowed against his chest. Shit. He pulled the thick duvet over them, tucking it in behind her and settled in, hoping she'd fall asleep quickly.

"Slater?"

"Try to get some sleep, Rocki. We'll talk in the morning."

From the way her body stiffened, that was the wrong thing to say, but he was afraid she'd ask about what happened with him at the hospital. He couldn't go there. Not again. Just the thought of it sent his heart racing and made him feel sick with dread. He wasn't sure what it was about, and he had no great urge to explore the phenomenon—just the opposite. He'd do anything to avoid feeling like that ever again.

Instead of thinking about it, he massaged Rocki's neck and moved down her back, chasing away the tension he felt coursing through her as he examined the room by the light of the almost-full moon.

The room was painted a soft antique blue and was filled with white Shabby Chic–like furniture Dominique had wanted him to buy—the kind that looked real—not the stuff you buy new that's just made to look old and well loved. A bookshelf lined the wall beside the bathroom, containing what he figured a teenaged girl would save: books, pictures, trophies with ribbons dangling from them, and a stuffed animal or two tossed in for good measure. Framed photos he was unable to make out sat on a long bureau with a mirror hanging above it, reflecting the light coming in through white lacy curtains. The curtains matched the duvet cover, which was made of a bleached white fabric with intricate flowery cutouts. All told, the place had a real girly feel without being overly prissy.

This bedroom was so different from Rocki's apartment—he couldn't believe they belonged to the same person. It was a definite disconnect. This room had a history. It was clearly decorated by someone who had a deep love for its occupant. Maybe it wasn't Rocki's room. Maybe Grace and Teddy had given Rocki their daughter's room to use. But when he thought of Rocki, the way she moved through the house as if she'd done it all her life, the way she walked into this room, took a deep breath, and looked as if she'd finally come home, it sure as hell seemed as if this was her childhood bedroom.

Home.

Grace had mentioned that it had been too long since Rocki had been home. Had she meant home to New Hampshire, or home to the mansion? And if Rocki had grown up in a mansion, what the hell was she doing living over a Chinese restaurant in a walk-up on Mott Street?

The more he got to know Rocki, the more questions he had, and the more intrigued he became. The woman was a mystery wrapped in an enigma and rolled in a paradox.

Tomorrow he'd figure her out, but right now, with her body curled against his side absorbing his heat, all he could do was concentrate on how holding Rocki O'Sullivan or Racquel Sullivan—whoever the hell she was—felt right in a way he'd never before experienced. Yeah, that was just one more thing he couldn't dwell on, so he closed his eyes and did what he did best—he wrote code in his head, trying to come up with a fix for a problem he had with one of the new programs he was developing. He was in bed with a beautiful woman practically lying on top of him and he was writing code. What a geek.

He stayed still and listened to Rocki's rhythmic breathing. He'd give it another ten minutes and he'd go to his own bed and try to sleep.

No matter how much code he wrote, he couldn't let go of what had happened in the hospital, so he finally gave up and went there. Or tried to. He put himself back in that place—the ICU room—and tried his damnedest to remember. Every time he felt as if he was almost there, it disappeared. The sick feeling still sat cold and heavy in his stomach. The fear was alive and well, but he couldn't, for the life of him, remember what caused it.

It was in the wee hours of the morning when he finally gave up trying and moved to get out of bed but Rocki held on to him. Every time he moved, her grip tightened. She mumbled something in her sleep and didn't settle until he wrapped his arms around her again. So much for going back to his own room—not that he was complaining. There were far worse things than spending the night holding Rocki . . . like trying to remember his past. He pulled her closer and settled in for a few hours of shut-eye. He was glad he was exhausted, because sleeping next to Rocki was dangerous.

Slater came awake and looked right into Rocki's shock-widened blue eyes. She was all warm and rumpled and her leg was thrown over his hip. His hand was wrapped around her upper thigh, and her nightgown had either ridden up or he'd pushed it. He wasn't sure if her shocked expression was from finding herself glued to him—trapped by her leg, or because she rode the erection straining the buttons of his 501s. From the red coloring her face he surmised she was either really embarrassed or completely turned on. Either way, he wasn't about to let her go. "Morning." He slid his hand farther up her thigh to her ass, shifted her beneath him, and kissed her.

It took a moment for Rocki to realize she hadn't been dreaming. Of course, there wasn't much to do about it now that Slater was lying on top of her with his tongue in her mouth. It was nice. She supposed *nice* wasn't the best descriptor—hot, amazing, groan-worthy—any of those would have definitely fit the bill. She wasn't sure if the groan she heard was his or hers, but by the way her back arched off the bed, she didn't think it mattered.

Her hands tangled in his hair and her legs had somehow ended up wrapped around his waist.

Her brain screamed no, but her body screamed giddyup. Still she needed to put a stop to this—unfortunately.

By the time she wrapped her mind around the problem, Slater had dragged his lips down her throat and was unbuttoning her nightgown. The man had incredible manual dexterity and that wasn't the only thing that was impressive about him. He kissed like a dream, which was exactly what she'd thought he was. She wasn't supposed to be kissing the real Slater Shaw.

"Slater." She dragged in a breath. "I need a do-over."

"No problem," he mumbled against her neck and slid his tongue over a sensitive spot she hadn't known existed. "We can do this over and over and over again."

He tugged the gown open over her breast and covered it with his mouth, sucking every thought of stopping this fiasco from her head. Every tug of his mouth on her breast was met with a thrust of his hips and she couldn't think of anything except getting more, getting closer, and getting into his pants.

She clawed at the button fly and with just a yank, the rest of the buttons popped open. It was a good thing his jeans were well worn. Wasting no time, she dipped her hand into the waistband of his boxers and grabbed hold.

His erection sprang free as he reared up and dragged her nightgown over her head before tugging his own T-shirt off.

They stared at each other, neither of them saying a word, but then sometimes words were superfluous. He should have looked ridiculous with his jeans and boxers pushed down around his knees, but he looked anything but. Every muscle in his body seemed to ripple with barely controlled energy. He reached for her and brushed the back of his fingers over her cheek in a whisper of a touch.

A knock sounded on the door, "Raquel, are you awake, dear?"

Ice filled her veins in a heartbeat and she froze for a millisecond before her face and body seemed to incinerate. Oh God! "Grace," Rocki called out, "yes, I'm up. Give me a minute and I'll be down to help with breakfast."

The door opened just a crack and Rocki shoved Slater off the bed and onto the floor. She yanked what she could of the covers over her, and motioned Slater to hide.

He groaned and kicked his pants off.

"Hide," she whispered.

The man looked up at her from the floor as if he was holding back laughter. "You're kidding, right?" he whispered back.

Rocki held her breath as the door yawned open a

foot, but Grace didn't come in. "Will you get Slater up, dear?"

"Yes, I'll wake him." She slapped at Slater, motioned him to hurry, wondering if a body that big could even fit under the bed. She dragged her nightgown over her head and tripped over the bedclothes on her way to the door. She couldn't seem to get any of the buttons to cooperate so she grabbed both sides of the button band, held it closed, and slipped out, careful to close the door behind her.

"I just woke up, Grace. I'm sorry if I overslept."

Grace's eyes went wide and then she looked away before she backed toward the stairs. "It's fine, Racquel, you and Slater take your time. Come on down whenever you're ready."

"Okay . . ." Rocki's voice trailed off as Grace scurried away like a woman who'd just remembered she'd left something on the stove. Rocki took a sniff and didn't smell anything burning other than her temper—she wanted to kill Slater.

When Grace turned the corner to go down the steps, Rocki pushed the door open and found Slater lying naked in her bed with a huge grin on his face right before he laughed.

She couldn't believe he was laughing. She dragged her eyes from his body—she figured it would be impossible to stay mad at him if she was drooling. "I can't believe you think almost getting caught in the act is funny."

Slater cleared his throat and looked as if he were doing his darnedest to stifle the laughter but failing. "I don't think almost getting caught making love is funny. What's funny is the sight of you going out there to talk to Grace with your nightgown on inside out."

She looked down at herself and cringed. "Oh God. She knows."

"Yeah, and she's smart enough to know we're going to be a while." Slater got out of bed and pulled her into his arms. He stood there butt naked and fully engaged, or should she say engorged—how was a mystery. He acted as if the last five minutes hadn't happened. As if Grace hadn't hit them full force with the equivalent of an ice-cold fire hose. As if he'd had the slightest chance of getting her back in the mood for what they were just doing. He was delusional. He kissed her neck.

It was so not working. She refused to let it. She ignored the way her heartbeat drummed against her breastbone like the machine gun double bass in a Metallica song. "I can't believe this."

"What?" He slid her nightgown back up while he nuzzled her ear, sending sparks into places that should still be iced over. The man was a living, breathing blowtorch or blowhard—she wasn't sure which.

"Cut it out." She tried to step away but he had her right where he apparently wanted her—up against him, and any move she made only made things worse—worse for her and her plan to somehow get out of this catastrophe. Slater just seemed to enjoy it. "Slater, we can't do this."

"I have to disagree with you there, sweetheart." He slid his hand from her ass to her thigh and tugged it over his hip—earning a groan from her. "I think the last few minutes just proved the opposite. I'll bet my next year's salary that when we do, it's going to be amazing. Since we've already been essentially caught and we're going to suffer the consequences regardless, we might as well enjoy ourselves before the morning-after tap dance around the breakfast table and the man-to-man talk with Teddy. He's going to want to know my intentions. It won't help your cause any if I had to say that I intend to get you horizontal as soon as humanly possible."

"You wouldn't dare."

"No, but that's what I'll be thinking."

Rocki wasn't sure how he did it; he slid his lips over hers and kissed her into submission. Within a minute he had her hotter than ever, breathless, and, well, needy. That was a new one on her—she'd never needed anyone—at least not that way, but damn, Slater was a whole different animal.

He pulled away but still held her tight against him, which was a good thing because if he hadn't, she might have oozed onto the floor after that last kiss. "I just want to make sure you know I don't plan to suffer alone. Misery loves company. I'm giving you fair warning. I'm not going to be the only one hot, hard, and wanting. I'm not going to be the only one looking for the nearest broom closet or empty bed. And I'm not going to be the only one imagining us ripping off each other's clothes. This, I guaran-ass-tee."

"What?" She wasn't able to take her eyes off his lips, and she wasn't able to think about words when his body was sending secret messages to hers, causing reactions she had no hope of controlling. "What are you saying?"

"Think about it. It'll come to you eventually." He gave her a perfunctory smack on the lips right before he dropped her leg and gave her a matching smack on the ass. "I'll just be on my way now." He stepped back, grabbed his jeans, and tugged them on, watching her while he tucked and buttoned. "I need to mess up my bed unless you want to join in the fun."

That damn smile of his broke through her good sense and a little bit of her wanted to sigh. He was a sight, wearing nothing but a pair of threadbare 501s only partly buttoned. She wanted to step forward and spend the next hour just exploring his body.

"We'll have as good a time messing up my bed as we did yours. I promise." His gaze zeroed in on the bed. "From the looks of it, it's a miracle the mattress didn't slide off the box spring." He stepped beside it and gave it a hearty nudge with his thigh. "That must have happened when you tossed me over the side. Thanks for that, by the way."

Oh God, she'd thrown him off the bed. She wanted to hide her face, but she knew he'd just enjoy her discomfort. Instead she did her best to meet his eyes and smile. "My pleasure. If you had moved, I wouldn't have had to resort to that."

Slater picked up his boxers, tossed his Henley over his shoulder, and grabbed his boots. "I guess we're both in for cold showers this morning. Enjoy yours, sweetheart. I'll see you downstairs."

Rocki watched Slater strut out of her room as if he hadn't a care in the world. And she supposed he didn't. What did it matter to him that Grace had almost walked in on them? And what the hell had happened? One minute he was warm and comforting, saying he'd only stay until she fell asleep, and the next thing she knew she was waking up wrapped around him like the sleeve on an ice-cream cone.

She'd love to blame Slater for the entire thing, but she couldn't. She'd dreamed of exploring his body with her hands and her mouth. She'd done things to him in her dreams that she'd only heard about. Things she'd never once considered doing to another man, but with Slater, they felt as natural as breathing—until she'd woken up anyway.

Okay, her internal lie detector was calling bullshit. She wished she could say that it had changed when she'd woken up but it hadn't. If Grace hadn't shown up when she did, there was no telling how far she'd have let things progress. She shook her head and tried to get the very clear image of Slater kneeling over her out of her mind. Oh yeah, she knew exactly how far she'd have let it go—they'd have gone all the way and she imagined it would have been just as amazing as he'd said.

Rocki's phone rang and her heart stopped, stuttered, and then pounded like a battering ram against her breastbone as if it were trying to break out of her chest. She jumped on the bed and reached for the phone as pictures of Jackson flew through her mind at warp speed, each more macabre than the one before. God, she'd been making out with Slater while her brother had been fighting for his life. "Hello?"

"Rocki, it's Bree. Are you okay?"

"Bree?" Relief flooded through her. "Thank God. I thought it was the hospital."

"Oh, Rocki. I'm so sorry. How is your brother?"

No words of censure, no why-didn't-you-tell-me-you-had-a-brother? questions. "As far as I know there's been no change. The hospital said they'd call if anything happened. He's in a coma. They did a ventriculostomy to relieve the pressure—his head is all wrapped up like a mummy. He was so still—if not for the respirator making his chest move, I'd swear he was dead." She wiped the tears off her face and wrapped her arm around herself, wishing Slater was there with her. "I'm just getting ready to head over to the hospital—visiting hours start at nine."

"Okay, I'll wait to hear from you. We're all praying and sending good thoughts your way."

"Thanks, Bree. And thank Pete for me. Slater drove me up here—he's been so . . . I'm glad he's here. I don't think I could have gotten up here without him."

"Slater has a definite way about him—that's for sure.

He's got this quiet strength that's pretty amazing. Give him our love. We'll talk to you soon. We love you, Rocki."

"I love you guys too." Rocki ended the call and realized she hadn't even asked Bree about her honeymoon. What kind of friend did that? The kind who only doles out need-to-know information. Suddenly all the reasons she had for keeping a huge part of her life a secret didn't seem nearly as important as she once believed. But then maybe that was because with Slater here putting two and two together, any choice of keeping her past and present separate might be out of her hands.

Rocki dug through her bag and tossed a change of clothes on her unmade bed—the bed she and Slater had been rolling around in less than fifteen minutes ago. It was amazing how much could change in a quarter of an hour. She just hoped that from now on, the only changes in her life would be for the better.

CHAPTER 10

"Damn, talk about piss-poor timing." Slater figured the only way it could have been worse was if Grace had knocked on the door ten minutes later. But then, if she had, he had a feeling he and Rocki would never have heard her.

He put his hand on the crystal doorknob one room over, which, if he remembered correctly, was the room he was supposed to have slept in. Right now, he just wanted to knock his head against the door. It wouldn't help the problem he had going on in his pants, but it might take his mind off it.

Slater stepped into his assigned room, let out a frustrated breath, and tossed his boots on the floor beside his duffel.

He hadn't planned to go there with Rocki. It had just happened, but he couldn't say he wasn't happy about it. He'd taken one look at her big blue eyes and all he could do was kiss her. Once he had a taste, once he felt her beneath him, neither of them had thought of stopping—until Grace's interruption. Yeah, that was the death knell. Rocki had stepped so far back she might as well have been in the next state.

From the first second he set eyes on Rocki, he wanted her. Want, he could handle. He didn't think the fact that he wanted her more than anyone he'd ever met was concerning—after all, Rocki was pretty extraordinary. It was all the other stuff he was having a problem with. Like the way he thought about her—even when he knew he shouldn't go there. It was as if she had somehow implanted the image of herself in his brain and invaded his thoughts at the weirdest times. Then there was the way he saw red that first night they'd met when he heard she was taking the subway home alone at two in the morning. He had no idea why that bothered him. If it had been anyone else, he wouldn't have given it a thought. After all, they weren't together, and it wasn't as if she didn't have a ride to the train. All he knew was that he wouldn't have slept if he hadn't seen that she'd gotten home safe and sound. At the time, he wasn't sure why he cared, but the problem was he did, and unfortunately, it was just getting worse, and he didn't know what the hell to do about it.

He unzipped his bag and dragged out a clean pair of jeans. Okay, maybe not freshly laundered but at least they didn't look as if they'd been slept in—he hoped. He dug through his duffel for a T-shirt—a white one, and then grabbed the only collared shirt he owned. He shook it out with a snap, and then gave it a once-over. It was a little wrinkled, but what the heck. He threw it over the hook in the bathroom and hoped the wrinkles would steam out—that was if he turned the water to hot. Right now, he had his doubts. If things with Rocki kept going the way they were, he wouldn't be able to take a hot shower while they were in the same country—maybe the same hemisphere.

Slater hated taking cold showers almost as much as

he hated stopping things when they were just getting good; sexual frustration was not his friend. So he chickened out, hopped into a hot shower, and took himself in hand and wondered if Rocki was doing the same thing. He let his imagination run wild, and it took all of a few minutes to find his release.

He hadn't been looking forward to spending the day half-hard, but then he didn't think it would hurt to keep Rocki's mind on something other than her brother's condition. Slater looked forward to taking her mind off her troubles just as soon as he had a minute alone with her.

After he dressed, he halfheartedly messed up the bed he hadn't slept in, and then pulled the sheets back before heading toward the kitchen. He hoped beating Rocki downstairs would take some heat off her. He liked Grace and Teddy, and as funny as it was that Rocki felt like a teenager getting caught making out, he didn't want to make her any more uncomfortable.

Slater slipped out of his room and heard Rocki's shower going. He did his best not to picture her naked with water running over her body and failed miserably. Shit, he wasn't the kind of pervy guy who pictured every woman he knew naked—well, not until he'd met Rocki at least.

He ran his hand through his still-wet hair and did his best to put the brakes on that particular train wreck. Shit, he'd gotten off less than fifteen minutes before and his dick was already working on a zipper tattoo. He might as well have been a horny teenager.

He needed a few minutes, so he spent some time looking around the house. Last night he'd been too concerned about Rocki to fully appreciate the place. It was just as nice as he suspected when he'd first set eyes on the mansion. He blew out a low whistle when he stepped into what he thought might be the living room. "So this is how the one percent live." The Turkish carpets looked old and worn, but beautiful. The furniture was probably antique and every piece had been polished to a shine. The crystal chandeliers gleamed in the morning light, a baby grand piano was dwarfed by the size of the room, and fresh flowers were scattered throughout.

He followed the scent of bacon frying through the massive formal dining room to the kitchen, stepped in, and spotted Teddy sitting at the table. "Good morning." He met the man's eyes over the newspaper.

"So I hear."

There was no pussyfooting around with Teddy, apparently. Slater couldn't help but respect him. The man went right for the jugular.

"Theodore." Grace shot the old man a warning look and then turned a smile on Slater. "I hope you slept well, dear."

"Yes, it's a very comfortable house. Thank you."

Teddy stood and gave Slater the hairy eyeball treatment before picking up his coffee and heading to the counter. "Is Racquel on her way down?"

"I don't know, sir. I heard the shower going when I passed her room."

Teddy didn't look as if he bought it, but then Slater really didn't care. He was pleasantly surprised when Teddy grabbed a mug from the cabinet. "Coffee?"

"Yes, please."

Grace stepped beside him. "Cream and sugar is on the table. I'm making a batch of huckleberry pancakes. We picked the berries last summer when the kids were here. They're Racquel's favorite. With any luck, she'll eat. I hope you're hungry."

Teddy poured the coffee, delivered it to the table,

and set it down without throwing it at Slater. That was a plus.

Maybe things weren't looking so bad after all. Still, he planned on sticking close to Grace. He wasn't chicken—not at all. He chose to think of it as being strategically safe. "Grace, is there anything I can do to help? I'm pretty good in the kitchen." Not to mention a total suck-up.

"No, thanks." When the woman smiled, she lit the whole room—no wonder Rocki loved her so much. "I'm used to doing things on my own. Just relax by the fire, and if you're good, maybe Teddy will share the paper with you." Grace shot him a wink and a smile.

Teddy didn't look as though he was happy about the idea of sharing anything with Slater. Besides, he tended to get his news on the Internet. "Do you have Wi-Fi here? I wouldn't mind checking my e-mail before we leave for the hospital."

"Of course. Jackson does so much of his work on the computer—he's in investments and such—that we've had it installed. Teddy, get the password from the office for Slater, please."

Teddy's scowl told Slater he wanted to refuse, but after one look at his wife, he obviously reconsidered and motioned for Slater to follow.

Slater had known it was coming—he had just hoped it wouldn't be so soon, not to mention before his morning coffee. Since everything was better with caffeine, he grabbed his messenger bag and the cup before following the old man to a study on the other side of the house.

When Teddy closed the heavy wood door behind them, Slater raised his eyebrows. It had been a long time since he'd received a talking-to by the father of a girl he'd dated. Actually, now that he thought about it, this would be the first.

He set his bag on the floor beside the desk and looked for a coaster on which to set his mug. Seeing none, he decided to just hold it, took a fortifying sip, and waited.

Teddy settled behind the huge desk and didn't look as if he was in any hurry to find the password.

The situation reminded Slater of the time when he was an E-2 and was forced to stand at attention for more than an hour, waiting for his commanding officer to acknowledge his presence. He took another swig and assumed the position as best he could while holding a mug. The minutes ticked past and Slater didn't move a muscle.

After what seemed like a half hour but was probably closer to ten minutes, Teddy's gaze met his. "Grace seems to think there's something going on between you and our Racquel."

Slater took that as an order to stand at ease. He'd never done so while holding coffee, but he did his best. "Sir, with all due respect, don't you think that's something you should be discussing with Rocki?"

"If I did, I'd be talking to Racquel."

One thing he learned well in the navy was that if you weren't asked a direct question, it was best to keep your mouth shut. It had served him well until now.

"Racquel may be a grown woman, but she'll always be our little girl. She's been through a lot and she doesn't need a broken heart on top of the situation she finds herself in with Jackson. Those two are closer than any siblings I've ever seen. God forbid—" Teddy turned away and scrubbed his face with his hands.

Damn. Slater felt for the guy, he really did. He didn't know much about love except for seeing how his father felt about him and his brothers and vice versa. It looked as if Teddy felt the same for Rocki and Jackson—the man must be going through hell. "Sir, it's not my intention to do anything to hurt Rocki. I'm here to help."

Wary eyes met his. "So that's what they're calling it these days?"

Slater's fingers tensed on the cup. It was one of those heavy earthenware mugs and had it been something fragile, it would have been in pieces. "I realize this is an upsetting time for you and your family. I don't know Jackson, but I know Rocki." And when he thought about it, he realized that he did. He knew Rocki, maybe not as well as he wanted to, but he knew enough to know the woman wore her heart on her sleeve—it might be encased in armor but he had a feeling he knew her heart as well as he knew his own. In that respect he and Rocki were surprisingly similar. "You have nothing to worry about, sir. If I ever did anything to hurt Rocki, I'd have to answer to my father, and believe me, I'm the last person in the world who wants to tug on that particular tiger's tail."

"Your father?"

"Pete Calahan."

Teddy's eyebrows rose and a smile played across his troubled face.

"I assume you know my father?"

Teddy gave him a nod.

Of course he did. Slater was sure Pop knew everything there was to know about Rocki. It just made sense that over the years, Pop and Teddy had become pretty well acquainted. "Pop asked me to bring Rocki up here. I'm to stay with her, take care of her, and make sure she gets whatever she needs. I think Rocki's stronger than either of you give her credit for, but no matter what happens with Jackson, we'll make sure Rocki lands on her feet. She has an amazing number of people in Red Hook who love her and would do anything for her. I'm just one of many.

"Last night, Rocki needed a shoulder to cry on and someone to hold her. That's what I did. And with all due respect, sir, anything else that goes on between Rocki and me is up to Rocki. Nothing you say or do is going to change that."

Teddy gave him a hard, assessing look, and Slater felt as if he were back in the navy under close inspection. "What happened to your face?"

Ah, back to the third, fourth, and fifth degree. "My brother disagreed with something I said to his girlfriend. I was wrong. He was within his rights to come after me."

Teddy cracked a smile. "I'm assuming you have a job."

"I spent eight years in the navy. I just completed my secondary degree in computer security and I have a contract pending with OPEC, a job offer with Microsoft, and then there's always the option of finding something here on the East Coast."

"I see." Teddy grabbed a piece of paper and scrawled something on it. "Here's the password, Slater." Teddy pushed the paper across the desk toward him and rose. "I think we should get back to the women now before Grace comes after me. Grace might look like a nice lady, but she's just good at hiding her claws. Talk about yanking on a tigress's tail. If you have any kindness toward me at all, keep an easy smile on your face for the next hour or so."

Slater took the first deep breath he'd taken since he'd walked into the study and nodded. "Yes, sir. I'd be happy to, sir."

Rocki slipped down the back stairs leading to the kitchen like she'd done since she was little, wanting to eavesdrop, and get the lay of the land before jumping headfirst into unknown waters.

Grace flipped pancakes and turned the bacon at the stove—it looked as if she were cooking for a crowd. Rocki sure hoped Slater was hungry because she couldn't imagine eating more than a few bites.

The men sat at the table discussing something in the newspaper while Slater's hands flew over his computer keyboard at lightning speed. Whoever said men couldn't multitask had never seen Slater Shaw in action at his computer, or in bed.

Rocki shook her head. She couldn't believe her mind went there after she'd spent her time in the shower lecturing herself about the necessity of avoiding all thoughts of Slater's naked body, the way he kissed, and the size of his—

"Racquel." Grace's voice interrupted her X-rated thoughts. "Are you going to stand there all morning or are you planning to join us?"

Rocki's face felt as hot as the griddle Grace flipped pancakes on. It only got worse when Slater turned and gave her a look that made her face feel like it was under a broiler. The worst part was that she seemed physically incapable of looking away.

He raised an eyebrow and looked as if he was holding back a laugh. That was all it took to spur her to move.

She made a beeline for the coffeepot. Maybe some caffeine would help. At least holding a cup would give her something to do with her hands. She poured herself coffee and then slid four plates out of the cabinet to set the table. When she turned, she almost ran into Slater.

"Good morning, sunshine." He held the plates between them, leaned in, and kissed her right on the lips. Right in front of Grace and Teddy.

Rocki was so not expecting that—especially not a lingering, nibbley kiss, the kind of kiss that leads to longer, openmouthed kisses. A smacking kiss would have been bad enough, but a nibbley kiss was way out of bounds. It was a good thing Slater had a grip on the plates, because if it had been up to her, they'd need a broom.

He licked his lips and gave her a look that promised more to come. "I'll just bring these to the table for you."

She heard Grace sigh beside her.

Rocki looked at Teddy, expecting him to pull his usual indignant, overprotective father figure act, only to find him folding the newspaper he'd been reading, and straightening the place mats for Slater, as if her being kissed by a man in this kitchen was a daily occurrence.

Grace wrapped her arm around Rocki's waist. "That boy of yours must have a golden tongue."

Rocki flushed. Grace had no idea.

"Teddy took him to the study and I was afraid he would threaten the poor boy's life. You know how protective he can be when it comes to his little girl, but when they came back to the kitchen they were all buddy, buddy, sharing the paper, and talking sports. Look at them—thick as thieves, setting the table together. If I didn't know any better, I'd think Teddy gave your young man his blessing."

"Blessing? Blessing for what exactly?" Was it just her or was everyone going mad? The dreamy expression on Grace's face made her certain they'd all gone nuts. "Stop looking at me like that," she whispered.

Grace returned to the stove, making more pancakes than any of them knew what to do with. "I have no idea what you're talking about, young lady. Now, why don't you get the syrup out of the refrigerator and put it in a pitcher to warm?"

"You're not getting out of this that easily, Grace."

The woman gave her a knowing smile that only some-one who had changed her diapers could pull off. "No, I don't expect I will, but right now we have more pressing matters to deal with than your love life—"

"I don't have a love life."

"Oh that's right, these days it's called a sex life, isn't it?" Grace clicked her tongue and shook her head before she crossed herself. "Racquel Olivia Sullivan, your mother would be rolling over in her grave if she found out you were having indiscriminate sex—"

"I'm not having sex," she whispered.

Grace lifted an eyebrow.

Okay, she'd almost had sex, and last she checked that didn't count. Besides, it's not as if she planned it. And as far as she was concerned, there would be no more mat-tress aerobics with Slater. No, she had enough to deal with; she didn't need to add a man like Slater to the mix.

Rocki left Grace and her eyebrow of truth, and went to collect the silverware and heat the syrup. She just wished the microwave was in a different room.

Setting the pitcher of warm syrup in the middle of the table, Rocki reached around Teddy, giving him a kiss on the cheek and placing his fork and knife on either side of his plate. She moved toward Slater and avoided his gaze. Looking at the man could be dangerous. She stood well away from him, set his knife down, and shrieked when he tugged her onto his lap. "What do you think you're doing?"

"Sweetheart, if you don't know by now, you're worse off than I thought."

Teddy lifted his head and shot Slater a man-to-man grin she'd never seen before. "She's always been a little on the hardheaded side."

Grace laughed and set the platter of bacon on the table as if there was nothing at all unusual about the fact that Rocki was trapped on Slater's lap. "Racquel has always been one to boss everyone around. I used to watch her as a tot and think that the man who ends up with her would certainly have his hands full."

Slater rested his chin on her shoulder as if the Grace and Teddy Show was the most fascinating thing he'd seen since his first *Playboy*.

Teddy laughed. "Come on, Gracie. You used to look at Racquel and say, 'I pity the man who marries her.'"

"I never said that—"

"Not to her face. But you certainly said it to me often enough. But then it did take both you and her mother to handle one baby girl. Who knew such a little thing could cause so much trouble?"

Rocki looked from Grace to Teddy and back again. She'd heard it all before—ad nauseam. She'd always known she'd been a nightmare baby. They'd made no secret of it. Hell, half of New Hampshire had heard the stories, but did they have to tell Slater?

Teddy laughed. "We used to call her Stone Face because our little Racquel didn't smile until she was almost two."

Grace set the platter of pancakes on the table. "I always thought she was angry because she didn't come from the womb walking, talking, singing, and dancing." She took her seat and passed the bacon to Slater with a smile.

When Slater let go of Rocki to grab the bacon, she took the opportunity to slide off his lap and take her own seat.

Grace clucked her tongue. "Racquel rolled over before she was a day old, and at two weeks she managed to crawl from the foot of a king-sized bed to the top in less than five minutes. She started screaming because she was banging her little head on the headboard." She took a sip of her tea. "I had put the pillows on either side of her because I knew she rolled. I just didn't know she could crawl."

Slater put a half dozen slices of bacon on his plate and passed it to Rocki without ever taking his eyes off Grace. "Is that unusual? The crawling part, not the screaming part. Even I know babies cry."

Grace laughed. "You don't have much experience with babies, do you?"

Slater shook his head. "None."

"Most babies don't start crawling until they're between six and eight months old. Rocki had always been way ahead of the curve—we had to take down her crib when she was seven months because the little monkey kept climbing out and walking off. By the time she was nine months old, she was running like a racehorse. Lord, I didn't know if her mother and I would survive her first year."

Rocki nibbled on a piece of bacon and took a pancake before handing the platter to Slater who, thank the good Lord, took a pile and covered it with syrup. "So what kind of baby were you?"

Slater shrugged. "I have no idea. I don't remember my parents. I was probably a handful because I got tossed from one foster home to the next until I ended up with Pop."

Slater didn't look at any of them; he just stared at his plate and shoveled a vast amount of food into his mouth.

He'd mentioned that not all foster homes were like Pete's. And from the way he practically shut down, Rocki knew he needed an out. It was just too bad that she wasn't sure how to give him one. "Well, I guess that saves some embarrassment. No one knows your past but you." It was the best she could do, but, unfortunately, it didn't seem to help. It was amazing how a person could be sitting right next to her and still be light-years away.

Slater had never hidden his past—and for the first time in his life, he'd been tempted to. He didn't want Grace and Teddy to think less of him. Not for his benefit. He wasn't trying to impress them; he just didn't want to embarrass Rocki.

He worked on eating, not wanting to see Grace and Teddy look at him and wonder why he'd been dumped by his family, or worse, see pity in their eyes. No, he could handle anything except pity. When Rocki went back to eating, all he felt was relief.

Slater knew what Rocki looked like as a little kid— hell, there were pictures of her all over the house. She was cute, with long blond hair and a mischievous grin. He was able to picture her, but he had no idea what he'd been like.

He always told himself it was better to look ahead than back. Maybe he'd always said that because when he did try to look back, all he got was the blue screen of death. There was nothing there. He remembered a few foster homes—just vague memories of some of the rooms he'd slept in. One house had a dog—Slater remembered him—but then he hadn't been there for very long.

Slater's case manager had given him a memory book and made it a point to put photos of foster families in there—not that he ever wanted to see those people again. He'd only kept it because whenever he left a place, she always asked if he'd remembered to bring it. Like he had so many belongings he could actually forget something. Now that he thought about it, he wasn't even sure what the hell he had done with it. He'd stashed it away when he got to Pop's place and couldn't remember seeing it since.

He'd never thought about his lack of memories until now. It wasn't as if he and his brothers sat around reminiscing about their time in foster care, or in Storm's case, his life with an abusive prick of a father.

He'd always thought that before moving in with Pop and his brothers, there hadn't been much worth remembering.

The lack of memories had never bothered him much—until yesterday.

When he'd walked into Jackson's hospital room he got a rush of something so terrifying it knocked the wind out of him. The only thing keeping him from getting as far away as he could from that hospital room was Rocki. She might not admit it, but he knew by the way she held him all night that she needed him.

He'd slept with his share of women, but not one of them had held on to him like she had. No one had ever made him feel as if he was necessary. Just Rocki. The woman might fight it, but he knew she needed him.

The thought of someone relying on him, of someone needing him—the way Rocki had looked at him that morning as if he were the only person in the world she wanted to be with—should scare the shit out of him. Okay, maybe it did scare him. But if he was afraid of anything it wasn't of her wanting something from him. He was afraid he'd be incapable of giving her whatever it was she needed—or just not knowing what she needed. He only had one relationship that he thought had been about more than just sex. The only thing he learned from the whole Dominique fiasco was that he was completely clueless. There should be an instruction manual for shit like this.

Rocki had barely touched her food, and when he got the guts to look at Grace and Teddy, instead of looking at him with pity, he found them watching Rocki push her food around her plate.

Worry lines furrowed Grace's brow, and Teddy had lost the smile he'd worn when he'd teased Rocki about being a nightmare baby.

Rocki pushed her plate away and touched his shoulder. "Are you almost ready to go? I'd like to get back to the hospital when visiting hours begin."

"Sure." He checked his watch. "I guess we should leave in about ten minutes then." Damn, just the thought of going back to the ICU was enough to make his insides turn to liquid. "Why don't you try to eat a little more?"

Rocki took a sip of her coffee and shook her head. "I'm full."

He didn't believe her—he'd seen birds eat more than she did, but he wasn't about to call her on it.

Thanks to his time in the navy, he'd learned how to eat even when the food sat like lead in his stomach. He shoveled in the rest of his food because the last thing he needed was Rocki wondering why he'd suddenly lost his appetite. She had enough to worry about without him and his newfound fear of hospitals. No, she'd needed him with her last night, and it looked as if she'd need him again today. He would have to buck up, just like he always did. If he concentrated on Rocki, he wouldn't have to think of all the crap in his own life he'd yet to deal with.

Unfortunately, he'd have to handle it all sooner rather than later. That was something else he'd learned in the navy. Things have a way of biting you in the ass at the most inconvenient times—like meeting a woman who has the ability to seemingly take over your brain function right before you're supposed to begin a five-year stint in Bahrain. Rocki was nothing if not inconvenient as hell.

CHAPTER 11

There weren't many women who impressed Slater. He'd always thought he had nearly impossible standards. But after spending the day in the hospital watching Rocki with her brother, he couldn't help but think she was seriously exceptional.

She went from being all business while meeting with Jackson's doctors to being the cheerleader at his bedside.

Jackson's doctors said they'd started weaning him off the medication that was keeping him in the drug-induced coma. All indications were that he should have come around by now, and the longer they spent there, the more tense and agitated Rocki became.

She'd spent the entire day holding Jackson's hand and regaling him with story after story. Some were about her friends in Red Hook. She talked about the band, Pop, Bree, Nicki, Storm, and the rest of the gang at the Crow's Nest. Others were about the two of them when they were kids.

Rocki was loving and brave. Slater would have had to be blind not to see how much the act cost her. He saw it in her slightly green pallor, in the way her hand shook when she brought it to her mouth to keep from sobbing, saw it in the way she blinked back tears, never once letting them drop.

Rocki held it together for Jackson, and, hell, maybe even for him because being back in this room had shaken him yet again. The only thing that kept him grounded was the sound of her voice, clear and strong.

Whenever Rocki came close to losing it, she'd start joking. One time she even threatened to hit Jackson over the head with Nicki's good-luck rock if he didn't come back to her soon.

Slater couldn't help but think Jackson was one hell of a lucky guy to have a sister like Rocki fighting so fiercely beside him.

Sibling love was one thing, but Slater had a feeling that if it hadn't been Jackson, if it had been any of Rocki's other friends, she'd have done the same thing.

From what he'd seen, when Rocki loved someone, she went for it full steam ahead. There was no holding back, no self-protection that he could see. She might keep much of herself hidden, but that didn't seem to change the fact that she was totally invested in each of her friends—friends she held as close as family. He saw that in the way she treated Pop, Teddy, Grace, and Nicki. He saw it in everything she did and every smile she bestowed on them—even the way she teased Patrice and Francis.

Slater hid behind his computer in the only other chair in the room, and pretended he was working. Made sure to make keystrokes every now and then. Just when he'd start to feel as if he'd faded into the wallpaper, Rocki would look at him as if she needed to make sure he was still there.

During the torturous day at the hospital, Slater learned more about Rocki than he suspected anyone other than Jackson knew. Rocki would keep going until she fell over but he wasn't about to let that happen.

"Rocki, it's time for a break."

"No, the nurses said I could stay."

He stood and stretched. "We've been here all day and you've hardly moved. Come on. Let's go to the cafeteria and get you something to eat. Teddy and Grace should be here in a few minutes."

Rocki looked at him with those bright blue eyes full of fear. "You go ahead. I'm not hungry." She returned her attention to Jackson.

Nope, that wasn't going to work. Slater stepped between her and the bed and pulled her right out of her chair, trapping her against him. God she felt good. "Sweetheart, you're going to either take a break and get a bite to eat, or I'm going to take you home. Look at you; you're shaky from low blood sugar. You didn't eat a thing at breakfast—"

"I ate pancakes—"

"Pushing food around your plate is not eating."

She rested her head on his shoulder and her arms tightened around his waist. "What if he doesn't wake up?" she whispered.

"He will. How could he not? If I knew you were waiting for me, I'd move heaven and earth to get back to you. Jackson loves you. If he's half the man you think he is, he'll fight to come back. You're not going to do him any favors if you refuse to take care of yourself."

"I don't want to leave him alone. There's nothing worse than being alone."

A flash of memory hit Slater with the speed and force of a meteor. Blinding bright lights, shadows of masked people moving over him. He couldn't speak—he couldn't move. When he'd tried, pain radiated through his chest and then the world had gone dark. Alone and scared and then in an instant it was gone. The only remnant was the thundering of his heart, the taste of bile rising in his throat, the sick sense of loss, and the cold sweat that sprang out of nowhere.

"Slater? Slater, you're shaking. Are you okay?"

Rocki. He pulled her closer and held on tighter, breathing her in, erasing the scent of hospital and disinfectant, if only for a moment.

"Come on, we're getting out of here. Jax, we'll be back soon." She pressed herself against Slater's side as if she thought he needed help walking, and led him out.

His first instinct was to run, but where the hell would he go? Rocki needed him. He was there for her, not the other way around. He just needed a minute to get his shit together. "I'll meet you at the cafeteria."

He brushed her off and headed for the stairs. It would take him a lot less time to run down than to wait for the damn elevator, and if he didn't get out of there, he might totally lose it.

"Oh no you don't." She called his name as he made the first turn in the stairwell.

He jumped over the rail as soon as he was able to on every floor, her footsteps following. He hit the lobby door at a run and forced himself to slow to a fast walk. The sun was setting and the automatic doors weren't fast enough for him, so he wedged them open. His only thought was to get out. To breathe fresh air. To get the hell away just long enough to make sure he didn't lose it in front of Rocki.

Rocki had never seen a man move so fast. Slater had literally flown down the stairs. He might as well have sprouted wings. Rocki was fast, taking the steps two or three at a time, but she wasn't nearly fast enough. By the time she made it to the hospital's front door, she didn't know which way to turn and Slater was nowhere in sight.

She didn't think he'd leave without her. She hoped he wouldn't but when she thought about the way he'd looked, the terror she'd seen in his eyes, there was really no telling.

She skirted the perimeter of the hospital, turned a corner, and found him leaning against the brick wall, his breath coming out in huge clouds, and his hands pressed against his eyes.

"Slater, it's just me. Rocki."

"Fuck."

She didn't think he'd be happy to see her, but she'd never heard him curse. He just didn't seem the type to curse in front of women. Pete was a stickler about that. Hell, he charged her five bucks every time she let one fly.

She didn't know if she should turn around and leave Slater alone. She knew it was what he'd prefer and she knew just how he felt. She'd never wanted him to see the terror bubbling inside her just waiting to boil over. She would rather have dealt with it alone, but he wouldn't let that stop him. He'd never once left her side. He didn't have to do much—hold her hand, put his arm around her—but just by him being there it calmed her. His presence had meant the world to her. He gave her strength when she thought she had none left and it was only right that she returned the favor, whether he liked it or not.

"Flashbacks are a bitch. But it'll be okay." She grabbed his wrists and pulled them away from his face. He avoided her eyes, and that was fine. He was a proud man, so she just stepped between his open stance, wrapped his arms around her waist, and once she was sure he wouldn't push her away, she stepped closer and leaned against him, winding her arms around his neck and holding him. "If you want to talk about it, I'm all ears. If not, that's okay too. I'm still going to be here."

He pulled her closer, lifted her off her feet, and buried his face in her hair. "I'm sorry."

"Sorry for what? Being human?" She took his face in her hands and forced him to look at her. Okay, there was no way on God's green earth or white earth—since it was currently covered with snow—that she could force the man to do much of anything. He was probably the strongest man she knew, aside from Francis, but he was nice enough to go along with it. His eyes were glassy, bloodshot, and so wary. She did the only thing she knew would help him. She kissed him.

Rocki thought she was prepared for the kiss; after all she'd initiated it. It wasn't as if they hadn't kissed before—heck, they'd spent a pretty good amount of time lip-locked just that morning. Granted, he was the best kisser she'd ever known, but nothing could have prepared her for the strength of the connection she'd felt when her mouth met his, for the electricity that buzzed through her, the way his muscles trembled at her touch, and the sense of possession she felt.

Slater took the kiss and turbocharged it. She wanted to be a balm to soothe his soul; instead he'd turned it around and lit a fire inside her. He'd taken what she had to give, added it to whatever energy he had, and turned it into something entirely different. It was raw, it was powerful, it was frightening, and it was oh so good, so natural, so damn satisfying she couldn't pull away if she'd wanted to.

He dragged his lips from hers, his breath rushing from his mouth like a wisp of smoke. "Are Grace and Teddy here?"

"Yes, I saw them in the waiting room."

"Good." He didn't bother putting her down; he just stepped away from the building, grabbed her ass, and wrapped her legs around his waist.

"Where are we going?"

"Back to the mansion to finish what we started this morning."

"Is that a good idea?"

"Probably not." His steps didn't slow. He looked at her as if there was no one else in the entire world that he'd wanted as badly as he wanted her. He held her as if she was the most precious thing in his life. "All I know is that right now, I don't care about anything but you. I don't want to think about anyone but you. I need you, Rocki."

"Then let's go, because I need you too."

Slater kissed her all the way to the car and then set her in the seat without her feet ever touching the ground.

She didn't know what it was about him, but she had a feeling that even if he'd set her down, she'd still be floating.

The look in his eyes shot so much heat through her, she was melting from the inside out. It didn't matter that neither of them had coats; before Slater even hit the driver's seat, the windows were fogging over.

She reached for him, and before she knew it, his seat was pushed back and she was straddling him. They were eye to eye, and she couldn't look away. She'd heard people say they'd gotten lost in someone's eyes; she'd just never understood it. Not until now.

Slater's hands wrapped around her waist and slid under her sweater. Her stomach muscles tensed and he drew her closer, surging up and hitting that perfect spot. She let out a groan and then his hands traveled up, flicked the front clasp of her bra open, and the next thing she knew her sweater was off, his mouth was on her, and her hands were tangled in his hair. "Slater? Oh God, Slater."

She'd never been one to go off without a hell of a lot of work on the part of her partner, and she'd never once come close with her pants on, but then she'd never known a man like Slater either. He seemed to read her mind, giving everything she needed and more. His mouth on one breast, his hand on the other. Every tug on her breast was met with a roll of his hips; together it was magical. Then he dipped his other hand into the waistband of her pants, cupping her ass, sliding his fingers over the crack, a little naughty, a little hot, and a lot unexpected. He'd worked her up so high, she had no idea she could even go there. Nothing but nothing could have prepared her for the way she went off. When she opened her eyes, she looked in his, and while she felt all wonderful and floaty, he looked as if he was in some serious pain. "Are you okay?"

"Not as good as you are, but damn, it just about killed me not to join you."

"Oh God, I'm sorry." She pressed her face to his shoulder and he kissed the top of her head.

"Nothing to be sorry for, sweetheart. The great thing about being a woman is that you can come three, four, five times at a go."

Seriously? "Where? In Fantasy Land?" She lifted her head and all she saw in his eyes was confidence, certainty, and conviction. She didn't believe it. She wasn't sure why she'd gotten off—that had been one heck of a shock. Maybe it had been the heat of the moment or maybe it was because she'd had the world's longest dry spell, but whatever the reason, when it came to sex, she'd always been more than satisfied if she even came close to having one orgasm. They'd always been elusive little suckers. Two orgasms were unheard of, and a hat trick was nothing less than a chimera.

The corner of Slater's mouth quirked right before he kissed her and revved her engine just enough to make her wonder if a hat trick was a possibility. She was certain of one thing: She'd have a hell of a time giving Slater free rein to try.

Slater slid her bra straps over her shoulders and fastened the front clasp without a hint of fumbling—he was definitely gifted in the manual dexterity department. She wanted to smack her own head. Slater Shaw was gifted in every department. He helped her into her sweater, kissed her, and then lifted her off his lap and set her in her seat.

Slater was sweating. He wasn't sure if it was the whole hospital thing or if it was the way Rocki squirmed in her seat. The fact that she was still squirming was enough to leave him throbbing.

It had been bad enough when she'd given him his own personal lap dance in his father's car, of all places, but then she'd gone off like a Roman candle and it was all he could do not to embarrass himself. Thinking about it, remembering the way she looked when she shuddered in his arms had him writing complicated code just to keep his breathing under control.

He drove, doing his best to keep his inner Stig under wraps, and pretended instead that he was an octogenarian on a leisurely Sunday drive. It was a total cop-out, but he needed a minute, or an hour. He didn't trust himself not to pick her up, throw her over his shoulder, and carry her to bed like some knuckle dragger.

By the time he pulled up to the garage he thought he had himself under control—Rocki was a whole other matter. The woman had her seat belt off and the door open before he put the car in park.

He slid his hand off the shifter and onto her leg. "Let's go and find what Grace left us for dinner." There. That should buy him some time.

Her head whipped back toward him and she blew out a breath wrought with frustration. "You're kidding, right?"

Damn. Rocki made him want to forget that, for the most part, he was a gentleman. "Where's the fire, sweetheart?"

Her gaze went from his eyes to his crotch and his dick jumped. "I thought the fire was in your pants. Maybe I was mistaken."

He let out a laugh, hoping to relieve the pressure. "Rocki, I'm a big boy. You don't have to worry about what's going on in my pants." That was his job.

"I wasn't worried. Interested, yes. Worried, not so much."

He swallowed hard and fought to keep his touch light. "We have all night." He strung out the word, hoping she'd give him a break. "And believe me, that's how long it's going to take, but you'll be dead on your feet before round two if we don't get some food into you." He leaned in and kissed her, doing his best to keep the kiss on the sweet side, and followed it up with an affectionate leg squeeze. "But thanks all the same for your concern."

The look she gave him told him in no uncertain terms she didn't want sweet and affectionate. No, she wanted hot and sweaty and possibly a little dirty. Sweet was definitely not cutting it. He wondered if she had any idea how transparent she was.

He stepped out of the car trying his damnedest to

look as if he had nothing on his mind except her nutritional needs.

Unfortunately, she went from hot and horny to pissed in less time than it took to get out of the car. She humphed all the way to the door and practically kicked the darn thing open. She let her shoes fly and they both hit the wall of the mudroom.

Damn. He scrubbed his hands over his face. Not trusting himself around her, he kept a wide berth and went straight to the refrigerator, stuck his head in, and wished it were a deep freeze. "Grace said she made lobster salad. She also said there were killer rolls in the breadbox. Whatever the hell that is."

Rocki gave him a *you've-got-to-be-kidding* look and pointed to the stainless steel box on the counter. "That's the breadbox. Grace must have gone to the market after we left this morning." She opened the thing up and pulled out what looked like oversized hot dog buns while he emptied the refrigerator of all the food he thought she might eat. Lobster salad, green salad, and some scalloped potatoes Grace said just needed to be nuked. He watched Rocki put the buns under the commercial-sized broiler. "It's good to see you've finally found your appetite."

"For something anyway," she mumbled and cast him a sideways glance.

Rocki was not taking this well at all, although he had to admit that a pissed-off Rocki was hot, and a vast improvement over the depressed one he'd spent the day with.

He didn't know what the hell she had to complain about. She wasn't the one left hanging and walking around with a hard-on. You'd think that wanting to make sure she ate a little something before getting to the good stuff was a capital offense. "You're pouting?"

"I don't pout." She brushed up beside him, stepped

between him and the counter, her sweet ass brushing his fly, and then leaned way over in the guise of checking out the food.

The woman was pure evil and damned if he didn't like it. A lot.

He held his breath and did his best to keep the mask of disinterest on his face. It was the only way he knew to get through this. "You'd better check the broiler. You wouldn't want to burn your buns."

She blew her bangs out of her eyes and slid away, tossed a hunk of butter in a little glass cup, set it in the microwave and slammed the door.

Shit. He was in some real trouble now.

She set the timer, hit start, and then proceeded to lick the butter off her fingers.

Slater held back a groan, turned his attention to the counter, and grabbed the closest thing he could—the salad. "Why don't you toss this?" Maybe if she took her frustration out on the salad she'd leave him alone until after she ate.

She slammed the bowl on the counter—it was a good thing it was wooden and not glass—then retrieved the rolls and brushed them with melted butter while she sang a sexy little tune to herself and shimmied that ass of hers. She was trying to kill him. He was sure of it.

Slater tried to be a good guy. After all he was there for Rocki—and he had a strong feeling that when Pop asked him to take care of her, he hadn't meant in the biblical sense. The woman was driving him mad. Singing that suggestive song— "Beer?"

Rocki didn't even bother to look at him. "Sure. Whatever."

Slater's jaw throbbed in time with his dick. She didn't just pull the *whatever* card, did she? He might not know much about women, but shit, he read his e-mails, and every man with a pulse knew that in woman-speak the word *whatever* means "fuck you."

"That did it." He turned, grabbed her, and tossed her right over his shoulder.

"What the hell are you doing?"

"Just what you want. I'm taking you to bed unless you want to do it right here on the damn table."

"No, bed is good."

"I thought so." He stomped out of the kitchen and when she wiggled too much, he let his hand come down on the ass she'd been teasing him with. He expected a squeak, maybe a squeal, but the deep, throaty groan she let out made his balls draw up. He blew out a breath. "Here I was, trying to be a nice guy, trying to take care of you and what do you do?"

"I—"

"That was a rhetorical question." He took the steps two at a time. "I'll tell you what you did. You pushed me too damn far. You want sex?"

"Of—"

"Another rhetorical question, sweetheart. I'll make you a deal." He threw open the door to her bedroom, tossed her on the bed, followed her down, and landed on top of her, making sure not to crush her.

Rocki looked like a cat that had gotten her tail stuck in an electrical outlet. Her eyes shot fire, her hair stuck straight up, and her back arched trying to toss him off. If he hadn't been holding her hands on either side of her head, he was sure she'd have drawn blood. Rocki obviously wasn't used to not being in control. It looked as if anger warred with excitement with just a hint of that naughty tease-him-till-he-comes-in-his-shorts part of her he was beginning to really like.

"We'll make love one time. But then you have to promise to eat."

Rocki tried to get out of his grip and failed. She blew out a breath, and her eyes bore into his. Man was she pissed. "I can't believe you're bribing me with sex."

"That's the deal. Take it or leave it. If you want to go two or more rounds, you're going to eat. Got it?"

"Two or more?" Her eyes sparkled and her mouth turned up into a smile. "You're not a one-shot wonder?"

"Sweetheart, I figure the first half dozen times will just take the edge off."

She didn't look as if she believed him. It was going to be his pleasure to prove her and her cute little ass wrong. Right after she ate something.

He straddled her hips, and pulled her sweater off, tossing it over his shoulder. With one flick of his fingers, her breasts spilled out of the lacy bra he'd refastened less than half an hour ago—the longest half hour of his life. He looked his fill, damn she was gorgeous, but he didn't allow himself to touch.

Her nipples puckered under his gaze and a blush ran from her chest to her face—excitement? Embarrassment? He didn't know; all he knew was the woman didn't have a damn thing to be embarrassed about.

"Is it a deal?" he straddled her, making sure he applied pressure at just the right spot and watched her stomach muscles tense.

Her gaze slammed into his, her eyes dark as she chewed on her bottom lip. "What?"

"You'll eat after round one?" His face hovered above hers, close but not touching. He wanted to suck on that lip she just chewed and soothe it, then nip it again.

Rocki lifted her head, her mouth moved toward his.

That pretty mouth of hers was too tempting. One more taste and he'd forget all about the deal. "Say it."

"Fine, I'll eat. Now will you kiss me?"

"Oh yeah." He brushed a kiss over the tip of her nose, and both eyelids.

"You're such a tease."

He didn't bother hiding his laugh. "Me a tease? You're one to talk." He nibbled her earlobe. "This is just payback, but don't worry." His lips slid down the side of her neck, teeth nipping, tongue soothing. "You'll enjoy it, I promise."

Damn. Rocki had heard paybacks were a bitch, but this was ridiculous. Her breath came out in bursts, every kiss, every lick, every touch of Slater's lips to her skin made her squirm beneath him.

She couldn't even move, but he had free rein of her body. He tempted and teased and tortured her with his mouth.

She held back a groan, not sure if it was because whatever he was doing felt amazing or if it was just pure unadulterated frustration. Okay, it was both. "Slater, let me touch you."

"Not yet. Be patient."

Patient? "Kiss me."

"I am kissing you." He kissed her shoulder, shooting tingles to her breasts, looked his fill, and then moved on without so much as a touch.

She felt his lips turn up against the hollow of her collarbone before his teeth raked against the throbbing pulse in her neck. "You're pissing me off." Who knew her neck was so sensitive and had the ability to get her all sorts of hot and bothered? He hadn't even laid a finger on her, and she was primed and ready and wanting. Her inner muscles vibrated with need so she arched her back, just wanting to increase the pressure.

"I'm not pissing you off. I'm driving you crazy—it's not the same thing." He slid her hands over her head, clasped one paw around both her wrists, and drew her breast into his mouth.

Finally! She tried to rear up again but then he rolled off her. God, was he trying to kill her?

Slater's mouth should be classified as a torture device. He sucked and nibbled and bit—pleasure mixed with pain—and left her wanting. A hand skittered down the length of her arm, thrummed over her ribs, which probably resembled bellows, her breathing was so rapid and choppy, and the next thing she knew he had the button and fly of her jeans undone.

Slater released her breast with a satisfied pop, raised his head, and tugged on her jeans.

She hadn't even noticed that he'd let go of her hands until he pulled off her jeans and panties and sat beside her. His eyes raked her body, sending sparks of need through her every pore.

She rose up on her elbows. "Lose the clothes."

He dragged the shirt over his head.

The man had an amazing chest—strong, lean, sculpted but not overblown. God, just the sight made her mouth water. She'd always had a thing for tattoos and Slater had a nice one she hadn't really noticed the night before—an intricate Celtic band encircled his biceps. She took a deep breath, wanting to drink him in, wanting to trace that tat with her tongue and then explore the rest of the playground that was Slater Shaw with her mouth. "Now your jeans."

He shook his head. "That's not a good idea."

She sat up, smiled, and scooted closer; steam sizzled

off him like an overheated radiator on a '57 Chevy. "I think it's a great idea." She'd wanted to kiss him for what felt like forever so she anchored her hands in his hair, and slid her mouth over his. Slater tasted like beer with a splash of hot, spicy man. She wanted to drink him in. God, she could get lost in his kiss.

It only took a second for him to wrestle control from her, but he was such a wicked good kisser, she couldn't really complain. He didn't so much kiss, as possess—he tamed, tempted, teased, and tortured.

Before she knew it, he had her flat on her back, and his hands and his mouth were on the move. When his tongue slid into the dent of her navel, his fingers slid between her inner thighs. Her legs fell open and then his mouth joined his fingers and manual dexterity took on a whole new meaning.

Rocki had had sex before. She'd even had a few boyfriends who enjoyed oral sex, but nothing had ever felt like this.

No one had ever shot her up so quickly and then made her hang on to the edge of the cliff for so long, she wondered if she'd survive. Her heart pounded so hard, she could hardly hear her own cries over the blood rushing through her ears. She didn't know whether to thank him or kill him.

He played her body like a master, controlling her, pushing her up, then letting her drop back, just to push her higher each time. "God, Slater, please."

One minute she was almost there, and the next she felt the bed dip and nothing but cool air. She heard a curse, the rip of a condom wrapper, and before she could yell at him to hurry up, his mouth was on hers. He took it with the same intensity as he took her body. He gripped her hips and slid home in one long, slow thrust that still knocked the wind out of her. She finally had her hands on him and she didn't know what the hell to do first. She felt stretched to the limit—pleasure mixed with pain, pushing her even closer to the edge.

As if he could read her mind, Slater dragged his mouth from hers. "God, whatever you do, don't move."

He had to be kidding. He'd held her on the edge, and now, now that she was able to actually do something, she was supposed to stay still?

She focused on his face, which looked as if it had been carved in stone. Every muscle she was able to touch vibrated beneath her fingers. His jaw ticked and the veins in his neck throbbed.

A moment later he blew out a breath and slid out, with torturous slowness.

Slater held on to his control by a quickly unraveling thread. He'd known this was a mistake; not the making love part, no that was anything but wrong. The timing, however, couldn't have been worse.

When Rocki wrapped her legs around his waist and locked her ankles, urging him forward, digging her heels into his lower back, every muscle in his body strained with such force he thought he might have cracked a few teeth. She obviously didn't know the meaning of the words *don't move.*

He'd been doing all right ... Okay, he'd been barely holding on, but then he'd made the mistake of looking into her eyes and, shit, all bets were off. Rocki's eyes dragged him in, took all his good intentions—all thoughts of gentle lovemaking—and threw them under a crosstown bus. What he saw was wild need, raw down-and-dirty want, and lust so elemental it incinerated the thread with enough heat to melt steel.

He lost himself in Rocki, in the way her body grabbed

on to him and drew him in as strongly and urgently as her eyes had, obliterating every ounce of his control. She single-handedly unleashed the part of him no one had ever dared to tempt. He lost all finesse, all gentleness, and let go. He slid his hands under her ass, changing the angle and went deeper, harder, and sent her over.

Slater was too far gone to give her a breather. He rode out her orgasm and then drove her right back up. He needed her as mindless as he felt; he wanted her as overwhelmed, as out of control, as raw.

She pulled him down and dragged her teeth over his neck and then, simultaneously, nipped his shoulder, grabbed his balls, and clenched her inner muscles, shooting him across the finish line with an intensity he'd never known. He thought she joined him, but he was in the midst of an orgasm so incredible, his vision blurred. He collapsed on top of her and thought he might have blacked out for a second . . . or ten. He wasn't really sure. He knew he should roll over, but his muscles were not yet responding to his brain's commands. Rocki might just have fried his hard drive.

He felt her laughing . . . from the inside out. "Wow. I guess the only thing left to say is, 'Welcome to Fantasy Land.'"

CHAPTER 12

Rocki lay pinned to the bed and stared at Slater, who seemed in no rush to move, which was okay because she was still having delicious mini-orgasms shooting through her that were strong enough to curl her toes and were as good as any orgasms her past lovers were able to elicit.

"Slater?"

"Hmm?"

He rose on his elbows, taking some of the pressure off her chest and, in doing so, slid farther into her, shooting off another round of toe-curling flutters that had her rolling her hips and groaning.

"Don't you dare start. I'm calling a time-out for sustenance. We had a deal, remember?"

Rocki kissed a puckered spot on his chest and wondered what had caused a scar like that. "Is it my fault round one has yet to end?"

"Sweetheart." He kissed her soundly but ended it way too soon. "Round one ended a while ago."

"Says who? It seems to me that things are anything but over." She clenched her inner muscles and if she wasn't mistaken, the way his dick seemed to jump up and take notice, and the groan that followed proved her point, stealing her breath.

Slater moved as if to pull out, but she still had her legs locked around him so he couldn't really go far. "Rocki." His voice dropped the octave and a half lower to what she'd labeled his bedroom voice—that voice alone was enough to get her going. "You promised."

"I promised I'd try to eat," she said, nuzzling his neck, drinking in his scent, and getting more turned on by the minute. "That's the best I can do. Tension goes right to my stomach—"

He slid back in, either to tease her or to start round two—God, she hoped he'd given up his quest to feed her. "Sex is a great tension reliever. You should have no problem eating now." He took her mouth in a kiss so hot she experienced a full-body sigh—every part of her relaxed and melted into the kiss. And the next thing she knew he slipped out and then rolled off her. "I'm starved. So how do you want it?"

"The sex?" She scooted a little closer.

"No, dinner. Do you want to go down to eat, or do you want dinner in bed?"

"In bed?" What was it with him and food?

Slater rolled off the mattress and headed, bare-assed, to the bathroom before Rocki could get her head together enough to even sit up.

He came back, and pulled his jeans on, tucking himself in carefully.

"I can come down and help."

A smile quirked one side of his mouth and all she could think of was everything that mouth had done to her; she was ready for more. "Oh, no. You're too much of a distraction. Stay here, stay naked, and I'll be right back with food. If you're good, I might even eat my dinner off you."

She crawled toward the edge of the bed and focused on the growing bulge in his pants. "If I'm bad can I use you as a plate? Just the thought of it makes having to eat much more appealing."

Slater's eyes darkened and his stomach tensed as if he were waiting for a punch to the gut. "You're a definite distraction." She kneeled on the bed, and he tugged her against him for a kiss that didn't end the way she wanted it to. "Sweetheart, you can eat off whatever you want but you'd better eat. Believe me, you're going to need the calories."

He grabbed his T-shirt and pulled it on as he headed out the door. The man looked as good going as he did coming. Rocki threw herself back against the pillows and, for the first time in forever, she actually followed instructions. It was amazing what sexual satisfaction could do to a person.

Slater hit the kitchen at a run. He gathered the food, beers, a bottle of white wine and a wineglass, stuffed napkins and forks in his back pocket, and was out of the kitchen and back to the bedroom in less than three minutes.

He didn't know what it was about Rocki but, damn, she had a way of fogging a man's mind—she was all-consuming. He just hoped it was something that wore off after a few go-arounds, because if not, he was in real trouble. But then, as far as trouble went, Rocki was the kind he wouldn't mind having over and over and over again.

He pushed the door open with his bare foot, amazed to find Rocki right where he'd left her, all spread out like a freakin' wet dream. He set the beers down on the bedside table, handed her the wineglass and bottle, and put the plates right on the bed. "Eat fast."

"I'm missing my plate." Shit, the way she looked at him had him swallowing hard and ripping at the buttons on his pants.

He stripped and climbed into bed before she even got the cork out of the wine bottle.

She didn't bother with the glass. A woman after his own heart. Then she proceeded to feed him and eat her entire dinner off his stomach. By the time she'd eaten her fill, he was messy and hot and hard and more turned on than he'd ever been in his life. Next Rocki slid between his legs. She had one hand wrapped around his dick, the other around the neck of the wine bottle. She took a swig of wine and then slid her mouth over him. Cold wine, hot mouth, just the right amount of tongue and teeth and he almost came right then and there.

He definitely hadn't expected that. He hadn't expected her to revel in her ability to drive him to the edge. And he certainly hadn't expected her to have him at her mercy. Shit. When exactly had he lost all control of the situation? Right at that moment he was tempted to beg. He was in serious trouble and she knew it. She hummed around his dick and shot whatever control he had left. He dragged her off him before he lost it completely. "God, tell me you're clean and on the pill."

"Yes, and yes."

She sucked his tongue into her mouth as she slid over him.

He'd never had sex without a condom before. Not once. He had never known what the hell he was missing, but then maybe it was just having sex with Rocki that made everything more extreme. Hotter, wetter, tighter, and so damn soft—Rocki had a way of turning up the volume on everything.

She had amazing rhythm and moves that had him

praying he could hold on just because he didn't want this to ever end. She was so beautiful and everything about her was a turn-on—the sounds she made as she rode him, the way she took what she wanted but gave with the same intensity, the wonder that flashed across her face as she climaxed, drawing him deeper, and the way she looked into his eyes and kissed him as if she wasn't close enough to him. They were connected in every way possible.

It was the kiss that drew him in, strung him out, laid him bare, and then breathed new life into him. It was the kiss that sent him flying over the edge. It was the kiss that shattered whatever resistance to Rocki he'd possessed. It was the kiss that made him feel things he didn't know existed, had no way to label, and scared him to his very core.

Rocki collapsed on Slater, incapable of any further movement. She'd either just hit her sexual prime, or the combination of her and Slater was seriously explosive. She wished she knew if that was a good thing or not. Right now, she considered herself lucky she still had the energy to draw breath.

When he'd gone downstairs for their dinner, she'd told herself that their first time together had been a fluke. But if she'd learned anything since, it was that whatever they had was no fluke, and round one wasn't nearly as incredible as round two. If round three got any better . . . She might not survive but she'd have one hell of a story to tell when she got to the pearly gates.

She kissed his chest and slid her tongue over the puckered scar. "How did you get this?" She ran her finger over it.

He shrugged. "I don't know. It's been there for as long as I can remember."

"Does it hurt?"

"No." He slid from beneath her. "We should probably get a shower. I don't know about you, but I'm sticky." He finished his beer and cracked the second. "Thirsty?" He held the bottle out to her.

Okay, she could take a hint. "No, thanks. I had quite a bit to drink earlier, remember?" She licked her lips and was relieved when he smiled.

"Oh yeah. That's not something I'm likely to ever forget."

Just like a man; he'd remember a blow job but not whatever caused a two-inch puckered scar on his chest. "Let me just call the hospital and check on Jax."

Once she talked to the nurses and found out that Jax was resting comfortably, Slater set his beer on the bedside table, and then pulled her along with him as he rolled out of bed. "Let's get a shower. I've wanted to see you wet for the last two days."

"That long, huh?"

"Sweetheart, thirty-six hours is a hell of a long time when you consider we've been practically connected at the hip. You have no idea how many times I've pictured you wet and soapy."

"Ah, a window into the male mind. Unfortunately, it appears to look more like a porn flick than anything else."

The naughty smile she was beginning to love slid over his face. "You have no idea."

He dragged her to the bathroom and it took only a few minutes for her to get a very accurate picture of what his fantasy entailed, and it was a hell of a lot more than just her wet and soapy.

By the time they dried off, they'd drained the house's hot water tank, they were both pruney, and Rocki couldn't remember ever being more relaxed, exhausted, and sexually satisfied.

Six hours later she was rudely awakened from the most erotic dream she'd ever had by what felt like an earthquake, only to find out what would qualify as a six-point-five on the Richter scale, wasn't an earthquake at all. It was Slater.

Rocki didn't know what was going on, other than she was in bed and Slater was shaking like he was deep in the throes of a nightmare. "Slater?"

Daylight crept through the window. It wasn't sunshine, just the usual winter early morning when the sun doesn't really rise, the world just grows light.

"Slater, wake up."

His face looked pale and his eyes raced beneath his lids, every muscle in his body tensed.

She reached across his chest, grabbed his arm, and tried to shake him awake.

"No!"

The next thing she knew, she was beneath two hundred pounds of a wild-looking Slater.

He had both her hands pinned to the bed, and his wide hazel eyes stared into hers.

"Slater. You're okay."

She watched the realization of what happened slam into him. He went from crazed, to confused, to horrified. "God, did I hurt you?"

"No, you didn't hurt me." He'd scared the crap out of her, but then she was more afraid for him than for herself.

He tried to pull away but she wasn't going to let him go that easily.

"Stay. Tell me what happened."

The man above her seemed to deflate before her eyes

and his head sank to rest on her chest. "Shit, Rocki, I wish I knew."

"What happened yesterday?"

"When?"

"When you ran out of the hospital, remember?"

"I remember."

"Yet you're not answering the question."

"I would if I knew how. If I understood what the hell happened, it wouldn't freak me out so much. One second I was holding you and the next—" He shook his head. "I don't know if it was a memory or a freakin' nightmare. I just saw this bright light, and people wearing what looked like surgical scrubs looking down at me."

"How old were you?"

"I don't know. It was just a flash. I remembered being scared to death and in pain. Then it was gone. I just don't get it."

"Where was the pain?"

"Everywhere."

She slid her finger over the scar on his chest and he jumped. "It sounds like a flashback. You said you didn't remember how you got this." She kissed the scar. "Maybe being in the hospital is dredging up old memories. It happens."

He let his weight come down on her and nibbled on her earlobe as he slid between her thighs. "Not to me."

She didn't bother telling him that it *was* happening to him. He was just fighting it. "Oh, that's right. You superhero types are so tough—nothing ever gets to you."

"Nothing does." He slid his hand under her thigh and lifted her knee.

His erection teased her entrance and she held back a groan. "I can see that."

"Good." He stared into her eyes as he slid into her

with exquisite slowness. "Nothing gets to me. Except you. It had to be you."

Rocki didn't know if he thought that was a good thing or not, but couldn't ask since she'd lost all ability to speak coherently.

His kiss was possessive, powerful, brutal—dragging her through his torment and into the heat. Slater had a way of stringing her so tight she vibrated like a tuning fork. He took her to places she hadn't known existed, he made her feel things she'd never felt, and when he looked into her eyes, she seemed to absorb his need, desperation, pain, and fear. He might not be able to speak the words, but he didn't need to. When it came to sex, they were on the same wavelength, they could communicate without words, and they could give each other what the other desperately needed. And right now, he needed to consume her, and she let him.

The feeling running through him into her sent her heart stuttering in her chest and brought tears to her eyes. She couldn't contain them any more than she could stop the waves of orgasm crashing through her—too fast, too intense, too much. She buried her face in his neck and did her best not to blubber. God, she was so overwhelmed, and he drove her even higher, as one orgasm rolled into another without so much as a break. He gripped her hips, raised her, and threw her headlong into something so cataclysmic she lost it completely.

Slater cursed, groaned her name, and stilled, huffing into her neck.

Tears rolled down the side of her face and no matter what she did, she couldn't stop them. She wanted to push him off her and wipe her face. She wanted to run, because this wasn't supposed to happen. She wasn't prepared for anything like this. She was supposed to be having hot sex and, last she checked, hot sex did not include tears and overwhelming feelings. It didn't include anything but scratching an itch.

"Hey, sweetheart? What's wrong?"

Shit, shit, shit.

He raised himself off her and brushed her tears away. Before she could stop it a sob escaped.

"It's okay."

"No . . . it's . . . not."

He shushed her, brushing away the tears streaming down her face. "Making love sometimes breaks down the dams—it's a physical and emotional release."

They weren't making love—at least she wasn't. She just wanted sex. Sex with Slater was a wonderful way to escape the labyrinth of her mind. For a while it took her away, allowed her to forget, made it impossible to think— all she could do was feel. And Slater made her feel incredible. Sex with Slater had given her that, and God help her, even after this embarrassing display, she still wanted more. "I thought we were having sex."

"What's the difference?" He slid out and rolled off her onto his side, pulling her to face him.

She missed the connection. She missed Slater's weight grounding her. She missed the way he held her beneath him, blanketing her with his warmth and caring. That alone scared the crap out of her. "The way I see it, the difference between sex and making love is sex is the act without the emotion."

He didn't move, but she felt him pull away.

"Slater." She slid closer and tossed her leg over his, trying to cross the invisible divide that suddenly separated them. "Try to understand. Since Jackson's accident I've been on an emotional roller coaster. I can't trust my feelings right now—I just can't."

Slater watched her and no matter how hard she tried, she couldn't tell what he was thinking. He just stared, blank faced.

"Look, it's nothing personal. How can I be sure what's going on between us isn't just a reaction to a crisis or if it's something more? The last thing I want to do is grab on to you for the wrong reasons. It wouldn't be fair to either of us. So right now, sex is all I can handle. Sex is all I can commit to."

He rested his head on his hand and looked at her. "Nothing personal? So this was just sex with no emotion?"

"Right." She felt a lot of things but she didn't think she could trust those feelings. That was the whole point.

"Do you really think you can pull that off?"

"I'm going to try. You should too. It'll be safer that way."

Slater brushed away the bangs over her eyes, as if he needed to see into her very soul, and part of her wondered if he could. "Every roller-coaster ride comes to an end, sweetheart. When it does, we'll both have to deal with the fallout."

"I know." And for some reason, she didn't think it was going to be an easy thing to do. "We can't afford to read more into this affair, sexcapade, or whatever it is than what it actually is—temporary. Slater, you said yourself that you're leaving for Bahrain in a month. I need to make sure my brother is healed and then I'll go home." And try to salvage the life she'd built for herself in Red Hook.

He gently slid her leg off his hip. "We need to get to the hospital. You can call this making love, sex, or whatever you like." A smile teased his lips but didn't reach his eyes. Slater pulled on his jeans. "I'm going to get breakfast going. Since Grace left dinner for us last night, I think the least I could do is fix breakfast for everyone."

"I can come down and help."

He held out his hand to stop her and looked as if he couldn't get out of the bedroom fast enough. "No, I'll take care of it. You get yourself ready to go."

"Slater, we need to talk about this—"

"Hey, we talked. I heard every word you said. Are you trying to get out of eating again?"

"No, I'm just wondering what lit a fire under your ass, that's all."

"No fire, I'm just hungry." He shrugged on his oxford and walked out, leaving her feeling oddly bereft.

Something was going on with him, and she didn't think it was the making love versus sex thing; maybe it was whatever freaked him out so badly at the hospital and the nightmare. Whatever it was, she got the impression that although he might want to get away from her, she shouldn't give him the opportunity. She got up, pulled on his T-shirt, and slipped down the back stairs.

Slater had had a lot of sex before, but sex had never been like what he'd just experienced with Rocki—not even with Dominique. Not even close. He'd never felt more in tune with anyone, more connected, more everything.

Shit, he rubbed his chest and felt the scar Rocki had kissed. It was as if she'd opened something within him and he was flying at light-speed, being bombarded from all sides with emotion, feelings, needs, and fears so intense, it scared the hell out of him—but not enough to stop.

He shook his head, trying to clear his mind. Maybe this was just the aftereffect of outrageously great sex.

He headed down the steps. Maybe Rocki was right

about the difference between making love and sex. But then, could anyone really control his or her emotions? He could compartmentalize—that he was good at. He should be thanking his lucky stars that Rocki wasn't the demanding, clingy type.

So, okay, the whole "nothing personal" thing made his ass twitch, but it wasn't as if people didn't say that all the time. Maybe the conversation with Rocki reminded him a little too much of his last conversation with Dominique— but she'd lied to him, used him. Dominique had made it clear she thought he was great for a roll in the hay but wasn't good enough for anything more. Rocki didn't. That wasn't what Rocki had said. But no matter how many times he told himself this was different, there was that little voice in his head wondering if that hadn't been exactly what Rocki had meant.

His phone vibrated in his pocket and he answered, almost thankful for the interruption. "Hello?"

"Any news to report, son?"

"Hi, Pop. How are you and Nicki doing?"

"We're fine. Storm has the restaurant covered, and Bree's found my stash of stogies so I'm left looking for a new hiding place. Nicki's working on all of us to buy her a bike for Christmas. It's all good—except for the stogies. How's Jackson?"

"No news yet. Yesterday the doctors were weaning him off the meds they had him on to keep him in a coma, but he didn't come out of it as quickly as they had expected. Rocki was worrying herself sick last night so I brought her back to the house to try to get her to eat." And screw her senseless, but Pop didn't need to know that.

"I'm glad you're taking good care of her." If Pop only knew exactly how he was taking care of her, Pop might not be so thrilled. "She needs you there."

Slater laughed. "Come on, Pop, cut the bullshit. I had an interesting discussion with Teddy yesterday morning, and I know for a fact that the two of you know each other well. You knew all along that Grace and Teddy were here and could take care of Rocki. She doesn't need me for squat."

"Slater—"

"I'm not complaining, but I would like to know what the hell you're up to." He didn't like the feeling that his dad was playing him. And he didn't want Pop to think he wasn't on to his schemes. He might not know what Pop's grand plan was, but he knew enough to know Pop had one. The old man was definitely up to something.

"I just thought that Grace and Teddy would have their hands full looking after Jackson. He and Rocki are like their own kids. With you taking care of Rocki and staying at the house with her, it gives Grace and Teddy leave to stay at their own place and not feel as if they have to move back into the main house for the duration. Old folks like us aren't good at sleeping in strange beds. Besides, I thought you could use the time to wrap your head around the changes in your own life and get some perspective on a few things."

"What do you mean? Grace and Teddy don't live here?"

"Damn, son, are you blind?"

Apparently he was.

"Grace and Teddy have a house on the property and take care of the place."

"They're caretakers?" He stepped into the kitchen and noticed that Grace and Teddy had returned the coats he and Rocki had forgotten at the hospital last night, and left a note saying they'd be at their home if he or Rocki needed them, along with a phone number—for his benefit he was sure.

"How the hell was I supposed to know? Rocki and I went to bed before Grace and Teddy that first night. I just assumed they lived here. They were cooking breakfast by the time I came down yesterday morning." All the hair on his neck stood on end. He turned and caught Rocki standing in the back hallway. He looked her straight in the eye. "Whose house is this anyway?"

Pop had no way of knowing Slater hadn't asked him the question. The old man cleared his throat. "It's Rocki and Jackson's home. I thought you knew that."

Fuck, this place was Rocki and Jackson's? They owned a freakin' estate? If she owned an estate, what the hell was she doing living in a second-floor walk-up in Chinatown?

Slater sat hard on the chair and scrubbed his hand over his face. God, the scent of Rocki was all over him. He looked up and watched a very guilty-looking Rocki approach him. "Look, Pop. I have to take off."

"Okay, son, you take good care of my girl and keep us informed about Jackson's condition."

"Will do. I'll call you just as soon as we hear anything. Bye, Pop." He ended the call and tossed his phone on the table, let the wave of anger roll over him, and blew out a breath. "I thought you were getting dressed."

Rocki stood there looking too damn good in his shirt. She wrapped her arms around herself and shivered. "I can explain."

"No need, I get it." He rose, grabbed a few pieces of newspaper, crumpled them, and tossed them in the fireplace. "I'm a chauffeur with benefits. It's not a hard concept to grasp. It's cold in here. Go get dressed while I build a fire."

"Slater—"

"Rocki," He didn't turn to look at her. He just picked

up a couple of logs and tossed them on the grate. "Do us both a favor and just let it be."

"No, dammit. Let me explain."

"Explain what exactly? A: Why you've lied to me ever since the day we met? Or B: Why you've spent three years lying to everyone in Red Hook—everyone you claim to care about? Or C: That I'm a good lay, and fun, but I'm not pedigreed enough for a woman like you. But then there's always D: All of the above."

"I didn't lie and I don't know what you're talking about with the whole pedigree thing."

"Not lying and telling the truth are two different things, sweetheart. Now, go get dressed."

"I'm not finished."

He lit a match and tossed it on the paper, watching it go up in flames, the fire licking the dry wood. "You may not be, but I am." He wished he could go upstairs, grab his stuff, and get the fuck out of Versailles, but he was stuck there. He grasped the mantel with both hands and stared into the flames. He didn't trust himself to look at her.

"Slater." She slid in behind him, wrapped her arms around his waist, and rested her head against his back. "I never lied to you. I just . . . look, money changes everything."

"So Cyndi Lauper said. Are you going to start singing again?"

"No, just listen to me. As soon as people find out about the money, things get weird."

"So you pretend you're what? Normal?"

"I am normal."

He let out a laugh. It was one thing to slum it for a while, but she'd never know what it felt like to wonder where your next meal was coming from. But maybe that wasn't normal either. Hell, he was so far from normal himself, who was he to judge?

"As soon as I graduated from college I was free to be whoever I wanted to be. I didn't have to answer to my uncles anymore. I've been making it on my own ever since. I work for my money, I live on what I make, and I'm happy for the first time in my life. Don't you see? If everyone knew about my trust fund, they'd treat me differently. I should know. I've dealt with this all my life."

He turned and stepped away. She was too close and if he didn't get some space, he'd do something stupid. Because when it came to Rocki, he was a stupid shit. He didn't need her and he didn't need to be played. Again.

"I never lied. I just didn't tell anyone my net worth. It's no one's business but my own."

Looking at her was a bad mistake—Rocki's blue eyes drilled a hole in him and damned if he didn't feel himself faltering.

"I never fit in with the girls at the French boarding school my uncles stashed me in. I mean, do I look like someone who would fit in with the debutantes?"

He wanted to groan when she did that whole blinking-back-tears thing. He had to cross his arms to keep from reaching for her.

"No matter how hard I tried, I didn't fit in with anyone. I'd just lost my parents, my brother was in another country, Grace and Teddy were here, and I was alone. I was alone for nine years. I was alone until I moved to New York, started my band, and got the gig working for Pete and Bree. That's when everything changed. For the first time in my life I had friends who liked me simply because I'm me. I don't want to lose that."

A tear slid down her face and he stopped himself

from brushing it away. He was about to fold like an old accordion. "Poor little rich girl."

"Fuck you, Slater." He expected her to cry and run away; he hadn't expected her to go ballistic. And that was what she looked as if she was about to do. He couldn't decide if the fire shooting out of Rocki's eyes was the real thing or a reflection. He was so busy staring, he was completely unprepared when she hauled off and slugged him. Hard.

She knocked the wind out of him. The pain radiating through his gut took his mind off the pain hitting him from all other directions. He had to give the girl credit; she threw a hell of a punch. He didn't fight his urge to smile, knowing it would piss her off more. A pissed-off Rocki he could handle, a crying Rocki did weird things to his insides. "Been there, done that—several times, and look at this"—he grabbed her and pulled her close—"you even got the T-shirt."

She raised her hand to slug him again.

He'd had enough. He caught it before she connected with his face and brought it behind her back, which only served to plaster her to his chest. Bad, bad mistake. "Apparently fucking is all I'm good for. That and chauffeur duty. But hey, if that's what you're after, what the hell, I'm game."

"You son of a—"

The second his mouth came down on hers, he was sucked into a tornado of emotions so strong and powerful, it nearly brought him to his knees.

Bad, bad, bad mistake.

CHAPTER 13

Slater might have been kissing Rocki, but the kiss was unlike any kiss she'd ever received—it was hard, brutal, raging, and raw.

She tasted anger, pain, confusion—all of which she'd caused.

She'd known deep in her bones that once Slater realized who she was, what she was, everything would change. It always did.

She hadn't expected it would be this ugly.

She hadn't expected to feel so much pain; she'd wanted to hurt him back.

She hadn't expected the fear when he pulled away.

She'd known he'd be angry, but she hadn't expected him to take a sledgehammer to the walls she'd erected and decimate them.

She couldn't think; she couldn't breathe. All she could do was hold on to Slater for fear of being sucked into the maelstrom of emotion swirling around them, through him and into her.

She tried to process what had just happened.

She'd hit Slater.

She'd never hit anyone—okay, she might have popped Jackson once or twice, but she'd never hit anyone with the intention to hurt him. Until today.

How could she do that?

And how could he laugh at her and then kiss her as if kissing her was necessary for life?

Weirder yet was, how could she kiss him back?

She heard a door open, and a cold breeze brushed her legs. Then she heard the stomping of boots. Oh, God. Grace and Teddy were here.

"Racquel?" Grace called out from the mudroom.

Rocki pulled Slater's T-shirt over her bare ass, dragged in a breath, and ran for the back stairs.

Slater cleared his throat. "No, it's just me. Rocki's still upstairs."

She flew to her room and stood there not knowing what the hell to do. She should get in the shower. She should get dressed and get back to the hospital. But all she wanted to do was curl up in a ball and cry. She wanted to erase the last hour of her life. She wanted to be back in Slater's arms, making love, and staring into his eyes.

There was a knock on the door, and as if her thoughts had called to him, Slater stuck his head in.

She took a step toward him but the look on his face made her freeze midstep.

He stared through her—his eyes hard, cold, and empty. "Jackson's out of his coma. We need to get to the hospital. We're leaving in fifteen minutes."

She hugged herself to keep from reaching out to him, to keep from shaking, to keep from falling apart.

"Did you hear me?"

She couldn't speak. She brushed away tears that fell unbidden and nodded.

He shut the door quietly, politely, and so resoundingly that the echo of emptiness slammed through her brain like a cymbal. Slater had never been quiet and polite; he'd been hard, demanding, aggressive, honest, and real.

She took a deep breath—she couldn't think of Slater now. Jackson needed her. She trudged to the bathroom and showered, letting the water wash her tears down the drain, and wished she was as good as Slater at shutting people out.

Slater was dressed and ready to go long before Rocki came down. He drank a cup of coffee that Grace had prepared, and tried to figure out how soon he could get the hell out of there. He needed to get home and sort out his life. He needed to look over that contract from Bahrain.

Still, in order to do the right thing and get past his father's questions, he had to find out Jackson's long-term prognosis. As soon as he heard Rocki's brother was on the mend, he'd be out of there so fast, he'd leave skid marks. It was nothing personal, but he didn't have time to be Rocki's bed buddy when he had a life of his own to piece back together.

Slater leaned against the counter, too antsy to sit, and watched Grace and Teddy work in tandem in the kitchen as if it had been choreographed.

Grace refilled his coffee. "I'm making Racquel a breakfast sandwich to eat on the way to the hospital. Are you sure I can't fix something for you?"

"Positive. I've already eaten, but thank you." Sure, it was a lie, but he knew better than to stuff anything more down his gullet today. Between the nightmare he hadn't been able to shake and the fight with Rocki, he'd already had his fill.

He closed his eyes and pressed his fingers to his sockets, trying to stop the images that ran like a slideshow on warp speed. Pictures of Rocki—too many to process, but all of them indelibly imprinted on his mind—and blurry images and feelings from the nightmare that, without context, made no sense. It was as if he searched for a word on the tip of his tongue. He couldn't get a handle on it and didn't know how, or even if, he wanted to bridge that gap. Just thinking about it was enough to set off a fight-or-flight response that he, even while wide awake, had a difficult time controlling.

When Rocki woke him in the throes of the nightmare, Slater's first instinct had been to protect her—but from what? From whom? Then he was swamped by a feeling of loss so deep and familiar he had to claw his way out or he'd drown in it. He did the only thing he could do—he lost himself in Rocki. She'd been naked beneath him and seemed to know what he'd needed. She'd been there for him, made love to him—or at least he thought she had.

He rubbed his chest, the phantom memory of searing pain made the numbness of his scar more noticeable than ever. He had to think about something else. Get the hell out of the wasteland that was his own mind. Focus on the present.

"So, Grace and Teddy, how long have you worked for Rocki and Jackson's family?"

Teddy looked up from the newspaper. "Close to thirty years. We manage the estate, rent out the cottages, and make sure the main house is ready if either of the kids want to come up."

"You seem more like family than caretakers."

"We are in all the ways that count. If it had been up to Grace and me, we would have kept Racquel and Jackson with us after their parents died, but their uncles had other ideas. It was hard to be so far away from them.

Still, we were lucky to stay on. The kids had already lost so much, we didn't want them to lose the one place they always thought of as home."

Grace refilled his coffee cup. "This is the only part of their parents' estate the kids held on to. We've been looking forward to the two of them filling this house to the rafters with families of their own."

Teddy took Grace's hand in a gesture that looked almost unconscious. "We hope you and Racquel will spend more time here now that you're together. And maybe if Jackson ever decides to settle down—"

Grace let out an infectious laugh. "Maybe the conk on the head will knock some sense into the boy. He and Racquel always run as fast as their feet will take them as soon as they get close to someone of the opposite sex. Slater, you're the first man Racquel's ever brought home. Maybe Jackson will see how much you two obviously care for each other and realize that relationships give you more than just the ability to be hurt. I don't think the poor boy's ever gotten over his parents' loss."

Slater took a sip of his coffee to hide his shock. Either Grace saw something he didn't or she was so far off the beam there was no hope for the old girl.

"But then maybe it takes falling in love to give them the incentive to take a chance on happiness."

Slater inhaled his coffee and choked.

Grace was smacking him on the back when Rocki slithered down the back stairs.

Rocki didn't even look at him. She gave Teddy a hug and then held him at arm's length. "What did the hospital say?"

"Jackson's awake and he's already giving the nurses a hard time. He's asking for you, honey. He knows you came home to be with him."

Rocki's mouth was so pinched her lips were turning white. "So he's okay?" She ran nervous hands through her hair, leaving most of it sticking straight up. It should have looked ridiculous, but it didn't—not on her. Red, swollen eyes searched Grace and Teddy's faces, "You're not keeping anything from me are you? Jackson's able to move all his limbs. He's not paralyzed or anything?"

Slater was just about to go to her, but Grace saved him the trouble, and pulled Rocki into a hug. "Oh, baby, no. We're telling you everything we know. Slater, help Racquel on with her coat." Grace held a breakfast sandwich wrapped in a paper towel. "Racquel, you can eat breakfast on the way to the hospital. See that she does, Slater, will you?"

"Yes, ma'am."

"Good. Now you two go on ahead. Teddy and I will be over just as soon as I clean up here."

Slater held Rocki's coat for her, doing his best not to touch her.

Grace handed Rocki the sandwich. Slater could tell by the look on her face, she had no intention of eating it.

"Are you ready?" Rocki asked, as if he hadn't been cooling his heels until she got her ass downstairs.

He waited a beat—hoping she would look at him. Time was up and so was his patience. "I was born ready, sweetheart. Let's go." He held the door for her and she stomped out.

He was back to being the chauffeur. This was just great. He brushed the snow off the Jeep's roof over the passenger side with his hand, opened the door for her, and then handed her the keys. "Warm up the car."

Rocki took the keys without a word. That was just fine with him. He had heard enough out of her for a lifetime.

He got busy cleaning the snow off. It took her three

tries to get the car started. He made a mental note to check the oil before he left town. When he climbed in, he threw it into four-wheel drive, and they drove to the hospital in dead silence.

Rocki shot out of the car before he cut the engine and hightailed it to the doors. The car was still in the throes of its death rattle as she tossed her untouched sandwich in the trash on her way in.

Shit. He should have told her to eat the damn thing. He had to double-time it just to catch up with her.

Slater found Rocki at the elevator, smashing her finger on the UP button.

"That's not going to make the elevator move any faster."

"No, but it makes me feel as if I'm doing something. Right now, that's enough."

She stepped into the elevator as soon as the doors opened and started abusing the button to the ICU floor, practically daring him to say more.

"Rocki, I'm not here to upset you. If you want me to wait in the cafeteria, if that would be easier for you, I will."

She finally looked at him and damned if he didn't want to just take her in his arms and kiss her. "Is that what you want?"

"What I want is immaterial."

"Not to me it's not." And the way she looked at him right at that moment made him wonder if she was having just as difficult a time separating sex from emotion as he was.

The doors opened and Slater put his hand on her lower back, and steered her out. "Let's see what's going on with your brother. We'll deal with everything else later. Don't worry about it now."

"I tried to explain and you . . . You . . . You . . . kissed me."

"That's what you said you wanted. Sex, no emotion." Even though there was more than enough emotion on his side for both of them. "You want a bed buddy. I get it." He didn't like it, but he wasn't really sure what he could do about it except do his best to change her mind.

"Slater—"

A nurse came toward them. "Oh good. You're here." She gave Rocki a relieved smile. "Your brother's anxious to see you. We're trying to keep him quiet—"

"He's talking?"

The nurse's eyes went wide. "Nonstop. He's been quite demanding. We're trying to keep him still."

"God, it sounds as if he's just about back to normal. Unfortunately for you, the words *quiet* and *still* aren't in his vocabulary."

"He can't change the elevation of his head compared to the valve. We've been monitoring him and raising the elevation of the valve over the last day and a half, and everything looks good. His pressure is almost normal, and we hope to remove the valve late tonight or early tomorrow, but he has to keep still."

"Or what?"

"He could lose more brain fluid than is necessary. The fluid is there for a reason."

"Okay, I'll talk to him. Hell, I'll sit on him if necessary."

Rocki grabbed Slater's hand, gave it a squeeze, and dragged him into Jackson's room.

The bandages were off Jackson's head, all except for a square piece of gauze covering the incision site close to his hairline. His face bore the colorful bruising and swelling of a man who'd played chicken with a Mack truck and lost.

Jackson's eyes opened at the sound of Rocki's sharp intake of breath. They were the same startling blue as Rocki's.

Slater hadn't noticed it when he'd seen the picture of them together in Rocki's apartment. He'd assumed the man was a lover, not her brother. He didn't even want to contemplate what that said about him.

Jackson's eyes met his and filled with questions. His gaze traveled from Slater's face to his and Rocki's joined hands. "It's about time you got here. Can you please tell the nurses I need to get up? They won't listen to me."

Rocki strode toward the bed, pulling Slater along with her, and then stopped, staring at Jackson as if she couldn't believe her own eyes. She seemed to examine him like one would a newborn, checking to see if all the fingers and toes were working and accounted for. She cleared her throat. "They heard you. They just don't want whatever is left of your brain coming out through the hole in your head. Jax, you'd better stay still or I swear I'll duct tape your empty head to the bed myself."

Jackson's lips twisted from a sneer to a smile. "And to think I've missed you."

Rocki reached for Jackson's hand, and it was as if all the fear and emotion she'd been holding back for the last couple of days broke through the dam.

Jackson's smile faltered and turned into a look of sheer panic.

Rocki crumbled right in front of Slater. She shook, tears and sobs racking her body.

Slater moved in, not sure if Rocki falling on her brother was the best idea. He wrapped an arm around her waist, holding her up. "He's okay." He captured Jackson's panicked gaze. "Shit, man, tell her you're okay."

Jackson raised his eyebrows and then grimaced.

"Rocki, I'm fine . . . well, except for the hole in my head. But they said they'd take the tube out and it would heal over."

"See, he's going to be fine. It's okay, sweetheart, just breathe." Slater sat on the chair beside the bed and pulled her onto his lap.

Rocki curled into him, clung to his neck, watered his shirt, and gulped for air. "I was so scared. I thought I was going to lose him too."

"I know." Slater wished he was one of those guys who carried handkerchiefs, but he wasn't. He kissed the top of her head and waited for the storm to pass. It was going to be a while, so he just held her close, murmured soothing words, and rubbed her back, all under Jackson's watchful gaze.

"I'm sorry." She kissed the spot on his shirt that covered his scar and he knew she was apologizing for more than just watering his shirt, but he wasn't sure how much more.

"Me too."

She looked at him, her face all blotchy, her eyes even more red and swollen than they'd been before, and he couldn't help but think she was the prettiest woman he'd ever seen. "So we're good?"

His stomach dipped and something inside him took a tumble. "We're good."

She wrapped her arms around his neck, kissed him, and damned if she didn't fry his circuits again.

Jackson cleared his throat. "Does someone want to tell me who the hell you are and just what is going on between you and my little sister?"

Rocki slid off Slater's lap but didn't drop his hand. She couldn't. Slater was the only reason she could hold it together now. She didn't know why, after all this time, she'd fallen apart, but she had. And just like with everything else, Slater knew what she needed, even after everything she'd said and hadn't said, and was there for her.

She took a stuttered breath, wiped her face, and then looked at Jax. "Slater Shaw, Jackson Sullivan. Jax, Slater's my . . . friend."

"Uh-huh. Sure. I might have an extra hole in my head, and it hurts like the devil, but I'm not dumb."

"Do you remember the accident?"

"Not really, but I hear the tree looks worse than I do."

Slater gave her hand a squeeze, and pulled her closer. "Why don't I go so Grace and Teddy can come in? I'm sure they'd like to see Jackson."

"You're leaving?" She didn't want him to leave.

Jackson made a face she didn't think had anything to do with his considerable headache. "That'd be great, thanks."

Slater and Jackson looked as if they were having a weird telepathic conversation, the kind one needed a Y chromosome to follow.

Slater gave Jackson a curt nod. "No problem. It's good to meet you, Jackson."

Jax had obviously lost his manners along with the cerebral spinal fluid they'd drained from his cranium because he didn't return the sentiment.

Slater didn't miss a beat. "I'll be right outside if you need me. Maybe I can create a diversion so that Grace and Teddy can both get past the nurses."

If anyone could, it would be Slater. He could cause a diversion just by breathing. "Thanks. I'll be out in a little bit."

"Take your time. It's all good."

Rocki watched Slater leave and turned on her brother. "You could have said it was nice to meet him too, Jax."

"I would have if that's the way I felt. The guy was all over you."

"He was not. He was being supportive."

"Supportive, my ass. So tell me, Racquel, what's the deal with you and Mr. Macho?"

"Racquel?" He only called her Racquel when he was pissed, and right now he had absolutely no reason to be pissed at her. Rocki couldn't believe him. "You almost kill yourself and you're asking me about Slater?"

"Damn straight I am. I talked to you last week—at least I think it was last week—and you never mentioned you were seeing anyone."

"It was last week, and obviously a lot has changed. God, Jax." She grabbed his hand—the same hand she'd been holding for days. "I've spent the last two days expecting you to die. You scared the shit out of me."

"I'm sorry. But if it makes you feel any better, it wasn't a picnic on my end either. You would not believe the scary, crazy dreams I've had. It was one long nightmare. I just didn't know I was dreaming. Even after I woke up, I didn't know. I had to ask the nurses."

He tried to sit and she pushed him back down. "You can't lift your head."

"So does your boyfriend allow you to hug your brother?"

"It's not Slater you have to worry about—it's the nurses. I'll hug you, but don't move that thick skull of yours, okay?" She reached over Jax, and gave him a hug. Drinking in the scent of her brother mixed with hospital soap.

Jax's arms came around her and squeezed. "I love you, Rocki. I'm really sorry I scared you."

"You did. You're all the family I have left."

"That's not true. You'll always have Grace and Teddy."

The tears started coming again. "I know, and believe me, they've been great. But please, don't you ever scare me like that again."

"It's not in the plans, but it looks as if you've been doing okay. So tell me what's going on between you and curly locks."

Rocki pulled away and looked at her brother. "It's complicated."

The door opened and Grace and Teddy stepped in.

"There's nothing complicated about what I saw in that man's eyes. I've just never seen that look aimed at my little sister before. I don't like it."

"Jackson Finneus Sullivan." Grace's scolding tone brought a smile to Rocki's face. "That's quite enough." Grace marched herself right up to the bed, leaned over Jax, brushed the hair off his forehead, and kissed his cheek. "I always knew you'd come back to us. Thank the good Lord."

"I'm sorry I worried you, Grace."

"I've worried about you both since the day you were born; it's a hard habit to break." Grace clucked her tongue and straightened Jax's covers. "Still, it doesn't give you leave to behave badly. Slater has been a godsend to Racquel. He not only dropped everything and drove her here, but he's sat with her at your bedside for two days. He never left her side."

"I can imagine."

"Hush. You should be thanking that young man for taking such good care of your sister."

"I don't like the way he looks at her."

"I think it's romantic."

Rocki blew the hair out of her eyes. "Would both of you stop talking about me like I'm not even here?"

Jackson went on as if Rocki had never opened her mouth. "I'm out for two days and when I come to, I see some strange dude has set his sights on my little sister. What do we know about this guy, anyway?"

Teddy patted Jackson's leg. "I know his father. Slater was regular navy and served for eight years. When he got out, he went to some high-falutin' computer school in Seattle and got his master's degree in computer science. He works in cyber security. The young man has been offered a contract with OPEC. He's selling them some kind of security program he designed and he also has an offer from Microsoft."

Rocki felt as if she were watching a tennis match. "Teddy, how do you know that?"

Teddy shrugged. "I asked him. You don't think I'm going to let you get involved with someone unless I check him out first, do you?" He turned back to Jackson. "If anything, Slater downplayed his experience. Did you know he was a chief warrant officer, fourth class? That young man has to be exceptional to achieve that rank in only eight years."

Rocki didn't know any of this. "He told you that?"

Teddy shook his head. "Of course not. I made a few phone calls."

Rocki couldn't believe it. "How could you do that?"

"I did nothing that any good parent wouldn't do."

"Jackson." Grace gave Rocki her trademark keep-your-mouth-shut pat. "Slater's a good man. And he looks at Racquel like she's the light of his life. A woman can't ask for any more than that."

Rocki's eyes almost jumped out of their sockets. "He what? No, Slater and I . . . It's not serious."

Both Teddy's and Grace's eyebrows rose in unison.

"It's complicated. And the timing is all wrong. Slater is leaving for Bahrain after the first of the year."

Teddy rocked back on his heels. "He was sure to tell me that he had a lot of options if he chose to stay on the East Coast."

Rocki couldn't believe what she was hearing. "What did you do, Teddy? Interrogate him?"

Teddy's gaze didn't stray from Jackson. "Slater's a nice young man, and he's got a hell of a backbone. He's not going to buckle under when Racquel starts getting pushy."

"I'm not pushy!"

All three heads turned to stare at her. Jackson groaned. Good, he deserved it. "Rocki, I love you but you're the pushiest broad I've ever known, and the only reason I'm telling you this now is because I'm in a hospital bed and you wouldn't dare hit me with Grace and Teddy here."

Rocki put her hands on her hips and shook her head. "I can't believe that Jax just came out of a coma and all the three of you can talk about is me and Slater Shaw. What's wrong with this picture? Shouldn't you be fawning over Jackson?"

Grace smiled at her and then Jackson. "You're probably right, but unfortunately, either of you showing up with a member of the opposite sex in tow is more unexpected than Jackson running into a tree and ending up in a coma."

Teddy let out a laugh and threw his arm around Grace. "It's a sad commentary on the state of their love lives, but the truth all the same. You have an amazing way of pointing out the obvious to the oblivious."

CHAPTER 14

Slater stood outside the hospital entrance and looked to the sixth floor wondering how long Rocki was going to be in her brother's room. "Pop. It sounds as if Jackson's going to be fine as long as he stays still for a while longer. He and Rocki seem to have the same problem when it comes to following directions."

Pete laughed. "She's one hardheaded woman, but then I've always considered that just part of her charm. Life with Rocki will never be boring."

"Jackson's not charming any of the nurses—that's for damn sure. Rocki's already threatened to duct tape his head to the bed if he gives her any more trouble."

"Is there a problem?"

"No, but until they remove the tube, he has to keep still. All I can say is it's a good thing they're talking about taking it out later today."

"Thank God for that. So when do you think you and Rocki will come home?"

"I can come home at any time. As for Rocki, I'm not sure. I guess that depends on her."

"You haven't talked about it?"

"When were we supposed to do that? We didn't find out Jackson was out of the coma until this morning and we had no idea what kind of shape he was in until we saw him."

"What's he like?"

Slater didn't think he'd make any points with his dad if he told him that Jackson seemed like an overprotective egomaniac. "He and Rocki look a lot alike, but other than that, I don't know. I didn't stay any longer than it took to meet the guy and make sure Rocki was okay. I wanted to let Grace and Teddy get in to see him."

"Why don't you and Rocki bring Jackson home with you? I'm sure she'd love to have her brother around to make sure he's healing, and with the holidays coming up, it would be good for Rocki to have her whole family with her. Besides, everyone here is curious about him."

"I can imagine. I'll mention it to her, but don't get your hopes up."

"Why's that?"

"Because Rocki's kept her life up here hidden from everyone in Red Hook for a reason. She's weird about the whole money thing."

"Money thing?"

"Come on, Pop. You know as well as I do that she kept a tight lid on the fact that she's a trust fund baby."

"You can't blame the girl for wanting to make her own way in the world."

"Rocki thinks that if it becomes common knowledge that she's a walking, talking Brink's truck, everyone will treat her differently."

"What do you think?"

"I think she's spent the last three years lying to everyone. I don't know, maybe she had valid reasons, but I don't give a shit how much money she has or doesn't have—neither will any of her real friends. But then you've known Rocki's little secret all along, haven't you?"

"Her story had more holes in it than Jackson's head, so I may have done a little checking."

"Why didn't you ever say anything to her?"

"Because it doesn't matter to me. It matters to her though, and she has to learn to trust people enough to make herself vulnerable. That's something all you kids have a hard time doing. Maybe now that you know, you can show her that everything doesn't have to change, and the life she's made for herself here doesn't need to come to an end."

"I don't like being made a fool of."

"No one does, but the thing is, son, this is not about you. It's about Rocki. You didn't give her a hard time about it, did you?"

Slater tried to decide just how much to tell his father.

"Shit, son."

He must have waited too long to answer.

"I can't believe even you would be stupid enough to give her grief with everything else the girl has going on. Did you at least wait to see if Jackson was going to be okay?"

"A heads-up would have been nice, Pop. What the hell did you expect?"

"I expected you to use the brain God gave you. Rocki's a woman and all women have their secrets. They're entitled. So what happened?"

"Before or after she slugged me?"

"After."

"We kissed and made up." At least he hoped they had. "I think. We were interrupted."

Pop let out a shotgun laugh. "I suggest you make sure the next time you get the girl alone."

"So that's your angle then? You're trying to fix us up?"

"It looked to me like you were already on the chase, son. I was just nice enough to help you out. If Rocki wasn't interested, you wouldn't have gotten past first base."

"I guess you're right. I'd better get back up to ICU." Which was the last thing he wanted to do. He should be getting used to being there by now, but he wasn't. He was just getting better at hiding his reaction.

"You make it sound as if you're headed to the gallows."

Okay, maybe he wasn't improving as much as he'd thought, but then it could be just Pop. Pop always had a way of knowing things there was no way in hell he could possibly know.

"Are you okay, son?"

"I'm fine. I just haven't been sleeping well."

"That could be a good thing or a bad thing. Which is it?"

"A little bit of both. I'll handle it."

"Are you sure?"

No, but what the hell could he say? "I'm fine."

"You know where I am if you need anything."

"Thanks, Pop. I'll talk to you soon." He ended the call, took a last breath of fresh air, girded his loins, and headed back to ICU.

He stopped at the nurses' station on his way to the waiting room. "Racquel hasn't come out of Jackson's room yet, has she?"

The nurse who had been so frantic earlier actually smiled at him. "No, not yet. Last we checked she and the Watkinses were still in with him. Jackson must be listening to your wife; he hasn't set off any monitors lately."

It was all he could do not to laugh at the wife comment, though he didn't correct her. Maybe that's why they'd let him into Jackson's room in the first place. "Good to know. So how long will Jackson be here?"

"Barring complications, they usually release patients like Jackson about twenty-four hours after removing the tube. If there aren't any setbacks, he should be home in the next day or two."

"That's good news, thank you." With any luck, he and Rocki would be on their way home before the weekend.

The nurse's face broke into a smile and she leaned toward him. "I think your wife is looking for you."

Slater turned, took one look at Rocki, and felt something shift inside him. The ball of stress that had been lodged in his throat since he'd gotten off the elevator seemed to unravel when the corners of her mouth turned up into one of her sexy smiles. He walked toward her and she slid right into his arms, wrapped hers around his waist, and went up on her toes for a kiss.

She ended the kiss but didn't let him go. "Jackson's impossible but he's my big brother so that shouldn't come as a complete shock."

"It's not."

She wrinkled her nose like she did whenever he teased her. It only made him want to kiss it. God, he was beginning to really worry about himself.

"I was expecting Jackson to be better but not that much better. I was so shocked and relieved and well . . . I don't know what happened. I'm sorry for losing it in there."

"You're doing okay?"

She held him tighter and rested her head on his chest. "I am now." She took a step back and grabbed his hand. Hers were a little clammy. "Do you want to get out of here?"

She had no idea how much. "Sure. But what about your brother?"

She smiled a smile that made him wonder if she wasn't

hiding a pair of horns under that spiked hair or was somehow distantly related to the Wicked Witch. "Grace and Teddy have decided to take the first shift. We've been released for good behavior."

Getting out of here with Rocki sounded like heaven. "Okay, I'm all yours."

Rocki had taken one look at Slater talking to the flirty nurses and couldn't believe her sense of relief—not that the sight of him flirting was a good thing, but after everything that had happened in the last two days, it didn't even cause a blip on her radar.

She'd been relieved because a big part of her had expected Slater to take off the moment they'd heard Jax was going to be fine. She had visions of having to steal Grace and Teddy's car and chase him. She wouldn't have blamed him if he had left. She hadn't meant to, but she had a strong suspicion that she'd hurt him.

"So, you're all mine?" She didn't bother hiding her smile when she threw his words back in his face—maybe he needed to hear them.

Slater's brows went up, and not in a sexy *are-you-in-the-mood?* kind of way. He didn't look happy that she'd picked up on that. It looked as if he'd pulled on a set of armor since leaving Jax's hospital room.

"It's a figure of speech."

Not many people would, but she took his aloofness as a good sign, and grabbed his hand. "Come on. I don't know about you, but I'm starving."

"You are?" The poor boy looked completely confused. She supposed it was a good thing. At least she wasn't alone.

"It's amazing what finding out my brother's going to be okay does for my appetite."

"You want to go out to breakfast?"

"No." She pressed the DOWN button on the elevator. "I want to go home. There's plenty of food there and everything else I have a taste for."

"Okay." He strung the word out, making it sound more like a question.

Rocki didn't want to show her hand so she ignored it. It was more fun to leave him wondering. She pulled him into the elevator and took great interest in watching the numbers above the doors.

Slater stepped away from her and leaned against the back wall. "I called Pop and told him the good news."

"I should have thought to do that." She turned to face him. "Is everything okay at home?"

"Everything is fine." His face broke out into a grin that she was sure had nothing to do with her. "Except Bree found Pop's cigar stash. Nicki has been working on everyone trying to talk them into buying her a bike for Christmas. And Pop was wondering when we'd be returning. He invited Jackson for the holidays. It sounds as if everyone would like to meet him."

Jackson and the crew of the Crow's Nest? She wasn't sure she could handle that. "You must not have mentioned what an ass he can be. After Jackson's behavior earlier, it makes me wonder why you didn't. I am sorry about that."

The doors opened and all she could think of was getting the heck out of there.

Slater followed her. "Jackson cares about you and I think you shocked him. Most guys don't know how to handle tears. It's not a big deal."

"It is to me. I think he was more shocked to see me with you than he was that I lost it. He's never seen me with anyone before and he didn't take it well. It took both Grace and Teddy to set him straight."

She thought Slater would say something but he just shrugged as if he didn't care. And maybe he didn't. He didn't even reach for her. He just stuffed his hands in his pockets, and walked to the Jeep.

Okay, so that was a bit of a letdown. When she ran out of Jackson's room, she thought of nothing but the feelings winging around her heart and mind. She hadn't known what to do about them, and wondered if Slater felt the same. All she could think of was finding him. All she could think of was being with him.

Once the worry and fear about Jackson's condition was over. Once she knew Jackson would be fine, she'd expected her feelings for Slater to dissipate. She hadn't expected her need for Slater to still be there, and she certainly never expected it to grow stronger. Shit.

Slater opened the door to the Jeep, and when she got in she had half a mind to bang her head against the dashboard. Falling for a man who was leaving the country in a matter of weeks was so not what she'd planned. Actually, she hadn't planned to ever fall for anyone. Let's face it, she didn't do well with loss, so she thought the best way to avoid it entirely was just to keep everyone at a comfortable distance and she'd done exactly that for so long, she didn't know how not to.

But then Slater walked into the bar, took one look at her, and somehow slipped past her every defense.

She just wished she knew what the hell to do now.

Slater pulled out of the parking lot. "Did you have a good visit with your brother?"

"Good? I guess so, if you consider an inquisition good. At least there seems to be nothing wrong with his mind—well, nothing new anyway. You'd think he'd be happy to be alive, but instead he was more interested in what was going on between you and me."

"He's protective."

"Teddy and Grace sang your praises though. They seem to have formed a Slater Shaw Fan Club."

Her statement was met with silence. She decided not to fight it; Rome wasn't built in a day. She just didn't like the feeling that he was slipping away from her, but there wasn't much she could do about it while he drove. They'd be back at the house soon enough. Not that she knew what she could do other than jump him. "Teddy mentioned that you might not go to Bahrain."

He looked at her and then returned his attention to the road. "It's a possibility."

"Why does he know this and I don't?"

Slater pulled into the drive and headed up the mountain. "You never asked." He parked in front of the garage and got out without saying a word. He just shook his head when she let them into the house through the side door. He had a thing for locking doors and for feeding her, and she wasn't sure why, but it bothered him to no end that, until now at least, neither interested her.

It should make his day that she was hungry, and not just for him.

She kicked off her shoes, dropped her bag, headed toward the refrigerator, and did an inventory. "It's not breakfasty but there's lobster salad. Did you eat this morning?"

"No, but don't tell Grace. She tried to feed me but I wasn't hungry, so I lied and told her I'd already eaten."

"You lied?" She spun around to look at him.

His face took on that carved-in-stone quality that made her want to wipe it right off it. "You heard me."

"Yeah, but you're all pissed off at me for supposedly lying—which I didn't even do—but it's okay for you to lie to Grace?"

"I was trying not to hurt her feelings. It was a little white lie."

She just raised an eyebrow.

Slater pushed himself off the counter he'd been leaning against and stepped toward her. "I might have overreacted a little about you keeping secrets."

That was something, at least.

"My last girlfriend pulled one over on me, and I didn't like the feeling."

She took a step forward and looked into his eyes. "What happened? She didn't tell you she was loaded?"

"No, she never made a secret of that. She didn't tell me she was engaged."

So, okay, she could see why he'd be just a bit sensitive. "Did you love her?" Just the thought of Slater in love with anyone was enough to ruin her appetite all over again.

"No, not even close."

Wow, that was a definite no. And why did that make her feel so much better?

"She just wounded my pride. I don't like being made a fool of." In his expression she saw nothing but anger—it was still a sore point. "She told me that it was nothing personal. So this morning when you said the same thing . . . I might have overreacted."

"Yes, about that."

"My overreaction?"

"No. What I said this morning."

"What about it?" Man, it was amazing to see his walls go up. His whole body tensed—even his nostrils. It was as if he were just waiting for a body blow. She'd never had so much power over anyone.

She put her hand on his shoulder and then slid it down to his belt buckle. "I was scared this morning. Overwhelmed and, well, I reacted badly."

His hands went around her waist and squeezed as if he wanted to hold her, but didn't trust himself. Or maybe he just didn't trust her. She wasn't sure.

"What scared you?"

"What scared me? What didn't? Look, I don't know how to do this, Slater. I'm not in touch with my inner anything. Hell, until I met you, I didn't even know I could have these kinds of feelings and I'm just not good at this. I mean it's one thing to have really great sex—that's safe. But great sex wasn't what we had. Great sex doesn't include tears and feelings. I freaked out and tried to put you back in that safety zone. But then you left me—"

His hold tightened but he didn't pull her close. He looked as if he was trying to decide whether to push her away or strangle her. He was just a little bit pissy. "I didn't leave."

"Bullshit. When you came upstairs and told me Jackson had come out of the coma, you looked right through me. You might as well have been gone."

"I was just doing what you said you wanted. Just sex, no emotion, remember? I left the emotion at the door."

"Yeah, well, it sucked."

"It was no picnic for me either, sweetheart."

"I was afraid that after we found out Jax was going to be okay and you left the room—" She took a deep breath. "I was afraid you were going to leave."

He actually looked affronted. Leaving damsels in distress must be against the superhero bro code. "I told you I would wait."

"Hey, I didn't say any of this made sense. I'm just telling you what happened."

"Fine, I'll shut up."

"Good. Now where was I?"

"You were afraid I'd dump you at the hospital even though I said I'd wait."

"Oh right. When I came out, I expected you to be gone, but then I caught you flirting with that nurse—"

"I wasn't flirting." It was the affronted look all over again.

She really needed to get that rule book. "That's not the point."

He opened his mouth to say something, so she held up her hand to stop him. "The point is, I can't tell you how relieved I felt when I found you waiting for me. I couldn't even get pissed about the whole flirting thing."

He blew out a breath and gave her another squeeze. "I was not flirting."

Exasperation can really be sexy. "Whatever."

"That nurse thinks we're married."

"And married people don't flirt?"

He opened his mouth and then shut it. Which was a good thing because she knew for a fact married people flirt all the time and not always with their spouses. "Fine, you have me there, but I wasn't flirting."

"Would you just forget about the flirting, please?"

"It's not hard to forget something I never did."

"Good." She shook her head. "I think I won, but then this wasn't supposed to be a fight. Darn it."

He didn't look real pleased either.

She rested her head against his chest. "I always thought I was a good communicator until today and you're not helping matters. Why can't you just read my mind and then decipher it for me? Is that too much to ask?"

He let out a laugh. "Now that's a scary thought. But

even if I could read your mind, it would never work. Sweetheart, you didn't trust me enough to know I'd stick around, so what makes you think you'd trust what I said?"

"It wasn't that I didn't trust you. It's just that I seem to have a habit of pushing people away, and I was afraid that's what I'd done. I didn't mean to push, but then I've been told that I'm the pushiest broad my brother's ever known. Do you believe he said that?"

Surprisingly, Slater didn't look the least bit shocked. As a matter of fact, he looked as if it was all he could do not to agree or laugh, maybe both.

"I'm still here. When I decide to leave, I promise you'll know. As for figuring out what's going through that mind of yours, just give it some time. Maybe things will sort themselves out and start to make sense."

She got the guts to look into his eyes and he finally pulled her close. It was like a puzzle piece locked into place and she didn't want to move, but then her stomach growled. "So, are you hungry?"

"I can eat."

She pulled away and raided the refrigerator, hoping Slater knew what he was talking about when it came to what was going on in her head. She was confused, and that was a new one on her. She'd always known what she wanted and went for it. Right now, the only thing she knew was that she wanted Slater—she just didn't know exactly what for or why.

CHAPTER 15

After eating brunch, Slater washed the dishes and Rocki dried. At least she'd eaten, but since that weird conversation, she hadn't said much. "When are we supposed to be back at the hospital?"

Rocki had been lost in thought, and from the looks of it, she was doing some deep thinking. "I'm supposed to bring Jax what he considers real food—a burger and fries from his favorite hole-in-the-wall. I thought the three of us could have dinner together."

"And he's okay with that?"

She shrugged. "I didn't ask him. The way I see it, if he wants to eat, he can learn some manners and behave himself."

"Well, that sounds like fun."

"Even when he's badly behaved, he's usually entertaining. In any case, it will be an improvement over the last two days."

Maybe for Rocki. For Slater, he wasn't so sure. Now he not only had to deal with the whole hospital thing, but an überprotective older brother. With any luck they'd move Jackson out of the ICU and into a regular room that might help. It couldn't hurt. He gave Rocki a nudge and handed her a frying pan to dry.

He'd been doing his best to understand the conversation they'd had. The only thing that was crystal clear was that she went to bed with him expecting to have sex and completely freaked out when just sex turned into making love. That he could understand. It threw him off his game too, just not as far off as it had thrown Rocki. And women were supposed to be more in touch with their emotions. Whoever said that had never met Rocki.

Slater understood that she wanted him. And Lord knew, he wanted her. The problem was that neither of them knew what to do with all the emotions involved. It was like the blind leading the blind across the Long Island Expressway on a summer Friday afternoon. In other words, one of them better see the light or they were both likely to end up being road pizza. He finished washing, pulled the plug, and drained the sink.

"Why don't you go on into the living room and start a fire? I'll make us hot buttered rums and bring them out."

He looked over the sparkling kitchen. "We just did the dishes."

"All this takes is hot water, some mix I found all prepared in the freezer, and rum. Don't worry—I've got it covered."

He couldn't help it, he raised an eyebrow. "I've seen you behind the bar, remember?"

She wrinkled her nose. "I don't like tending bar so I may have played up my ineptitude a little bit."

"Ya think?"

"Hey, it worked, didn't it? I'm the last person they ask to watch the bar and that's just fine by me. Go start a fire. I'll be there in a few minutes."

No one could destroy a bar as quickly as Rocki.

"Fine." He dried his hands on the towel she'd thrown over her shoulder, leaned in, and kissed her. "If you make a mess, you're cleaning it up."

"I told you, I got it covered."

"That's what I'm afraid of."

He headed out of the kitchen, but not fast enough to avoid the towel she snapped at his ass.

Building a fire in the living room consisted of nothing more than opening the flue and lighting a match. He strolled around the room and picked up a photograph of Rocki and her family riding bikes. Rocki looked to be about Nicki's age, maybe a little older—all long-limbed and skinny. Rocki's blond hair was longer than she wore it now, and Jackson was probably fifteen. Their mom was a looker. Rocki had her legs and her smile. The stunning blue eyes and stubborn chin though, were from her father.

"Those are my parents with me and Jackson. We used to take our bikes and ride into town to get ice cream just about every day. We rode bikes everywhere."

"I never had a bike." He ran his finger over the picture. He would have given his left arm to have a bike like Jackson's when he was a kid. "Sometimes the family I was with had bikes I could ride, but they weren't mine. I never did get my own bicycle."

"Maybe that's why Nicki wants one so badly."

He shrugged. "Probably." He returned the photograph to the mantel.

Rocki curled up on the couch. "I remember the day my dad taught me how to ride. I was so scared and excited. He held on to my seat and ran beside me for the longest time. I didn't fall until I realized he'd let go of me. It scared me. I didn't think I could do it on my own. But my dad was great. He picked me up, made sure I was okay, and told me I was riding on my own for a while before I fell. He said I already knew how to ride, I just didn't know I knew. So we did the whole thing again. But that time, he warned me before he let go and started cheering me on. It wasn't so bad the second time because I was prepared."

"Did you fall?"

"Nope. I just circled around and rode back to him. He made a big deal out of it. You know how dads are."

"The ones on TV at least. By the time Pop took me and the guys in, we were all twelve or thirteen—way past the stage when Pop could teach us much of anything."

"Pete taught you everything you need to know about love, trust, and relationships."

"Hardly. Rocki, I look at you and I wish I knew what to do. I wish I knew how to get through to you."

"What are you talking about? I thought we cleared all that up. I told you how I felt."

"No, you accused me of flirting and said you were confused. I think that was right before you asked me to read your mind and tell you what it all meant."

"Okay, so I didn't do such a great job of saying it, but we didn't just have sex—at least I wasn't having sex. I totally meant to have sex but then something happened and it turned into more."

He kissed her—the kind of kiss that made it clear that he wanted her. All of her—the mixed-up emotions, the love she had no problem showing but seemed unable to label, and the confused, sexy woman with the voice of an angel who could mesmerize a crowd. The woman who had so much love to give, she couldn't stop herself from spreading it around while expecting nothing in return, the woman who loved so fiercely she believed in everyone she cared for more than she seemed to believe in herself, and the lonely girl who was afraid to get too close. "Making love with you was something else, and I can't wait to do it again."

"Making love doesn't scare you?"

"Sweetheart, we were making love before we knew it. It was like the way you learned to ride a bike. Once we realized what we were doing we took a tumble, but now that we know what to expect—it'll be even better." He stood and she wrapped her legs around his waist and let out a groan.

"Slater, I'm not trying to give you a big head or anything, but if it gets any better, I don't think I'll survive."

"I guess it's a good thing I know CPR." He kissed her as he made his way toward the bedroom. She tasted like rum and spices and Rocki. Halfway up the stairs, he pressed her back against the wall. She felt so good, it was all he could do not to just drop his pants and take her, but this was supposed to be about more than sex. This was supposed to be making love.

He was fine with the concept, but he'd never done it intentionally, and he'd only made love with Rocki. He wasn't sure how one got started—he'd only stumbled into it. This time, he didn't want to stumble. He wanted to do it right. Shit, nothing like a little pressure.

When they reached the bedroom Slater set Rocki on the bed and stared at her through all-new eyes. Sex was a no-brainer, but love? Did the fact that he'd made love to Rocki mean that he loved her? Could someone fall in love within two weeks of meeting a person?

What he felt for her had been immediate—sure it had turned into more as he'd gotten to know her, but love?

He knew lust, and that was certainly a star player in his thoughts, but there had always been something between them that was so much bigger than lust. Something he'd never felt before. It was as if her happiness and well-being meant more to him than his own. Which was probably why he spent the past two days torturing himself in the hospital. If it had been anyone else, he would have told her to go without him.

The thought of leaving Rocki . . . of going to Bahrain was really not something he even wanted to contemplate. He'd had a hard enough time just leaving her in her brother's hospital room without knowing she'd be okay without him. How would he feel being a half a world away? Damn, talk about bad timing all around.

"Slater?"

He had her sweater off and had already flipped the front clasp of her bra open on the way up the stairs. "Do you have any idea how beautiful you look?"

"That's not a fair question. But the way you look at me makes me feel beautiful."

"The first time I laid eyes on you, you were behind the bar, and I wanted to offer you my jacket so no one but me could see you in that dress. I think I was sunk then."

Her nose wrinkled and a wave of something soft and warm broke over him. Tenderness? Yeah, tenderness. He didn't know he had it in him, but then Rocki seemed to bring out a lot of things in him he'd never known existed.

"I didn't see you until I went on stage. Then I had to sing what I will forevermore think of as my come-on set. I never noticed before, maybe because I never sang it to anyone in particular, but every one of those songs was embarrassingly suggestive."

A picture of Rocki on the stage singing to him made him smile. A blush had covered her face. "Yeah, I caught that." He'd dreamed of her and the way her eyes had held him spellbound. That first night, he'd wanted to pick Rocki up and carry her off like some kind of caveman.

He smiled at the memory of when she'd driven him to do just that.

He slid down beside her and took his time tugging her leggings down, the same way he'd savored opening presents his first Christmas at Pop's—when he realized he could keep everything he'd received. When he realized that no one was going to take his gifts away from him. When he realized he had a home.

Slater knew at that moment, with every fiber of his being, that Rocki was a gift he wanted to keep and never wanted to lose. When he looked at her, he experienced that same rush of emotion he'd had when he looked at Pop and his brothers that Christmas and felt, for the first time in his life, as if he belonged. With Rocki, it was even stronger. With Rocki it was overwhelming. With Rocki it was love.

Rocki wondered if she was growing gills because when Slater brought his mouth to hers and kissed her, it was so overwhelming she couldn't remember breathing.

Even the way he looked at her before the kiss had taken her breath—the way she suspected being hit with a sonic boom might; the force was nothing she could see, but its impact was earth-shattering.

He'd said that now that they knew how making love felt, it wouldn't come as such a shock. He'd been wrong. It was one thing to find yourself laid open before someone else, and a completely different thing to do it intentionally. The fear still existed. The trust was tenuous. The risk was great. But it was the need that drove her.

She needed to feel connected to Slater in every way. That connection suddenly seemed necessary to life and that alone was enough to trigger her fight-or-flight response. Every muscle in her body seized and she found it impossible to breathe.

He held her close and kissed her forehead. "Look at me, Rocki. I've got you. I'm not going to let you go. You're mine."

When she met his gaze, she saw that same fear reflected in his eyes. Her big, tough superhero was just as afraid of breaking this fragile bond as she was.

"Breathe, sweetheart."

It was like dancing with a partner—trying to learn steps that neither knew. But he wasn't letting fear stop him; he spoke with such certainty, with such belief, that she had no choice but to follow, glad he was taking the lead.

She drew in a breath, drew in the scent of Slater and rum and spices, drew in his warmth and tugged his shirt over his head while he kicked out of his pants.

Slater pulled her over him, and she melted, finding that spot on his chest just made for her to rest her head. His heat surrounded her, the beating of his heart fast but steady beneath her ear centered her, and his hands traveled, soothing and exciting in equal measure.

The bridge of the song she'd written created a soundtrack in her mind. "Him." She'd written it for Slater. The notes slipped through her consciousness, hammering away at her fear, ebbing and flowing on the tide of feelings he'd stirred since the beginning.

Drawing her deeper, he slid inside her, mind body and soul, filling her, riding the crest of desire, want and need.

She felt whole, she felt cherished, and she felt loved, and that feeling turned her inside out, sent her flying, over and over again.

She heard the music, she saw the starbursts, and when Slater lost hold of his control, he never left her, taking her with him, cushioning her fall.

"Slater?"

He rolled them over to their sides and drew her leg over his hip—keeping their connection. He kissed her, running his hand through her hair, then pulled her closer, kissed her harder and ended it with a smile. "I know, sweetheart. I love you too."

"You do?"

"I do. I love you like crazy."

"How . . . How did you know?"

He rolled over on top of her and slid farther in, curling her toes, and stealing her breath. "How did I know that you love me?"

"Yeah." The word came out as more of a groan than a question.

"I'm good at reading code. I'm learning yours." He took a long, leisurely slide back so she wrapped her ankles around his waist and tensed around him.

"Okay, so what am I saying now?"

He kissed her, teasing her with his tongue, with his hands, and then raised her hips and slipped back in. "You love me and you can't get enough of me."

"You're definitely not lacking in self-confidence."

He rose up on his forearms. Her back arched when he hit that spot and stilled. "Am I wrong?"

"God no. Just don't stop."

"You want more?"

She tried to move, but he had her trapped. "Yes. More."

"Then say it. Come on, Rocki, it's only fair."

What was this—an X-rated version of *Barney*? "Please? Thank you?"

"Try again. Come on, you can do it."

"Are you always going to be this demanding?"

He slid farther out. "You can count on it."

The man was impossible. He was going to force her to

say it. She might feel it, but saying it was . . . difficult. She tried to move, to get him to change the subject but nothing worked and she needed him to move, like she needed her next breath. "Slater, I love you."

The only movement was his eyebrow. "You can do better than that. Come on, once more with feeling."

She reached up and kissed him, dragged her mouth away from his and looked right into his eyes. "Slater, I love you but if you don't start moving, I might be forced to hurt you."

"Now that was real." He slid back in and laughed. "Grace and Teddy were right."

How he could do what he was doing and carry on a conversation was beyond her. "'Bout what?"

"The man who ends up with you will certainly have his hands full. Lucky for you, I love pushy broads."

He'd pay for that . . .

But then he went and did something magical that made her feel amazing and she was more intent on having another orgasm than in retribution, so she went with it.

He'd pay later.

Much later.

And if she didn't survive this round, she'd haunt him because that's just the kind of girl she was.

CHAPTER 16

The flashing lights on Rocki's phone woke her. She grabbed it and tried to focus her eyes. "Patrice?"

"Rocki, you've been gone for days and you didn't think to call me?"

"Three days, and I've been a little busy." She stretched and tried to get some of the kinks out. It was going to take a hot bath or at least a very long shower. Alone. "Besides, Slater's talked to Pete. I figured he'd pass the word."

"Yes, he did, but it's not the same, girl, and you know it."

"Right, it's that horse's mouth thing again, isn't it? And today, I'm the horse?"

"You'd be correct. Now hurry, before I have to leave to pick up the girls from school and preschool."

Slater was nowhere to be found. "What do you want to know?"

"How's your brother?"

"Better. Thanks for asking. They should be able to remove the tube today. Except for a wicked bad bruise on his face, a matching headache, and an extra hole in his cranium, he seems like he's no worse for wear."

"And how is Slater?"

"Tell her to pretend she's reading a fortune cookie." Bree's voice came through the phone loud and clear.

"Why would she do that?" Oh God, Patty had put her on speakerphone.

"Because," Bree continued, "when you read a fortune cookie you always follow it with the words 'in bed.' Don't you know anything?"

Rocki groaned. Shit, if she knew she'd ever be in this position, she'd never have given Elyse, Bree, and Skye such a hard time. So okay, she would have given them a hard time, but she'd just stop answering the phone. "Do you two need me here for this?"

"Yes, answer the question." They answered in stereo.

"Did you two practice that?" God, the two of them ganging up on her was just too much.

"Girl." Patrice put on her scary voice and Rocki thanked God she was out of smacking distance. "Don't you mess with me. You leave here without so much as a good-bye to see to your sick brother—the one you never once mentioned you had, and now you're giving me lip?"

"Fine. I'm sorry. It's just that Slater's . . . Well, he's . . . and we're . . . you know . . ."

Bree's laugh cut through Rocki's embarrassment. "So which is it? Great, inventive, and going at it like bunnies? Or is it wonderful, caring, and madly in love?"

"A little of both?" She was just glad she wasn't on FaceTime. She swore she heard a high five and then a bunch of giggles.

"I knew it." Patrice sounded as if she was bouncing in her seat. "I knew you couldn't keep out of each other's pants."

"Patty," a deep voice cautioned.

Oh God, Francis was there? He'd heard? She groaned

into her pillow. It was one thing for the girls to hear, but Francis?

"Hi, Rocki." And Storm?

"Hi, guys." Did she just squeak? "Please tell me you just walked in."

Silence. Dammit. "A little warning would have been nice, ladies. What is everyone doing there? Aren't you supposed to be at the restaurant?"

"It's Monday. It's our day off," came Storm's reply.

"Right."

The background noise disappeared as if the phone was taken off of speaker. "So um . . ." Storm's voice came on the line. "Is Slater around?"

"He's probably around somewhere. I was just napping."

"Can you call him?"

The house was way too big to just scream and expect an answer. "Why don't you just try his cell?"

"I did. There's no answer."

"Is there a problem?"

"I don't know. Look, just have him give me a call when you see him. Okay?"

"It's not Nicki, is it?"

"No, Nicki's just fine. It's business."

"Okay, hold on. I'll see if I can find him." She tossed the phone down, pulled on Slater's shirt, and took the back stairs down to the kitchen. He wasn't there but he'd been there—the mess she'd made with the hot buttered rum had been all cleaned up.

"You still there, Storm?"

"Yeah. How big is that house of yours anyway?"

"Big enough." She headed to the living room. Slater sat in his jeans and no shirt with his head buried in one of the photo albums Grace always left out. He turned the page and she saw a flash of baby pictures. Great.

Slater spotted her and smiled that sexy smile that had her thanking God he was hers. "You're awake."

She held out the phone. "It's Storm. He said you weren't answering your phone."

Slater took the phone from Rocki—who didn't look happy about something. He set the photo album he'd been looking at on the coffee table, pulled her into his lap, and kissed her before he put the phone to his ear. "Hey, what's up?"

"You apparently from the conversation I overheard. Going at it like bunnies was mentioned, Casanova." No wonder Rocki looked a little upset. "Look, I don't know how to say this nicely, but if you mess with Rocki and hurt her, Francis and I will have to take you out."

He pulled Rocki tighter to him. "Oh yeah? Well, you'd have to get in line. I don't think Rocki's brother likes me much—he's got dibs."

Rocki buried her face in her hands and groaned. "I can take care of myself you know."

"Did you hear that, Storm? Rocki said she could take me out all on her own if I step out of line. So did you just call to threaten my life or was there something you needed?"

"Some guy stopped by the restaurant today to see you. He's a lawyer for OPEC and said he's your contact if you want to make any changes to the contract."

"You have his card?"

"Not with me, but it's in the office."

"Great. I'll look at it when I get back. Thanks for calling—"

"Wait. I want to talk to you about Nicki."

"What about Nicki? Is she okay?"

"She's fine—physically."

What the hell was that supposed to mean? Storm was the eldest of the three of them, or at least they thought he was since Logan's birthdate was nothing more than a guess. Still, according to the paperwork, Storm was the big brother and Slater was the baby. Unfortunately, Storm never let Slater or Logan forget it. Storm put on his big brother voice—he might have gotten away with it ten years ago when he was twice Slater's size, but now he could just go to hell.

"Are you going to threaten me again? Because listen bro, once a day is about my limit."

"No, I'm just wondering if your plans have changed now that you know you have a daughter. Pop tells you that Nicki's your kid, and the next thing I know you're running away to New Hampshire."

"What the fuck? Pop didn't tell me a damn thing." Slater lifted Rocki off his lap, went to the study, and closed the door. He stood there looking out the window at the late-afternoon sky—it looked like snow. Cold, gray, bleak. "Storm, slow down. What the hell are you saying?" It sounded as if a million bees had just invaded his head. He could hardly hear over the buzzing. His skin felt tight and tingly, his heart rate tripled, and he grabbed the windowsill to keep from falling. He was missing something; he knew it.

"I'm saying that Nicki needs a father, she needs a family, and right or wrong, you're the lucky bastard who won the daddy lottery."

Slater dragged in a shallow breath—deep breathing seemed beyond him at the moment. Daddy lottery? He forced the breath out through his lips. Storm thought that he was Nicki's father? A picture of Nicki so crisp, so clear came to him. "What the fuck are you talking about?" There was silence on the other end of the phone—or at least he thought there was. It was hard to tell over the ringing in his ears. "Why would you think I'm Nicki's father?"

"Pop said he was going to tell you."

"Yeah, well, he didn't."

"Oh fuck. Bree's gonna kill me. Pop might too."

"I'll kill you myself if you don't tell me what the hell is going on."

"Do you remember Marisa Sotto? She worked as a waitress. I was almost eighteen, you were seventeen. She was hot, Latin, and curvy."

Slater sat in a chair beside the window. A guy never forgot his first time—even if he wanted to. "I remember her." Slater's cheeks burned.

"Nicki is Marisa's daughter. Marisa told Pop Nicki was his granddaughter when she dumped Nicki off."

The blood drained from Slater's face and he braced his hand on the arm of the chair so tight, his knuckles were probably white. "Marisa?"

"Yeah, I never slept with her and Logan's paternity test came back negative."

"Nicki can't be mine. I used protection. I only slept with Marisa once," he mumbled to himself. And it wasn't all that successful. For most guys the thought lasted longer than the act, and he'd been no different. All he remembered was that when it was over, Marisa hit the door and said something about having to be back on the floor. He'd been nothing more than a fifteen-minute diversion on a twenty-minute break. It had been embarrassingly awesome.

"Yeah, well, condoms aren't one hundred percent effective you know. Congratulations. You made a hole-in-one and she's gorgeous."

She, as in Nicki? As in Marisa's daughter? As in his

first time? Holy shit. He made the connection and he did not like the outcome. What the fuck was he supposed to do with a daughter? What was he supposed to do with a girl? "Storm, are you sure?"

"The only way to be completely sure is to take a paternity test, but shit, Slater, we're ninety-nine point nine percent sure."

Slater rose, and then sat back down. There had to be a mistake. It was a big, big mistake. "Marisa could be lying. This could just be wishful thinking on Pop's part."

"Nicki looks just like you."

"The same can be said for Logan, but you said yourself she's not his."

"She walks like you. Hell, Slater, she even has your attitude. Everyone knew it the second we saw you two together. Everyone but you."

"You've suspected all this time and no one has bothered to tell me?"

"Pop said he was going to the day you took off. I thought—"

"You thought I ran away."

Storm didn't say anything. He didn't need to. Slater knew that was exactly what he'd thought.

"Just because you and everyone else thinks there's a resemblance still doesn't mean Nicki's my kid." But what if she was? What if Nicki was his daughter? What the hell was he going to do? All his plans, all the work he'd done . . . He couldn't go to Bahrain. He would lose a multimillion dollar contract. All his dreams would be flushed right down the toilet. It wasn't Nicki's fault. Shit, she was just the unexpected product of raging teenage hormones, an overactive libido, and a few brain cells shy of common sense.

"The only way to be sure is to take a paternity test."

Did that involve needles? "Fuck."

"So what are you going to do, little brother?"

Slater tried to brush the little brother thing off, but it was difficult. He was a grown man. A grown man who could possibly have a ten-year-old daughter who scared the crap out of him. "I'll do what needs to be done."

"She's an amazing kid. Any man would be lucky to have her as a daughter."

"I said I'll do what needs to be done. So, do us both a favor and drop it."

"Nicki's not a fuckin' obligation, Slater. She's a little girl."

"And she's not yours." If they had been in the same room, he'd bet that Storm would be in his face. But Slater wouldn't take a step back. Not this time. The muscles across his shoulders bunched. "If Nicki's mine, I'll take care of her. Now, back the hell off."

"When you get home you and I are going to talk. I don't know what the hell is going on in that computer-like brain of yours, but I suggest you pull it out of your ass before you get back. I love Nicki, and I'll be damned if I let you or anyone else mistreat her."

"Fuck you, Storm. Don't go there. Don't you dare." Anger unlike any he'd ever experienced turned his blood to ice and he saw a flash of memory—a man's face twisted in fury. Mad. Crazy. Frightening. A monster. He didn't recognize the face, but he knew the eyes. The eyes were his.

His heart pounded in his ears so loud, he wasn't sure if Storm said anything. "This conversation is over." He ended the call and if it had been his phone, he'd have thrown it through the plate-glass window. Instead, he pressed his fingers to his temples, willing the vision to recede, and blew out a breath, trying to slow the racing of his heart. He had to get out of there.

He opened the door and headed toward the stairs.

As soon as Rocki saw him she wrapped her arms around him.

Slater couldn't stand to be touched. Not now. "Don't." He shucked Rocki's hands away and turned for the stairs. He needed to get dressed. He needed to escape. He needed to figure out what the hell was going on with him. "I'm going for a run."

"Slater, wait."

"Leave it alone, Rocki. If I'm not back before you have to leave, take the Jeep." He didn't bother looking at her. He couldn't. He just needed to get out, and fast.

Rocki stared after Slater and the slam of the back door made her jump. She called Patrice.

"Rocki?"

"Put Storm on."

"Look, maybe—"

"Patrice, put Storm on the phone now." She blew out a breath and ran her hand through her hair.

"You people need to calm down. Take a breath."

She was breathing. If she breathed any more, she'd hyperventilate.

"Rocki, it's Storm. Are you okay?"

"Of course I'm okay. Slater's the one I'm worried about. What the hell did you say to him?"

"Look, Rocki, no offense, but this is between Slater and me."

"Bullshit. I care about him and I've never seen him so upset. What the hell did you say?"

"It doesn't matter. The fact is, he freaked out."

"Everyone does once in a while. I heard you freaked just driving through the Red Hook Houses."

"Low blow, Rocki."

"Yeah? It's nothing you don't deserve. What do you think you just did to Slater? He's the best man I know."

"Oh man, Rocki. Don't tell me you've gone and fallen in love with him."

"What? You think Slater doesn't deserve to be loved?"

"Oh no, that's not what I said. But Rocki, as much as we all love Slater, he's not like the rest of us. I don't want to see you get your heart broken expecting that love to be reciprocated."

"You really know nothing about your brother, do you?"

"I—"

"That's a rhetorical question. Storm, you and Slater haven't seen much of each other for ten years. You might want to spend some time getting to know him again before you start making blanket declarations. People change. Heck, just look at you."

"People don't change that much. He buries himself in his computers for a reason, Rocki. He doesn't feel things like other people do. Don't say I didn't warn you."

"And don't say I listened to you. But don't worry. You'll see. Slater's going to prove you wrong."

"I only want the best for all of you. For your sake, I hope to God you're right."

"I am. I'm sure of it. We should be home as soon as Jackson's okay. Tell Pete I'll call and let him know when to expect us." She didn't wait for a reply before she ended the call.

Slater hit the driveway at a dead run. The pounding of his feet matched time with the pounding of his heart. He didn't know if he was running toward something or away.

Nicki could be his daughter. If that wasn't mind blowing enough, his own brother thought that he was capable of mistreating a child. His child. He thought he'd been angry before, but shit. From what Storm said, everyone knew since the day he came home, and he was just finding out about it now? Only because Storm stuck his size twelve foot in his mouth. Had Rocki known too?

He had to release some of this anger Storm had stirred up or he'd explode. Just the thought of his brother had him punching the air. He'd never allowed himself to feel the anger he felt at that moment.

Storm was wrong about him having a computerlike brain. Just because he kept a lid on his feelings and emotions didn't mean he didn't have them. He had so many emotions and feelings running through him, he was swamped by them. Especially if you took into account the amount of anger he felt. Yeah, right now, anger was a biggie and that's what scared him.

He remembered the way Rocki looked at him when he'd yelled at Storm when she was on his lap. He saw fear in her eyes and the thought that she might be afraid of him sliced him to his core.

It didn't help that his own brother thought he was capable of mistreating Nicki. What the hell was that about?

Sure, maybe Storm thought he was unfeeling, but Slater had never once been abusive. He'd never hurt anyone who hadn't asked for it and then only if they left him no choice. It took a lot to make him use force. He'd taken down a guy who was attempting to rape one of the locals just off base. Even that night he was in control. He froze as soon as he knocked the guy out. He'd made sure the girl was okay, offered to call the police, and put her in a cab home when she'd refused to involve the cops. Hell, he'd even picked up the petty officer and carried him to the infirmary to make sure he was okay—and to file a report.

The one time he remembered losing his temper had scared him enough to make sure he never did it again. He'd been nine or ten, and had gone after one of his foster fathers when the man took a strap to his own daughter. No one deserved to be whipped like that. Slater had broken the guy's nose and it took two of the neighbors to pull him off the man. Social services had Slater out of the house before the end of the day.

That feeling of being out of control, of wanting to hurt someone badly enough to ensure that the man would never hurt anyone ever again, scared the life out of him and that's exactly what he felt when Storm accused him of mistreating Nicki. If the two of them had been face-to-face instead of on the phone, Slater didn't know what he'd have done—and that's what scared him most of all.

He might not know much about his past, but he knew the man's face he saw in the fragment of memory used anger like a weapon. He fed on it. He'd embraced it. He was a monster. And Slater knew he was somehow connected to that anger. The man's face might have looked like something out of a horror movie, but the thing that scared him the most was that the man stared at him through eyes so like his own. The eyes he saw every day when he looked in the mirror.

Tears ran down his face, either from the cold or from the anger—or hell, maybe he was just crying and didn't know it. Right now, nothing would surprise him.

He stopped, wiped his face on his shirt, braced his hands on his knees, and tried to catch his breath. He wasn't sure how far he'd run or how long he'd been gone but knew Rocki must be worried. Shit, how the hell was he supposed to explain this to Rocki when he didn't know what to make of it himself?

He jogged back toward the house amazed at how far

he'd run. By the time he made it up the hill, his calves were screaming. He got to the door, stretched out his quads and calves and stood there trying to come up with something to tell Rocki. When the cold froze his sweat-soaked shirt he knew he'd have to wing it.

Slater pushed the door open and caught Rocki, who launched herself at him.

"Are you okay?"

"No." He was gross and sweaty and cold but he didn't have the strength to put her down. He drank in her scent, and just the feel of her in his arms calmed him. "But if anyone is going to teach Nicki to ride a bike, it's going to be me. I'm her father. I'll teach her, dammit." Just the thought of one of his brothers teaching Nicki to ride a bike, and his blood pressure shot through the roof. The beating of his heart pounded in his ears.

"What?" Rocki's blue eyes were wider than he'd ever seen. "Did you just say that Nicki's your daughter?"

Shit. He ran his hand through his hair and led her back to the living room. "I didn't know." He paced to the window, turned on the frozen landscape, and made his way back. Rocki stared at him the entire time. He saw no judgment in her eyes, just patience. She looked as if she'd wait forever for him to answer. "I didn't know. Storm just told me."

"You're Nicki's father." It wasn't a question—it was a statement. She tried it on for size and nodded as if she agreed with the fit.

He certainly didn't. He could relate to the wild mustangs he'd seen out west. They would capture part of the herd, break them, and sell them. He'd heard mustangs made great mounts once they accepted the saddle—but the first time they put one on, it was scary. He'd always felt bad for the horse. It couldn't be easy to go from completely free to saddled. Giving up freedom for three squares and a nice stall didn't seem like a good trade to him. "I don't know if Nicki's mine or not. Everyone seems to think she is. It's a possibility—Marisa and I hooked up once. When she dumped Nicki off at Pop's, Marisa said Nicki was his granddaughter."

Rocki slipped her arms around his waist and leaned in, holding on, her head tucked beneath his chin. "What are you going to do?"

"When I get home, I'm going to take a paternity test. And if Pop's right—" He shook his head. "I don't know, Rocki. I don't know how to be a dad. I can't remember my father—there's no picture, no memory, no nothing"

"You had Pete."

"I was half grown when Pop took me in."

"He's still your father. Look at you. You're amazing."

Slater laughed. "Yeah, I'm so freakin' amazing my parents dumped me in the foster system. Hell, I don't even know why. I don't remember them."

"If you don't remember then how do you know it was something you did? Have you ever asked Pete?"

He shook his head. Every time he thought about it he was paralyzed with fear—which was something he wasn't about to tell Rocki. She teased him about being a superhero. Little did she know that he was nothing but a coward.

"It's not as if she's a baby. Nicki's ten."

"Ten and a half. Nicki's a little girl. She deserves someone who knows how to be a dad."

"Parents aren't parents until they have kids, Slater. It's on-the-job-training. You learn as you go. Nicki's a great kid. She's easy to love."

"I know that. It's not Nicki. It's me. I've never wanted to have kids. I don't want to screw anyone up like I am.

I'm not father material. The last thing I expected when I went home was to find out that I'm a single dad with a ten-year-old daughter."

He raked his hands through his hair. "I'm supposed to leave the country by the first of the year and now I don't know what the hell is going to happen. I can't take Nicki to Bahrain. I've worked toward this for years, and it's finally coming together. I've been offered a multimillion dollar contract, and now I'm not even sure they'll want the program if I'm not there to implement it."

"Slater, it's a contract. It's only money. Nicki's your daughter. Do you have any idea how lucky you are?"

Spoken like a true trust-fund baby. Money is only a problem when you don't have it, or in his case, when you've never had it. He didn't mention that—it wasn't as if he didn't understand where she was coming from—but shit, he'd worked for ten years and everything he'd worked toward was within reach. "Lucky?" Even if he didn't take the contract into consideration—he knew he could find a job tomorrow if he wanted one—that wasn't the problem. He was too terrified to feel lucky. "I probably sound like an uncaring bastard, but I hardly know Nicki. I look at her and God, Rocki; she's still so small. She asks questions I don't know how to answer, and she needs stuff—stuff I don't have."

"Stuff?"

"Emotional stuff, security, a home. Stuff I've never had except for my time at Pop's."

Rocki pushed him down on the couch, straddled his legs, looked right into his eyes, and then kissed him. It wasn't an I-want-you're-body kiss, it was more of a it's-going-to-be-okay kiss.

Too bad his dick didn't seem to recognize the difference. Especially when she scooted up to him, her breasts pillowed against his chest, her fingers combing through his hair. As if they had a mind of their own, his hands went straight to her ass and tugged her tighter against him.

"Slater, listen to me. You're everything in a dad that Nicki could ever want. If you're afraid you won't be able to give her all she needs, it means you care enough to try. Look, my parents were wonderful, but they weren't perfect. No one expects that, not even Nicki. If you're Nicki's father, you'll be a wonderful dad. I know you will. And besides, everyone is involved in Nicki's life; you're not in this alone. It takes a village, and you have a pretty amazing one. You have Pete, Storm and Bree, Logan and Skye, Patrice and Frankie, and you have me."

His eyes locked on hers and held on like a lifeline. "I have you? Still?"

"Did you think this would change how I feel about you? I love Nicki. I love you."

"I love you too. But right now that's the only thing I'm sure of."

Rocki nodded. "You need to talk to Pete. You need some time. I understand."

"Listen." He looked into her eyes. "I promise we'll talk about this—just not now. Now I've got to get cleaned up so we can take your brother his dinner."

"Okay." She still looked worried but he was glad she didn't push. "I can go to the hospital by myself if you want."

Man, he wished he could take her up on that, but it would be a cop-out. "No, it's fine. Why don't you call in the order for pickup. Give me ten minutes." He gave her another kiss and forced himself to set her down. If he brought her upstairs, there was no telling how long it would take him to get cleaned up.

"What do you want?"

Her laid out in a bed, but that wasn't going to happen. "Whatever you're having is fine." He'd be lucky if he could eat. His gut felt as if someone had used him for kickboxing practice.

He felt better after a minute under the scorching water—that was all the time he had. He pulled on some clothes, hoping he didn't look as trashed as he felt, ran a comb through his hair, and headed back down.

Rocki tossed him his coat. "Want me to drive?"

"Do you have a license?"

"No, but I know all the cops."

"Yeah, I think not. Thanks though."

"So I let my license lapse—it's not as if I'm not a good driver."

"I'm sure you are. Renew your license and then you can be the chauffeur."

She shot him a sexy smile and laughed. "A chauffeur with benefits?"

"Sweetheart, you can be whatever you want. You'd sure look cute in the hat."

CHAPTER 17

Jackson was relieved to be out of ICU. He'd hated that place. The pain in his head was lessening. He wasn't sure if it was because he was no longer hooked up to all those damn noise machines or just because the lighting was better. Either way, he was thankful for walls that weren't made of glass and the fact he could actually get up and take a piss without help. He learned early on, no matter how cute the nurse—and damn, there were some really cute nurses—there were just some things a man liked to do without an audience.

Rocki pushed through the door without knocking—not that Rocki ever knocked. She'd barreled through more doors than a SWAT team, and with more force. "I hear you have one less hole in your head."

The scent of grease hit his nostrils and his mouth watered. "Yeah." He rubbed his hand over the gauze-covered wound.

"Did it hurt?"

"Not as much as I thought it would, it just felt really strange."

Rocki's "friend" Slater didn't say anything but he

didn't need to. He looked as if he wanted to be any-where but there. Jackson could definitely relate. He just wasn't sure why. What did the guy have to be nervous about?

Rocki carried a bag already riddled with grease spots. "I don't know how you live on a steady diet of this stuff. It's amazing your arteries aren't clogged." She put one on the rolling table beside his notebook computer, reached over, and kissed his cheek.

She looked as if she hadn't slept in a week. There was bruising under her eyes and her normally pink skin was pale. Shit, he'd known what she'd gone through when they'd lost their parents. It looked as if for her, the last few days had been a recurring nightmare. "Did you get me bacon cheese fries and onion rings?"

"Yes, and a burger with the works. Hold the mayo."

"I knew there was a reason I kept you around."

She passed a bag to Slater. "Jax, you remember Slater."

How could he forget? "Your friend, right?"

Rocki snatched the bag of food right off the table, almost taking out his computer. She'd always been too quick for him. "Jackson, if you don't behave, I swear this is going right in the garbage and you can eat whatever the nurses want to serve you."

Shit, all they'd given him was clear fluids for hours, and then they gave him what would be considered gruel and soft foods. God, all he wanted was a juicy burger and french fries.

Slater cleared his throat, and Jackson looked over to where he'd pulled a chair. "Give the man back his food, Rocki."

Maybe Teddy was right about this guy after all. No one Jax had ever known had the guts to tell Rocki what to do. If nothing else, this little visit would be entertaining. It had been a while since he witnessed Rocki let someone have it. "Whose side are you on, anyway?"

"Ours. Depriving him of a good meal isn't going to make him any happier about his sister going out with a guy like me."

Jax had to hand it to Slater; at least he knew where he stood.

"A guy like you?" Rocki shoved the bag back into Jax's hands and shot him a warning look before turning her attention back to Slater. "I happen to think you're amazing, and my bullheaded brother is just going to have to get used to it."

"Hey, I'm not deaf, Rocki." He pulled a fry out of the bag, and gave Slater a nod while wondering what he'd drugged Rocki with. "Thanks, man. I was worried there for a minute."

"I would be too if I were you."

So maybe this guy did have his Rocki's number after all. Just the thought of it brought a smile to his face. Rocki ran roughshod over every guy who seemed at all interested in her and once she conquered him, she lost all interest.

"I don't know who to smack first. But at least you're getting along. Why you have to bond while ganging up on me is the question."

"So, Jackson." Slater ignored Rocki, which worked for him. "Are you on any pain meds?"

"No, man. They took me off the juice yesterday. Today it's nothing but Tylenol."

Slater reached into his pocket and pulled out a beer. "You want one?"

Okay, so maybe Slater wasn't a complete waste, but Jackson still didn't like the way he looked at Rocki.

Rocki grabbed the beer out of Slater's hand. Damn, foiled again. "No, he doesn't want a beer."

Jax sat up straighter and the pain in his head made itself known. "Like hell I don't."

Slater hadn't even fought her over the beer. Jax started to rethink his admiration. Still, there was something in his eyes. Rocki turned and Slater shot him a warning look. "Think fast." He pulled out another beer and let it fly.

Good thing he'd played catcher all through high school and college. The beer connected with his hand— he still had it. "Thanks. Maybe you're not so bad after all."

Rocki just shook her head and put her hands on her hips, giving Slater what he was sure was her stink-eye. "Did you think to bring me one?"

Slater smiled, "Of course, sweetheart. I always think of you." He slid another out of a pocket and twisted off the top. "Man, I love this jacket."

Jackson had to concur; he had one just like it. "You ride?"

"I have an old Harley Sportster I rebuilt."

"I ride a Ducati." Jackson cracked his beer and took a swig.

"A crotch rocket?"

"No, I went for the Diavel."

Slater whistled through his teeth. "Nice."

He shrugged. "I like it." He didn't get to ride it enough, but then that was the story of his life. No time.

"What's not to like?"

Jax unwrapped his burger. He hadn't wanted something so badly since the first time he'd had a hot, naked woman in his bed. Though the way he was feeling right now, he'd probably leave the woman and take the burger.

He was starving. He took a bite, groaned in ecstasy, and talked around the mouthful. "So where do you ride?"

"I took a trip from Seattle to Banff this fall. It was fun—cold as hell, but fun."

"Sounds like a good time. I've skied there. It's beautiful; it must be nice with all the fall colors. But nothing beats New Hampshire and Vermont when the leaves change. If you're around next fall, we should go out for a weekend."

He caught Rocki's surprised look. "What? I can be nice."

"When plied with alcohol."

"It certainly doesn't hurt."

Slater laughed and raised his beer. "So what do you do when you're not tree skiing?"

"I'm in investments. I'm a fund manager."

"Aren't you a little young for that?"

Slater didn't look any older than he was. He was one to talk. "I graduated high school early and went into Wharton's five-year BA, MBA program."

Rocki hated what he did and he saw her gearing up for another onslaught of lectures. "It didn't hurt that he had family connections. The uncles are grooming him. All work and no play makes Jackson a boring man."

"Hey, I was taking time off. You're the one who couldn't get away. Which makes me wonder why you couldn't take a long weekend." He looked from Slater to Rocki and back. "How long have you and Rocki known each other?"

"A couple of weeks. We met when I went home to help out my old man—he owns the bar where Rocki's band plays."

"You're Pete Calahan's son?" Shit. He set his burger and beer on the rolling table "Teddy said he knew your father, but he didn't elaborate and I didn't put it together."

"You know Pop?"

Oh yeah, he knew Pete—what kind of brother would he be if he hadn't checked out the place where his sister played. But then over the years, he and Pete had done some business—not that Slater and Rocki needed to know that. "We've talked."

"Yeah, why doesn't that surprise me?"

"How's he really doing after the heart attack?"

"I don't think he's a hundred percent yet, but he's doing well."

Jackson rested back against the pillows. "That's good." He liked the old man, and he liked the fact Pete kept an eye on Rocki.

"Pop invited you down for the holidays. He thought it was about time you met the whole crew."

Jax caught his sister's eye and smiled. Oh yeah, she was going to be pissed. "I'm out of here in two days and can't go back to work right away. Since Grace and Teddy are going on a cruise, that would be great."

Rocki's brows furrowed. "Since when?"

"Since we bought them the cruise for their Christmas present. I sent you the e-mail. They're heading over to Europe on the twentieth."

"Oh, well that was nice of us."

"I thought so. I was just going to hang out here alone since Rocki wasn't planning to come up, so this will be great. I'd love to spend the holidays in New York and meet all of your *friends*."

Rocki rolled her eyes.

He wondered if Slater realized he just handed Jax an engraved invitation to play concerned big brother and keep an eye on her and Slater.

"Jax, Slater has to get home soon. When do you think you'll be able to travel?"

"As soon as I'm discharged. I just have to come back in six weeks for another CT scan."

"Are you sure?"

"That's what the cute nurse said when she asked me out. I'm not allowed behind the wheel though—she offered door-to-door service."

Rocki held up her hand. "Please, I really don't want to know."

Jackson looked into his bag. "Hey, either of you have any extra ketchup?"

Rocki searched her bag. "No."

"Would you mind taking a run to the cafeteria and getting me some?"

She shot him a warning look but really couldn't get out of going. After all, a guy needed ketchup when he ate onion rings.

"Fine." She stood and looked from him to Slater and back, as though she was worried about the man. "Do you want anything while I'm down there?"

Slater looked over his half-eaten meal. "No, thanks, sweetheart. I'm good."

Teddy had said he checked out Slater—but then Teddy was a whole lot nicer than Jax was. After all, Teddy still thought Jax was a great guy. Maybe he was in some respects but when it came to dating—not so much. He certainly wouldn't want a guy like him dating Rocki.

Jax waited for the door to click shut before he began the interrogation. This first session would have to be fast—knowing Rocki, she'd be back in less than five minutes.

Rocki had been a mess since leaving Slater with Jax in his hospital room. Now that they were home, she was even more worried. Slater hadn't needed another grilling after the day he'd had, and if she knew her brother—and she did—he'd been waiting to jump all over Slater's case.

When she'd returned with the ketchup, Slater looked no worse for wear, but Jax was quiet—especially after she asked him if he was finished doing his impersonation of Colonel Klink.

Slater hung his jacket in the mudroom after depositing the empty beer cans into the recycling. He apparently spent the entire drive home counting to ten... over and over and over again. He put his arm around her and kissed her temple. "Rocki, I love you but you have to understand, I'm not some wet-behind-the-ears kid who can't handle a man-to-man talk."

She walked into the kitchen and grabbed a bottle of water. "Yeah, well, I'm not a teenage girl who needs her big brother to check out her boyfriends." She pretended the cap was Jax's neck and still couldn't rip the damn thing off.

Slater took it from her, cracked the seal, and handed it back before he grabbed another beer. "I know that, and you know that; unfortunately it's news to your brother. But, sweetheart, you don't need to protect me. I handled it, and then you come in like an avenging angel intent on rescuing me. Your brother didn't bother me. You thinking he could does."

"So do you have a rule book I can have a copy of? Because right now, I'm feeling pretty clueless. Oh, and if you're mad at me for what I said to my brother, you're going to be really pissed after you find out what I said to Storm."

He groaned. "You called Storm?"

"If someone upset me the way Storm upset you, wouldn't you want to blister their ears? And you might want to think long and hard about what you say now, because this conversation has all the earmarks of making you sound like a male chauvinist pig."

"Is it chauvinist for me to want to protect you?"

"No, but it's chauvinist for you to think that I don't want to do the same for you."

He shook his head. "There's no way I'm ever going to win this one, is there?"

"Nope, so you might as well concede gracefully."

"Fine, but you have to understand that I'm just a guy with the whole fragile male ego problem. We live to feel needed and we're protective of our women. If our women try to protect us, we get accused of hiding behind their skirts and that's a hard thing to overcome."

"So this is about male hierarchy?"

"Yeah, pretty much. We may have evolved but we still pound our chest—it's in the genes, sweetheart. And come on, admit it, you wouldn't want it any other way."

"Maybe. But you can't expect me to stand aside when I see someone taking potshots at you either. I might not pound my chest but I do believe in sharpening my claws."

"Right. I have a mental picture. What did Storm say?"

"Not much, the man couldn't get a word in edgewise. I reminded him that not too long ago he was the one freaking out, just driving through the Red Hook Houses, so he had no room to talk."

"Man, you're cruel."

"Only when warranted."

He tugged her toward the back stairs. "Come on, let's go to bed. I just want to hold you, make love to you, and forget the rest of the world exists for about eight hours. Can we do that?"

She looked into his eyes; he still had a shadow of that tortured look he'd worn since his conversation with

Storm. "Yeah, we can do that. But I'm not forgetting about your promise. We need to talk eventually."

"I know, but not now. Not yet. Right now, I just need to be with you."

Slater rose early the next morning, left Rocki sleeping, and headed downstairs to make coffee. He'd been up all night, wondering about his parents and thinking about Pop, Nicki, and Rocki. God, he was a mess.

He grabbed his phone and called his dad while he waited for the coffee to brew.

Pop picked up on the second ring. "I was just going to call you. Storm told me what happened. I'm sorry, son. I should have been the one to tell you."

"Why didn't you?"

"I was about to when Rocki ran in upset with the news on Jackson. I needed someone to take care of her and you were the only one available. I was going to tell you just as soon as you came home. It's not a conversation you have over the phone."

"Storm had no problem with it."

"Storm didn't know I hadn't gotten the chance to tell you. He loves Nicki. He's worried about her. He's worried about you and Rocki too."

"Why didn't you tell me as soon as you suspected. What the hell were you thinking?"

"I was thinking you needed time to get to know Nicki. You needed time to fall in love with her the same way we all did."

"Pop." Slater ran his hand through his hair, trying to clear his head. "I don't know how to be a father. You're the only father I remember. I don't know what it is, but I can't help but feel that Nicki would be better with anyone other than me. I wasn't cut out to be a dad."

"Slater, listen to me. You're going to be a wonderful father. Nicki already loves you. If I had any question about whether or not you could handle Nicki, I would never put either of you in a situation—I've seen the damage that can cause. I've raised you, I know you, and believe me, I have no question that you're going to be an incredible father if that's what you want."

"If you're right about Nicki's paternity, what I want is a moot point."

"Not necessarily—there are always options. Have you decided what you want to do?"

"I don't know what I want, but I know what I have to do. I'm going to do what needs to be done. I'm going to take a paternity test and go from there."

"Have you talked to Rocki about this?"

"She knows Nicki might be mine, but as for any plans, no, I haven't."

"Secrets are never a good thing—they make a relationship more like an obstacle course than a Ferris wheel ride. Now that Jackson's on the mend, it sounds as if it's a good time for you and Rocki to sit down and have a conversation. Oh, and as for the paternity test, all you have to do is go to a lab and have them swab the inside of your cheek—no needles involved. You can take care of it when you get home and we'll see if we can't put a rush on it. Still, it has to be done at an approved lab. That way it will be admissible in court if you ever have the need to fight Marisa for parental rights."

"That doesn't look like it's going to be an issue."

"It might become one if you sign the contract with OPEC that FedEx just dropped off. Money might not make a difference to the friends Rocki has made here, but if Marisa catches the scent of money, you can bet your ass she'll be circling like a shark at a blood bath.

Best to have incontrovertible proof that Nicki's yours. Do you want me to overnight the contract to you?"

"No, not yet. Let me see what's going on here first. I'll let you know."

"Okay. And Slater, I'm really sorry you had to find out this way, but I'm proud of you, son."

Slater only wished he could be half as proud of himself. He felt like a total failure as a man. Chances were he had a kid, a great kid, and the whole idea of it scared him more than anything in his entire life.

Slater had never been so happy to see Red Hook. Anything was better than being stuck in a car with Jackson Sullivan for six hours. "We're here."

He nudged Rocki awake and checked the rearview and spotted Jackson checking his e-mail again. The man's hand seemed to have grown around his phone.

"Jackson, Pop said you could crash in the extra bedroom. My brother Logan and his girlfriend, Skye, seemed to have worked things out and are staying in the other apartment, so Rocki and I will just go back to her place tonight." And not a moment too soon. He needed some time alone with Rocki.

Slater parked, carried Jackson's bag upstairs, and was greeted by the welcoming—or in his case, the not so welcoming—committee. Pop, both brothers, and their significant others were there. Shit. Storm and Logan looked as if they were sharpening their axes. Pop, Bree, and D.O.G. were the only ones happy to see him.

The dog barked and gave him a doggie hug and Pop boosted himself out of his chair. "Hey, you're home. How was the trip?"

"Long." He dropped Jackson's bag and looked around. "Where's Nicki?"

Storm mumbled something that sounded a lot like "Surprised he noticed she isn't here."

Slater chose to ignore the comment.

Pop stepped in front of Storm. "Nicki's spending the night over at Francis and Patrice's place."

"Isn't it a school night?"

"Yeah, but Patrice is taking her and the girls to Nicki's school tomorrow. Nicki's in a play and Patrice made her costume so she's going to see it with Cassie and Callie. I'd go, but I have a doctor's appointment that can't be rescheduled."

"I didn't know Nicki was in a play."

Pop looked surprised that he cared—what did Pop think he was, an ogre?

"She has the part of Gerda in *The Snow Queen*."

He'd never heard of it. "What time?"

"The information is on the bulletin on the refrigerator where it's been since you were in school."

Rocki and Jackson made their way in, so Slater turned to make the introductions. "Jackson Sullivan, this is Pete Calahan."

Pop shook Jackson's hand, "Good to finally meet you, son. You had all of us worried. I've never seen Rocki so upset. Do you want to get off your feet?"

Jackson laughed. "No, thanks. I've been off my feet for days. It feels good to stand."

Slater cleared his throat. "My brother Storm Decker and his wife, Bree, are over there by the kitchen, and my brother Logan Blaise is on the couch with his girlfriend, Skye Maxwell.

"It's nice to meet everyone."

Rocki made the rounds hugging everyone—even Storm. Bree played hostess. "Have you eaten already? I made sure to make plenty for dinner. Can I make you each a plate, get you something to drink?"

Slater nodded. "I'd love a beer. Jackson?"

"Water for me, thanks. I have to take my antibiotics and then if you don't mind, I'd like to crash. I'm sorry I'm not good company tonight, but the drive took a lot out of me."

Bree shot Slater the same look she'd always used when they were kids and she was about to boss him around. "Sure, not a problem. Slater, take Jackson's bags to the spare room and show him where everything is. I'll send Rocki in with the water."

Ten minutes later, he and Rocki were out the door. As soon as it was shut, he grabbed Rocki, pushed her up against the wall and did the one thing he'd been waiting all day to do. He kissed her, long and hard and deep.

So long and hard and deep he realized too late that he should have waited until they got to her place. Once he had a taste of her, he wanted to do anything but stop. The only reason he did was because he didn't think either of them would appreciate being caught making love at the top of the stairs, and his brothers were certain to come out of the apartment anytime. He removed his hands from her ass and backed off.

Rocki's eyes were wide, her lips were swollen, and her cheeks were flushed. "What was that for?"

"Think of it as an appetizer. I've been hungry for you all damn day, but I didn't think I could get away with making out with you in front of your brother."

"You're probably right." She took his hand and took off down the steps to the street. "How fast can you drive?"

Chapter 18

Slater watched Rocki take a sip of her coffee and stare bleary-eyed at him. "Are you sure you don't want me to go with you?"

"To Nicki's school play? Sweetheart, if your brother wasn't at Pop's apartment with a bunch of strangers, I'd say, hell yeah, but one of us should be there with him on his first day, and I have a feeling he'd prefer to see you."

She looked exhausted and he felt a twinge of guilt. It hadn't helped that he and Rocki had slept in her twin bed—though to say they slept was a real stretch. Slater soon realized that sleeping practically on top of each other wasn't conducive to sleep—it was conducive to making love. Not a hardship for him, but the lack of sleep was really catching up with Rocki.

"Take lots of pictures."

"I will."

"And tell her to break a leg."

"Okay."

"And give her back her lucky rock. She might need it."

"I will."

"Tell her if she gets nervous, to just picture the audience in their underwear."

What? "No way."

"Why? It works every time."

"I don't care. I don't want Nicki to picture anyone in their underwear—ever."

Rocki started giggling—something he'd never heard before. The woman had a great laugh, but he'd never heard her giggle.

He ended up taking her coffee out of her hands because she looked about ready to spill it. "What's so funny?"

"You are. You sound just like a father. My dad used to say I wasn't allowed to date until I turned forty." She wrinkled her nose. "Jackson obviously agrees with him."

Slater was beginning to appreciate exactly why Jackson didn't like him. He couldn't imagine liking anyone who might look sideways at Nicki—even if she were Rocki's age. "I'm thinking Nicki should join a convent. That whole chastity thing is suddenly very appealing."

"You're Catholic?"

"No, but I'd be willing to convert."

"Yeah, well, good luck with that."

He dropped Rocki off at Pop's and went to Francis and Patrice's place. He parked the car and headed up the walk.

The storm door flew open and Nicki was out like a shot, running right for him. "Slater! You're back!"

He caught her when she leapt into his arms and gave her a hug—at least someone was happy to see him. "How are you doing, squirt?"

"Great now that you're home." She wrapped her arms around his neck and pressed her cheek against his. "So, did my lucky rock work?"

"Yeah, Nicki. It worked great. Rocki kept it with her the whole time."

"See, I told you nothing bad can happen when you have my lucky rock with you."

He pulled the rock out of his pocket and handed it to her. "Rocki asked me to give it back to you in case you needed it today. I hear you're the star of the play."

"Not the star—I think the Snow Witch is the star, I'm just the hero."

"Heroes are stars too, Nicki."

He held on to her, not that he'd had any choice. The kid was a real monkey with her too-long arms wrapped around his neck. She smelled like Johnson's Baby Shampoo and peanut butter—her drug of choice. He waited for that weird feeling he always got when he saw her, and though it was there, it wasn't as overwhelming as it was the last time. Maybe he was getting used to her.

Patrice stuck her head out. "You two get back in here. It's cold and Nicki doesn't even have her coat on."

Slater smiled at Patrice and carried Nicki into the house. "Hey, Patrice, thanks for letting me go with you this morning."

He set Nicki down and Patrice wrapped him in a hug and kissed his cheek. Visions of Francis killing him made the already awkward hug even worse.

Patrice smirked at him and gave him a *get-used-to-it-buddy* look. "I'm just finishing up. Give me a minute and we'll go." She headed back to what he guessed was the kitchen.

He bent down to Nicki's height. "Is she always so affectionate?"

"You mean hugging and kissing and stuff?"

He nodded.

"Yeah, but don't worry about it. You get used to it after a little while."

"I don't think so."

"I didn't either, but then she hugs and kisses me every time I see her and every time I leave. After a while I realized I didn't hate it so much."

"I guess that's a start."

"That's what I thought too and she always smells real nice. Bree and Rocki too—they're all big-time huggers."

"So if you don't like hugging much, how come you always hug me?"

Nicki shrugged her shoulders. "'Cause like Storm and Logan, you're real big and strong but you need hugs as bad as I do. They're like medicine. You don't like taking it but it will make you feel better eventually—at least that's what Pop and Ms. Patrice say." Nicki tugged on his hand and gave him a commiserating look. "But until it starts workin' it's not fun."

"How long does it take?"

"Pretty long." She shivered. "But now, don't tell anyone, but it's kinda nice sometimes."

He tried to swallow the lump that seemed to have lodged itself in his throat like the hot dog he'd choked on once. "I can see that. Hugging you doesn't weird me out as bad as it used to."

Nicki wrapped her little arms around his waist, looking up at him, her chin resting on his chest with eyes so big and trusting and familiar. One look at her see-into-your-soul eyes and tenderness melted through him like warm syrup over pancakes.

Patrice stepped out of the kitchen with two little girls in tow and a knowing smile on her face. "Coats and hats on everyone." She shoved a bag against his chest. "Hold Nicki's costume."

"Got it."

Patrice took both her girls' hands. "Let's go."

Nicki grabbed his hand and pulled him outside the door. "Handholding is a big deal with Ms. Patrice too," she whispered.

"Yeah, I caught that. So you want to ride with me or with Patrice and the girls?"

"I'll go with you. I don't want you to be lonely." Nicki jumped into the back of the Jeep. He wasn't sure why, but didn't want to ask. He still had a lump in his throat over the whole hugging thing and that smile that felt like some kind of precious gift.

When they arrived at the school, he was left in the auditorium with Patrice's two kids. The three-year-old climbed on his lap and she and her big sister told him about their visit with Santa. Slater wondered if Nicki believed in Santa—hell, he wondered if she ever believed in Santa.

Patrice had gone to help Nicki get into her costume and didn't return until the lights lowered.

Once Nicki stepped on stage he was mesmerized. Nicki charmed everyone in the audience. For a little kid, she was amazing. Something welled up inside him and it took him a while to figure out exactly what it was since it wasn't something he felt often: pride. Bone-deep pride. The kid got a standing ovation and he had been the first one on his feet.

Patrice nudged his arm. "Your little girl did an awesome job there, Slater."

"Yeah, she did, didn't she?"

"Look at you. You're practically beaming."

Nicki came to meet them and he swooped her up in his arms. "You were incredible, squirt." He planted a big kiss on her cheek and watched a blush cover her face. "I'm so proud of you."

Nicki put her hands on his face and looked at him. "Really?"

"I don't think I've ever been so proud of anyone—ever." He gave her another hug, set her down, and watched all the parents with their kids, wondering if he stood out as a newbie. He didn't look much different from any of the other guys shuffling around the lobby—a little younger maybe, but hey, he had been just a kid when he and Marisa had hooked up.

Nicki stood beside him, holding Callie's hand. Nicki was small, but damn, Callie was tiny. If Nicki was his daughter—he'd missed so much. It hadn't bothered him before, but then when Francis and Patrice's chubby-cheeked little girl climbed into his lap earlier, he'd tried to picture Nicki at that age and drew a complete blank.

Nicki tugged on his hand. "I gotta go back to class now. Thanks for coming."

"I wouldn't have missed it, squirt." When she smiled, he realized he'd meant it. He didn't want to miss anything ever again. "I'll be by to pick you up this afternoon. Okay?"

"You promise?"

"Yeah, Nicki. I promise." He watched her get in line to go back to her classroom. She looked over her shoulder at him, smiled and waved, and just like that, he knew what he needed to do, and he was going to do it today.

Slater walked Patrice and the girls back to their car. Patrice buckled Callie into her car seat. "Slater, are you coming back to Pete's apartment with us? I promised I'd show him the pictures of Nicki's play."

Damn, pictures. "Good thing you were there. Rocki told me to take pictures and I forgot."

"You were too busy puffin' up. I swear you men are

somethin' else. You'd give Francis a run for his money in the proud papa department."

"You go ahead, I've got something I need to do. I told Nicki I'd pick her up after school. We'll be back after that."

Patrice's eyebrow rose but she didn't ask. "Okay, I guess I'll see you later then."

He waved her off and then phoned Pop.

"Hey, how'd Nicki do?"

"She did great. The kid might just have a future on the stage."

"Oh good, I'm glad to hear that. Nicki was nervous."

"Pop, where's that lab you told me about? Do they have Nicki's DNA?"

"It's on file. All you have to do is show up. I'll e-mail you all the particulars."

"You know how to e-mail?"

"Shit, son, I might be old but I'm not that old. I'll send it to you. Just give them the case number and tell them to put a rush on it."

"Will do."

"I'm proud of you, Slater."

"Thanks, Pop." Slater jumped into his father's Jeep and smiled, because now, at least, he could relate.

Rocki sat at the family table in the back of the Crow's Nest—they weren't open yet, not for another hour or so, but Skye had decided it was easier to cook breakfast for a crowd in the Crow's Nest kitchen than in Pete's apartment.

The mushroom-leek frittata she made was orgasmic and the fact that it was on Pete's diet was amazing.

Storm had been keeping his distance, which was fine with Rocki. He and Jackson talked boats all through breakfast, and last she saw, they were heading upstairs to check out the plans for a racing boat Storm had just designed.

Skye cooked, so Logan had been relegated to dish duty. It looked as if everything was back to normal with the two of them, since Skye was wearing an engagement ring. Another one down.

Rocki pushed aside the feeling of the last woman standing—or in her case, falling—and told herself she was not jealous. After all, she'd never once thought about getting married. She'd never thought she'd ever find anyone who would love her just for herself and not for her trust fund. But then she'd never met someone like Slater. To him, her money was more of a detriment than an asset. She didn't agree with that either, but maybe it was better that way.

She stared into her coffee cup and wondered when Slater would be back. It was weird; he'd dropped her off a couple of hours ago at most, and she already missed him.

"Oh, I've seen that face before—just not on you." Bree pulled up a chair and sat. "If it's this bad now, what are you going to do when Slater takes off for Bahrain?"

Rocki shrugged. She didn't know how much Bree knew about Slater's situation with Nicki, and as much as she'd love to talk to Bree about it, she didn't think she should.

Patrice flew through the door, waving her phone. "I just dropped the girls off so I'm free—for a few hours at least." She hurried over to the table. "You wouldn't believe how great Nicki was in her play!"

Bree moved over, making a spot for Patrice. "Let's see the pics. I was so bummed I couldn't go. Damn meetings."

Patrice held her phone so everyone could see and

flipped through the pictures. From Rocki's perspective, it looked as if Nicki lit up the stage.

Patrice sighed. "I swear Nicki stole the show. She didn't forget one line. You should have seen Slater. He had a smile so wide—it could span the Brooklyn Bridge."

Rocki scanned the restaurant. "Speaking of Slater, where is he?"

Patrice shrugged. "He said he had something to do. He was all hush hush about it—like it was supersecret or something."

"Supersecret?" He hadn't told her he was going out. But then she didn't know if that's what people did when they were seeing each other. It wasn't as if he had to check in with her or anything, but if she were going out, she'd probably tell him what she was doing. Maybe. Shit, she didn't know how to do this relationship dance.

Patrice turned her *tell-me-all* gaze on Rocki. "So spill."

Rocki looked up from her coffee. "Spill what?"

Patrice did her Cher hair flip. "All the details. And don't go pretending it's all casual between you and Slater—after you reamed Storm—that's not gonna fly, girlfriend."

"Yeah." Bree smiled. "I haven't seen Storm look so dazed since that night I hit him with the frying pan. It's really impressive you could get a reaction out of my husband with only the threat of bodily harm."

"You're not mad?"

Bree laughed but it wasn't a funny ha-ha laugh, it was a *you'd-better-talk-or-we'll-torture-you-for-a-long-long-time* laugh. "Are we mad that you kept a world of secrets from us, or that you threatened my husband's ability to reproduce?"

Guilt rushed over Rocki like a tidal wave. "Both, but mostly the first one."

Patrice rocked in her chair. "Rocki, look, we love you—you know that—and we've discussed this."

Of course they had. Knowing Bree and Patrice, they had a plan to extract information in the most efficient and possibly painful way.

"We realize that when you first met us, you didn't know who you were dealing with." Patrice ran her hands up her sides, framed her face, and did a little shimmy. "You had no way of knowing how absolutely fabulous we are. So okay, we understand why you didn't trust us enough from the get-go to let us in. But, girlfriend, that doesn't explain why we're just hearing about it now."

"Because if I had said something, I would have come off like either a liar, or a showoff or both." She sipped her cold coffee. "But mostly, I didn't want to change our relationship. Money changes everything."

Bree looked from her to Patrice. "I think that's a bunch of bunk. Frankly, I couldn't care less if you're rich as Roosevelt—"

"But you were weirded out with Storm and Thomas's friendship because the man owns a ten-million-dollar boat." Bree was so busted.

"So I had a few moments—mostly because I knew what kind of women Storm dated—women who were rich and beautiful—"

"Like me?"

"No, not like you. You'd never be the yacht-club, mean-girls type, no matter how much money you have."

"That's true enough. I never fit in and believe me, I went to school with women who were the very ones you feared."

"I know not everyone in your tax bracket is like that, but I imagined the ones he knew were. How does some-one like me compete with that? It was a natural fear. But

I got over it and you know I did, so you can't use that as an excuse."

"I was afraid and I saw no reason to complicate things. I've been happier here, living on what I make, being my own person, than I have ever been before. I love you guys."

"And we love you." Bree and Patrice said in stereo.

"I don't want to lose that. I don't want to stop shopping at thrift stores or going out and scoring deals at Macy's just because I can afford to pay full price."

Patrice nodded. "I totally get that—shopping is a sport."

"Exactly. Besides, I don't think of the family money as something that's mine. That's not how Jackson and I were raised. The family trust is a responsibility. Kind of like a family heirloom—you have to protect it, take care of it, and make it grow until you can hand it down to the next generation."

"So you can't spend any of it?"

"I could if I wanted to. I can't tell you how many of the girls I went to school with blew their fortunes. I just think that's really tacky and stupid."

"Totally." Bree nodded.

"Me, I stopped drawing from my trust fund after I got this gig. I wanted to prove I was able to make it on my own. I wanted to prove I'm more than just the balance of my trust fund."

Patrice went to the coffee station and brought a pot back, refilling their cups and taking one for herself. "So what do you do with all the money?"

"Jax and I have a foundation—the Sullivan Trust. We give a certain amount each year to worthy causes. I have my favorites—I like to give money to schools and rec centers in support of the arts, especially around here. I want to make sure the music programs aren't cut so I gift money earmarked to buy instruments, pay music teachers' salaries, and support after-school music programs. But other than that, I don't have much to do with it—"

Bree sucked in a breath. "The Sullivan Trust? You gave a grant to the Red Hook Revitalization Committee?"

Rocki shrugged. "I thought it was a great cause."

"I didn't know. Thank you."

"You weren't supposed to know. See"—she shook her head and threw her hands up—"now it's getting weird."

Bree let out an oh-please groan. "Dramatic much? It is not weird at all. I thanked you when you volunteered your time to help clean up the park and that wasn't weird."

"I don't have much to do with the trust or our investments. Jax is the numbers guy in the family and he deals with all that and sends me updates."

Patrice looked at her and then looked down. "So the reason you didn't tell us wasn't because you thought we'd turn into a bunch of moochers, was it?"

"No."

Patrice relaxed and then smiled. "Good. Now let's get to the juicy part. What's going on between you and Slater?"

"I don't know. He's wonderful but he's going through a lot of stuff and I was too. It wasn't a great time for either of us to get involved. We're just taking it a day at a time and we'll see how things shake out."

Patrice sat back. "Well, he's a hottie—he certainly doesn't look like he did when we were in school together. He was skinny and geeky and, well, now he could be on the cover of *Playgirl*." She stared at Rocki. "I'm right about that, aren't I? I mean I've only seen him with clothes on."

"Patrice!" Bree tried for indignation but missed the mark by a mile.

Patrice gave a halfhearted shrug. "You can't blame a girl for tryin'."

"All I will say is that nothing about the man is a disappointment."

"What, no pictures?" Patrice pouted, her lower lip sticking out just like Callie's did right before she threw a temper tantrum.

"It's not gonna work."

"At least Skye gave us the goods on Logan."

"Yeah, but we had to get her drunk first. Then we were on Logan's shit list for a week. I'm not going to repeat that mistake. No way. I have a feeling Logan is a whole lot more understanding than Slater would be."

"So he's the shy type?" Patrice's brows drew up.

"No, just private. Besides, I don't ask questions about Francis."

Bree shivered. "Francis is like a brother to me. The last thing I want to know is what he's like in bed."

Rocki laughed. "Slater's your brother-in-law but that's all right?"

Bree thought about it. "It shouldn't be, but strangely, it is. None of Pete's kids have ever been remotely sibling-like to me."

Rocki couldn't help but laugh. "I'm sure Storm would appreciate it if that changed."

"If what changed?" A deep voice had the three of them turning their heads. Storm. Too bad he missed the inquisition. Rocki wondered if the men talked about them the way they talked about the men. God, she hoped not.

Bree blushed furiously and that sent her and Patrice into a fit of giggles.

Jackson just watched with one eyebrow raised. "Maybe we shouldn't ask."

Rocki nodded. Jax was always the smart one.

CHAPTER 19

Slater snuck down the back stairs and heard Rocki doing her version of "Santa Baby." Her singing that song never failed to give him a hard-on—add to that the Naughty Elf costume she wore and he was toast. He stood in the hallway and watched her shimmy her way through the chorus. As if she felt his eyes on her, she looked over her shoulder and smiled when she saw him.

No matter when he came down, somehow she always knew he was there—as if she had some weird kind of radar.

He slid into their booth, waved to Wendy for a beer, and did his best to make Rocki forget the words. Damn, just one *I-can't-wait-to-kiss-you* smile added a little huskiness to her voice.

They'd been home a little more than a week and had fallen into an easy routine. Neither had done Christmas shopping so they went while Nicki was at school. Sometimes he and Rocki picked Nicki up from school together, sometimes he'd go alone, but he always went. Nicki would skip beside him and tell him all about her day. He'd thought he'd get tired of listening to her chatter, but he hadn't—the little squirt was a trip. One part innocence, one part streetwise, one part snark, and one part sweet.

Rocki usually joined them for an afternoon snack before he dragged Nicki upstairs to do homework, then, time and weather permitting, they'd take Nicki and D.O.G. to the dog park for a good run. He didn't know who got more exercise, Nicki or the dog. Just watching them tired him out.

Most nights dinner was a family affair; then Rocki would head to the bar and he'd go down after Nicki was tucked into bed.

Jackson fit right in with the clan—he was pretty good at doing his own thing even though he was never far from his phone or computer. But then the same could be said for him. The two of them had no problem hanging out, working on their own projects while Rocki played piano.

Rocki signed off, grabbed her water glass, straightened her little elf's cap, and headed to the bar for a refill. Bree slid into the booth. "You're not helping business, Slater."

"What? I always pay for my drinks."

"Yeah, but you're scaring off all the single men."

"Just the ones who bother Rocki." She was going to be the death of him. She had every man fantasizing about her shimmying on his lap. He should know. That was exactly where his mind went.

"Looking at Rocki and watching her perform is not bothering her. She doesn't need a bodyguard. She worked here for three years and the only man she ever went home with was you, and that's only because you practically forced her."

"I persuaded."

"Still, I'd appreciate it if you'd stop growling at the customers."

"What are you talking about?"

"You heard me. If someone even looks cross-eyed at Rocki, you get all puffed up. It's pretty cute actually. I used to think Storm was possessive, but you take it to a whole new level."

"I'm not possessive, just protective. There's a difference."

Bree raised an eyebrow. "The two of you are playing house and you're practically connected at the hip." She lowered her already deep voice and leaned in. "Are you still planning to take off for Bahrain after Christmas?"

"What are you, her mother? It's not bad enough I have to deal with her brother and Pop, I have to answer to you too?"

"I'm her best friend."

He didn't like it, but shit, he didn't want to get on Bree's bad side—the woman was scary. "I'm trying to renegotiate the deal with OPEC and I have to see what happens—"

"With the paternity test?"

"God, are there no secrets here?"

"What do you think? Nicki means a lot to every one of us. And believe me, I know you care about her. How can you help but love the little scamp?"

"I just want what's best for Nicki, regardless of what happens with the paternity test."

"If you're her father, you'll be what's best for her. If not, we'll jump off that bridge when we come to it."

"How do you know, Bree? God, I look at Nicki, and no matter how much I want it, the whole idea of parenthood scares the living crap out of me. It's like I have some unnatural aversion to it."

"That's natural—"

"No, Bree, it's not."

Maybe she heard the self-loathing tone in his voice, because when she looked up at him, her eyes went wide.

"I don't want to feel like this. It's not about the money I could lose. Look, I'd love to be rich, but hey, it hasn't made Rocki very happy. I know I could earn a decent living. I'm not that shallow. But it's as if every cell in my body is telling me to get away from Nicki for her own good. It's not that I don't care about her. I really do. God, I care about her so much it scares me." He ran his hands through his hair and shook his head. "I'm not making any sense."

"You're making perfect sense; you're scared. The only thing I don't know is why."

"I don't understand it either and I felt it the second I laid eyes on Nicki. And before you say it's about not being used to little kids, that's not it. I never get that weird feeling with Francis and Patrice's kids. Hell, I had Callie crawling all over me—I was fine."

"Is it getting better?"

"Yeah, but it's still there."

"Have you talked to Rocki about it?"

He shrugged. "A little. But shit, I feel like a heel. Here's this great little girl, and she might be my kid, and just looking at her scares me."

"Maybe she reminds you of someone. What did your parents look like?"

A flash of the monster shot to the forefront of his mind and he squeezed his eyes shut. "I don't know. I have no memories of them."

She looked at him and then drew a line through the ring of condensation on the table with her finger. "I think you need to talk to Pete. He's seen your file. Pete would know."

"That's what I'm afraid of. Maybe I'll talk to him, but not tonight. Hell, it's Christmas Eve."

"But you'll talk to him?"

Everything in him screamed no, but he didn't know what else to do. "I'll talk to Pop after Christmas." He had a feeling it would be a total mind-fuck, at least for him, and he didn't want to spoil his or anyone else's Christmas.

"Talk to Pete about what?" Rocki slid into the booth and leaned in for a kiss.

Slater scooted over against the wall to give her more room. "Business." He spent his nights and days wanting Rocki wrapped around him, except for now. Now, he really didn't want to be touched. "Would you excuse me?"

Rocki got up to let him out of the booth and bit her lip. Shit.

He shot her what he hoped was a *be-right-back* smile and headed to the men's room. He needed to get his head on straight. Damn, nothing but nothing made sense—he was really wondering if he was losing it.

Rocki threw herself back into the booth and grabbed Bree's hand. "What was that about? What did you say to Slater?"

"Calm down. We were just talking about Nicki. I didn't say anything—I just listened."

Rocki tried to relax her muscles that tensed the second Slater had moved away from her. "But he's doing great with Nicki. He adores her."

"I know that, and you know that, but Slater . . . something's bothering him and he's not even sure what it is. Something has him really scared and it sounds to me like it might have to do with his past."

"It has to be. He's had nightmares. He screams 'No' and the next thing I know he's on top of me shaking.

Like he's trying to protect me from a bomb or a bullet or something. It's like something out of the movies."

"He didn't mention nightmares but then he probably wouldn't have told you either if you hadn't lived through them. I just told him he needs to talk to Pete. Slater might not know anything about his birth family or how he ended up in foster care, but Pete sure as hell does."

Rocki wanted to hit her head against the back of the booth. She was a total washup as a girlfriend. Slater had never even told her what freaked him out so badly when he'd talked to Storm and she'd let him get away with it. She hadn't wanted to push him. "How come he can talk to you but he can't talk to me?"

"Because he's not in love with me. I'm his sister-in-law; he doesn't really care what I think of him."

"Yes, he does. He cares about everyone here. Even Storm and Skye."

Bree patted her hand. "Slater apologized to Skye and explained his leap to the wrong conclusion. Skye accepted his apology and she's fine with it. As for Storm— I think you had more to do with Storm's apology than I did, even though I told him he was dead wrong. He can be so stubborn. I think your threat held more water than a subtle nudge from his wife."

Rocki felt herself smile. "Yeah, well, we do what we can."

"It might be easier for Slater to talk to me because I'm not as close to the situation as you are. He's obviously in love with you and he's a man. Men are supposed to be big and bad and strong. They're supposed to rescue their women, not the other way around. It's stupid, but it's in their DNA."

"So he says. I swear, I need a copy of the *Dating for Dummies* handbook—actually the CliffsNotes would be good."

"You're always in such a rush. Some things take time, Rocki."

"That's the problem. I don't know how much time Slater and I have left. I thought I was fine with just fooling around with him—I wasn't prepared to fall for him. It's never happened before and—"

"Hey, it's not like he has his plane ticket and his bags packed."

"Bree, Slater never bothered unpacking. Except for buying a queen-sized bed because the two of us didn't get much sleep in my twin, he hasn't made one move to make things permanent."

"That you know of. Maybe he's waiting until he knows what's what. No need to get your hopes up if all his plans are dashed. He's working on figuring things out. Just be patient."

"Right. And what the hell am I supposed to do in the meantime?"

"Just love him, talk to him, and be supportive. That's all we can ever do. If it's meant to be, it will work out."

"And if it's not?"

"Then you'll get over it."

"Like you got over Storm?"

"Rocki, you're the bravest person I know. Life is too precious to waste time the way I did. If the worst happens, you'll do what you always do. You'll pick yourself up, brush yourself off, and use what you learned in your next relationship."

"Wow, that's encouraging."

"It's a real possibility, but I don't see that happening. Slater doesn't want to leave you any more than you want to leave him. Just be patient, put a smile on your face, and move over. He's on his way back."

Bree got up and took her empty glass. "I'm going to

head out. I guess I'll see you two in the morning. Text us when Nicki gets you up."

Rocki gave Bree a hug good-bye and slid into the other side of the booth. "Did you get Nicki's bike all put together?"

Slater nodded. "I have it in Rex's office. Once you're done here we can put the presents around the tree."

She'd really been looking forward to doing that, but now, not so much. "Do you still want me to stay with you on the pullout in Logan and Skye's place?"

"Don't you? My back isn't looking forward to it; I've actually slept on that torture rack before. But I don't want to miss Nicki's first Christmas with us."

"First Christmas?" *First* insinuated that they would have more than one. She sure hoped he was right.

Slater rested his forearms on the table and leaned toward her. "I love the costume, Rocki. I just don't love the way other guys are looking at you, like they want to lay you under their tree and unwrap you. Couldn't we keep some of these costumes to ourselves?"

"It's a naughty-elf costume, but not that naughty. It's Christmas Eve, Slater. Don't be such a Grinch."

Chaos—that's the only way Slater could describe Christmas morning with the Crow's Nest family. Everyone showed up to watch Nicki open her gifts so they ended up having to take the party down to the bar. There just wasn't enough room in the apartment.

Their family had expanded exponentially and, damn, there were a lot of people and even more presents. He doubted Nicki had ever dreamed of hauling in such a bounty.

Of course, Nicki's favorite present was the bike he bought her—a Schwinn Sprite—black with splashes of purple, pink, and orange, a basket, and even a horn. Very cool. Unfortunately, her size didn't come with training wheels. He did have the forethought to buy her a helmet, wrist guards, elbow pads, and knee pads, thanks to Rocki. He even considered padded-butt biker pants but they didn't come in her size and Rocki said no woman any age would ever wear something that expanded the size of her ass. Fashion always outranked pain. Rocki did insist on color-coordinating the ensemble though.

Nicki raced over to him, her neon Vans slapping against the hardwood floor. "Can we go now, Slater?"

She'd been asking for a trip to the park to learn how to ride since five o'clock that morning. She actually lasted longer than he'd expected. "Yeah, we can go. Ask Rocki if she wants to come with us."

Nicki ran off to find Rocki. Five minutes later they appeared and Nicki looked like Nanook of the North.

Slater took one look at her and laughed. "Did Bree do that to you?"

He thought he caught a nod, but it was hard to tell. Nicki wore her new coat, hat, scarf, and gloves.

He got up and put his mouth close to where he hoped her ear was. "Don't worry. We'll unwrap you once we get in the car. I've already loaded your bike." He'd bought a bike rack so they didn't have to put down the back-seat.

"Can we take D.O.G.?" Even her voice sounded muf-fled. "He wants to see me ride my bike."

He gave Rocki a *what-do-you-think* look.

Rocki put her hands on Nicki's highly padded shoul-ders and squeezed. The poor kid probably didn't even feel it. "Sure, why not? He's been cooped up all day. A run would do him good."

Five minutes later they were on their way to Prospect

Park. Nicki had one arm around D.O.G. and bounced in her seat. She was so hopped up on sugar, it was amazing the seat belt held her down.

Slater held Rocki's hand in his the whole way there—a habit he'd had since their drive to New Hampshire—and parked in the biggest parking lot he could remember. It was on the east side of the lake and was thankfully deserted.

They left the dog in the car while Slater took Nicki's bike off the rack.

Rocki fit the helmet to Nicki's head and put on the rest of her safety gear, making her look like a little purple Michelin Man.

Slater adjusted the seat and held the bike as Nicki climbed on. "Okay, you pedal forward to go. It has coaster brakes, so all you have to do is press back lightly on the pedals to stop."

"Okay." Nicki looked like she was doing a math problem. She screwed her face up in concentration, biting her tongue. Where had he seen that before?

He shook his head. Shit, it didn't matter. "Okay, Nicki, start pedaling and I'll run along beside you. Just circle around the parking lot."

"You're not gonna let go, are you?"

"I'll let you know before I do, okay?"

"You promise?"

"Promise. You're gonna be great." Slater held on to her seat and her handlebars to get her going and then let go of the handlebars. The kid wobbled a little, and the first turn was a little iffy, but man, once she hit the straightaway, she was off. He had a hard time pacing her. "You got it, Nicki. I'm gonna let go, but I'll try to stay with you."

"Okay."

He had to really run to keep up. She took an easy

curve around and headed back toward Rocki. "I'm riding! Look at me!"

Rocki had a huge smile on her face and D.O.G. was pulling for all he was worth to get to Nicki.

"Slow it down, squirt. Just lightly press back on the pedals."

Nicki didn't seem to know the definition of the word lightly and locked up the back wheel.

Slater caught her and the bike right before she tipped over. "Lightly, Nicki. That wasn't light, but it was effective. Remember, when you stop, you have to put a foot down so you don't fall."

"I didn't fall."

"You would have if I hadn't been here to catch you."

"Maybe, but I knew you would catch me. I wasn't scared."

"That makes one of us." Maybe this bike wasn't such a good idea. The kid was fearless.

Rocki and D.O.G. ran up to them. "Nicki, you were awesome. Good job. You too, Slater."

"Thanks. Can I go around again?"

Slater rubbed his hands together. "One more time around and then let's get our gloves on and take D.O.G. for a walk. Do you want help getting started? That's the hardest part."

"No, I want to do it by myself. Just, you know, stay close by in case I fall—at least until I'm going real fast, okay?"

Slater blew out a breath. At least he'd work off all the junk he ate today. It was hell having a chef in the family. He stood beside Nicki, adjusted her pedals for an easy start, and got ready to run.

Nicki had a few wobbles at the start but she had great balance so she corrected it and then really took off.

Slater tried to keep up with her, but stopped once she made it around the first turn. He walked back to Rocki and watched the kid ride like the wind around the parking lot. He tried to get her to stop but she breezed right by him.

"Just one more time around, okay?"

He was afraid to tell her no. If she slammed on the brakes, he wasn't sure he could catch her. "Okay, but coast in and then brake lightly." He wrapped his arms around Rocki, who was shivering.

"She's a natural. Look at her go."

He rested his head on hers and stood there just drinking in the happiness. Even the dog had a goofy grin on his face. "This is nice."

"It's the best Christmas I can remember."

"Yeah, I think so too."

Nicki came in a little fast, but stopped without killing herself—or them. "That was epic!"

She jumped off the bike and forgot to put the kickstand down before throwing herself into Slater's arms.

He caught both Nicki and the bike.

"Slater, this is the bestest present I ever ever got. Thank you."

"You're welcome. And you did great. But next time, don't forget the kickstand." Slater put the bike on the rack and locked it in. "Come on, let's take D.O.G. for a run and then we'll go home and get some hot chocolate, what do you say?"

D.O.G. heard the word *run* and made his intentions clear.

Slater looked around—no one was there, so he let D.O.G. off the leash. D.O.G. and Nicki took off, and he and Rocki followed at a more sedate pace. He yelled, "Nicki, stay away from the lake."

"Okay."

Nicki disappeared through the trees and Slater walked faster and kept his eye on her purple jacket.

He caught a glimpse of her tossing a stick for the dog and settled back into a walk.

"D.O.G. No! Don't go on the ice!"

As soon as Slater heard Nicki cry out he took off at a run. His heart double-timed against his ribs. Damn! He should never have let her out of his sight. "Nicki!"

He raced through the trees, just as he heard what sounded like a shot. His adrenaline went into overdrive and a memory, so real, so crystal clear, so Technicolor, it blasted his senses like a 3-D Hitchcock horror flick — the kind that leaves you awake for months. The kind that has you looking over your shoulder when you walk alone. The kind that leaves you in a cold sweat on a sweltery summer morning.

His mother holding him behind her while the monster — God, the monster was his father — held a gun to her head. "NO!"

Nicki's scream cut the vision. D.O.G. ran for shore.

Nicki turned, took another step, and fell through the ice. All he could see was her head.

He dove onto the ice and slid on his belly. "Nicki!" He edged toward the hole. "Nicki!"

Hands clawing the icy edge. Purple lips. Wet, stringy hair freezing in the cold air, and puffs coming from her mouth. Her eyes filled with terror. His mother's eyes. His mother's terror.

"Slater!" She reached for him; and like the creature from the black lagoon, Nicki stood — water lapping at her waist.

He grabbed her, dragged her along the ice with him, and once he hit shore, he picked her up and ran to the car.

Her teeth were chattering and she shivered so violently her body convulsed. He couldn't lose Nicki. God, he couldn't lose her too.

Rocki ran after them. "Slater?"

He stripped Nicki out of her wet clothes as fast as he could, dragged his shirt, sweatshirt, and jacket off and pulled them over her quaking body.

Rocki caught up with them, just as Slater put Nicki in the car.

He was mumbling, his eyes wild, and he shook—of course he was half naked—but she had a feeling it wasn't just from the cold. He looked as if he was going into shock.

He tossed her the keys and paced behind the car. "Get the heat on."

Nicki was crying. "D.O.G. Where's D.O.G.?"

"Fuck the dog. Get in the car. Rocki, drive to the hospital." Slater clenched and unclenched his hands almost as if he wanted to punch something—or someone. His face was ashen, his eyes haunted, as if he'd witnessed the horrors of Auschwitz—or lived through it. Rocki grabbed his arm.

He shook her off as if her touch electrocuted him and stepped back. Rocki counterstepped to his movements without touching him and locked him in her gaze.

"Slater, look at me."

His eyes came into focus when she dropped her voice and projected like a barrel-chested drill sergeant berating a new recruit on the first day of boot camp. "You need to calm down. You're scaring Nicki. You take the keys, start the car, and get the heat going." When she saw the nod, she turned her attention to Nicki. She reached into the back of the Jeep and touched her face. "Hey, sweetie. How are you doing?"

"C-c-cold."

"We'll get you warmed up real soon."

D.O.G.'s bark was close by. Tears streaked Nicki's face. "I'm s-s-s-sorry."

"Shh, hush now. You're okay."

The dog pushed past Rocki, jumped into the car, and laid his head against Nicki.

Rocki pulled the seat belt around Nicki's little shivering body and clicked it into place.

"Slater, get in the passenger's seat. I'm driving."

She grabbed her phone as Slater got out of the car, and speed-dialed Pete. "Meet us at Methodist Hospital. Nicki fell through the ice—I think she's gonna be okay. It's Slater I'm worried about. Hurry." She ended the call, got in the car, and took off.

It had been years since Rocki drove—but she figured it was like riding a bike. Of course, she'd never driven a car this large before so she went over a few curbs—Slater didn't seem to notice. It looked as if he were in some kind of freaky trance, gripping the dashboard and staring off into space.

"Slater, are you okay?" Nicki's teeth chattered between syllables.

Rocki glanced at him. There was no reaction; the man didn't even blink. She caught Nicki's eye in her rearview. "Nicki, honey, Slater loves you, and he just got really scared when he thought you were hurt. That's what grownups do when their kids fall through the ice."

Rocki kept one eye on the road and one eye on Slater with an occasional glance back at Nicki through the rearview mirror. She was pretty sure Nicki was going to be just fine after she was wrapped in some warming blankets. Slater, on the other hand, looked like he'd just gone to hell and back and lost his luggage.

She reached over to take his hand and he startled so badly, his head hit the window. God, he was out of it. "It's going to be okay, Slater."

He looked at her as if he'd just discovered the bogeyman really did exist and she was it. She wanted to comfort him, but she didn't dare touch him for fear he'd throw himself out of the speeding car just to get away.

Rocki kept up a constant stream of chatter for Nicki's benefit, asking her questions; afraid she too might go into shock.

Nicki answered through tears while D.O.G. whined beside her.

Rocki broke just about every traffic law between the park and the hospital and was amazed there wasn't a fleet of cop cars following her. She skidded to a stop at the emergency room and found Francis waiting. She'd never been so happy to see anyone in her life.

She jumped out of the car. "I'll take Nicki. You deal with Slater. Physically, I think he's fine. But there's something wrong. He's probably in shock. Be careful. He doesn't want to be touched."

Rocki got Nicki, and closed the door on D.O.G. "Come on, baby, let's get you all warmed up."

"I want Slater."

"I know, baby, but Slater needs to talk to Francis. You'll see him in a little while. I've got you now."

CHAPTER 20

Slater heard the fighting. God, they were always fighting. Fighting about him. Slater's back still stung from the last whipping he'd received. Momma had put something on it, gave him Tylenol, and put him to bed early. "Don't leave your room, baby," she'd cooed. "Just stay here. Momma's gonna handle it."

But then Momma screamed and sounded scared. He snuck down the hall to the living room, being really super quiet.

He wiped the sleep out of his eyes and saw his dad—he'd turned into a scary monster again.

Momma's scream made him feel sick, his back hurt where his shirt stuck to his cuts, and tears stung his eyes, but he couldn't cry. If he cried, the monster just gave him something else to cry about.

The monster held Momma by the hair—her long brown curls hung like a horse's tail. Momma's eyes were wide. She saw him and waved him away, then clawed at the monster's face.

The monster screamed and threw her into the wall.

Momma crumbled like one of his block houses when he drove his fire truck through it.

"No! Momma!" Slater tackled the monster's legs. The monster picked him up by the neck and threw him. He landed hard, tasted blood, and rolled over, crawling backward to Momma.

The monster raised his arm and pointed a gun at them.

Slater heard a shot and then felt like someone kicked him. He fell back, felt the heat and searing pain.

Another shot rang out, echoing in his ears.

He yelled but made no sound. He reached out for his mother and turned his head. Momma's face was covered in red. He tried to scream, to cry, to move.

The monster put the gun in his own mouth and pulled the trigger. He hit the wall, sliding down to the floor, leaving a bright red stripe.

Slater tried to breathe and heard bubbles popping. He liked bubbles. The room got dark and quiet.

"Slater, it's Francis. You with me, Slater? Can you hear me?"

"Nicki." Nicki had his mother's eyes and Slater had the Monster's.

"Nicki's gonna be just fine. Can you get out of the car, buddy?"

"I gotta get to Nicki."

"Rocki's with Nicki. Let's get you inside. I'm just gonna open the door, real slow. Okay?"

"Yeah. I gotta make sure Nicki's okay."

"She's gonna be fine, buddy. Let's get you inside and have you checked out. You're cold and wet."

"I'm fine. I need to save Nicki." Slater got out of the car and had to hold on until the world stopped spinning.

"Nicki's being taken care of—Rocki has her." Francis

put a blanket or something around him, pushed him into a chair, and through the doors.

The next thing he knew he had a blood pressure cuff on one arm and an IV in the other. He hated hospitals. He remembered now. He'd been in one for a long, long, long time. He'd been all alone and scared.

"How you doing, son?" A hand squeezed his shoulder but didn't let go.

Pop? Slater opened his eyes. Pop looked fuzzy and pale. God, everything was so distorted. "Pop, Nicki—"

"Nicki's fine. You saved her. She's perfectly fine."

He saw Nicki's face and it kept morphing into his mother's. "No. I watched her die. Momma died because of me. She told me to stay in my room. She told me to stay away, but I didn't listen."

"Slater, look at me."

He tried to focus on Pop's face.

"That was a long time ago, you were just a little kid. It wasn't your fault. He'd already written a note. He'd planned it. You did not cause it. If you hadn't walked in on it, he would have shot you in your bed."

Slater's face was wet, his heart raced, and he felt sick. "The monster killed my mother. I saw it. I remember everything." He remembered the scent of terror, the hate pouring out of the monster, the metallic taste of blood.

"I know, Slater. I know. God, son, I'm so sorry."

Slater rubbed his chest. "He shot me. He tried to kill me."

"You're okay and he's dead. You're okay."

The cold sweat of fear covered him. The tangy taste of bile rose in his throat, and the weight of guilt settled in his chest. "How can I be okay, Pop? That monster was my father."

"No, I'm your father. That man was no father to you,

son. You're mine. You've been mine since the day I saw you. You'll always be my son."

"The monster is in me. I know it. I feel it. It's always been there just waiting to come out."

"No, son. There's nothing of him in you. I know you. I love you. You're nothing like that madman. You're no monster."

"I'm tired. I need to see Nicki, Pop. I need to see her."

"I'll see what I can do. You rest. I'll be back."

Slater closed his eyes; he felt a big hand on his forehead, then a kiss.

"I love you, son."

Love? How do you love a monster?

Rocki ran from Nicki's bed to find out where Slater was as soon as Bree and Storm came and relieved her. Nicki was fine. She was cold and shaken, but that was to be expected. It couldn't be any fun to fall through the ice, even if it was in just a few feet of water. The kid had gotten soaked and she was half frozen, but it was Slater's reaction that had scared Nicki the most.

Rocki turned the corner and almost ran into Pete. She took one look at him and the tears she'd been holding back and the terror she'd been ignoring hit her at the exact moment her adrenaline bottomed out. She walked into his open arms and completely lost it. He wrapped her in a bear hug and held on while the tidal wave of emotion ran over her. "Where's Slater? Is he okay?"

"They've sedated him. He's going to be fine." Still the worried look in Pete's eyes told her he wasn't so sure.

"What happened to him?"

Pete took her hand. "Come on, let's go get a cup of coffee and talk."

Rocki pulled away and wrapped her arms around herself. Slater had seemed unreachable and that scared her more than anything since her parents' deaths. "I don't want to talk. I want to see him. I have to. He can't be alone. You don't understand what he's like in hospitals."

"Yes, I do." Pete wrapped an arm around her and nudged her toward the cafeteria. "They have enough drugs in him to sedate an elephant. He's not going to know he's alone until he comes out of it."

Rocki leaned into Pete and allowed him to shuffle her along. Before she knew it, she sat at a corner table with a cup of coffee in her hand, and stared at Pete who looked pale. "Okay, talk."

Pete raked his hand through what was left of his hair. "Slater went through hell when he was just a little tyke, and then he was in the foster system for almost seven years before I got him."

"He told me. He doesn't remember much. He doesn't remember his parents and has only vague memories of the houses he's lived in."

"Yeah, well, that changed. He remembers everything."

"Is that good?"

"I don't know. I'd have been happy if he'd never remembered it. The shrinks told me that he'd eventually remember when he was strong enough to handle it. I didn't think anyone was that strong—apparently I underestimated Slater."

"What did he remember?"

"When things like this happen, the person remembers it like he's experiencing it for the first time. He sees it through the eyes of the victim—in this case, through the eyes of a five-year-old little boy. It takes a while to be able to extrapolate the memory and be able to look at it through the eyes of the man he's become."

"What did he remember?"

"When Slater was five—"

Rocki pictured a smaller, lighter, male version of Nicki and realized that Nicki and Slater had the same smile.

"He walked into the living room, interrupted a fight between his parents. His father shot him—"

The sound of the ocean filled her ears; she wasn't sure she heard Pete right. "Shot him?"

Pete nodded.

"Oh my God—that scar on his chest is a bullet wound." Sweat beaded on her hairline, tears filled her eyes, all the air left her lungs, her heart hurt, and bile burned the back of her throat.

Pete nodded. "Slater watched as his father shot and killed his mother, and then turned the gun on himself."

Now she knew she was going to be sick—and the way her stomach dropped, it was going to be bad. She would have warned Pete but she couldn't speak.

"Slater was the only survivor. He was in the hospital for weeks."

How does one survive that? It was horrible losing her parents, but it was an accident. She couldn't imagine how Slater was going to go on now that he knew. Rocki looked for a ladies room but it was too far away; she'd never make it. She took off through the doors to the courtyard and emptied her stomach by a bush.

When she finished, Pete handed her a napkin and a bottle of water. "That didn't go well. I'm sorry."

Rocki gulped air, trying to stop the flow of tears—tears for the little boy Slater had been and for the man he was now.

Pete pulled her into his arms. "He'll be okay. It might take some time, but he'll get past this."

"Pete, how? How the hell do you get past something like that? Those were his parents."

"I'm his father, dammit, and that's what matters. That monster, as Slater calls him, was nothing more than a sperm donor. I raised that boy. He's strong, he's successful, he has you and Nicki. He has to come through this. It's just going to take some time, Rocki. He's going to need all of us."

"I couldn't reach him."

"Look, he thought Nicki was going to die in that lake. That fear obviously triggered the rest of it. Now he just needs time to process it."

"What if he can't? How can someone process something that horrific?"

"I don't know, but the human mind is amazing. Look at all the survivors of the concentration camps."

"Slater was a baby. He was Cassidy's age." Nicki thought of Francis and Patrice's oldest daughter, Cassidy, going through something like that and almost lost it again.

Pete patted her back and held her. "He might have been Cassidy's age then, but he's not now."

Rocki sat beside Slater on a hard plastic chair and watched him sleep. She didn't know what they'd given him, but he hadn't so much as stirred in the last four hours.

She'd spent more time in hospital rooms lately than she ever wanted to. With as much time as people sat and waited in these chairs, you'd think they could at least make them comfortable.

The door pushed open and Rocki wiped the tears off her face.

Jackson stuck his head in.

Rocki stood and motioned for him to be quiet, then

walked right into his open arms and started crying again. God, she wished she could turn off the waterworks.

He pulled a hanky out of his pocket and held her chin in his hand, just like their father had every time he'd dried her tears. "Are you okay?"

"No, I'm not going to be okay until I know Slater is."

"I'm sorry, Rocki. No wonder he always looked so freaked out at the hospital. He's not going to be happy when he wakes up here." He pulled a chair close to hers and sat, crossing his long legs at the ankle and held her hand in his.

She just wanted Slater to wake up, but then part of her wished she could get him home before he did. She pictured him sprawled out in their new bed with her draped over his chest, listening to the comforting beat of his heart. She wanted to wiggle her nose and transport them to Chinatown but that wasn't going to happen. "How's everyone at home?"

Jackson smiled and shook his head. "Man, Rocki, you've been talking about these people since you moved here, but I always thought you were exaggerating. You weren't. If anything, they're even tighter than you led me to believe. Storm is a mess—I guess he lit into Slater before we came back and is now regretting it big-time."

"He should."

"It looks as if the guilt is eating him alive."

It seemed that Jax had more sympathy for Storm than for Slater and that didn't sit well but she didn't say anything—it wasn't worth fighting about.

"Patrice is clucking over everyone. Francis is running roughshod over the kids and grumbling about sleeping on the couch for life if he pisses Patrice off. Skye is cooking—"

"She cooks when she gets nervous."

"Bree is organizing. She sent me over to your place to get a change of clothes for Slater." He held up the bag. "How long do they think he'll be out?"

"I don't know but I'm staying. He can't wake up alone—not after what happened."

"Would it be better for Pete to be here?"

"No. Slater needs me and I need him. God, Jax, I'm so scared."

"After you see him, do the guy a favor, give him some space, Rocki. He has a hell of a lot to deal with. He might not want you around when he's doing it."

"What? That's just bullshit."

"No, it's not. It just goes against what you want. Guys are different. We like to lick our wounds without an audience. He's not going to be able to take care of you and get his head straight at the same time."

"I don't need taking care of. He does."

"No, he doesn't. He needs to deal with his baggage and that's a one-man job. The last thing a guy like Slater's going to want is you treating him like an emotional cripple."

"I wouldn't do that."

"You wouldn't be able to help yourself. Shit, Rocki. You're a fuckin' force of nature—you're going to take a battering ram to whatever walls he puts up for self-protection. You always do."

"I love him."

"Yeah, well, you might just have to do it from a distance, because, little girl, there's nothing you can do to fix this. It's all up to him."

"I don't want to fix him."

"Rocki, I love you and I know you better than you know yourself. You spend your life fixing things and people or at least trying to. Pay attention to the signals. If he pushes away—give the man space. I imagine he's going to feel like a caged tiger at the zoo. Everyone's going to be watching him deal with something that no man should have to. If it were me, I'd get as far away from everyone I knew as fast as I could, and then I'd lock myself in a hotel room and deal with the fallout on my own."

"You're not him."

"I know, but he's a strong, proud man. He's spent his life alone for a reason—hell, if I'd gone through what he did, I would have too."

"You've spent your life alone, Jax; what's your excuse?"

He stood up and shook his head. "Oh no, there's no way I'm getting into this with you. I'm fine. It's you I'm worried about. I'm going to crash at your place tonight. I think the family would appreciate some space, so head over to Pete's when you're done here. Everyone's worried about you. Patrice left some clothes for you in my room. She said you'd have everything you need."

Rocki stood and wrapped her arms around her big brother. "Thanks for coming down."

"Call me if you need anything. I'm just going to check on Nicki before I leave. They say she'll be released in a little while. She's a lucky little girl."

"No, we're the lucky ones. God, if anything had happened to her—"

He shook his head. "Don't do this to yourself. She's fine. She's as tough as her father is."

Rocki just raised an eyebrow.

"Shit, Rocki. I knew the minute I saw her. She's her daddy's daughter—the resemblance is amazing. She's got his nose, his smile, his hair, and his walk."

"Slater didn't know about Nicki until the day you came out of your coma."

"I figured that out all on my own. Slater might be a lot of things, but he's not a the kind of man who would shirk his responsibilities."

"No, he's not. He loves Nicki."

"She's a hard kid not to love. Bree asked me to bring her a rock. Why, I don't know, but I wasn't about to ask any questions."

"Yeah, okay. Give her my love when you see her."

"Call me if you need anything. No matter what time."

"I will. I just need Slater to wake up."

Jax kissed her and held her tighter. "Remember what I said. If he pushes you away, you need to give him space. If you love him, you'll let him deal with his shit the way he needs to—even if it doesn't include you. If you really love him, you'll give him that."

Slater rolled over and felt a tug on his arm. His eyes shot open. Where the hell was he?

"Slater, it's me, Rocki. You're okay, you're in the hospital."

Shit, everything was so blurry. He felt drugged—hung over. Something happened, something bad. "Nicki?"

"She's fine, baby. You saved her. She wasn't hurt, just cold and wet. They're releasing her soon."

Nicki was okay. Rocki was here. She called him baby in the sweetest voice. He smiled. Momma used to call him baby. He remembered her kissing him good night. "Don't leave your room, baby. Just stay here. Momma's gonna handle it." God, he remembered and when the pain hit, it stole his breath.

"I'm here, Slater."

He looked at her, but she was blurry, either from the drugs screwing with his vision or it could be the tears he was trying to look through. "Rocki?" He pulled her right up on the bed, wrapped his arms around her, and cried like a fuckin' baby.

She cradled his head against her chest. "It's okay. I have you."

She smelled like Rocki, like heaven, like home. He'd never needed anyone so badly it scared him. He did his best to stifle his sobs. God, he was acting like a pussy.

"I'm okay." He wiped his eyes on her shoulder so he could look at her.

"I'm not. I need to hold you."

Shit, she was crying. What kind of guy cries all over the woman he loves and doesn't even notice she's bawling too? "I'm sorry, sweetheart. I'm so sorry."

"For what? For being a hero? Slater, you saved Nicki. You kept it all together until she was safe."

"I'm no hero. It was my fault she was in danger in the first place. I almost lost her. She could have died."

"Nothing is your fault and Nicki is just fine."

He couldn't look at her. "I remembered everything, Rocki."

"I know. Pete told me. I'm so sorry, baby, so sorry."

He blinked back more fucking tears. He had to get his shit together. "I'm okay now." He wanted to hold her forever, but pulled away. "You'd better get off the bed before someone comes in."

She held his face in her hands and looked into his eyes and by the look on her face, she'd seen it all. Questions, sympathy, love, and fear.

"Don't look at me like that."

She looked confused and adorable and hurt—God he'd rather kill himself than hurt her.

"I love you."

For her sake, he wished she didn't. She'd be better off without him. She should run as fast and as far away from him as she could get, but he didn't have the balls to tell her that. He needed her. Right now, he'd take what he needed. Tomorrow . . . he wasn't so sure. He couldn't think straight. There was only one thing he was certain of, there was only one thing he could promise her— something she should know. "Rocki, I'll love you for the rest of my life."

CHAPTER 21

Pete opened the door to Slater's room and stuck his head in, holding Nicki back by her collar.

Rocki was on the bed and she and Slater were wrapped around each other.

"Rocki." Slater's voice was low and pained. "I'll love you for the rest of my life."

Shit. Pete knew that tone and it sent dread running through his veins thick and heavy and hot like lava burning everything it touched. He was losing his boy—they all were. There was no question, the only question he had was if Slater would ever come back.

Slater kissed Rocki with a desperation Pete had never seen. He let the door close without a sound.

Nicki tugged on his sleeve. "Pop, I wanna see Slater."

Nicki looked up at him, her big brown eyes showed every emotion. She squeezed the teddy bear Jax had bought her to her chest, held her lucky rock in the same hand, and tugged on Pete's with the other.

"Slater's okay, just give him a minute with Rocki."

Nicki leaned against the wall and groaned. "Are they kissing again?"

"Nicki—"

"Gosh, Pop. They could be doing that for hours. I just don't get it. How come it's okay for them to kiss each other but it's not okay for me to kiss D.O.G. At least I keep my mouth closed. They don't—I seen 'em. It's kinda gross."

"Nicki—"

"Okay, I'll shut up now."

"And whatever you do, don't talk about the kiss. Okay?"

"Sheesh—even I know better than that. Slater's in the hospital. I'll just file it away in my arsenal for later."

Pete laughed. "Do you even know what the word *arsenal* means?"

Nicki rolled her eyes. "It was a vocabulary word. Ms. Patrice helped me with it. She said she's got an arsenal too—but hers is full of shoes and handbags and lipstick—she really loves lipstick. Ms. Patrice said those are female weapons."

Pete groaned. What the hell was he going to do with Patrice? Then he laughed. It was Patrice—no one could do anything about that woman. He wasn't sure if he pitied Francis or envied him.

He'd had about all he could handle of Nicki's fascinating commentary, so he knocked on the door and slowly pushed it open, keeping Nicki behind him. "Can we come in?"

Nicki broke out of his hold and ran for the bed, jumping up and throwing her arms around Slater. "You okay, Slater? I didn't mean to scare you so bad. I'm sorry."

"I'm okay now that you're here. But if you ever go out on the ice again without permission, I swear you'll be grounded until you're my age."

"Like I'd ever do that again. I was so scared. But then you were there and I knew it would be okay. You fix everything—even when I mess up bad."

"God, Nicki, what if I couldn't get to you? You could have died. You took ten years off my life."

"Huh?"

"You scared me to death, squirt."

"I'm real sorry. D.O.G.'s sorry too. He didn't know any better—he's just a dog."

"It's okay. I'm not mad at D.O.G. either."

Nicki settled her head on Slater's chest and closed her eyes. "When are you coming home?" she asked in a little voice.

Pete rubbed his eyes. Damn, he knew that voice too—tears weren't far behind.

"I don't know, squirt. I just don't know. But Pop's gonna be there and Logan and Storm."

"But I want you."

Pete saw the plea in Slater's eyes and the tears he held back. Pete cleared his throat. "Come on, Nicki. It's time to get you home and tucked into bed. You heard the doctors."

"Can't I just stay here with Slater?"

Rocki rubbed her back. "No, baby. But I'll stay with Slater and make sure he's okay. You need to go home and rest."

She turned her big brown eyes on Slater. "Please, Slater, tell them I can stay."

Slater kissed her forehead. "It's against the rules, squirt. You go home with Pop and behave. I don't want to have to worry about you, okay? Can you do that for me?"

Tears rolled off Nicki's cheek onto Slater, but she nodded. "You'll come home soon, though, right?"

"As soon as I can, Nicki. Now give me a kiss and go wait out in the hall with Rocki. I need to ask Pop something."

"Is it supersecret?" she whispered.

"Yeah, squirt, it's supersecret."

"You'll tell me later, right?"

"Maybe."

"All right. Here." She handed him her rock. "You need this worse than I do. I can lend you my teddy bear too. Jax gave him to me for being brave, but you're way braver than me. Besides, I have teddy bears at home."

"Thanks, Nicki. I'll keep the rock with me, but you'd better take your teddy bear. We wouldn't want to hurt Jax's feelings."

"I guess not."

"Now give me a kiss and go on out with Rocki so I can talk to Pop."

Nicki gave him a big hug and a kiss on the cheek and then whispered something in his ear.

Pete watched Slater squeeze his eyes shut and blow out an unsteady breath.

"Me too, squirt, now go on, get out'a here." He looked over at Rocki. "Take her outside, sweetheart. We won't be long."

Rocki shot Slater a questioning look, hit Pete with one too, then took Nicki by the hand and led her out.

Slater waited until the door clicked shut. "Pop, you gotta take Rocki home with you."

"And how do you propose I do that?"

"I don't know. But she can't be here. Please, Pop. I can't have her here."

"Are you sure, son? Rocki's not going to understand."

"Maybe not, but at least she'll be safe. I need to know Rocki and Nicki are safe."

Pete pulled Slater into a hug. "You might not believe it son, but the safest place for Rocki right now is with you. I'll take her home, but know this: You will never be a threat to that young lady. Take all the time you need to figure it out. Until then, the only threat you pose is to yourself."

Rocki kept it together for as long as it took to get back to Pete's. She slipped up the back steps, ran into the room and lost it royally. She sobbed and sobbed and sobbed. Once she finished, she called Jackson.

"Hello?"

The sobbing started all over again.

"Are you at Pete's?"

"Yes."

"Are you bleeding?"

"N-n-no"

"I'll be right there."

It took a half a box of tissues for him to get there.

Jax walked in, pulled her onto his lap, and held her like he used to when they were young. "He had Pete take you home, huh?"

"He didn't even say good-bye."

"Rocki, give the guy a break. How could he say good-bye to you without breaking down? Honey, he loves you. He's afraid, he's confused, he needs space, but he loves you."

"I know but when he told me . . . He said he'd love me for the rest of his life—he didn't say he'd spend the rest of his life loving me—there's a difference. A big, big difference."

"Give him time. He's a smart guy; he'll figure it out. Have some faith in him."

"What if I lose him?"

"Why do you think I'm single? I'm not as brave as you are." Jax hugged her close and rubbed her back.

She didn't know when it happened, but she must have cried herself to sleep. She awoke with a big dog in her bed and a little girl standing next to her.

"Rocki, I got scared. Can me and D.O.G. sleep with you?"

"Sure, baby, crawl under the covers." She held the blankets up for Nicki and pushed the dog down to the foot of the bed. "Did you have a bad dream?"

"I dreamed that Slater went away and I couldn't find him. I kept calling for him and he never came. I got so scared."

"I know, baby." Nicki was a perceptive little girl—Rocki had the same feeling, so she didn't want to tell her it wouldn't happen. "Slater loves you. Even if he's not here with us, he'll always be in our hearts."

"I don't want him in my heart. I want him here."

"Yeah, me too."

Nicki snuggled up close. "Is he gonna leave because of me?"

"No, baby. Slater needs some time to deal with a grown-up problem. Men are different, when they have problems, they go into their caves to figure things out."

"What do girls do?"

"We eat chocolate, talk to our best friends, and shop." She thought she should leave out getting stinking drunk. Nicki was only ten after all.

"Where's Slater's cave?"

"I don't know, but it's not a real cave. It's just a place where he can be alone to brood."

"Yeah, Storm told me about that. Boys brood and girls cry."

"You can cry if you want to, Nicki. I have tissues, and I know where Bree keeps her stash of chocolate."

"You do?"

"I certainly do. We can have a little girly picnic. But D.O.G. can't have any."

"'Cause he's a boy?"

"No, because he's a dog. Chocolate makes dogs sick."

"Okay."

"And no smudges on the sheets."

Nicki smiled. "That would just be a waste of good chocolate."

"Exactly. Maybe tomorrow, you and I can go out for some retail therapy. Think of all the after Christmas sales."

Nicki's face screwed up into a complicated knot.

"What's wrong?"

Nicki shrugged. "I don't have any money. And really, everyone bought me so many presents and stuff, I don't need anything and I don't want to ask Pop for money. It doesn't seem right."

"That's okay. Let me tell you a little secret."

"Do you want me to pinkie swear not to say anything?"

"We can if you want. But I trust you, Nicki."

"You do? Okay, what is it?"

"I have lots and lots of money, so we can go on a shopping spree on me."

"You're rich? Like Scrooge McDuck?"

"No, not that rich."

"How come it's a secret? Mr. Thomas is rich—he's Scrooge McDuck rich, but instead of a helicopter he has one of Storm's boats. A super-big boat—but he doesn't try to keep his money secret."

Rocki shrugged. "It sounds stupid, but I wanted to make sure everyone liked me for me, and not because I have money."

Nicki leaned back against the pillows. "You're right, it sounds stupid. No one here would do that. If you were mean or something, it wouldn't matter how much money you had, they'd still not like you. Look at Logan's old girlfriend, Payton. She's rich and we couldn't stand her. Logan said she was a good person, but I didn't think so. I think she was a big meanie."

Yeah, Nicki was a real smart little girl. Rocki slipped out of bed. "You stay here. I'll get the chocolate. Do you want a glass of milk?"

"Yes, please. Oh and can you bring a cookie for D.O.G. so he doesn't feel left out?"

"Sure thing, I'll be right back."

Rocki shook her head. Nicki was so much like Slater it hurt. If Slater left, it would be hard to be around Nicki. If Slater left, it would be even harder to lose Nicki. At least she'd have a little piece of Slater in her life. If Slater left, Rocki wouldn't be the only casualty.

Jax stepped out of the shower and picked up the phone, his heart jackhammering like the guys ripping up the sidewalk two doors down. The last several calls he'd received had all been bad news and he had a feeling this one wouldn't be good either. He answered while dripping all over Rocki's bathroom. "Hello?"

"Jax, it's Pete."

Jax wrapped a towel around his waist.

"I need you to do me a favor."

"What do you need?"

"Can you bring me Slater's duffel bag and anything he left at Rocki's. I think his computer is here."

"It is. This doesn't sound good, Pete." Jax put the lid down and sat, holding his head in his hand. It sounded as if Slater was rabbiting.

"It's not. But there's nothing we can do. This is a road Slater has to walk, and for some reason, he thinks he needs to go it alone. He checked himself out of the hospital."

"Shit."

"He thinks he's doing what's best for Rocki and Nicki."

"Rocki's a mess."

"I know. This is hard on everyone. I need to fill Storm and Logan in on what's going on."

"They don't know?"

"I probably should have told them last night, but I just didn't have the stomach for it. It would really help me out if you could take Rocki and Nicki to breakfast— get them out of the house for a few hours."

"I'm happy to help. I'll get dressed and head over after I get Slater's things together."

"Just bring them to the bar, son. I don't want to upset the girls."

"Okay, but one of us is going to have to tell Rocki."

"I want to talk to Slater first and see how he's doing."

"Sure, just keep me in the loop. I'll keep the girls occupied."

"Thanks, Jax. It means a lot to me. Rocki means a lot to me too. She's like another one of my kids. I hate to see her upset."

"Let's just hope Slater gets his head together and doesn't do something stupid."

"From your mouth to God's ears."

"I'll be there in under an hour."

He made the trip to the Crow's Nest in no time. Packing for Slater was as easy as zipping the guy's duffel. He obviously hadn't made himself at home. He was definitely military—everything was neatly folded—probably regulation. The man traveled light, which was another bad sign.

He dropped the bag off with Pete, made it to the apartment, and found the girls curled up together asleep like kittens in a basket. D.O.G. opened one eye and then rolled over using Rocki's feet as a pillow.

Jax remembered the way Rocki woke up every day after their parents died. She'd open her eyes, smile, and then she'd remember. He would see the black veil of pain cover her face. He didn't know how to stop it. He couldn't stand seeing it. He did the only thing he could do. He made her laugh. Shit, he hadn't done this in years but it looked as if he was going to have to resurrect his stunning performance of The Blob. He just hoped it still worked.

He crouched at the foot of the bed and started the sound effects—the guttural beat of a heart. When Nicki opened her eyes, he made a funny face and oozed onto the bed. Rocki awoke, heard him and found Nicki grinning from ear to ear.

Rocki feigned a B-flick scream queen, but couldn't stop her laughter. "Nicki. Help! It's—"

"The Blob." He strung out the word till he ran out of air, holding his hands in the air like a bad impression of Boris Karloff's mummy. He felt dumb. He pushed D.O.G. off the bed and started his sideways roll over them.

"Jax!" Rocki yelled. "You're heavy!"

"The Blob is coming for you." He grabbed Nicki and tickled her until she was fighting for breath.

Rocki beaned him with a pillow, and then Nicki got into the act and bedlam ensued. D.O.G. jumped around barking.

Nicki laughed so hard, happy tears streaked her face, and Rocki tackled him.

Shit. Rocki knew all his ticklish spots. He finally yelled uncle and ended up lying in the middle of the bed with an arm around both girls. Once he caught his breath, he gave them each a kiss on the forehead. "I'm here to take my two favorite ladies to breakfast. How fast can you get ready to go?"

Nicki shot out of bed. "I gotta ask Pop."

"Already done."

"D.O.G. needs to go potty."

"I'll walk him while you and Rocki get dressed."

"Okay!" Nicki tore out of the room.

"Brush your teeth, Nicki," Rocki yelled before turning her gaze to him. "Okay, what's going on?"

"Do I have to have an ulterior motive to want to take you out to breakfast?"

"No, but you do. I just want to know what it is. Is something wrong with Slater?"

"Nothing that wasn't wrong with him last night—at least as far as I know."

"Don't lie to me, Jax."

"I'm not." Okay, he wasn't telling her everything, but as far as he knew, Slater was no more screwed up than he had been last night. That was the truth at least.

"Nicki doesn't need to be hanging out in the apartment missing Slater. I thought you two could take me around the city today."

"Well, we did talk about going shopping."

Jax smiled. Shopping he could do—it might kill him, but he'd do anything to keep a smile on their faces. "It just so happens that I have an American Express Platinum Card burning a hole in my wallet. I never did get to buy you a Christmas present."

"Only Platinum? I thought you'd go Black."

"Rocki—I'm not that pretentious. Besides, it costs seventy-five hundred dollars a year just to have one."

"You're pretentious, but you're also cheap."

"I'm a fund manager. I make money and I spend it, but I hate to waste it."

"I guess I should get ready."

"Yup. I'm thinking we should hit FAO Schwartz, Toys R Us, and maybe Tiffany."

"And shoe stores—you know how much I love shoes."

Shoes. He groaned inwardly. God, she was really going to kill him—and make him pay first.

Slater stood outside his hotel, counting the cracks in the sidewalk. He ignored the rumble of the elevated subway down at the end of the block, inhaled exhaust fumes, and waited for Pop. He scrubbed his face with his hand, thinking he should shave. His beard was getting itchy, but then the rest of him felt itchy too. It felt as if he were about to crawl out of his own skin.

He needed to get his computer. He needed to do serious research. He needed to know where he came from, who he came from, why his own father hated him so much—he'd murdered Slater's mother and tried to kill him.

Pop stopped beside him, dropped Slater's duffel and messenger bag, and leaned against the same graffiti-covered wall Slater was holding up. "You couldn't find a dumpier hotel?"

"I wanted to make sure you wouldn't tell Rocki where I was."

The look on his father's face screamed disappointment. Slater just wished he could feel enough to be ashamed, but he didn't have it in him today. He was numb. Maybe it was from the cold, but he had a feeling it was from pushing Rocki away. She took his heart, and without one, a guy might live, but it made feeling anything more than pain difficult.

"All you had to do was ask me not to tell Rocki, son. I'd respect your wishes. Why don't I call my buddy and get you a room at the Millennium? At least they have room service."

"No, Pop, I'm fine."

"You'll get bedbugs here."

"I've had worse."

"Slater, I don't ask much—"

"Fine." God, he didn't want to hear a sermon, but Pop had that look Slater had seen a million times—the look that was always followed by a lecture. "Call your friend and give me the address, but if Rocki shows up, I'll leave."

Pop put a hand on his shoulder and it was all Slater could do not to shrug it off. Pop was already upset— Slater saw it in his face. He didn't want to make things worse for anyone—that was why he had to get away.

"Son, I'm not going to put Rocki in a position to be hurt any more than she already has."

"I'm not hurting her. I'm protecting her."

"I know that's what you think you're doing. That's the only reason you're still standing. You're making a huge mistake. I know it in my bones, but there's no way you'll believe me. I just hope you come to your senses before it's too late."

A lump formed in Slater's throat that no amount of swallowing could reduce. "I don't know what to believe. Pop, I lost my temper once. I went after some asshole beating on his own daughter. I wanted to kill him and if I hadn't been nine years old, I would have." Shit. The lump filled his throat as if he were intubated. Every time he tried to swallow, he fought the urge to gag. He'd spent the last twenty years afraid he'd turn into a murderer. He'd been capable of it at nine. He was more than capable now. Knowing that, knowing that his own father was a killer, told him every fear he'd ever had was warranted.

"You would have been justified. I read the report. That man deserved whatever you did to him. He went to jail for child abuse a year or so after you were pulled out of that house."

Slater sucked in a breath and met Pete's gaze. "Was Kendra okay?"

"She lived."

Slater rubbed his eyes. He'd been remembering so much, his brain was flooded with Technicolor horrors. It was like the dam broke and feelings and images rushed through every part of his past, breaking down all the walls he'd built, destroying everything in its rapid descent to the bottom. He just wished he knew when he'd hit the floor. His head pounded, his heart raced, his fingers tingled with pins and needles, and beads of sweat popped out on his forehead even as a chill ran through his entire body.

"Slater, you're not a nine-year-old boy protecting a little girl from a man three times your size. You're a grown man. You're the man I raised. You're in control."

"I almost lost it when Storm accused me of mistreating Nicki." He dragged a hand across his brow and squeezed his eyes shut. "If he had been in front of me instead of on the phone, I don't know what would have happened."

"You would have beaten the snot out of him. But you wouldn't have hurt him. I saw you and Logan go at it, remember? You pulled every punch, hell, you let him pummel you."

"I deserved it."

"Maybe, but you were in control."

"I'm not now."

"No." He pursed his lips in irritation. "You're right. You're letting a ghost control you." He spoke slowly, as if Slater's IQ had been cut in half. "That's your problem. I hope you bury that bastard where he belongs and have a happy, fulfilling life just to spite him while he rots in hell."

"I'm not letting anyone control me. I'm trying to get control. I'm doing my best, Pop."

Pop's shoulders dropped and he widened his stance, rocking back on his heels. "You're not in this alone. You have me, your brothers, Rocki—"

"God, don't do this." Slater ran his hand through his hair and gave it a tug, then paced to the curb, turned and paced back, stopping right in front of Pop, meeting his gaze. "You can't fix this for me." Spitting the words out around the lump lodged in his throat was painful. He swallowed and tried not to lose his coffee. "You can't make it go away. No one can. I just need to learn to live with it. I need to understand what happened. I need to find a way to move past it."

"Love heals all wounds, son."

"Now you're quoting the Bible?" Slater wanted to bang his head against the brick wall; it would do more good than arguing with Pop.

Pop gripped his shoulder again and squeezed. If he wasn't mistaken, Pop was fighting the urge to cuff him upside the head. Not that he didn't deserve it. "No, if I were to do that, I'd tell you that *love bears all things, believes all things, hopes all things, endures all things . . .*

It's in Corinthians. Check it out smart-ass. They'll probably have a Bible in your room." Pop released him and stepped back. "Go to the Millennium in Times Square. Jerry Schmidt will have a room waiting for you. All I ask is that you contact me once a day and let me know how you're doing."

"And whatever I say won't be repeated to Rocki?"

"You have my word." Fire flashed in the old man's eyes and Slater wished he hadn't had to ask.

"Okay, I'll talk to you tomorrow. Remember, take care of Rocki and Nicki and don't tell them where I am."

"I've been taking care of my girls long before you got here. I don't need you telling me what to do, especially since you're doing such a piss-poor job of it yourself." Pop gave him another disgusted look, then walked away.

Slater rubbed his chest. Okay, maybe he could feel shame after all. Fuck.

CHAPTER 22

Pete had had some rough days as a parent, but the last two were ones for the *Guinness Book of Parenting Nightmares*, and the future wasn't looking bright and sunshiny.

He thought that once the kids were grown and out of the house, his job would get easier. Shit. Was he ever wrong.

He stared across the bar at Storm and Logan's desolate faces and cursed the man who had caused his boys so much pain.

It was bad enough that Slater had to live with it, but telling Storm and Logan made it even worse. Pete would have kept it to himself, but they were grown men—something he kept reminding himself—and they had to be told. Slater needed them. Maybe they'd knock some sense into him. Lord knew, nothing Pete had said worked.

For the last sixteen years, Pete had prayed every morning that Slater wouldn't remember, and he'd gotten down on his arthritic knees to thank God every night that Slater hadn't. Tonight though—if he survived this little shindig—he and God were going to have words.

Storm looked about ready to hurl. "His father shot him? That scar on his chest is a bullet wound?"

Pete just nodded.

Logan sat down hard on the barstool.

Pete looked at his watch; it was barely ten a.m. Aw, the hell with it, it had to be noon somewhere. He pulled his bottle of Macallan 18 off the top shelf and poured them each four fingers. They were going to need it. He sure as hell did. "Where is Bree?"

Storm eyed the bottle. "She went with her mother to return the clothes that didn't fit Nicki."

"Good." Pete slipped his hand into the V of his sweater, pulled out a stogie, and lit it.

Storm shook his head. "Man, you're really asking for Bree to come down on you like a woman PMSing and having a bad hair day at the same time — which is exactly the kind of day she's having."

PMS, his ass. The woman was pregnant. Of course, she hadn't figured that out yet, but he saw the signs. This wasn't his first rodeo. He'd already started a name-the-birth-date pool with his buddies.

Storm gave him that *I-know-my-woman* superior smirk and continued. "It's gonna get ugly, and don't think you're hiding behind me when she comes after you with the cast iron."

"Don't worry about me, son. I've been dealing with your wife for a lot longer than you have. I've got it down to a science." Although a pissed-off, pregnant Bree was an unknown. Still, a man deserved a cigar on days like this, dammit.

Logan was still processing things. The poor kid had no memory of his parents either. He and Slater had that in common at least; now Logan was probably wondering if his father was a homicidal maniac too. This was just getting better and better.

They each took a belt of scotch.

Logan stared at the bottom of his glass; Lord only knew what he saw. "Slater's dad shot his mom in front of him?"

"Shot her in the head. It was a messy crime scene. It wasn't even in my precinct but I remember hearing about it. It's a miracle Slater lived. God was watching over each of you boys."

Storm let out a sarcastic laugh but knew better than to say anything.

"Slater checked himself out of the hospital this morning."

A look of surprise widened Logan's eyes. "Is he upstairs?" He stepped away from the bar.

"No. He's staying at the Millennium in Times Square." Slater told him he couldn't tell Rocki, but he never said anything about his brothers. "Rocki can't know or Slater said he'd leave. That means we can't tell any of the women."

Storm looked pissed. Good. "Why in the hell didn't he just come home?"

"Because he's afraid—" Shit. Tears filled Pete's eyes and his heart broke a little more. "His father lost it and killed Slater's mother and damn near killed him, but not for lack of trying. He's not feeling emotionally stable right now, and he's scared to death he'll hurt Rocki or Nicki."

Storm blanched and sat hard, almost toppling the stool. "God, it's my fault." He rested his elbows on the bar and pounded his fists against his forehead. "I accused him of mistreating Nicki. I didn't know."

Pete reached over and grabbed Storm's joined hands. "Look at me."

Storm lifted guilt-filled eyes to his.

"Slater took it the wrong way. You had no way of knowing how he'd interpret it. It's not as if you knew his history."

"Thanks, Pop, but shit, I can't let myself off that easily. I crossed the line. I sure as hell knew we didn't end up in foster care because we came from stellar families."

"No, but there aren't many who have had as bad a time of it as Slater."

Storm shook his head, looking paler by the minute. "I'd have given anything to have Nicki for a daughter—both of us would—and there's Slater. I thought he found out he might be the father of this amazing little girl and a few hours later, runs away to New Hampshire. I was pissed. Nicki deserves better than to have both her parents run out on her."

Okay, so maybe Storm deserved a little guilt. "I told Slater to take Rocki home. She was so upset about her brother's accident, she was in no shape to go anywhere by herself."

"Yeah, I got that from Rocki once she stopped chewing on my ass long enough to ream me out."

Pete blew out a breath. "So you fucked up. Go out there and talk to him."

Logan drained his second scotch. "And say what?"

"Tell him you're on his side. For God's sake, you've been there. You two boys know better than anyone what a nightmare the foster system can be. It can't be that huge a stretch to put yourself in Slater's shoes. He needs to know you trust him not to go postal. He needs to know that he's not the monster his father was." Pop pointed at Storm. "Any more than you're an abusive husband because your father used you and your mom as a punching bag." He aimed his finger at Logan. "Or that you're going to abandon your child because you were dumped by your parents."

Storm set his drink down and shot Pete a *get real* look. "Will he even talk to us? You know how he is. He's probably got his head so buried in his computer, he won't notice we're there."

"Shit, boys, I don't know. I hope to God he listens to you because nothing I've said to him can get through that thick skull of his."

Storm looked at Logan and both nodded. "Okay, but we're going to need ammunition."

"What's that?"

"A bottle of 1812, a bottle of Macallan, and a bottle of Jack."

Logan got up and headed toward the storeroom. "Oh, and cover for us with Skye and Bree."

Pete smiled and snapped his rag on the bar. "You got it." He tossed Logan the keys to the storeroom and finished setting up. "I love you boys. Call me if you need me and even if you don't."

Slater stuck his key card in the door, dumped his duffel on the bed, and prayed Pop hadn't forgotten to pack his shaving kit. He needed a shower, a shave, and about ten hours of sleep sans nightmares.

He tugged the zipper on his duffel, stuffed his hand in to feel around for his ditty bag, and pulled out an accordion file. He saw his name on the cover and opened it. His case file. Shit. He didn't know if he wanted to kiss Pop or strangle him. He tossed it on the bed, sat beside it and, elbows on knees, tried to breathe. His chest felt as if someone had parked a car on it, and not a smart car either—more like a Hummer.

He looked at the folder and forced himself to pick the damn thing up. It wasn't going to get any easier to look at. He opened the thick file and blinked, trying to muffle his inner voice screaming for him to burn it. He felt as if he were standing on the edge of a cliff with a raging wildfire licking his back—he had to either jump onto jagged rocks, or be burned alive. It was a sucky versus suckier situation. He just wasn't sure which was which. Still, he couldn't live in this weird state of limbo because his ass was getting burned either way.

He dug through the crypt of his life and ignored the ring of his cell phone. He ignored the knock at the door. He ignored the incessant ringing and flashing red light on the room phone. He ignored the fear, the urge to flee, the pain stealing his breath.

The description of the crime scene had him heaving.

He was raw and scared and felt as if he were doing his best to exorcise his demons and praying it worked because he couldn't imagine living through this again. He wouldn't. He couldn't.

He pulled a picture of his momma out of the file and it was as if he was caught in a freeze-frame. He remembered her scent, the sound of her voice, and the way he'd climb onto her lap, lay his head against her breast, and listen to her heartbeat mingling with the sound of her voice while she read him books. He remembered the hugs, the kisses, playing in the park. He remembered having picnics on the kitchen floor in the middle of winter and pretending they were on Coney Island in the summer. He remembered her singing "Baby, Mine" to him every night after they said prayers, and he remembered praying. Praying for his father. Praying his business would survive. He hadn't understood what that meant, but said the words while he prayed the monster would go away. He remembered when he stopped praying.

He picked up a copy of the suicide note, not ready to deal with that. The bastard had it planned—that's all Slater needed to know at the moment.

The door opened and slammed against the wall and his brothers stormed the room like Ghost Busters.

Slater dropped the note. "What the hell are you doing here?"

Logan held up the key card. "Pop had to call his buddy to get us in. Why didn't you just open the door?"

"Because I wanted to be alone, you idiot."

Storm leaned against the wall holding the suicide note Slater had dropped. "He's wallowing."

"Fuck you!" Slater got in his face, shaking with rage. "Get out."

"Make me."

Logan put a hip on the dresser, set up a makeshift bar, and poured tequila. "Got any ice?"

Slater's head whipped around. "What?"

"Ice. You know, frozen water."

"No."

"Fine, I'll get some." Logan looked as if Slater hadn't threatened to rip Storm and him a new one. "Do you want a Coke to go with your Jack?"

"No, I don't want a fucking Coke. You need to leave. Both of you."

Logan just shook his head like he would to Nicki, refusing to hear her plea to stay up late. "You want us to leave, you're going to have to make us. It's two against one." He smiled and rubbed his hands together. "Should be fun. I don't have a problem rearranging your face. Again."

"You only did it the last time because I allowed it. You couldn't fight your way out of a wet paper bag."

Storm stood behind Slater. "Maybe Logan can't, but I sure as hell can. So here are your options. We can sit down, have a drink, and talk about this, or Logan and I can beat the crap out of you, sit down, have a drink, and talk about this. Your choice."

If he took the two of them on, he could toss them out—after he retrieved the other key—and then have a drink by himself—or a bottle.

Storm walked around him, "Oh, and Pop asked his friend Jerry to give you a room slated for a remodel in case we break anything."

Shit.

Logan raised an eyebrow. "I'm going to get the ice and maybe we can order room service. I'm kinda hungry. How about you?"

Storm the human garbage disposal just grinned. "I can eat."

Slater fisted his hands so hard, his almost nonexistent nails cut into his palms. "Okay, what's it going to take to get you guys out of here?"

Storm crossed his arms and leaned back against the wall, still holding that damn suicide note. "We'll leave once you prove to us you're not going to do anything stupid. It might take a bottle of Jack for you to do that."

Logan shook his head. "Don't forget room service. I'm hungry."

Storm went over to the bedside table and picked up the phone. "Slater, what do you want?"

"For you to leave."

"I'm talking food."

"Nothing."

"Okay, I'll get the usual." Storm ordered while Logan went to get ice.

Slater had to get that suicide note away from Storm. If he did, he'd just pick up his duffel and leave. He didn't need to stay there. But Storm had the note and he knew Slater wouldn't leave without it.

Big rare steaks and baked potatoes were delivered. Drinks were poured, and Logan and Storm settled in with their backs to the door. If he was going to leave, he was going to have to go through them and get the note.

Storm cut into his steak. "So, what's the deal?"

"I thought Pop would have told you."

"I want to hear it from you."

Slater reached over, picked up the file, and handed it to him. "I don't want to talk about it. You might want to finish eating before you open it—either that, or just stop eating now."

Storm raised an eyebrow. "That bad?"

"I lost my cookies, but then, it could have just been because it was my mother who ended up with her brain matter splattered all over the room."

Storm swallowed hard and pushed his food away, crossing his legs and resting the file over his lap.

Slater just concentrated on his food and tried to forget what his brother would read. If he was going to be drinking, he needed to fill up. He hadn't had much to eat since yesterday morning. The nurses had tried to get him to eat dinner and breakfast at the hospital but he just couldn't.

Slater cut into the perfectly cooked steak and took another bite. His gaze returned to Storm. He looked like one of those guys you see in Central Park impersonating statues, standing so still you can barely see them breathe. They change position and freak out whoever is nearby. One scared the hell out of Nicki when he and Rocki took her to the ice rink to skate.

Storm hadn't said a word—unusual for him. Logan had always been the quiet one—Storm, not so much. In the last few minutes Storm's face took on the character- istics of shrink-wrap. His skin clung to his bones, making him look almost gaunt, his cheekbones standing out in sharp relief, the color seeming to bleed from his face. Slater supposed he should feel sorry for the guy, but he didn't. No one forced him to look at his file. Storm chose to stick his nose into Slater's nightmare. He could deal with the consequences.

"Storm? Are you going to eat the rest of your steak?"

Storm didn't answer him; he just pushed his plate far- ther away.

Slater stabbed the meat with his fork and brought it over to his own plate. No sense in wasting good food.

Logan leaned toward Storm, took a closer look at the file, swallowed hard, and pushed his plate away too.

Slater had eaten his fill and, after a quick look at his brothers, figured it would be safer to 86 the rest of the food before someone spewed. He put the dishes on the room service cart and rolled it out to the hall, wishing he could take off. When he went back in, Storm was looking even worse. "If you're going to hurl, make sure you hit the can, man."

Neither Storm nor Logan said anything. Yeah, that damn file left him speechless too. So maybe they wouldn't do any talking after all. He wasn't sure he could handle talking. Not now, not ever, not about this.

Storm took the picture of his momma out of the file and looked at it for a long time. He handed it to Logan and then put the file away.

Slater let out a breath.

Both Logan and Storm stared at the picture.

He felt weird about them looking at her like they were. "Her name was Rachel Slater-Shaw."

Storm wiped his eyes, looked at her picture, and then back to Slater. "It's really incredible. You look so much like her. You have her smile, her hair, and Nicki—" He shook his head. "Nicki has her eyes."

"Yeah. I think that's why every time she looked at me it made me feel as if someone was stepping on my grave."

"Man, she could be a carbon copy of your mother— just with a darker complexion. You're going to have your hands full in a few years."

Slater had his hands full now. He took one look at that picture and any question of Nicki's paternity was erased.

Storm handed Logan the note.

Slater bit back his anger. "Do you mind? I haven't even read it yet."

Logan didn't bother looking at him. "How come?"

"Because he wrote a note. He planned it. It wasn't like he just went off." His voice got louder and his brothers watched him as if they were afraid he was going to go postal too. Hell, they should be afraid. The thought that he could scared him to death. He got a grip, crossing his arms to keep from falling apart or breaking something and lowered his voice. "The fucker planned it. He planned to murder Momma and me. I was going to read it . . . eventually. I guess. Then the two of you barged in." God, he so didn't want to do this.

Logan seemed to get a hold of himself. "Do you remember her?"

"Yeah, I feel as if someone just unlocked something in my head. I remember everything. She liked to sing. I can hear her voice and I even remember how she smelled—she smelled really good. She was fun—she made everything fun. She played with me, let me get as dirty as I wanted. She taught me to make pots out of the clay we fished out of a stream in the park we used to go to. She took me to church a lot. She was always praying—it never did any good. She always tried to protect me, but . . ." They knew what happened. He didn't need to paint them a picture—they read all about it.

Logan looked back at the picture. "Your mom loved you."

Storm shook his head. "Your mom died protecting you."

"I know. I remember. I watched him throw her into a wall like a fuckin' rag doll before he shot me. Then he shot her. She got herself killed protecting me." Slater couldn't sit there any longer. Storm and Logan were looking at him and he wondered if they saw more than just his mother in him. He had his father's eyes. Those fucking crazy eyes. He picked up his empty glass and poured them all drinks. Storm and Logan looked like they needed a belt almost as bad as he did.

He put their drinks in front of them and paced. He needed to move.

Logan stood and watched him. "Why didn't you come home when you left the hospital?" He looked hurt.

"Why the hell do you think? My father was a murderer, he was nuts—believe me. I saw him in action. The man was a monster."

Storm stood and blocked his path. "Yeah, we get that, but we don't get why you didn't come home?"

Slater smashed his glass down on the dresser. "Are you both stupid?" God, the Hummer was parked on his chest again. "Do you really want me spending time with

Nicki?" Just the thought that he could hurt her—he squeezed his eyes shut and tried not to picture her face looking up at him. She was so damn small. She was so damn trusting. She was so damn special. God, he missed her.

He walked right up to Storm and got in his face. "Do you want me around your wife?" He gave him a shove and Storm shoved him back. "Think about it. Do you trust me around Bree?"

He spun around and shoved Logan too. "What about you? Do you trust me with Skye? And what about Rocki? Do you want to take the chance that Rocki could end up just like my mother? I sure as hell don't. I left because I love them. I left because I want them to be safe. I left because they'll never be safe with me." His legs didn't feel as if they'd hold him up much longer and he sat on the bed.

He hadn't slept, he'd been afraid to close his eyes. He didn't want to deal with the nightmares; his day terrors were bad enough. He rested his elbows on his knees and pressed his palms against his eyes. Shit, he was crying. Crying in front of his brothers was the last thing he wanted to do. He still hadn't recovered from the humiliation of breaking down in front of Rocki.

The bed dipped. "Shit, that's gotta suck." Storm's arm came around his shoulders.

Slater almost jumped out of his skin.

The bed dipped again and Logan threw his arm around him too. "What the hell ever gave you the idea you could hurt them?"

Blood pounded through Slater's temple and his head felt like a pressure cooker. Any moment he was going to blow. The only release was the tears raining down his cheeks. He took several deep breaths but he couldn't exhale enough and his lungs felt like overfilled balloons. "It was in the file. I almost killed one of my foster fathers. I wanted to. It took two men to pull me off him, and that's when I was nine and skinny. I lost it. I was out of control. I was my father. It scared the shit out of me."

"You were protecting your foster sister. Just like your mother protected you. Don't you think your mother would have killed that bastard if she could have? She gave her life for you—she'd have taken his if she were able."

Slater felt Logan's hand grab the back of his neck and squeeze. "You're nothing like him; you're like your mother. You're protective. I trust you with my life and the lives of everyone I love."

Storm cleared his throat and moved, shaking the bed. "You need to pull yourself together. You need to look at this."

Slater wiped his eyes on his sleeve. When he opened them, that damn note was in front of his face. He couldn't see through the tears that just kept on coming.

"That asshole thought he owned you and your mother. You were nothing more than possessions to him. When he lost his company, he couldn't live with the embarrassment, so he planned his suicide. He wanted to possess you and your mother—even in death."

"So?"

"So, you're willing to leave the two people you love most in the world just to protect them. You're willing to give up everything. You're willing to give up your family, all of us, and the only woman you ever loved. You're willing to give up your own daughter just to ensure her happiness."

"Of course I am."

"You're an idiot—you know that?" Storm got off the

bed. "Logan, explain it to him. You might want to speak slowly."

Logan gave Slater's neck another squeeze. "Does this mean we don't get to beat him?"

"What do you think?"

He stood and blew out a breath. "Okay, listen, and listen good because I'm only going to say this once."

"Slater, look at me, bro."

Shit. He wiped his face on his sweatshirt. "I'm looking."

"You're nothing like your father—but you're exactly like your mother. Think about it. The only time you've ever beat on anyone was to protect someone else. I remember talking to you after you took out that asswipe who was trying to rape a girl outside some bar. You beat the piss out of him."

"So, anyone would have done the same thing."

"Anyone with a shred of conscience. Anyone who respected women, and was protective of them. That monster was possessive—if he couldn't have you and your mom, no one could. If you were anything like him, you'd never be willing to give up Rocki or Nicki. So you have nothing to worry about. And you know what else?"

"What?"

"I spent six years of my life living with you. And the only time I saw you even come close to losing your temper was that time you took on three guys twice your size to save a dog they were abusing. They beat the snot out of us, but you were more concerned with the dog, remember? You're your mother's son, Slater. Your mother's and Pop's. He raised you. He's your father, just like he's mine and Storm's."

Storm kicked Slater's boot. "And we're your brothers. I trust both of you with my life, and the lives of everyone in the family. You'd sooner cut your own arm off than hurt any one of us. We love you, Slater." Storm's cheeks turned bright red. "In a totally brotherly kind a way."

Logan cleared his throat and then punched Slater's arm. Hard. He really did have a hell of a punch. "Yeah, what Storm said. Just don't make Skye cry again or all bets are off."

Slater looked up at his brothers and shook his head. They wore matching *you're-such-a-dumb-ass* grins. He rolled it around in his mind. He tried to look at it logically; he tried to look at only the evidence. He sifted through his memories, trying to remember ever coming close to losing it, to remember if he ever had that out-of-control feeling any other time. No, he hadn't. Just once on the phone with Storm—but it was then he'd remembered the monster's face. He'd seen a flash of the night of the murder. Just thinking about it had all the hair on the back of his neck standing straight up and kicking his heartbeat to the danger zone. Damn. "You really think so?" He sounded like a freakin' pussy.

Storm coughed. "Yeah. Logan, we might just have to beat the shit out of him." He started rolling up his sleeves.

Slater stood. "No, I'm good. I just . . . need time to think about it."

Logan shot Storm a *what-are-ya-gonna-do* look.

Storm shrugged. "You're not gonna do anything stupid, are you?"

"No. I just need to digest this. It's a lot to take in."

They both picked up their bottles and left his. Logan grabbed his coat. "Okay. We're right next door if you need to talk."

"You got a room?"

Storm laughed. "Shit, yeah, we did. Do you think for even one minute that we'd leave you alone to deal with this emotional clusterfuck? Besides, it's purely selfish. We need to keep you around. It's been hell having to deal with Pop all on our own. We're just trying to spread around the love. Thirty-three percent of Pop's attention is a hell of a lot better than fifty."

Logan grunted. "Damn straight."

They each hugged him and did their best to break a rib while slapping his back. God, they were such asses. He loved them, but shit. He'd be lucky if he didn't end up bruised.

"I'll see you in the morning. Thanks, guys."

Slater put the note back in the file where he didn't have to look at it again. He'd seen enough of that to last him a lifetime. He kicked off his shoes and lay back on the bed, holding the bottle in one hand and his mother's picture in the other. Nicki really did look a hell of a lot like her grandmother. He wished his momma could see her.

Rocki stepped into Logan and Skye's apartment across the hall from Pete's without so much as a knock. She was expected, and yes, the gang was all there—Patrice, Skye, and Bree. "Where are the guys? Downstairs?" She plopped down on the couch, kicked off her heels, and tucked her feet under her.

Bree shoved a wineglass at her. "You look as if you could use this—unless you want something stronger."

"No, but thanks. I've been off my feed since yesterday—wine is about as strong as I can take on an empty stomach."

Bree joined her on the couch. "The guys are MIA, except for Francis—he's got rug rat duty. Where's Slater?"

Rocki took a long drink of cold, crisp white wine—their wine selection had certainly improved since Logan had shown up. Where was Slater? She wished she knew.

It was as if he disappeared into thin air. "I don't have a clue. Pete said he's okay, but wouldn't tell me any more than that."

Skye shook her head. "Logan took off out of here like he had fire ants in his pants and was running for the water."

Patrice did her hair-over-the-shoulder toss and wrinkled her nose. "When I asked Francis to watch the girls, he didn't say boo. He must have known the guys wouldn't be here. They're up to something. Not that Francis would give me a hard time, Lord knows. I'm on momma duty full-time when he's on his shifts, but there wasn't even a groan; it was as if he knew I had to be here."

Bree laughed. "Either that or he was afraid of sleeping on the couch again."

Patrice sniffed as if she smelled something vile. "You're just jealous you don't have your man as well trained, but don't worry. It takes time and constant conditioning."

"Oh God, here we go again." Skye picked up her soda and took a drink as if she needed help getting through Patrice's lecture.

Rocki tuned out Patrice—she'd heard it all before—and watched Skye. She hadn't seen much of Skye since she and Logan came back from California—the girl was positively glowing. She was as sparkly as that diamond she wore.

Skye took another sip of soda. She probably hadn't had alcohol since Rocki and Patrice's unfortunate fact-finding mission. Get the girl drunk one time and she turns into a teetotaler. They'd certainly got the goods—interesting X-rated goods—and left Logan to deal with the cleanup. Logan, however, had yet to forgive them. The man could certainly hold a grudge. So they didn't take Skye's petite size into consideration when plying her with Logan's champagne. It wasn't as if they'd done it on purpose . . . well, not totally on purpose.

Patrice snapped her fingers in front of Rocki's face and made her jump.

"Do you mind? So I drifted. Sue me. What the hell do you expect? I'm worried sick. Okay? I mean, you didn't see Slater. I don't think I've ever seen someone so, so . . . haunted. And he kicked me out—"

Bree moved closer and pulled her into a hug. "He didn't kick you out, he just needed some space."

"Yeah. Then he disappears. How much space does he need?"

"He didn't go far."

"How the hell do you know? He could be in Bah-fuckin'-rain for all we know."

Bree pulled away and raised her eyebrows. "Well, it's like this. Storm and Logan both disappeared so you know the three musketeers are together."

Rocki shrugged. "Okay, that makes sense. So they wouldn't run off to Bahrain."

"And"—Bree shrugged—"I LoJacked Storm's phone. . . . All I have to do is pull up the app, and I'll know exactly where he is—within fifty feet and, therefore, we'll know where Slater and Logan are too."

Rocki let out a laugh, probably the first since Nicki took a dip in the lake. "I love you, Bree. I love every evil inch of you."

"Hey, I prefer to think of myself as slightly wicked. And believe me, Storm appreciates my wicked tenden-cies."

Patrice laughed. "Girlfriend, turn that thing on and let's find out where they are. Then we can plan our at-tack."

CHAPTER 23

It took a minute for Slater to figure out that the knocking was coming from the door and not the inside of his skull. The knocking amplified the pain—not good. He loved his brothers, he really did. And he'd never loved them more than today—or was it yesterday? But all the love in the world didn't keep him from wanting to kick their collective asses.

He laid the picture of his mother he'd fallen asleep with on the bedside table, pulled on his jeans, and opened the door as fast as he could, hoping one of them would be leaning against it and end up on the floor.

"Rocki?" Slater shook his head to make sure he wasn't seeing things. When she didn't disappear, he swallowed hard and almost choked.

She stood wide-eyed, staring at him. Man, her eyes were big to begin with, but when she looked at him like that, they were huge, and total backbone breakers.

He cleared his throat, or tried to. "Rocki? What are you doing here?"

She fooled with the hem of the sweatshirt she wore—

one of his—and with the cuffs all rolled up, it hung to midthigh.

"Did Pop tell you where I was?"

"No." She slipped through the door.

He didn't stop her; he couldn't if he'd wanted to, the look in her eyes just about gutted him.

"Pete didn't tell me anything. I know someone who LoJacked her husband's phone. She's just a little bit evil, but her husband seems to like that about her. Go figure."

"Storm and Logan are next door."

Rocki kicked off her shoes and sat on his bed. "We know. Jerry Schmidt, he's a regular."

"Not surprising." Slater sat beside her and watched, not sure where all this was going. "Between Bree and Patrice, they know everyone who's anyone."

Rocki took a deep breath and tucked her hands under her legs. "Sl—"

"Roc—"

They spoke at the same time.

Rocki looked relieved. "You go first."

He shook his head and regretted the movement. "No, you go ahead."

She bit her lip, which just made him want to kiss her. She really did have one hell of a mouth. "I didn't come to bug you. I understand that you need time."

"I'm sorry."

Rocki jumped off the bed. "Let me finish. Don't say anything. Then I'll leave you alone."

The thought of her leaving had his stomach visiting his toes. "What if I don't want to be left alone?"

"If you didn't want to be alone, why the hell did you come here?"

"I wanted to be alone when I came." Now he didn't know what the hell was going on. All he wanted to do was hold her. He caught her by the waist and pulled her toward the bed, so she stood between his splayed legs and rested his forehead against her.

"Has that changed?" Her hands cupped his head, her fingers threaded through his too long hair.

He didn't know. God, he couldn't afford to be wrong about this. He squeezed his eyes shut, not sure what to say. "You're wearing my sweatshirt."

"It was with Nicki's things when we brought her home from the hospital. It smells like you."

Damn, what the hell kind of father was he? He didn't think to ask about Nicki until Rocki mentioned her. "Is Nicki okay?" He didn't want to look at Rocki; he might not have been able to feel shame before, but he sure as hell felt it now. Heat shot up his neck like a geyser. What kind of father ran away from his own child? What must Rocki think of him?

"She's afraid that you left because she fell through the ice. I told her it wasn't about her, but she's a kid. They think everything is about them."

"Damn."

"She'll be fine."

"I never wanted to hurt her. I never wanted to hurt you, but I hurt you both. I wanted to protect you. That's why I left."

"Protect us from what?"

"From me."

Rocki's fingers tensed in his hair and she pulled his head back so he had to either look her in the eye or risk going bald. "What the hell are you talking about? Explain, dammit."

He'd seen Rocki pissed, and tonight there were sparks

shooting out of her eyes without the aid of a fireplace. Yeah, that was all her. God, he loved her.

"I remembered everything ... I was afraid that ... no, I was terrified that something in me could snap, and I'd turn into a monster and end up hurting you and Nicki, and not just your feelings. I was afraid I'd hurt you."

"Because of your birth father?"

"It's not that much of a stretch, Rocki."

"It's ludicrous."

"How do you know?"

"Because"—she pushed him back onto the bed and straddled him—"I know you." Rocki walked her hands up his chest. "I've watched you." She kissed his scar, nuzzled his neck, and stretched out on him. "I've slept with you. I've seen how protective you are of both Nicki and me. When you had that nightmare, you rolled over me like you were protecting me from whatever it was you dreamed about."

"I dreamed of him." He wrapped his arms around her and held on to her like she was some kind of security blanket. God, he was a grown man, and was talking to his girlfriend about nightmares.

"I know you did. I'm sorry. But what you have to remember is your first thought was to protect me. You saved Nicki's life. You'd have gone in after her and done whatever it took to make sure she was okay. Heck, the first day I met you, you insisted on taking me home to make sure I was safe. You just don't have it in you to hurt anyone."

"How can you be so sure? Rocki, I'm related to a murderer."

"So? You lived through that. You're not a monster. If you were going to turn into a psychopath, it would have happened by now. But your father—Pete—raised you to be the man you are today. The man I love. I trust you and I will spend my life loving you."

"It's that easy?" God, how could she do that? Be so fucking certain?

"Slater, it's never easy, but it's not complicated. I love you and that's just the way it is. I can't change it, and I wouldn't if I could. So take all the time you need. I'll be here waiting for you."

"You mean it?" He looked into her clear blue eyes. "Just as easy as that?"

"Like I said, it's not complicated. Definitely difficult, but not complicated. Slater, there's no one else I want. No one I love. No one I trust more than you. Only you. It had to be you." She wrapped her arms around him, pulling him into a kiss, the kiss full of understanding, desperation, passion, and love.

One kiss, a melding of breath, the mating of tongues, the touch of her lips, and the nip of her teeth, and he was sure of one thing: He never wanted to live without her. He'd planned to, but she had a way of bending the steel of his resolve into a pretzel. He was putty in her hands and her hands were all over him. God, only Rocki could get him hard on the third worst day of his life. Frankly, he was amazed he was functioning at all.

"Slater?" She stared into his eyes, taking his heart out for a spin. She tugged on the partially open fly of his jeans. "Make love to me."

His body felt like one big exposed nerve. Every touch, every taste, the scent of her, the feel of her body above him, and the way her hair felt against his skin had him shaking with need. By the time her clothes hit the floor, he feasted on her like she was his last meal. And as far as he was concerned, she was.

Rocki filled his heart, his soul; expanding places he

didn't even know he had. Her love wrapped around him like her body, surrounding him, driving him, pushing him to the breaking point, testing his limits, his strength, and his control over and over again.

Rocki might have been on top of Slater but he somehow controlled her every movement and it was driving her crazy. She didn't come here wanting to break the record for orgasms during one session. No, she wanted to make Slater feel. He was always so damn controlled, and if she had her way, tonight he was going to lose that control and realize that sometimes, control was highly overrated.

She moved down the length of his body, slapping his hands away, afraid he'd shatter her resolve. She kissed her way down his tight stomach, tracing the lines of his muscles with her tongue, nipping at his skin, and ignored the way he tried to tug her back.

She watched his eyes as she moved lower, slipping the head of his erection between her lips. He groaned and stilled beneath her. Damn his control. She had plenty of time, and she planned to use it. She ran her tongue around the head, pressing against the slit, tasting him.

His hands fisted in the sheets, his entire body shook beneath her. His groan sounded like a plea, one she ignored.

Rocki cupped him with one hand, the other followed her mouth up and down the length of his shaft. She used everything she knew, every weapon at her command — her tongue, teeth, suction, increasing the strength of her grip until he begged. She took control, took him high, just to back off, and tease him.

Slater's chest worked like bellows, his groans sounded animalistic, his eyes darkened until the irises disappeared.

It was a battle of wills she was determined to win. She backed off again and then watched him snap.

He flipped her over so fast, her head spun. His big body slid between her legs and he thrust into her with such force, it knocked the wind out of her.

He took her mouth in a crushing kiss, filling her lungs with his breath, taking her over so quickly she broke the sound barrier.

His dark eyes were wild, his every muscle strained as he drove her up again and slid his hands under her ass, changing the angle, going deeper, bucking harder, groaning with every thrust.

Rocki wrapped her arms around him and bit down on his shoulder at the same time she clenched her inner muscles, sending them both into an orgasmic whirlwind, ripping down their shields and leaving every emotion exposed.

Slater came so hard, so long, so strong, he thought for sure he felt the earth move, but maybe they'd just broken the bed. He'd taken her like a fucking animal; he'd completely lost control. His eyes burned and he squeezed them shut trying to stem the flow of tears as he dragged in a shuttered breath.

"Finally."

"Finally what?"

"I get the whole superhero thing, Slater, but it's nice to know you're human."

He rolled them over once he could move.

Rocki kissed the tears that streaked his cheeks. "I love you. I love the little boy you were. I love the man you are—even when you growl at my audience. I love watching you with Nicki—the way you look at her with your heart in your eyes, and I love the way you reach for me in your sleep like you don't feel complete without me."

She rested her chin on her hand, looking a little smug. "You don't have to wear your cape all the time. I love what's under the suit too. I love all of you."

God, he'd missed her. "That's a good thing, because I love all of you too. Can you stay? I don't want you to go. I need you with me tonight."

"Like you'd let me go off by myself at this time of night."

"You're right." He pulled up the covers and tucked her against his side. "I still need to leave. I have a contract. I need to get my shit together and I need to do this job—I need to do it for all of us."

"I know. When do you leave?"

"Day after tomorrow."

"You need to spend some time with Nicki. I can be there with you if you want."

"No, but thanks. I should be okay. I talked to the guys."

"Oh really? What did they say?"

"They said I was a stupid shit. They might have a point. I don't know. I need to think about it."

"Take all the time you need. Just don't shut me out again, okay?"

"I love you. You're a part of me. I couldn't shut you out if I wanted to. I've already tried that. It didn't work."

"Thank God."

Slater thought leaving Rocki that morning after he dropped her off at her place was the hardest thing he'd ever done. That was until he walked into Pop's apartment and dropped his bags.

Nicki and Pop both looked up from eating their breakfast, "Slater!" Nicki ran to him, her Hello Kitty nightgown floating around her long, spindly legs.

He caught her and pulled her to his chest, breathing in the scent of Johnson's Baby Shampoo and Cap'n Crunch. "Hey, squirt. How are you doing?"

"I'm good now that you're here."

He gave her a kiss, hugged her again, and then set her down. "I was thinking we could take your bike out today, just you and me."

"Really?" Nicki bounced on the balls of her bare feet.

"There's someone I need to see, and it's a great place to ride bikes."

"Okay."

"Why don't you get dressed—wear something warm. I'm just going to talk to Pop for a while and then we'll go."

He and Pop watched Nicki run to her room.

Pop took one look at him and motioned to the door. "Go ahead down to the office and I'll ask Logan and Skye to keep an eye on Nicki until we're done."

Slater rubbed the back of his neck. "Okay."

Pop went out the door and Slater grabbed his file from his duffel. He was done with it. He'd kept the picture of his mother—that was the only thing he wanted to take with him.

He took the back stairs, started a pot of coffee, and poured two cups before letting himself into the office. He set the file on Pop's desk. The place smelled of cigars and he was shaking his head when Pop walked in.

Slater turned and looked at his father, who pulled him into a hug. "I've been worried about you, son."

"I'm okay."

"Do I need to call Jerry? Did you boys break anything?"

"Just the bed, but that had nothing to do with fighting."

Pop held up his hand. "I really don't want to know."

"Rocki found me."

Pop laughed. "I still don't wanta' know. I didn't tell her a thing, so don't try to pin it on me."

"Bree LoJacked Storm's phone."

Pop ran his hand through his hair and shook his head. "Somehow that doesn't surprise me—she is her mother's daughter." He went around the desk and sat in his lecture chair. "So, when do you leave?"

"How did you know?"

"I knew the moment you walked in and saw Nicki. Guilt was written all over your face."

"I had no idea I was such an open book."

Pop shrugged and eyed the file. "I've known you a hell of a long time. You're my son. I know you as well as you know yourself, sometimes better."

"If I work this deal out, I'll make enough money to make sure Nicki won't want for anything for the rest of her life. I'm doing this for her. I want to make sure she's taken care of."

"Shit, Slater. Haven't you learned yet that money isn't a replacement for love? Nicki needs her father."

"I know, but I need to make sure that Nicki and Rocki will be better off with me than without me."

"Damn. I thought your brothers would have knocked some sense into that thick head of yours."

"I heard what you said; I heard what they said. But I couldn't live with myself if I did anything to hurt Nicki or Rocki."

"Don't you think you're hurting them now?"

"Give me a few months. Take care of Nicki and Rocki for me. I'll work it out."

"You'd better. Nicki and I will be here waiting for you, but I don't know about Rocki."

"Rocki said she loves me and she'll wait."

"You'd better hope to hell she does. Just know, she's not going to wait forever."

Pop took the file, unlocked the drawer to his desk, and put it back where it belonged. "What are you going to tell Nicki?"

"The truth. I'm going to take her for a bike ride and visit someone special. I'll have her home after dinner."

"Okay. When do you leave?"

"Tomorrow."

"Does Rocki know?"

"I told her. We already said our good-byes."

Pop got up and pocketed his keys. "I hope to God you know what you're doing."

"Yeah, me too." Slater rubbed the back of his neck. Every nerve in his body told him that leaving was wrong, but he had to be sure.

Slater parked the car at the gate of Green-Wood Cemetery and took Nicki's bike off the rack.

"What are we doing here? Isn't this where they bury people?"

"Yes, it is, but it's a really cool cemetery. There are a lot of great things to see. They even have parrots that live here all year-round."

"Parrots? I thought they just lived in jungles."

"Nope, there was a shipment of parrots that were flown into LaGuardia airport years ago. The crate broke; they flew away and settled here. They've been living in the cemetery ever since."

"Do you think they know about all the dead people?" Nicki whispered.

Slater smiled and helped Nicki with her helmet. "Probably not." He knocked on the lid after he snapped the chinstrap.

"So who do you want to meet?"

"My mom. She's buried here. I wanted to stop by her grave and say hi. I thought maybe she'd like to see you." He reached into the car and got the flowers he'd picked up that morning.

"That's just weird, Slater."

"She's in heaven, but I think she'd like to know we cared enough to see her."

"People in heaven can see down here?"

"I don't know, but I'd like to think so."

"So how'd she die?"

"She got shot."

Nicki put her arms around him. "I'm sorry. I didn't know."

"Thanks, squirt. I haven't seen her in a long time. I was even younger than you when she died."

"Do you know where she is?"

"Yeah, now I do. It's down this way." He walked through the parklike cemetery as Nicki rode around on her bike. About twenty minutes later, he found the spot. He hadn't known what to expect. He hadn't expected a beautiful headstone—that was for sure. He also hadn't expected to find flowers. Someone had left them not too long ago. He took the old bouquet and replaced them with his.

Nicki stood next to him and reached for his hand. "Her name was Rachel?" She whispered like she was in church.

"Yeah, and she was a wonderful mom and she was pretty, just like you. I miss her."

"I miss my mom too sometimes. I don't think she was all that great though." Nicki leaned against his side and stared at her grandmother's grave.

Slater put his arm around her. "I'm going to have to leave for a while, Nicki, but I promise I'll be back."

"No, don't leave. I'm sorry I went out on the ice, Slater. I promise not to ever do that again." Her eyes filled up and she dug her foot into the snow-covered ground, breaking through the grass, digging into the dirt. "I don't want you to go because of me. I'll be good, I promise."

Slater ignored the snow on the ground and got down on his knees so he was eye to eye with Nicki. "I'm not leaving because of anything you did. It's just that I have a job to do—that's the only reason I'm going. I have a contract to go to Bahrain and it's not a place I can take you. Besides, you have school."

"So I'm not the reason you want to leave?"

He pulled her into his arms and kissed the top of her head. "No, squirt. You're the reason I want to stay. I just have to do this job and then I'll come home. For good." He wiped the tears off her face and looked into the eyes that were so much like his momma's. Instead of it feeling weird, right now, it felt amazing, like everything was as it should be.

"You'll come home and stay forever?"

"Yeah, when I come home, it'll be forever. I might have to do some traveling, but I'll always come home."

"What about Rocki?"

"What about her?"

Nicki rolled her eyes. "I'm not a baby. I know Rocki loves you and you love her. Is she cool with you going away?"

"Rocki understands." He hoped to God she understood.

Nicki looked down at her feet again. She was getting her shoes muddy. "I don't know, Slater. Rocki just doesn't seem the type to wait around."

"Where did you hear that?"

Nicki shrugged. "Ms. Patrice was talkin' to Skye and Bree."

He tipped her chin up so she had to look at him. "Eavesdropping is not nice." He would really love to give those three a piece of his mind—but he figured after the last few days, he was lucky to have a mind at all. He probably couldn't afford to lose any of it.

"I know. You sound just like Bree and Pop." She rolled her eyes.

He was really beginning to dislike that eye-rolling thing.

"But how else am I supposed to find anything out?"

"Let me worry about Rocki."

Nicki eyed the gravestone. "So are you gonna talk to your mom or somethin'?"

"I don't know. I've never done this before. What do you think?"

"I think you could probably talk to her in your head, kinda like talkin' to God when you don't want anyone else to hear what you're prayin' for. Just close your eyes and picture her and let 'er rip." She wrapped her bony arms around him and squeezed, resting her head on his shoulder. "Do you want me to stay with you? I can hold your hand if you're scared. Sometimes that helps."

Damn. If she didn't stop, he was going to be crying. He hadn't cried this much since he was in that hospital alone when he was five. "No, I'll be okay, but thanks."

She bit her lip and looked at him. He must have passed some kind of test, because she smiled and gave him a kiss on the cheek. "Okay, I'm going get my bike and ride around."

"Stay where I can see you, and make sure you put your helmet back on."

Nicki waved and ran to her bike. He watched her for a

while. He cleared his throat. "Momma, that's your grand-daughter, Nicki. She looks so much like you, it's amazing. She has your eyes and the first time I saw her, she reminded me of you. I think that's how I remembered." He ran his hand over his mother's grave. "I remembered the love, Momma. I remembered everything, but I remembered you most. I miss you. I'm going away for a while, but I'll come back."

He thought he'd feel something . . . shit, maybe he did. There was a weight he'd been carrying around—that Hummer on his chest—that seemed to disappear, leaving only the throbbing pain in his heart. "I love you, Momma." He blew out a breath and headed to where Nicki was riding.

Nicki stopped her bike on a dime. The kid was a definite daredevil. "How'd it go—talkin' to your mom?"

"Okay, I guess. It wasn't as hard as I thought it would be."

"That's good, right? Maybe it'll get easier once you get used to it. I don't mind coming with you. I thought this place would be creepy, but it's not. It's kinda like a park—only with graves instead of swings and playgrounds."

"I heard that when they designed Central Park, they copied Green-Wood."

"Minus the graves, right?"

"Yeah, Nicki. Minus the graves."

She pushed her bike along beside him. "So, where are those parrots you told me about?"

"Down at the main gate—that's where they have their nests and there's a big bird feeder down there too." He patted his jacket pocket. "I brought some birdseed and bread; maybe we can feed them like pigeons."

"Cool!"

He and Nicki watched the parrots for a while. They were like people, some of them were quarreling, some of them seemed like lovers. They were a big hit with Nicki, and the bread and birdseed made Nicki the most popular little girl on the planet, in their eyes at least.

Once the birdseed was gone, Slater took Nicki to the Brooklyn Botanic Gardens. Then they grabbed a quick lunch, and walked hand in hand through the Steinhardt Conservatory. He smiled to himself; it looked to him like Nicki was just as much into handholding as she claimed Bree was, but he didn't mind, which surprised the hell out of him.

He gave her his phone and she took more pictures of flowers and plants than he ever imagined anyone could. He even stopped someone and asked if they would take a picture of the two of them—it was something he could take with him and also something to leave with Nicki. They hit every one of the gardens, but the desert was Nicki's favorite.

Slater wished he liked the desert as much as she did— he was going to a part of the world surrounded by desert, and he was really not looking forward to it. Of course, his work would take place in the financial centers of the country. The last time Slater spoke to his contact, he mentioned a trip to Venezuela and possibly the world headquarters in Vienna, Austria.

Austria would be nice. Maybe he could take Rocki and even Nicki with him if school was out.

Mr. Seville said they wanted to see how the program would run in Bahrain first, and if it went as well as Slater knew it would, he'd have his system running in every major OPEC office in the world.

Slater and Nicki headed back to Red Hook and ended up at the Pound for Lobster Rolls; if he was leaving

Brooklyn, he was going to binge before he left. They sat at one of the indoor picnic tables and pigged out on lobster rolls, corn on the cob, lobster mac and cheese, and even wolfed down a few whoopie pies for dessert. Nicki ate like a truck driver. Not only did she eat as if she'd never seen food before, but she had no problem making a mess. She was half asleep before they arrived home — maybe it was the overly full stomach. He helped her out of the car and when she tripped over her own feet, he picked her up and carried her to the apartment.

He was trying to fit the key into the lock when Pop opened the door.

Nicki's head lulled on Slater's shoulder.

"Looks like you wore her out. Go ahead and put her in bed. Just take her coat and shoes off."

She woke up when Slater unzipped her coat. "Hey? How'd I get up here?"

"You fell asleep so I carried you."

"I'm awake." She let out a huge yawn and stretched. "I can get dressed by myself. I'm not a baby."

He shrugged and hid his smile. She was real sensitive about the whole baby thing. "Okay."

"But you'll come and tuck me in, right?"

"Sure, Nicki. Don't forget to brush your teeth."

"Too tired for that, but I want to put my jams on. Can I skip brushing tonight?"

"Nope. You don't want cavities. After cramming in those whoopie pies, you'd better brush."

She rolled her eyes and let out a sigh. "That's what I thought you'd say."

He went out to the living room. "Pop, I took Nicki to see my mother's grave today."

"Oh, did you tell her?"

"No, I just told her it was my mother, and that she reminded me of her."

Pop sat back in his chair and muted the TV. "There will be time to explain everything later."

"There were flowers by her grave."

"Yeah?" Pop looked at his hands folded in his lap.

"And she had a really nice headstone."

"That's good." He still stared at his hands as if he'd never seen them before.

"Did you do that, Pop? The headstone and the flowers?"

He shrugged. "She's your mother and she needed a decent headstone. I might have taken flowers to her every once in a while over the years. I owe her that much — after all, without her, I wouldn't have you. Besides, I knew you'd want to see her taken care of. You always take care of the people you love. I just did it for you until you were old enough to take over the job yourself." Pop got up from his chair. "I better go and tuck Nicki in."

"Pop?"

"Yes, son."

Slater pulled him into a hug. "Thanks. Thanks for everything — for taking care of Momma, for taking care of Nicki —"

"They're mine, just like they're yours. It's what we do, son."

Slater cleared his throat. "I'll tuck Nicki in tonight. I was getting pretty good at it."

"Yes, you were. You're a natural. The only one who doesn't see that is you."

CHAPTER 24

Rocki tapped on the piano keys, trying to make some changes to her newest piece but nothing was coming to her. All she could see was Slater's face right before he kissed her good-bye.

He looked like hell. He was hung over, but it was more than that—he looked like she felt. Like he reached right into her chest and ripped her heart out to take with him. Still, what could she say? She'd promised to give him time; she just didn't realize how awful it would feel.

Jax threw the paper down on the table. "Rocki, you've played that at least fifty times, it's starting to get on my nerves."

She'd spent a week living here with Slater and had had no problems, but less than twenty-four hours in the same apartment with Jax, and she wanted to kill him. "If you don't like it, go home."

"And leave all this?" He gestured to her studio apartment. "Not a chance. What time does Slater leave?"

"Soon, in about forty-five minutes."

"Then what the hell are you doing here?"

She fiddled with a chord on the piano. "He didn't want

to upset Nicki—it sounds as if she's been trying to talk Slater into staying."

"And you didn't?"

"Jax, he's been through hell. He needs some space. That's what you told me."

"Right. I was thinking about that. I might have been wrong."

"What?" Rocki looked at her brother and she couldn't believe it; Jax was actually turning a bit red.

"I just realized that space never did either of us any good after our parents died. How's it going to help him? What he needs is the same thing you needed then and still need now. Love."

She tossed the music onto the top of her piano. She was wasting time trying to work now. "Slater loves me. He's going to come back."

"I know, but he doesn't need to leave in the first place."

"What the hell am I supposed to do about it? He has a job to do."

"Job, schmob. He could find a job tomorrow. Hell, I could hire him. He's running away and you're letting him."

"You're the one who told me to give him space!"

"Yeah, well, since when do you listen to me? If you fought for him the way you fight for everything else you want, the man wouldn't stand a chance. I think you're afraid."

"Afraid of what?"

"The same thing we're all afraid of. You're afraid of loving someone too much. You're afraid that if you spent more time together and lost him, you wouldn't be able to deal with it. But I have a news flash for you, you're already there."

"Thank you, Dr. Phil."

"So, what are you going to do about it?"

"Nothing. Leaving is his decision. I can't force him to stay."

"Fine. I never thought I'd see the day when my little sister turned into a coward."

"I'm not a coward. I'm being understanding, dammit."

"No, you're being stupid. If you want him, you have to at least try to change his mind."

"Jax, there are some things people just have to realize on their own."

He stuck his thumbs in his armpits and fluttered his arms. "Bock, bock, bock, bock, bock, begowwwwk."

"Oh, that's real mature."

"Go ahead and get down there. You might just be able to catch him before he leaves. I dare you."

"Shit, Jackson! That's so not fair."

"Oh, come on, I'm just giving you an excuse to do exactly what you want to do. Now go. Call me if you need me."

Rocki grabbed her purse, slipped on her lucky shoes, and headed out the door at a run.

She ran down Canal Street until she found a cab. "I need to get to Red Hook. There's a hundred bucks if you can do it in twenty minutes."

"Sure, lady. Fasten your seat belt."

They made it to Van Brunt Street faster than Rocki thought possible. "Let me out right in front of the Crow's Nest, and thanks." She tossed the driver the cash and was out of the cab and up the steps in no time. She knocked but the door was locked, so she grabbed her keys and let herself in.

Nicki stood next to the breakfast bar, her eyes red and

swollen from crying, both hands behind her back. The sad expression on her face was quickly eclipsed by guilt.

"Nicki?"

"Slater left already."

She stepped backward, heading toward her room.

"What's behind your back, Nicki?"

"Nothing?"

Rocki stuck out her hand. "Come on, hand it over."

"Fine, but I just opened it because the mail man said it's real important. It must be. I had to sign a paper—in cursive—and promise to give it to Slater." She handed it to Rocki and dug her sneaker into the carpet. "It says it's positive. What's it mean, Rocki? I don't get it."

Rocki didn't need to look at it, but she did. It was the paternity test. "It means that we're a family."

"It's for Slater, and he left. We have to get it to him."

"Yeah, we do. Where's Pete?"

Nicki dug her foot into the carpet again. "Everyone's downstairs. I snuck up. I just wanted to be alone."

"Get your coat. If we're going to deliver this to Slater, we need to leave now. I wonder if Pete will let me borrow the car."

Nicki pulled on her coat. "I thought you didn't have your license."

"Technically I don't." She grabbed Nicki's hand. "But it's probably not a good time to mention it."

"Oh, okay."

They ran down to the bar and it felt as if they were walking into a wake. Not good. Pete was nursing a scotch and Bree wasn't even giving him a hard time about it.

"Pete, Nicki and I need to borrow your car."

A slow smile spread over Pete's face. "It's about time you decided to go after him. Good idea taking Nicki, the boy doesn't have a chance." He handed her the keys. "You'd better hurry. He's at JFK. British Airways on the 6:25 to Heathrow. Bring him back with you, honey."

She gave Pete a kiss on the cheek. "I'll try." She grabbed Nicki's hand. "Come on, baby. Let's see if we can catch Slater. Get in the backseat and buckle up—it's going to be a bumpy ride."

"Yeah, I remember how you drive. Are you sure you don't want Ms. Patrice to drive us? Or Mr. Francis—he might be able to use his red light and everything."

"No, I'm a good driver. There's nothing to worry about. Just . . . when we get into the airport, I may have to talk us through security." She checked to make sure the road was clear and gunned it. "So whatever you do, don't say anything."

"How come?"

Rocki caught Nicki's wide-eyed gaze in the rearview. "Because I might just be forced to tell a few white lies. If anyone asks, be sure to leave that part out of the conversation—this is an emergency. I don't condone lying—"

"Unless it's an emergency, right?"

"That's right, but you didn't hear that from me."

Slater sat on his duffel and stared at the British Airways check-in counter. He'd checked in. He used to think it was cool that he could carry everything he cared about in a duffel bag. Now he realized he couldn't. He had a hell of a lot more baggage than he'd ever known. And that wasn't even counting Rocki and Nicki—his girls. They walked into his life and turned everything around. Suddenly the whole traveling-light-through-life thing had lost all appeal.

He checked his watch. He should get up and get his

ass in the security line but all he could think of was the way Rocki and Nicki looked when he left.

Rocki held back the tears, barely, but Nicki didn't. Pop had to peel her off his leg so he could leave.

If he had any part of his heart left, it was mutilated now. His chest ached. He'd almost told the cabbie to turn around a dozen times. He'd sat on his own hand to keep from pushing the door open.

Slater had left every place he'd ever been and he'd never had a problem. He never looked back. But now? Shit, now he couldn't seem to look ahead.

He pulled his phone out of his pocket and considered calling Mr. Seville to see if he could rework the contract. He still hadn't signed it. At first, he didn't want to sign it until he'd received the results of the paternity test. Now he didn't need a piece of paper to prove Nicki was his baby girl. After remembering his mother, seeing her picture, there was no doubt in his mind. But if he called Mr. Seville, he could very well flush the whole deal down the toilet.

He ran his hands through his hair. He had a bad feeling that leaving was wrong. Like he needed to stay. He told himself he was crazy. Pop said he'd look after Nicki and Rocki, and he was sure his brothers would too. But all the time he spent telling himself they would be okay didn't make that lump of fear go away, or even get smaller.

So, what if he did scuttle the deal? He could possibly lose millions. But then if he had a choice between money and Rocki—there was no contest. Rocki would end up on top every time.

"Shit." He thought back to the last time he was here in this airport. The last thing he'd wanted to do was stay;

it took him a whole day to get up the courage to go home. Now he couldn't seem to leave.

It wasn't as if he couldn't get a job here. Sure, they wouldn't be millionaires—okay, maybe they would if you took Rocki's trust fund into account, but he really wanted no part of Rocki's money. He almost wished she didn't have it. There was a definite feeling of I-am-man-and-will-support-my-woman going on inside him—she sure as shit wouldn't like it either. He almost looked forward to the fight; nothing turned him on more than Rocki with fire shooting out of her eyes.

"Slater!"

Damn, now he was hearing things. Maybe he should just cut bait and check himself into the nearest psych ward.

He heard the clickity-click of the sharp tattoo of heels racing across the tile floor and his heart matched the beat. Nobody ran like that—nobody but Rocki.

He shook his head and took a deep breath, praying he hadn't completely lost his mind, and looked.

Nicki sprinted right for him. Damn, his girl was fast. She held something in her hand and waved it like a flag to get his attention, as if her screaming his name wouldn't do it. God he loved the little squirt.

He stood, pocketed his phone, and caught her. She wrapped her arms and legs around him and he closed his eyes, willing his heartbeat to slow so he could hear her over the blood rushing through his ears.

Rocki was still running—the woman knew how to run in heels, and looked damn good doing it. She was creating quite a scene—even the cops wore the same look he'd probably worn since that first night he'd seen her. Rocki had rocked his world, and from the looks of them, she'd just rocked theirs too. Too bad for them she was his, and he'd be damned if he was ever going to let her go again.

He wondered if he looked as stupid as they did, but shit, he took a deep breath, the first deep breath he'd taken since he'd left her, and realized that if it were up to him, he'd wear that look for the rest of his life. He was just happy as hell to see Rocki and Nicki both. "What are you doing here, squirt?"

"Me and Rocki got something you have to see. It's important."

Rocki skidded to a halt. She was a hell of a runner, but wasn't good at judging distance—not that he minded since she ran right into him. Thank God he'd had the forethought to move Nicki to his hip, leaving him one arm to catch Rocki.

She was winded from the run, and her tight T-shirt and all her deep breathing had his blood flowing south, which was ridiculous since he had Nicki with them.

Rocki didn't loosen her hold on him; if anything she scooted closer. "Slater, what are you doing here? I thought for sure I'd have to talk my way past security to find you."

"If anyone could, it would be you."

Nicki jumped up and down. "Look, this came in the mail. It's really important 'cause I had to sign for it, and I had to promise to give it to you." She looked down at her shoes. "I opened it 'cause I didn't know how to get it to you. It says it's positive. That's good right?"

His smile made his face feel stretched. He bent down until they were face-to-face. "Yeah, Nicki, that's real good."

She started digging her heel into the tile. "Rocki said it meant that we're a family." She said it in such a small, timid voice, his heart sank, but then when she looked up at him, he realized she was nervous—and that just about killed him.

He swallowed hard and prayed he didn't screw this up. "Nicki, we've been a family ever since you showed up at Pop's place. But this paper is special because it proves that I'm your dad, and you're my little girl."

She blinked a few times and looked at him, almost as if she didn't hear him. "For real?"

"It says so right there."

Nicki shook her head and sat on his duffel hard. "I didn't know I had a daddy." She hugged the paper to her chest, and damned if she didn't start crying.

"I didn't know I had a daughter." He looked at Rocki—which was no help, because she was crying too. He picked Nicki up, took a seat on his duffel, and set her on his lap, holding his hand out for Rocki to join them.

"I always wanted a daddy of my very own."

"That's good, squirt, because I just realized I always wanted a little girl of my very own too. I'm so lucky you're mine. I love you, Nicki."

She looked at him through his mother's eyes, her lashes thick enough to hold her tears and get all pointy. "Forever and always?"

He had to clear his throat. "Forever and always." He kissed the top of her head and thanked God she was his.

"What about Rocki? Is she part of our family too?"

"I guess that depends on if she wants us."

"She must, because she raced like an Indy driver just to get here and talk you into coming home."

He looked from Nicki to Rocki. "You drove?"

"I'm a good driver."

Nicki wrapped her arms around his neck to whisper in his ear. "She parked on the sidewalk. If we can't talk you into coming home with us, I think we should call someone to pick us up. Rocki's scary when she's behind the wheel. And I'm not allowed to repeat the things she said."

"Nicki!" Rocki's affronted look made him laugh, and that horrible feeling in his chest burst like an overfilled water balloon, filling him with something so warm, so pure, so perfect.

He dragged his wallet from his pocket. "Nicki," he said, pulling out a twenty, "do me a favor and run and buy us some water and a few candy bars, but stay where I can see you."

"Are you guys gonna kiss or something?"

"Yeah, probably, so take your time, squirt. Here," he added, grabbing another ten and handing it to her, "get whatever you want."

"Cool. So does this mean that Rocki will be my new mom?"

"Let me see if I can talk her into the whole family thing first, okay, squirt?"

"Sure, Daddy, take your time, just don't screw it up."

"Nicki—"

"Yeah, I know. I'll shut up now. But don't screw it up, okay, Daddy?"

"I'll try not to." He threw his arm around Rocki and pulled her onto his lap. "Nothing like a little pressure. I hope you say yes. If not, you're gonna make me look bad in front of my kid."

"Well, you'd better not screw it up then."

"I couldn't get on the plane. I didn't even make it past security."

"Did they stop you?"

"No, I never got that far. I just couldn't leave you or Nicki. I thought about the contract and realized that there's nothing more important than you and Nicki. I felt as if I were leaving my heart and soul here. I just couldn't do it. I know this is really fast. I mean, we've known each other less than a month. So I was wondering, how do you feel about long engagements?"

"I guess that depends on how you feel about living in sin. I just don't sleep well without you anymore. I don't want to."

"We'll have Nicki with us."

"Of course we will. I love her."

"So you're cool with the whole instant parent thing?"

"Are you?"

"More than you'll ever know. I think I'm really gonna like this daddy business. I wouldn't mind doing it again to find out what I missed."

Rocki shot him her sexy smile and raised one eyebrow. "I'm sure that would make Grace and Teddy very happy."

"Sweetheart, the only people I'm worried about making happy are you and Nicki. Not that I don't think the world of Grace and Teddy. Hell, even Jackson's growing on me, but all I care about right now is what you think."

"I don't have to think. I know I love you. I'll spend the rest of my life loving you. I love Nicki too, and would be honored to be her mom. And as for other kids . . . let's get settled and then we'll work on that."

"So, how'd I do?"

"I don't know yet."

"Huh?" His mouth hung open. He knew it. "Seriously?"

"Asking me how I feel about long engagements does not a proposal make."

Slater glanced at the milling throng stationed around them. "Sweetheart, do you really want me to propose to you in an airport?"

Rocki's brow slid into position. Locked, loaded, and devious. "I think if you don't, you're going to have to explain the fact that you didn't to a ten-year-old."

He looked over and saw Nicki watching them. "Okay." He supposed if he was going to do this with an audience, he better do it right. He stood, set Rocki on her feet, and assumed the position. Shit, they were attracting a crowd. Some lady was even filming them with her camera. He looked at Rocki and realized that it didn't matter. "Rocki, I love you more than my own life. Will you marry me, be the mother of my children, and spend the rest of your life with me? Will you be my lover, my wife, my family?"

"On one condition."

"What's that? You might want to make it good, since right now, I'll agree to just about anything to get you to say yes." His knees were killing him.

"I'll marry you if you promise to always be mine, to be my lover, my friend, a father to my children, my hero, and never shut me out."

"I will if you will."

"Then yes, I'll marry you."

He stood, picked her up, and kissed her. Once they came up for air, he noticed the clapping and Nicki jumping beside them. He pulled her into a hug. "How'd I do, squirt?"

"I don't know. Did you ask her if she'd be my new momma? 'Cause I know I already have one somewhere, but I want a whole family."

"I'd love to be your new momma, Nicki. I love you like you were my own, anyway."

Nicki took his hand and grabbed Rocki's too. "We're a family then, forever and always?"

Rocki looked at him through her tears and nodded. "Forever and always."

Slater looked at his girls, picked Nicki up, and pulled Rocki into a hug. "Forever and always. Let's go home."

Nicki hugged him tight and whispered in his ear. "You drive, okay, Daddy?"

Rocki handed him the keys, and her eyes widened like dinner plates. "Oh gosh, I hope they haven't towed Pete's car."

Read on for a sneak peek at Robin Kaye's
Bad Boys of Red Hook novella,

HOMETOWN GIRL

Available now wherever e-books are sold.

"I can't believe I shaved my legs for Conan the Barbarian," Elyse Fitzgerald whispered to her friend Ronna. She walked down the sidewalk, trailing well behind her blind date, and was in no hurry to catch up. Elyse not only shaved her legs, but other places—places no woman would ever want to nick. "What's his name again?"

Ronna shot her a disapproving glare.

"Doug? No, Dan? Damn, that isn't right either. I know it's a 'D' name." Elyse snapped her fingers. "Dave!"

The moment she said his name, Dave turned and Elyse had the urge to duck into the alleyway, but then realized he wasn't turning to look for her; he was pulling the door open to the bar without gentlemanning up to wait for her. The man was a real prize.

A moment later, Elyse stepped into the Crow's Nest—the third bar they'd hit since coming to the Red Hook section of Brooklyn that night. She'd suggested leaving the first two under the guise of finding a decent band whenever Dave became too attentive.

Ronna nudged her shoulder to get her attention. "Dave's not that bad, and I hear he's really good in bed. Isn't that the point of this exercise?"

Elyse shot Ronna a skeptical look, wondering why, if Ronna was such a big fan, *she* didn't sleep with him. "Maybe, but I'm just not feelin' it."

Ronna tossed her long red hair over her shoulder and pulled her shirt down to maximize her cleavage. "Probably because you won't let him touch you."

Just the thought of Dave putting his meaty paws on her had Elyse stifling a shiver. She ripped her eyes away from her blind date du jour to stare at the bartender, who stared right back from across the crowded bar. "No. It couldn't be. That would be way too it's-a-small-world-after-all-ish."

"What are you talking about now?" Ronna hollered over the band and bar chatter.

"The bartender. I think I know him." Elyse elbowed her way across the crowded space for a closer look to make sure she hadn't imagined him. Hell, it wouldn't be the first time she thought she'd spotted her schoolgirl crush during the six years since they'd last met. She stepped up to the bar, and her mouth dropped open as she stared into the fathomless silver-gray eyes of none other than Simon Sprague. Elyse couldn't believe her luck and was suddenly thrilled she'd shaved in all those places. Carefully.

Simon Sprague hated full moons—especially on a Saturday night when the bar was packed. Full moons raised high tides, made dogs howl, and caused people to do things they wouldn't normally do—which was why the Romans had come up with the word *lunatic*. There was always a marked increase in three things: crime, bar fights, and admissions to emergency rooms.

The bar's house band, Nite Watch, kicked up the volume as Simon pushed a margarita, no salt, across the bar to the normally shy and quiet blonde auditioning for a place in his bed. The full moon was working its black magic on her, at least. He hadn't the time, energy, or interest, so he scanned the busy restaurant and bar, keeping an eye out for problems and locking in on the dark-haired, dark-eyed goddess who'd just entered.

He knew her from somewhere. She looked so familiar, but then he was sure he'd never forget a woman with the face of an angel, the body of a centerfold, and the knowing gaze of a courtesan. His fingers itched to sketch her, and the rest of his body went on full alert. His mind spun, trying to figure out their connection, and there was a definite connection between them. He'd make time for a girl like her.

"Simon? Are you okay?"

He blinked and turned to Bree Collins, his boss and good friend. "Yeah, I'm fine. I just thought I saw someone I knew."

Bree was a looker, a tall, green-eyed redhead with a wicked sense of humor, the biggest heart this side of the Hudson, and a temper that confirmed the redheaded Irish stereotype.

"I have the bar under control if you want to do a fact-finding mission." She pulled a bottle of Stoli from the well and poured. "Go ahead. I dare you."

"Simon?"

He turned toward the end of the bar to see the woman he'd been talking about pushing past the blonde.

"I thought that was you. How are you?" she asked.

She must have stepped on the rail to lever herself up, then leaned over the bar and pulled his head close to kiss his cheek.

He sucked in a breath. Her scent was soft, familiar, sexy, and subtle with a spicy kick that didn't hit until she pulled away, taking half his functioning brain cells with her. He stared, knowing he was supposed to say something but not remembering what it was.

"How are you?" she prodded, as her eyes danced with undisguised mirth, dimples appearing right where he knew they would, which he had the sudden urge to explore with his tongue. Damn, she was gorgeous.

"Simon?"

Shit. He shook his head, praying for his brain to reengage. "I'm great. How are you doing?" He studied each of her features, hoping something would jog his memory and at the same time wondering what the hell was wrong with him that he could even for a second forget this woman's name. Her mouth, which was a bit too wide for her face, broke into a beautiful smile; her lips quirked up and were full enough to make a man lose sleep wondering what she could do with them; and then those dimples appeared again.

"I'm good. Finishing up my master's at Pratt, looking for a job . . ."

She let that hang there and he couldn't help but think that whoever the beautiful woman was, she was looking for more than a job. Whatever else she was in the market for, he hoped he fit the bill.

"What field?"

"I have my BS in construction management and I'm finishing up my master's in regional and city planning."

"Wow. That's impressive."

"It's Pratt, not Princeton."

She knew he'd gone to Princeton. A clue as to how he knew her, but damned if he could figure it out. "You should talk to my friend Bree over there." He nodded to the bar manager. "She's on Red Hook's Revitalization Committee. I'm sure you'll have a lot in common." And maybe she'd introduce herself and he'd figure out how the hell he knew her. "Have a seat and tell me what I can get you."

"I'll take a Sixpoint Sweet Action, but I can't stay. I'm kind of with someone."

Simon put an iced mug under the tap and poured, thrilled that she was a beer girl and not into froufrou martinis. "Someone?" All the hot, sweaty visions he had of getting properly reacquainted with her went up in smoke.

Just then a big guy came from behind and wrapped his paws around her waist, pulling her against him. "Babe, we snagged a table close to the band just for you."

Damn, Simon knew this guy—he was a weekend warrior, the kind who drank too much and talked too loud. And on a full-moon Saturday night, that spelled trouble with a capital T.

Something clicked, something about her—damn, it was right there, yet he couldn't reach it.

The blockhead looked from Simon to the goddess and back, shooting him a warning that failed miserably.

She pushed away and looked at him over her shoulder. "I'm just getting my drink—I'll be there in a minute, Dave."

Dave released her and speared Simon with another look before sauntering away.

Simon gave the bar a cursory wipe. "Dave, huh?"

Elyse levered herself up against the bar and leaned forward as if drawn by the strong pull of attraction like metal to a magnet—invisible yet powerful. "What's that line from Casablanca? 'Of all the gin joints, in all the towns, in all the world, she had to walk into mine.' But in my case, I walked into yours." She couldn't decide if that was good or bad.

"Let's hope this meeting has a happier ending. If I recall in the movie the girl left Bogey standing alone on a runway as she took off with her . . . date." He looked in the direction Dave had gone. Simon seemed more put out about her date than he did about her presence, which in and of itself was reason enough to alert the media. He looked at her the way she'd spent most of her life wishing he would.

Elyse shook her head. Maybe she'd had too much to drink. Every time Dave spoke to her, she'd taken another sip of beer—her way to keep from having to make yet another excuse not to go back to his place for a little mattress mambo.

She took a draw of beer and watched Simon over the rim of her mug. It had been a *long* time since she'd seen him—probably since her and his sister Melissa's high school graduation six years ago—but then only from a distance.

She and Mel had been best friends since kindergarten, and she cringed when she remembered some of the stunts they had pulled on Simon until their freshman year of high school when he left for Princeton. It was no wonder he called her Trouble—her half of the dynamic duo he dubbed Double Trouble. Her face heated as memories of her most embarrassing moment flooded her partially inebriated brain—the day she followed Simon, like a lovesick puppy, into the bathroom. Before she realized where they were, he'd had to ask her to leave. God, she'd been the biggest dork, not to mention pest.

Looking at Simon now, she had to admit she'd always had great taste in men. Simon was tall. She topped out at five-foot-six, and he still had eight or nine inches on her.

He had her definition of the perfect body—commanding height, broad shoulders, thin waist, lean but muscular—more Iron Man than Thor. His dark, thick hair was cut short on the sides and longer on top, making her fingers itch to see if it was as thick as she remembered. His deep-set silver eyes and high cheekbones made his face look like something Michelangelo should have created, not Bitsy and Ralph Sprague.

Elyse had always wondered if he'd been adopted, and looking at him now—all filled out in glorious manhood—she still did. But then his sister, Mel, was beautiful too.

Melissa was the kind of girl Elyse didn't want to introduce to her dates. Not that Mel would even look twice at them, but she couldn't help the second, third, and fourth looks every straight man in the vicinity gave Melissa. The same could be said for Simon and the female population. The only female not staring at him was the other bartender.

Elyse's friend Ronna sidled up to her. "Dave's pissed and he's drinking like a fish. You'd better get over there. He's already looking for greener pastures, if you know what I'm sayin'. I think he likes the cocktail server."

"Good." Elyse set her half-empty beer on the cardboard coaster. "Ronna, I know you went to a lot of trouble setting us up, but Dave's not my type." She didn't spare Ronna a glance; she was too busy drinking in Simon's profile and checking out the way his khakis hugged his tush.

"And you think the hot bartender is?"

"You don't?"

"Fitz, he's everyone's type. Look around. He has you and every other woman drooling over him. If you really wanna do what you said you wanted to do—Dave's a sure thing."

"Would you keep your voice down? God, Simon is a friend of mine." Okay, so that was stretching it, but shit. Ronna could really be a pain in the ass. Elyse looked toward the band and wondered for the fifteenth time what she was thinking to consider a date with Dave, no less having sex with him. But then she always managed to find a reason *not* to sleep with the men she dated, which was why she was a twenty-four-year-old virgin. Unfortunately, it looked like this weekend wouldn't cure that problem.

Sure, she had all the best reasons: She was focusing on school, she was too busy to date, she wasn't desperate, but when she came right down to it, the main excuse was that not one of the men she dated made her feel one one-hundredth as much as Simon had always made her feel just by being in the same room. It was hard for a woman to consider losing her virginity to someone she felt nothing for. And so far, the only man who had ever turned her on, the only man she'd ever dreamed about, the only man she imagined in every romance novel she'd ever read was Simon Sprague.

He set a fresh beer in front of her and winked. "It's on the house. Sit tight while I fill these drink orders, okay? I'll be right back."

Elyse nodded, and then smirked at Ronna. "Tell Dave I ran into an old family friend, so I'll probably be a while."